KITTY-KITTY, BANG BANG

Dear Reader:

It is once again my pleasure to present a novel by Cairo, one of the hottest additions to the Strebor Books family. His first book, *The Kat Trap*, was so intriguing that it became an instant classic. Now Cairo follows up with its sequel and Katrina, Kat for short, is back with a vengeance.

The ruthless diva has tamed down as far as her guns are concerned, however, when drama surfaces, she settles the issue in her own style—the way she knows best.

Cairo's titles—*The Man Handler*, *Daddy Long Stroke* and *Deep Throat Diva*—all feature his unique brand of erotica: raw and lustful. He is fast becoming synonymous with the genre as he delivers novel after novel of wild adventure.

Hopefully, after you read this book, you will walk away analyzing your own sexual behavior, the decisions that you make in the name of love and lust, and how everything has its consequences. Cairo has once again penned a wonderful novel and we are all highly anticipating his future works. Stay tuned for his next adventure, *Man Swappers*.

Cairo has a weekly spot as host on Tuesdays at 10 p.m. on my social networking site, PlanetZane.org. Thanks for supporting the authors in the Strebor family and for the continuous love and support that you have shown me over the past decade. I love and appreciate each and every one of you. To find me on the web, you may also go to eroticanoir.com or Facebook / Zane Strebor.

Blessings,

Zane

Publisher
Strebor Books International
www.simonandschuster.com/streborbooks

ZANE PRESENTS

KITTY-KITTY, BANG BANG

A NOVEL BY

CAIRO

STREBOR BOOKS

NEW YORK LONDON TORONTO SYDNEY

Strebor Books
P.O. Box 6505
Largo, MD 20792
http://www.streborbooks.com

© 2011 by Cairo

ISBN 978-1-59309-303-7
ISBN 978-1-4391-8406-6 (ebook)
LCCN 2011928052

First Strebor Books trade paperback edition November 2011

Cover design: www.mariondesigns.com
Cover photograph: © Keith Saunders/Marion Designs

10   9   8   7   6   5   4   3

Manufactured in the United States of America

For information regarding special discounts for bulk purchases, please contact Simon & Schuster Special Sales at 1-866-506-1949 or business@simonandschuster.com

The Simon & Schuster Speakers Bureau can bring authors to your live event. For more information or to book an event, contact the Simon & Schuster Speakers Bureau at 1-866-248-3049 or visit our website at www.simonspeakers.com.

THIS BOOK IS DEDICATED TO
all *The Kat Trap* lovers who threatened to
hunt me down if I didn't bring their girl, Kat, back.
Well, she's baaaaaaaaaack!
And she's nastier, freakier and crazier than ever;
just how you like it.

Enjoy!

ACKNOWLEDGMENTS

Once again, to the sexually liberated and open-minded: Thanks for supportin' my books and for continuing to embrace the sexual revolution with me, responsibly and respectfully. Raise ya freak flags and let 'em fly high!

To my publicist, Yona Deshommes at Simon & Schuster: Thanks for continuously doing what you do best. Keep crackin' that whip and bein' ya boy's gatekeeper (smile)!

To the readers and fans (new and old), who continue to support my work, spread the word, and email me your comments and thoughts: Thank you, thank you, thank you! On some real ish, I 'preciate YOU and the luv!

A special shout-out to all of my Facebook Beauties and Cuties who hit me up behind the scenes, post on my wall, and/or poke me (even though I don't poke ya back, LOL), wanting more of the Cairo juice: Thanks for ridin' this wave with me!

To all my peeps who come thru and chill wit' me in chat every Tuesday night on Planetzane.org: Thanks for keepin' chat hot and for allowin' me to finally stay on topic. I enjoy the vibe!

To everyone who continues to visit my website and blog (and who keep returning for more of the Cairo juice): From China, Russia and Singapore to Italy, Greece and Egypt—and all over the U.S., the monthly stats are still lookin' real crazy. Thanks!

And to the members of *Cairo's World*, you already know how it goes down. Thanks for keepin' it real nasty wit' me.

To Zane and Charmaine: Thanks for everything!

To my beautifully talented, freak-nasty partner in crime, Allison Hobbs: Whew, I love you and ya sticky drawers. Thanks, baby girl, for always having ya boy's back.

And, last but not least, to the naysayers who still struggle with my style of writing: You inspire me to write nastier, raunchier and filthier; real talk. Yes, with more graphic, steamy sex and *less* story because I can. And because there's a growing audience of readers who want it, crave it, beg for it, just how I bring it: hot, nasty, and raw. Trust me. Nothing's gonna change. So thank you for being my motivation. But, uh, why you still readin' it?

One luv—
Cairo

CHAPTER ONE

Fly, exotic bitch wit' the long lashes and slanted eyes…smooth, buttery thighs…fat ass…soft lips…got niggas 'n they bitches tryna get up in these hips…got 'em turnin' tricks…beggin' to lick the clit…while I'm ridin' down on a nigga's dick…got muhfuckas lined up to get glazed wit' my cream…niggas tossin' 'n turnin'…can't get me outta they dreams…

'Scuse me, bitches! Can I have ya attention, please? In case some of you hatin'-ass Tricks and Hoes forgot who I am, let me reintroduce myself. I'm that cinnamon-colored beauty with that sexy swagger and straight-up bangin' body that keeps the bitches rollin' they eyes—and niggas recklessly eyeballin' me, undressin' and tryna mentally fuck me. I'm that chick rockin' all the fly wears and pushin' the hot-ass whip that all the other bitches wanna be like. I'm the chick bitches still wanna hate, but love to grin up in her face, always wantin' to be up in her space 'cause I'm e'erything they'll never be. Rich, fly and muthafuckin' F-I-N-E! Not braggin'; just keepin' shit real. Bitch, *whaaaat?*

Call me shallow, call me superficial; call me whatever the fuck floats ya boat, but know this: You'll never call a bitch broke, busted, or beat down. So keep hatin'. Keep poppin' shit. Keep pickin' ya face up. 'Cause a bitch like me feeds you dust. So, poof!

Annnnnnnywho, for my bitches and niggahs who I fucks wit', I was on hiatus for a hot minute. I had'a step outta the game to get my mind right. 'Cause on some real shit, after how shit went down in Atlantic City, it had a bitch's dome all jacked. Oh, trust. I heard how some'a them corny-ass broads were tryna come at my neck for puttin' a bullet in Grant's bucket. Predictable, they say? Uh, what the fuck them birds thought I was gonna do? Let the nigga walk after he done popped up in the room and saw I done bodied his fam? Bitch, puhleeze. You must be smokin' that shit if you thought I was gonna let that nigga get a free pass. Yeah, he had that bomb-ass dick. And yeah, the nigga's head game was sick. He knew how'ta tongue-fuck this pussy 'til a bitch shook. But, fuck what ya heard. Good dick, slammin' tongue, or not. My number one rule is: No witnesses, no evidence. Period! So say what the hell you want. I'ma paid bitch, not a dumb one.

Still, I'ma keep it raw wit'cha. For a hot minute, my soul ached. It ripped a bitch's heart to have'ta lay that fine, sexy nigga down. And yeah…I dropped a few tears. But there was no other option. Well, none that was gonna work for me. Prison, not! Him puttin' lead in me, not! Me stressin', wonderin' if the nigga's gonna be on some revenge-type shit, not! So, he had'a go. And for a bitch like me, it was for the best.

Like I told ya'll from the dip, I fucked for sport. But I murdered for business. *Yes*, you heard me. I said *fucked* and *murdered* as in past tense. Well, for now, that is. It's been almost two years since a bitch rode down on sum dick, then took the nigga's head off. Shit, a bitch ain't had no dick since…neva mind. I ain't in the mood to get into it right now.

My cell rings. I grab it off the nightstand, peepin' the digits.

"Bitch," Chanel snaps in my ear the minute I answer. "What took ya ass so long to answer?"

"Slut," I snap back, "the last time I checked I wasn't suckin' ya clit, so pump ya raggedy brakes 'fore you get ya fronts knocked."

She laughs. "Trick, puhleeze. Ya ass 'posed to pick up on da first ring. You know what it is, boo. Don't have ma-ma spank that ass." She laughs harder. *Oh, I see this ho is in rare form this mornin'*, I think as I try 'n hold back a yawn.

"Yeah, I know you better fall back wit' all that *boo* 'n *ma-ma* shit. I done warned ya ass 'bout that lesbo shit. It's too early in the fuckin' mornin' for that clit-lickin' bullshit."

She continues laughin'. This bitch is my girl 'n all, but I swear sometimes she be on some real extra shit. Not that I give a fuck if she's poppin' tits 'n clits in her mouth, 'cause she's gonna be my girl, regardless. But a bitch like me is only takin' a dick that's attached to a real nigga in the back of her throat and deep in her fat pussy. "Hahaha, hell, bitch. I can't stand nuthin' yo' cum-guzzlin' ass stand for."

"Yeah, right," she says, crackin' up. "That's what ya mouth says."

"*Whaaat*eva. Why the fuck is you callin' me, tramp?"

"Fuck all that you talkin'," she says, chucklin'. "Oh, before I forget, guess who I ran into the other night and was askin' 'bout you?"

"Who?"

"Patrice. And as usual ya aunt was dipped in some ill shit."

I roll my eyes. Yeah, I'll give it to her ass, though. The ho definitely knows how'ta throw it on. But, she still ain't as bad as me. And she damn sure ain't servin' me. *I bet her ass is still livin' up in da projects wit' Nana, triflin' bitch!* "Mmmph, where you see that roach at?" She tells me she ran into her at the Ledisi concert at BB King Blues Club and Grill in Times Square. "Well, I don't know why the fuck she was tryna check for me."

"She wanted to know what you were up to, then started talkin' 'bout how you done got all brand-new on e'eryone, changin' ya numbers 'n shit."

"Yup, fuck all'a them hoes. And I hope you didn't tell that bitch shit, either."

"Oh, she was tryna fish me, but trust…you already know. I got you. I kept it real cute."

"Good. They all dead to me."

"I hear you, girl. But, damn…that's kinda harsh."

"Harsh my ass. It is what it is."

"Kat, you know I usually keep my mouth shut, but this craziness between ya'll has been goin' on for too long. That's still ya family, girl. Don't you think it's time ya'll try 'n peace shit up?"

"Yeah, when that bitch's in a box and I spit on her grave. Then it's peace. Until then, that bitch is invisible to me."

"Well, alrighty then. Movin' right along. The reeeeal reason I was callin' ya ass is to find out when you bringin' ya dusty-ass back to the East Coast. There's this bangin'-ass party comin' up the end of next month and you need to have ya ass here for it."

"Umm, Sweetie, you know I ain't beat to be 'round a buncha played-out, dick-thirsty Wal-mart bitches."

"Trick, don't clown me. You know I wouldn't be callin' ya ass for no low-budget showdowns. This is all top-of-da-line dick and dollas, boo."

"Hmmph. Who's givin' it?" I ask, tryna decide if I wanna blaze. I glance at the clock. 8:45 A.M. I get outta bed and walk over to my armoire and open it. I pull out a bag of purple haze. Open it, then take a deep whiff, closin' my eyes. *Yeah, this that good shit right here, but I ain't feelin' it.* I reseal the bag, then toss it back in the drawer, pullin' out the chocolate thai. *Yeah, this is what'a bitch needs to jumpstart the mornin'.*

"Remember that baller nigga Thug Gee from Newark who gave that party at Studio 9 before the shit shut down?"

"Yeah," I state, pullin' out my Dutches. I lay my stash and cigars on the nightstand, then go into the bathroom. I sit on the toilet. How could I ever forget that party? That's the night I met Grant. The night I dropped down low, popped my hips, and pressed my juicy ass up against his cock and grinded into him 'til his shit bricked up. The night I knew I'd end up fuckin' him. It's the same night e'ery bitch on the floor wished they coulda been me.

"Well, he's throwin' another one in Manhattan at Eden...." Mmmph. She's talkin' 'bout that spot over on Eight Ave between Forty-sixth and Forty-seventh streets. It used to be the China Club back in the day. Anyway, it has a lil' rooftop area for peeps to sit 'n chill and get they drink on wit'out all that loud music beatin' 'em in the head when they tired of bein' hemmed up inside. And the music's real cute. But from what I remember, the two times I went there, the drinks weren't hittin' on shit and they had more bitches than niggas up in there. And most of 'em wasn't even dimes. And the few that did look like sumthin', they weren't no high-end bitches. And the truth is, I ain't have no business up in there wit' 'em.

"If I decide to come through, you need to make sure ya ass gotta back-up plan for us in case that shit is busted."

"Oh, trust. Word has it's gonna be fiiiyah. You know that nigga only rolls wit' them balla niggas."

I roll my eyes, wipin' my snatch, then flushin' the toilet. This thirsty bitch stays tryna find her next trick. "Umm, what's good wit' Divine?" I ask sarcastically, checkin' to see if the nigga's still dickin' her. I'm at the sink washin' my hands, admirin' my reflection in the mirror. *Hmmph, even wit' ya hair tossed all over ya head, and sleep in ya eyes, you still a hot, buttery bitch!*

She sucks her teeth. "He's just dandy. Thank you very much."

I step back into my bedroom, sittin' on the side of the bed while I split open a Dutch and pack it wit' my mornin' get right. "I'm glad to hear that. I've always liked that nigga. Is he still rabbit-fuckin' you, or has his stroke game improved?"

Now, typically askin' a bitch 'bout her man's dick game is a no-no, but since she's always put it out there in the past that his dick game was mad whack; that he be fuckin' her mad fast and whatnot, then nuttin' off in minutes—then it's a fair question.

"OhmyGod, I can't believe I told you that, and you remembered. Girl, he finally got that shit together. Took him two years to learn how'ta slow it down and not be so damn eager to nut. I mean, damn. I know I got that bomb pussy, but still."

I suck my teeth. "Ho, please. Ain't nobody tryna hear 'bout how ill ya snatch work is. I asked you 'bout Divine handlin' his. I'm glad he finally got that situation together, though. I'd hate for him to get fucked over 'cause he ain't fuckin' you right, even though the nigga's been damn good to you."

"Sweetie, don't think I don't know what you doin'. Fuck you."

I laugh, tightly rollin' my blunt. I spark it, takin' a toke. "Ho, I got nuthin' but love for ya silly ass. But that nigga Divine needs to straight dip on ya ass 'cause you ain't ever gonna 'preciate what you got."

"Bitch, how you sound? That shit ain't true. I know what I got."

"Oh, really? And what's that?"

"I gotta nigga in my bed," she snapped, servin' me up a dish of 'tude. "What'a 'bout you?"

I ig the 'tude and keep pressin'. "Ho, yeah, you might gotta nigga. But ya ass is still scrapin' the barrel tryna find ya next catch. I'm paid, bitch. I don't *need* a nigga. And a bitch ain't trickin' no niggas to make shit pop. *That's* what about me."

"Bitch, what-da-fuck-*eva*. You still need some dick in ya life."

I sigh, blowin' weed smoke up at the ceilin'. I swear. Hoes like her make me sick. They ain't neva satisfied wit' what the fuck they have. Always lookin' to chase down the next nigga wit' the biggest dick, or thickest knot. I don't know how the fuck that nigga don't know what time it is wit' her ass. Mmmph. A hot, fuckin' mess!

"Oh, sweetie, don't go there. How 'bout you not worry 'bout what I need, okay?"

"*You* need to get ya mind right, Chanel. Do sumthin' wit' ya'self."

"And like I said, you need to get ya back knocked. But you don't hear me comin' at ya neck all sideways 'n shit."

"Bitch, I ain't comin' at ya neck. I'm tryna get you to see you too damn fly to be birdin' ya'self out. You gotta good man. Get ya'self a hobby."

"Newsflash, boo: I gotta hobby. Checkin' niggas 'n runnin' they pockets. So instead of puttin' so much energy into my situation, how 'bout you focus on ya own shit."

I let out a disgusted grunt. See. You can't tell a bitch like her nuthin'. She's too damn hardheaded. A Miss Know It All bitch gotta learn the hard way. Then again, maybe she won't. She's been fuckin' wit' Divine's ass for two years and ridin' down on a few other niggas' dicks whenever she feels like gettin' her creep on, and his ass ain't peeped it yet. Either she done fucked him blind or the nigga just don't give a fuck 'cause he out there doin' him, too. Nah, that ain't his style. That nigga's big on Chanel's retarded ass. Like I said, this bitch gotta good-ass man who grinds hard e'ery day; a muhfucka who'd give her anything she wants, but she'd rather be out tryna trick another muhfucka up off a his paper. Go figure. The last time I got at this ho 'bout doin' sumthin' wit' her life—you know, goin' to school or gettin' her ass a job, she flat out told me, "Hustlin' these niggas is a job. And a bitch like me is gonna always hustle a nigga off his paper." So since then, I keep my dick sucka shut. Well, most of the time.

"Mmmph, do you, boo-boo. But, trust. When that nigga finally peeps ya game, you do know he's gonna knock ya whole grill out, right?"

She sucks her teeth. "Bitch, I ain't call ya ass for no Oprah special. All I wanna know is when you bringin' ya stankan' ass home. That's it. And for the record, there ain't shit for Divine to peep. All I'm doin' is lookin'. There's no harm in that."

I laugh. "Okay, answer me this: When's the last time you popped another nigga's dick in ya mouth?"

"No comment."

I keep laughin'. "Unh-hunh; just what I thought. What you get outta it? A new Louis bag and some jewels?"

"No."

"A few stacks?"

"Nope. An iPad."

What the fuck?! This bitch givin' up throat and she ain't get no paper. No ice. No wears; just a six-hunnid-dollar electronic gadget. No extras wit' it? OhmyGod, this bitch's fuckin' 'n suckin' for peanuts! Shit, she might as well fucked the nigga for free if you ask me. 'Cause six hunnid ain't shit, especially when you fuckin' over a muhfucka whose gonna snap and do a Chris Brown on ya ass if he ever finds out. The last time this ho gave up some charity pussy was when she fucked Cash's cousin Coal. And even then I looked at her ass like she still had the nigga's dick snot hangin' from her lips.

I pull the phone from my ear, starin' at it, then put it back to my ear. "*An iPad?* Are you fuckin' serious? Let me get this shit straight. You mean to tell me you tryna fuck up ya situation by fuckin' 'round wit' a muhfucka for some bullshit-ass gadget? Some shit Divine woulda bought ya ass."

"Whaaateva," she snaps, tryna front like she's heated.

"Hmmph. Ya nasty ho-ass is still my girl. But don't say I didn't warn ya trick ass."

"Bitch, you make me sick. I don't know why I waste my time even fuckin' wit ya ugly ass."

"Oh, get ova it," I say, crackin' up. She gets quiet. *I musta hit a nerve.* "Oh, so now you wanna be on mute? Let me find out you on some sensitive shit. I'ma fuck you up myself."

She sucks her teeth. "Kat, lick my ass. Ain't nobody on mute nuthin'. I was doin' sumthin'."

I take another pull off'a my blunt. "Oh, aiight. 'Cause I was about to say."

"Puhleeze. The only thing you need to be sayin' is when you gettin' here so we can shut shit down. I ain't got all day to be fuckin' wit' ya snotty ass."

"Trick, I just saw ya ugly ass two months ago when you came out here. I ain't fuckin' wit' you like that," I tease. Although I wasn't plannin' on goin' back home 'til the summer, it's been a minute since a bitch popped these hips, so I might make a special appearance. "When's this shit?"

She tells me it's the last weekend in April. Then says I should probably stay 'til after Memorial Day weekend so we can party in Miami. "Ho, don't be tryna plan my time."

"Oh whaaateva. It ain't like you punchin' a clock where you at. Besides, ya ass misses these East Coast niggas, and you know it."

"Yeah, but I don't miss ya ugly, yellow ass," I say, takin' another pull. "Look, hit me up later. You fuckin' up my high. You know a bitch don't like to make plans 'til after I done sparked a fatty."

"Ooooh, save me some."

"Bitch, take ya fiend ass somewhere and go suck a dick."

"Fuck you, wit' ya monkey ass."

I choke on weed smoke. "Ho, drink bleach. You smell like you been lickin' the back of a garbage truck." We bust out laughin', poppin' mad shit back 'n forth 'til we finally hang up. I walk over to the glass doors and open them, walkin' out onto the balcony. I take in the bangin'-ass view of Mt. Tam and the San Francisco Bay. Breathe in the crisp air. *Not bad for a bitch from da hood*, I thought, takin' two deep pulls off a my blunt. Never in a million years would I think I would be someplace like here. Quiet. No drama. No stress. No bullshit-ass niggas and family. I could get used to this. But, Chanel's right. I miss the East Coast. I miss the hustle 'n bustle of the city. I miss the swagger of the streets. I miss home. I take two last tokes of my blunt, tap out what's left, then toss it over the railin'.

For some reason, talkin' to Chanel's ass got me thinkin' 'bout summertime in New York. How that shit be live 'n poppin' wit' mad niggas and bitches gettin' they shine on, flossin' and flexin'; stereos blastin' the hot beats; muhfuckas gettin' they smoke on; hoes stuntin' on da dick; young cats poppin' off, bringin' heat to the streets. Whew, a bitch's pussy is startin' to overheat just thinkin' 'bout it. Yeah, Cali is cute. This quietness and scenery is real special. But it's time for a bitch to step back on the East Coast scene 'n shake shit up a bit.

I walk back into the master bedroom, pullin' off my wife beater, then removin' my panties. I lift open my Louis trunk, searchin' for the perfect toy to take the edge off. Sumthin' that's gonna stretch this pussy out. Sumthin' aggressive; sumthin' raw. I pull out the Slugger—a ten-inch, thick, jet-black dildo. *Oh, yes, I'ma ride the shit outta you*, I think, pullin' out its harness. I walk over to my closet and drag out my stool, strap the harness over the seat, then attach Slugger. I position the stool in front of the wall mirror. I wanna watch myself gettin' off. A bitch don't even need any Wet 'cause my juicy pussy is already leakin' wit' anticipation. I'ma ride this shit like I'm ridin' the streets of New York, fast 'n furious and full of power. I hit the remote for the stereo.

As soon as Jay-Z's "Empire State of Mind" comes on, I climb up on top of the stool, lower my hips down onto the head of my rubber companion, then slather Slugger wit' all of my creamy juices. I match my rhythm to the beat of the music. Imagine I'm on the top floor of the Empire State Buildin' fuckin' a nigga named New York. A nigga whose as mean and as gritty and grimy, and as rough as its streets. *"…These streets will make you feel brand new…the lights will inspire you…let's here it for New York, New York, New York…"*

"Oooooh, yes, New York…fuck me…aaaah…mmmm…beat this pussy up, nigga…" I buck my hips, slam my hips down onto Slugger; take it balls deep, rock back 'n forth. Scream out, "Newwwwwww York!" Then, just as I'm nuttin', a bitch falls off'a the muthafuckin' stool, bangin' her dome. I bust out laughin' as my juices spurt outta me. "Bitch, you done bust ya ass tryna get that nut. What'a mess."

I get up, wipe the cream runnin' down the inside of my thighs wit' my hand, then lick my fingas. *Pussy cream this damn good should be bottled and sold on the streets*, I think, climbin' my ass back into bed. I pull the goose comforter up over me, closin' my eyes wit' thoughts of New York, where paper is made and bitches are paid. The big city of delicious dick and muthafuckin' sweet dreams.

CHAPTER TWO

*Smilin' faces…changin' places…things ain't always what they
seem to be…sumtimes life becomes a charade…a mask of disguises…
dippin' outta sight…eliminatin' da fakes…flushin' out da snakes…
clown-ass bitches can't eva keep a butta chick down…fuck what
ya heard…cream always rises…*

The next day, I'm on'a ferry goin' over into downtown San
Francisco to get it in. It's mid-afternoon and packed on
this shit for a Wednesday from all'a the tourists and whatnot tryna make their way back to Fog City 'cause that's exactly
what the fuck it is. The shit can be so thick that it's almost
spooky. But I ain't gonna front; a few times I wished I was stuck
in the middle of the bay on a boat late at night or earlier in the
mornin' bein' fucked down lovely in it.

I guess some'a you nosey asses wanna know how I ended up
here. Well, on some real shit, I stumbled on Sausalito while I was
out here in San Francisco, handlin' a target three years ago—this
big, burly, light-skinned, Magilla Gorilla-type nigga wit' freckles.
Ugh, he made my fuckin' eyeballs ache lookin' at 'im. Anyway,
I thought Sausalito was *cute* 'n cozy wit' all'a its cafés and pricey
boutique shops. Although they ain't really servin' shit I wanna
buy, I was lovin' the vibe. So here I am.

After pickin' up a few cute pieces at Bloomingdales and Louis Vuitton, for some reason, I feel like playin' tourist today. I've been chillin' in the Bay Area for almost a year and have never done any of the touristy shit, 'cept go down to Fisherman's Wharf, which is a buncha shops, restaurants, and tourist attractions.

I decide to take a cable car ride. Sumthin' I've never done. Probably 'cause any time I'm downtown over on Powell or Hyde Streets, the muthafuckin' lines are long as hell. And a bitch ain't beat to be standin' in heels waitin' to be on some damn trolley. But, today...the lines aren't bad. Probably 'cause I hop on at California Street line at Van Ness. So I dare to be adventurous. Yes, this is what a bitch's social life has come to, shoppin' and sightseein'. I find myself laughin' to myself as we go through the financial district. Ugh! *Borrrrrrin'!*

By the time we make it to Chinatown, a bitch is ready to hop the fuck off'a this contraption. *I've had enough of this shit*, I think, glancin' at my timepiece.

WHILE I'M SITTIN' UP ON THIS TROLLEY, MY THOUGHTS DRIFT TO Grant—again. I try to blink the nigga's face outta my head. Usually I can. But, right now—for some reason, I can't. I ain't gonna sit here 'n front wit' ya asses. That nigga Grant haunted me. His eyes were filled with hate when he asked me if I was gonna smoke him, too. I had'a look that nigga dead in his grill, knowin' I was gonna slump 'im. And it made me so fuckin' sick to my stomach. And for the first time in my life, regret did creep up on me. But I had'a shake that shit off. I had'a remind myself that there was no muthafuckin' time for it. I had'a remember my rule. I had'a repeat that shit in my head a thousand times before I raised my gun and aimed it at him.

"It's what I do," I had'a tell him, shiftin' my eyes from his hurtful stare. The nigga had love and hate all wrapped up in his eyes. They were pleadin' with me. Even though he knew I was gonna blast him, he didn't blink. He was a real nigga. And that's what I dug 'bout him. But, at that moment, killin' was my life. And I wasn't goin' down on some soft shit for some dick—for you, or any-fuckin'-body else. Maybe if he hadn't tried to reach for his piece, maybe things woulda turned out different. Maybe it wouldn't have. I don't know. But what I do know is the nigga moved after I told him, warned him, not to. So, I took his head off. And his vacant brown eyes starin' up at the ceilin', his blood seepin' outta his skull, his lifeless body sprawled out on the mattress next to his people's—all those images had a bitch spooked for a minute. I stayed lifted for weeks, tryna keep that shit outta my head. But e'erytime I closed my eyes, he was there fuckin' wit' a bitch.

And when I stepped up in his funeral like I was the black Jackie O—the *real* Jackie O. Mrs. Kennedy, that is. Not that busted-ass rapper broad—laid out in my Chanel wears and bling, for one hot minute, all eyes were on me as I swayed my hips up to the double caskets. I touched the side of Grant's face, then leaned in and kissed his forehead; the same spot my bullet hit when I shut his lights. Then I walked over and took his grievin' mother's hand, slidin' her a card wit' ten crisp Ben Franklins in it while expressin' my condolences. She dabbed at her eyes, thankin' me. Then I took my seat in the back of the room among the sea of mourners and scanned the room, takin' in the faces of e'eryone. Oh, it was terrible listenin' to the family and some'a his man' 'n 'em scream and sob and fall out over the loss of two of their loved ones. I shifted in my seat a few times, dabbin' at my eyes. But sittin' through that ordeal was more torturous than B-Love's funeral ever was. It ripped a hole in my heart to sit through the whole service starin' at that nigga stuffed in a casket. Oh, it was terrible! But I survived it. And got over it!

And on some crazy shit, if I inhale deep enough, I can sometimes smell the muhfucka. His cologne and his sweaty, musky, I-just-finished-fuckin'-the-shit-outta-ya-ass scent is stamped in a bitch's head. Other times, I can hear him whisperin' in my ear, tellin' me how good and deep and juicy this pussy is. Or I can taste his dick 'n balls on my tongue. Then there are times when I am in bed and I snap up, feelin' the nigga's hands runnin' up 'n down and along the dangerous curves of my body.

For three months straight, the shit had'a bitch jumpin' up outta bed and flickin' lights on 'n shit. And that's exactly why—well, one of the reasons, I bounced the hell up outta Jersey when I did. It felt like the walls were closin' in on me. And it was rattlin' my fuckin' nerves. The other reason I dipped was if I had stayed I knew I would still be bangin' niggas' brains out. I needed to prove to myself that I could walk away; that a bitch wasn't controlled by the shit.

On some real shit, I've bodied a buncha muhfuckas and none of 'em ever fucked me up like what went down in AC. Shit. Even when I took B-Love's head off after I caught him fuckin' Patrice, I didn't feel any kind'a way 'bout it. Probably 'cause I plotted on that nigga. I knew what it was. But Grant...nah, there wasn't a bullet wit' his name on it, not from me. That shit was different. I was diggin' him. Wanted to build wit' him. Bottom line, the nigga wasn't supposed to be there. But he was. So the nigga had'a take one for the team. And that's what it is.

You already know when I was bodyin' muhfuckas there was no time for compassion or sympathy. And there was definitely no time for muthafuckin' regret. Unfortunately, Grant got caught up bein' at the wrong place at the wrong time, and got got. The shit wasn't personal. I couldn't let it be. It was 'bout clockin' that paper 'cause a bitch was gettin' paid by the body. Not gettin' clanked up. So fuck all that ying-yang ya'll been poppin'. I had'a do what I had'a do. And sheddin' a buncha tears 'bout sum shit I couldn't change wasn't gonna bring the nigga back. He was dead. And a bitch had'a keep pressin'. So, yes, I put back on my wig, slipped my chrome back into my bag and slid outta the hotel room, chokin' back tears. When I finally made it to my rental and had'a make that call to Cash, that was one'a the hardest things I had'a do. I remember, takin' a deep breath, tryna steady my voice as I told him, "I know why the caged bird sings."

Then after I told him that there was another body in the room, I had'a tell him that a bitch needed a break. I knew if I didn't bounce I was gonna end up snappin' or doin' sum other reckless shit. Like I told ya'll before I knew that shit was in my blood— killin'. Lookin' into a nigga's eyes, splatterin' his fuckin' brains while ridin' down on his dick did sumthin' to a bitch. Made my pussy hot, made it pop. The thrill of the kill turned me on. And it overshadowed the risks. But that shit down in Atlantic City cost me sumthin'. It cost me what was startin' to feel like love— well, at least the idea of it—and the chance to finally be free.

However, a bitch had'a get the fuck over it. Heartache and cryin' over a nigga ain't what I do. My name ain't Juanita, okay? Uh, duh, the neglectful bitch—yes, you heard me right. I said *bitch!*—who dropped me outta her hairy pussy for those of you who can't remember the script. Annnyway, I saw enough of that shit growin' up watchin' her dumb ass go nutty over the dick. I swore I would never, *ever* be her. And I mean that.

Speakin' of that bird, I haven't seen or spoken to her ass since that night she came to my spot with her face all banged the fuck up by that young nigga she was fuckin'. Then she had the fuckin' audacity to bring her sister Rosa wit' her ass. And that bitch came poppin' outta bushes tryna bring it, callin' me out to fight her like the ghetto-ass bird she is. Get real. I'm done wit' all of 'em. As far as I'm concerned I ain't got no family. And I made that very clear when I pulled my chrome out on 'em. And, hell muth-afuckin' yeah, don't get it twisted. I woulda put a bullet in both of them bitches. E'erything Juanita stands for makes me fuckin' sick. She's a weak bitch in my eyes. And I don't respect her. Nor do I have any love for her. But the crazy thing is I don't hate her ass either. I don't feel shit for her. I guess 'cause I learned to finally accept who she was, and is—neglectful, selfish, and straight pathetic. Which is why I had no problem lookin' her dead in her busted-up eyes and tellin' her flat out that I wanted nuthin' else to do wit' her, then slammin' my door in her raggedy-ass face. I meant that shit on e'erything I love. And that ain't much, trust.

Anywaaaaaay, enough 'bout all that shit. For the last two years, I've been doin' me. Lovely, I might add. So, fuck what ya heard. I'm stayin' away from fucked up family, niggas, and guns. Well, uh…shootin' 'em that is. 'Cause I still gotta few pieces I keep in my personal collection.

Waaaaait one muthafuckin' minute! Why the fuck did I spend the last ten minutes explainin' myself to you bitches? Uh, fuck that! I bodied the nigga, I ain't fuckin' wit' my family; period! So, let's save all that shoulda-coulda-woulda bullshit for the next bitch. It's a waste'a time 'n energy for a fly, butter bitch like me. A bitch is back, ohhhhhhhhkaaaaaaaay?! And that's all you need to know. I got shit to do, peoples to check, and paper to spend. So, let's get this shit poppin', muhfuckas.

CHAPTER THREE

Silky hair; pretty face...first glance...got 'em thinkin' a bitch's outta place...too soft for da streetz...gotta bitch ice-grillin' 'n talkin' slick...tryna punk'a fly chick...wrong move...it ain't neva that deep...now a bitch gotta knuckle up 'n creep up... trick-bitch gotta get put ta sleep...One, two...I'ma shatter 'er jaw...three, four...slide da whore to da floor...five, six...da bitch'll need 'er face fixed...seven, eight... puttin' a bullet in da stupid bitch ain't neva too late...

I'm dressed in my wears zippin' down I-580 East in my rental, a slick-ass XK convertible Jag, toward Oakland. It's bright skies and sixty-eight degrees out, and I'm chillin' wit' the top down, lettin' the cool breeze whip through my hair as I make my way down the highway. If I were in Brooklyn right now chillin' wit' Chanel we'd be blazin' and poppin' mad shit to niggas tryna push up on us. But, I'm here, and it's me on some solo type shit—for now.

Anyway, I'm on my way to meet up wit' this nigga Tone—a tall chiseled nigga who reminds me of a browner version of that sexy-ass Boris Kodjoe—for a hot meal. I met the nigga in one of my real estate classes I took a few months back. Uh...yeeeeeah, a bitch's been in school. And I've completed all'a my coursework;

just waitin' to take the exam for my broker's license. Thank you very much. What? Ya'll thought a bitch was layin' low, trickin' up my paper on wears 'n trips 'n dumb shit? Bitch, puhleeze. I'm tryna make power moves. I'm sittin' on stacks, and I'm tryna clean that shit up. So far, I've been fortunate not to have heat wit' the Feds or IRS, and I'm tryna keep it like that. So while I've been out here I decided I might as well do sumthin' constructive to occupy my time. Shit, there's only so much shoppin' and travelin' a bitch can do 'fore that shit gets played, anyway. Besides, I'm always gettin' at Chanel 'bout doin' sumthin' wit' her life, so I figured I needed to be a true bitch and step shit up a notch and do the same. The way I see it, I can get a Cali license, then go back to New York or Jersey and get my papers there, too. There's fetti to be made and I'm tryna get at it on both ends. And if Chanel decides to get her mind right, I'ma put her on, too. That's what real bitches do!

Anyway, this nigga Tone finally convinces me to meet up wit' 'im at this spot called Soul's Restaurant. Actually, it wasn't that he talked me into shit. The nigga caught me at the right time. I was bored, and wanted sumthin' to do. So that's what it is. He claims the shit is bangin', so we'll see. Although I'm not really feelin' him on any extras—aside from the fact that he's mad young; like twenty-four, he's a cool nigga. Partly 'cause he's a Jersey head and he got swagger and he's also tryna make moves, still...

My cell rings. I peep the number, and pick up. It's him. "Wassup?"

"Yo, ma, you left yet?"

"Yeah," I say, quickly glancin' at the GPS. "I'm actually gettin' ready to turn onto MacArthur Boulevard.'

"Oh, aiight. You almost here. I'll be outside waitin' for you."

"Aiight, peace." I disconnect, tossin' my cell onto the passenger seat. Five minutes later, I'm pullin' up into the restaurant's parkin' area. I spot Tone leanin' up against the passenger side door of a black S550, talkin' on his cell. He hangs up when he sees me pullin' up toward him. I park two cars down, shut off the engine, rake my fingas through my hair, then step out like the fly bitch I am in a pair of stone-washed jeans and a brown pullover and a pair of six-inch light brown python Gucci platform pumps. My Gucci jungle tote hangs in the crook of my arm. The nigga watches and grins as I sashay over to him. His eyes lock on the sway of my hips. I bet the muhfucka thinks I'm throwin' the pussy at 'im. Niggas!

He's rockin' a black True Religion long sleeve tee wit' the front tucked inside a pair of True Religion Joey jeans. He tops his wears off wit' a bangin'-ass pair of black Mark Nason square-toed boots and belt. The tee is clingin' to his muscles. *Goddamn*, I think, flashin' him a smile, *I mighta been sleepin' on this young nigga. This muhfucka got body for days.* He's lucky I ain't a bird. Otherwise he'd be pluckin' tail feathers tonight.

He smiles wider. "Damn, ma, you lookin' good."

"Oh, so what you tryna say?" I tease. "I'm usually busted?"

"Nah, nuthin' like that. I'm sayin'…you always do ya thang, but to finally get you outside of classes, you the truth, fo' sho. So can I get a hug?"

I smirk. "I guess. But don't be tryna press up on me too hard. I don't wanna have'ta slice ya grill." He laughs, pullin' me into his arms. He gives me a quick, but strong, manly hug and kisses me on the cheek. It's been a long time since a bitch felt a nigga's arms 'round her. I almost forgot what the shit felt like. I inhale his cologne. The nigga got the nerve to be wearin' one'a my favorites. My pussy twitches. "OhmyGod, I can't do this wit' you. You killin' me wit' that *Bora Bora*."

He frowns. "Damn, too strong?" he asks, soundin' disappointed, liftin' his arm and smellin' himself. "My bad, ma."

"*Too strong*," I grin. "Nigga, you tryna get ya'self some pussy wearin' that shit 'round me."

"Oh shit," he says, smilin', "then in that case let me go put on some more."

"Don't push ya luck, muhfucka."

He laughs, takin' me by the hand and leadin' me toward the restaurant's entrance. Surprisin'ly I let 'em get that. Even though I said I wasn't feelin' him on any extras, a bitch might need to take a moment to rethink that. *Damn, he got some big hands.* I peep how his jeans fit his ass and lick my lips wit'out thinkin'. Shit, fuck what ya heard. A bitch is horny! I want a warm, hard body to get it in wit'. A bitch's tired of fuckin' these fingas and a buncha dildos. *And the muhfucka gotta nice ass, too.* I imagine sinkin' my nails into his plump, juicy ass, pullin' 'im deep into this pussy. I quickly shake the thought.

Once inside, we're immediately seated. Five minutes later our waiter comes to the table to take our orders. I order the mac 'n cheese, collard greens, turkey wings and cornbread stuffin'. He gets the steak and shrimp combo wit' the same sides as me. We both order large pink lemonades. My stomach growls the minute the waiter returns and sits a basket of corn muffins on the table.

"So what do you think about that property management class?" he asks once the waiter dips from the table.

I shrug, placin' a muffin on a plate. "It's aiight, I guess. I'm not really interested in managin' properties. I'm tryna own 'em, ya feel me?"

"Oh no doubt. I'm with you on that. I already have a few properties; I just wanna understand the management side of things."

"Same here," I say to 'im. He tells me how he owns two houses in Jersey, a townhome in Delaware, and another spot out here. All this and the nigga's only twenty-four. When I ask 'im how he was able to make his moves, he tells me used the money and house his grandmother had left 'im in her will. I can't front, I'm impressed. And I tell 'im so.

"Thanks," he says, reachin' for a muffin, then bitin' into it. He swallows, then says, "By the time I'm forty, I'm tryna be set for life."

For some reason, my clit twitches. I'm not sure if it's 'cause e'ery time the muhfucka licks his lips I imagine it's my clit he's lickin', if it's 'cause the nigga's on his grind, or 'cause I'm mad horny and he happens to be the only muhfucka out here I've given any real convo to in a minute. Whatever the reason, I wanna fuck! I press my thighs together tryna pinch off the achin' in my clit. I am relieved when the waiter returns to the table wit' our orders.

While we're eatin', I peep Tone checkin' me on the sly, but I play it off 'cause I'm checkin' him, too. He grins. "What? Why you grinnin' like that? Is there sumthin' hangin' from my lips?"

He shakes his head. "Nah, I'm diggin' your style. You real cool peeps, Kat."

I smile. "Yeah, I bet you say that to e'ery chick you out wit'."

"Nah, not at all. I been out here for almost two years, and you the first real dime I've come across. And the fact that you from Jersey is a big plus."

I frown. "Nah, nigga," I state with much 'tude. "I'm *from* Brooklyn. I *rest* in Jersey. Don't get it twisted."

"Oh, my bad, beautiful. I stand corrected. And you feisty as hell. That shit's a turn on, ma."

"Oh, so that's what I'm doin'?" I ask, starin' in his eyes. "Turnin' you on?"

"No doubt." He stares at me for a quick minute, then switches up the convo, askin' if I gotta man out here. He seems surprised when I tell him no. "Damn. And how long you been out here?"

"I've been back 'n forth for a minute. But I been playin' it real heavy here for the last six months."

"And no one's tried to snatch you up?"

"A muhfucka can't snatch what I'm not givin' out," I tell him, sippin' my drink. "Besides, I ain't lookin'. What about you?" He tells me he's been on some solo shit for the last few months, but had been fuckin' wit' some chick that started wildin' out. States she was a real ghetto-bird. So he dipped on 'er. "Any baby mommas?"

He frowns. "Hell, no. I ain't ready for that. One day, though." He pauses as his foot brushes up against mine. "Listen…so, what's your deal, ma. You don't have a man, and you're not lookin' for one. Is it because you don't get down with 'em like that? You know you…you dig the ladies? Or you've been hurt real bad?"

I laugh. "Oh, trust. I'm all 'bout the dick, baby. And no, I ain't been hurt. The fact is I was fuckin' wit' someone for hot minute, but things didn't work out so that situation deaded."

"Oh damn. Sorry to hear that. What happened?"

I sigh, placin' my elbows up on the table, then claspin' my hands together. "He got murdered."

"Wow," he says, shakin' his head in disbelief. "That's crazy. I'm sure that fucked you up."

"You have no idea," I tell 'im, slowly shakin' my head while placin' my hand up to my chest. I know. Theatrics; oh well. "It tore me up. But, life goes on."

"So, how'd he get bodied, if you don't mind me asking?"

"A bullet to the head."

As he opens his mouth to speak, he's interrupted by this brown-skinned, thick in da hips chick wit' burgundy hair, stompin' up to our table wit' major 'tude. Cute girl, though. Kinda reminds me of a ghetto version of Jill Scott wit' a tore up weave.

"Ohhhhhh, helllllllll naw. So, this is why you ain't been picking up your phone the last two weeks. You traipsing 'round town with some other ho. And then you got the nerve to bring the bitch to my hood."

I blink, take a deep breath. Say a quick prayer, hopin' I don't have'ta come from outta chill mode and bring it to this bitch's face. He checks her. Tells her to step the fuck off, but the bitch ain't havin' it.

"Oh, so fuck me, right? You got me swallowing your babies and now you wanna break new. Nah, that ain't how we do it 'round here, homie. You think you gonna flaunt some bag ho…"

Bag ho? *Oh, she must see my work*, I think, glancin' over at my thirty-eight-hundred dollar bag. *Or is that some corny-ass west coast slang she's usin'?* I peep the bitch's grill piece and wanna throw the fuck up. *Ohmymuthafuckin'God! This Bama coon got a gold tooth in her mouth. What a late bitch!*

Now, I done heard how these Oakland hoes get down, so I really ain't beat for fightin' a buncha gorillas today. But, I tell you what…this amazon is 'bout to catch it Brooklyn-style real fast. I shift in my seat. Turn my head and stare out the window. Make the ho invisible as she's yappin' her gums at Tone, talkin' all greasy. I stick my hand down into my bag and slyly slip my blade into the palm of my hand in case I need'a bring it to her face. I sit my bag up on my lap, pullin' it close to me. She says sumthin' else, this time directed at me.

"Ho, how long you been bobbling him?"

"Yo, Shelly, word up. You need to get the fuck up outta here wit' that dumb shit."

I finally turn my attention to 'er. Stare the bitch *down*. Tilt my head. Tone catches how I'm grillin' this bitch. I peep she has a lil' fan club wit' 'er—three hood-booga bitches.

"What, you deaf, ho? I asked you a question."

I don't respond. I count to ten. Play this shit out in my head. Take a deep breath, then slowly exhale. I'm tryna keep it cute, but I already see I'ma have'ta turn it up a notch.

Now she's eyein' me, and I'm eyein' her right the fuck back, darin' the bitch to bring it. She shifts her stare back to Tone. "Yo, go 'head with the dumb shit, Shelly. Ain't nobody tryna hear this crazy shit today, yo. For real."

She slams her hand up on her hip. "Go 'head nothing, mother-fucker." The bitch is gettin' amped now, bringin' a buncha unnecessary attention to our table. I decide this is my cue to exit. A bitch ain't tryna be caught up in nobody's domestic shit.

"Look," I say, gettin' up, slippin' my bag on my arm. "Obviously ya'll have some unfinished business to deal wit' so I'ma let ya'll handle this wit'out me." I toss a Ben Franklin on the table. "Thanks for the meal, but I ain't sign up for the extras," I add, gettin' ready to step off.

She smirks. "Oh, so the ho does speak. Mmmph."

He quickly stands, snatchin' the money from the table. "Nah, fuck that. It's on me," he says, handin' the money back. "You don't have to leave. Just hol' up. Give me one sec...*please*." I can tell the muhfucka's embarrassed that this bitch done stepped to him all sideways. I twist my lips, shakin' my head.

"Nah, I'm cool. Holla back when you handle ya situation." Now instead of this bitch keepin' the heat on him, she starts tryin' it on my time; callin' me dumb shit like: Beezy, Bopper, Bootie Crack Corn, and some other shit that was definitely some Bay area lingo. A definite no-no. Now I'm ready to light her ass up. I guess the dusty bitch thought she was chasin' me up outta here. I stop in my tracks.

"Bitch," I snap, droppin' my bag down on top'a the table. "Speak English. Or invest in Rosetta Stone. A bitch like me don't understand bama-ass lingo. So what you betta do is step da fuck away from this table. Trust, I ain't tryna ride this nigga's dick, so whatever beef you got wit' 'im, you keep that shit between you and 'im. Don't pull me into it." I sit back in my seat, cross my legs, starin' this bitch *down*.

"Well, if you're sittin' here with him, then you get it, too."

"Shelly, will you go the fuck on," he says, lettin' out a frustrated sigh. "I'll call you later, aiight. Damn."

I smirk, shakin' my head. *This retarded bitch!* "Don't tell that bitch nuthin'. Let 'er keep standin' here talkin' shit."

"And then what?" she asks, glancin' back over at clique like I give a fuck.

I raise my brow, leanin' forward in my seat. "You know what, sweetie. I wasn't gonna fuck this nigga 'cause I wasn't feelin' 'im like that. But, the more you standin' here poppin' shit, the hotter my pussy is gettin'. And, trust…a hot, wet pussy has no conscience. So guess what? Now I'ma fuck 'im. And I'ma nut all over his muthafuckin' tongue, so that the next time you think 'bout kissin' 'im, you'll be tastin' me. Trick-ass bitch!"

The crazy bitch tries to lunge at me, but Tone grabs her. She pushes him back. I remain in my seat, smirkin'. Finally a manager decides to rush over and tells her to take that shit outta here before he calls the police on her retarded ass. Reluctantly, the bitch backs down as her girls decide to pull her away. *Mmmph, I wouldn't be surprised if this low-budget bitch's on probation or some shit.*

"Girl, c'mon," one'a the booga bears says. "Fuck this square-ass motherfucker and his stank-ass bitch. We'll catch 'em."

I clap my hands. "Catch me now, boo. You ain't said nuthin' but a word."

"Ho, I will break your fuckin' jaw," Booga One says.

I laugh, tossin' my hair to the side. "Sweetie, don't let this pretty face and long hair fool you. You do what you do, and keep it da fuck movin', okay?"

"Yeah, let's get the fuck outta here. But don't think I'm done wit' you, nigga," the Shelly bitch hisses at Tone. "I got something for you and that Boss Head you with."

I wave, tauntin' her. "Bye, bye, sweetie. Get the fuck outta here wit' that nappy ass weave, you raggedy-ass bitch. And, on ya way out the door, make sure you think 'bout me while I'm fuckin' what you can't have tonight; toodles."

I purposely say this to set her off more. And it works. She starts yellin' and screamin' a buncha extras while bein' pulled by the arm. I watch as she's bein' dragged outside.

Tone immediately starts apologizin', leanin' up in his seat. "Yo, I'm sorry 'bout all that. That broad is fuckin' crazy; that's why I stopped fuckin' with her. If I woulda known she was gonna be up in here I wouldna met you here."

"Don't sweat it," I say, watchin' her exit the buildin'. "That bitch don't really want it wit' me, trust."

After e'erything settles down, the waiter comes back askin' if we want anything else. I decide I wanna have dessert. That lil' ruckus done gave me the munchies. I order a peach cobbler. I watch as the waiter walks off, then asks, "So she's the bird you were guttin'?"

"Yeah, something like that. We met at a club a while back and kicked it a few times. But I cut her off when I found out she was on parole. She got too many issues for me."

I knew it! "Let me guess," I say, keepin' my eye on the door, "for assaults and weapons, right?"

He nods. "Yeah, and drugs. I ain't with that. I'm tryna make things happen. The last thing I need in my life is that kind of bullshit."

"Mmmph," I grunt, twistin' my lips up. "Well, looks like she done brought it to you."

"And you know they'll probably be outside waitin' with a crew. But it's whatever. My man's in 'em will be on alert in case shit pops off. I just feel bad that I got you all up in it."

I shrug, shakin' my head. "I'm not fazed. Like I said, they don't want it wit' a bitch like me."

He pulls his phone out and texts someone, then sits the phone on the table. He leans in toward me, restin' his forearms on the table. "Yo, so did you mean all that shit you was sayin' to her?"

"All what shit?" I ask, playin' stupid.

"You know. How you're gonna take me home with you...and you know..."

"Fuck you?" I finish for him.

He nods, pickin' up his phone when it buzzes, lettin' him know he has a text. "Yeah, that."

The waiter returns wit' my dessert. I wait for him to bounce, then say, "Is that what you want?"

He grins. "Hell yeah. Who wouldn't? You bad as hell, ma." He texts back, then sits his phone back on the table.

I rest my arms up on the table. "You gotta lil' dick?"

"Is eight-and-a-half little for you?" I peep the Shelly bitch slippin' back into the restaurant. She walks toward the bathroom as if no one sees her slide through.

Oh, that crazy-ass ho done sealed her fate, I think, grinnin'. My pussy starts to moisten at the thought. *She came at the wrong bitch, now I'ma bring it to 'er.* "We goin' to your place or mine?"

He smiles, lickin' his lips. "Mine. I'm right over the bridge."

"Have the waiter wrap this to go, then meet me outside by your whip. I need to use the bathroom real quick." I grab my bag and strut off.

On my way to the bathroom I unzip my bag and drop my blade back in, pullin' out another weapon of choice to do this bitch wit'—brass knuckles. I decide not to ice-pick 'er ass or slash 'er up; just break her damn face. I slip my fingas through the loops, then quietly push open the door. I'm relieved there's no one else in here besides her. She's still in the stall. I sit my bag on the sink's counter, and wait. And the minute she flushes the toilet, then steps outta the stall, I hit the bitch dead in her throat, knockin' her backward. She grabs her neck, gasps for air. I hit her in the mouth, splittin' her shit wide open. Blood gushes out. I hit her again. "Bitch, what was all that slick shit you was talkin'? Pop that shit now."

She is still gaspin'.

I kick her in the stomach, rammin' my heel into her stomach. "You ain't gonna fuckin' do shit, bitch!" She keels over, and I hit the bitch again. Got the ho all discombobulated. I hit her ass again, then take her by her weave and slam her face 'n head into the wall. "I don't know who the fuck you *thought* I was, but you shoulda did ya homework, Booga. I ain't that bitch. And you lucky I'm in a good mood, otherwise ya ass would be needin' plastic surgery. But if you ever"—I bang her dome into the wall again—"come at me sideways like that again, I'ma do a one-eighty 'cross ya face, then plant a bullet in ya skull." I let her go and she slides down to the floor wit' her grill all bloody, still gaspin' 'n holdin' her throat. I spit on her. "Dumb ass bird!"

I kick the bitch in her face, then step off, closin' the stall door. I wash my hands, rinse off my brass knuckles then drop 'em back into my bag, poppin' my hips out the door. Still fly, still fabulous…still that bitch! I glance at my watch, smilin'. *I handled that trick in less than three minutes, not bad for a bitch who's been outta commission.*

I can't front, seein' that bitch's blood spurtin' outta her face, gotta bitch's slit sizzlin'. I quickly strut out the restaurant door, past the three booga bears smokin' and waitin' on chickie to come back out. I overhear one'a 'em say sumthin' slick as I flip open my cell and hit Tone up. I peep him standin' by his car, waitin'.

"So, what's up?"

"You might wanna hop in ya whip, like now, and burn rubber," I quickly say, walkin' by him toward my rental. "It's 'bout to be a situation in the next few minutes, so peel out *now*. I'll follow behind you."

"Whatchu mean?"

"Nigga, get in ya whip and let's roll out. I laid that bitch out on the bathroom floor."

"Oh shiiit," he says, hoppin' in his ride, then pullin' off. I jump in my whip and do the same, followin' him over the bridge to his spot where I plan on rockin' his cock wit' thoughts of that bitch's bloody face.

CHAPTER FOUR

Muhfucka, don't front...who da fuck you foolin'...I see it all in ya eyes...hot like fire...nigga wanna bitch to cream on da dick...tight ass gotta nigga droolin'...got 'em wantin' to hit it 'n split it...ass clappin'...pussy snappin'...tongue lappin' round dem balls...ready or not...can't hold da nut...pressin' on da clit...muhfucka's dick's 'bout to spit...

"Yeah, muhfucka suck the walls outta this pussy...oh, shit, yeah...run ya long tongue on my asshole..." I'm lyin' on my back, smokin' a blunt wit' my right leg cocked up over Tone's broad, muscular shoulder, pressin' the heel of my foot into his back. I thrust my hips upward, grind up on his face. He's slurpin' 'n suckin' all over my pussy; lickin' 'round my ass, dartin' his tongue in 'n out. I let out a moan. Palm the back of his head while blowin' out weed smoke. "...Yeah, muhfucka, suck my ovaries out...aaah, yesssssss..."

He looks up at me; licks his sticky lips. "Damn, ma...your pussy tastes like cotton candy. And ya asshole tastes even sweeter. I can eat this shit all night."

"Then stop all that talkin'," I say, pushin' his head back between my thighs, "and get back on that clit." He does what he's told. I moan, again. This nigga's body is sick! Muscles for days, and his dick…well, it's thick as a damn can, but the nigga musta measured it usin' a defected ruler 'cause it ain't no where near eight—uh, eight-and-a-half—fuckin' inches. Try six; maybe six-and-a-half, tops. But, his savin' grace is that it's a pretty golden brown dick. And it's extra fat and juicy. *Hmmph. This nigga gotta stumpy, Humpty-Dumpty cock.*

See, had this been a mark, I mighta blew an extra hole in his skull for misleadin' a bitch. I take another pull off the blunt, hold it in my lungs, then blow circles into the air. He pulls my pussy open, dips his tongue, then darts it in and out. In and out. "Oh, shit…Mmmph…" I reach for him, pull him up. "Get on ya back, so I can ride ya face."

He grins, shiftin' his body. "You wanna get it in sixty-nine. That's wassup, ma."

"Nigga," I snap, pushin' him down on his back, "ain't nobody say shit 'bout sixty-ninin'. I'm tryna grind down on ya face. A bitch's tryna nut on ya tongue, then suck my cream off'a it while you pumpin' ya fat-ass cock in 'n outta me."

"Do you, baby," he says, layin' back on a king-sized pillow. I take the last three pulls off the blunt, place it in the ashtray on the nightstand, then grab the headboard, straddlin' his face, then droppin' down on his mouth. He slurps, licks and darts his tongue all around my pussy lips, then in 'n outta my slit. As I'm grindin' on his face, puffin' on my blunt, I'm all of a sudden not beat for the nigga. Yeah, I'm moanin', but his tongue work is only givin' me mini-orgasms. I switch up my position, thinkin' if I have my back to him and I stroke his dick that maybe I can get off lovely. I don't. It's not 'til I close my eyes and focus on that bitch's bloody face that my nut swells and gushes out all over his grill. "Aaaaaah…uhhhh…yessssssssss…" He gags, almost chokin' on the bucket of cream I dump into his mouth.

"Daaaaaaamn, girl," he says, catchin' his breath, wipin' his chin 'n lickin' his lips. "You got that sweet, creamy cum. And it gushes. I been with a buncha chicks but none of 'em ever shot a nut all over my face like this." He licks his lips—again, then sucks his fingas. "Damn, you got that goodie-goodie. You can fuck 'round and have'a muhfucka slippin'."

I grin, glancin' over my shoulder at him through hazy, weed-filled eyes. *This nigga's a cutie and his body is fuckin' sick, but I swear I'm really ain't beat to fuck 'im*, I think, reachin' for his extra meaty cock. *But I wanna see this fat-ass dick spit*. I squeeze it, then begin slowly strokin' it. I wrap both of my hands 'round it, spit on the head of it, then put in work. I rapidly jack his dick; edge the muhfucka to the brink of blastin' off, then slow down the pace, leanin' over and twirlin' my tongue 'round the head. The nigga moans. His dick gets thicker. And for some reason the muscles in my pussy start to contract.

"Bust this fat-ass dick, nigga," I say, strokin' him faster, harder. "Let me see this shit spit, muhfucka."

"Yo, ma...oh, shit, ma...You want me to nut?"

"Yeah, nigga...pop da cork, muhfucka." I spit on his dick some more, then spin his top wit' one hand while strokin' his shaft wit' the other. The nigga's right leg starts to shake. The head of his dick swells, the veins in his shaft pop, and the shit gets wider in my hand. *OhmyGod, this nigga's dick is fatter than a beer can*. On some real shit, a bitch is shocked at how this nigga's dick done expanded 'cause I ain't ever seen no shit like this in my life. And a bitch done handled a buncha dick in her time; particularly before deadin' a muhfucka. I close my eyes, picture that ho lyin' bloody on the bathroom floor. My pussy muscles clench. Steam oozes outta my slit. I decide to go for mine and fuck 'im real quick.

"Where ya condoms? I wanna ride down on this dick."

He catches his breath, leanin' up. "Hol' up…there right here." He reaches over toward the nightstand, pullin' open the top drawer. He snatches an opened box of Durex condoms, then dumps 'em out on the bed. I grab one, tear it open wit' my teeth, then roll it down over his dick. I swing my body 'round to face him, reach up under me, then guide his mini-bat in me, slowly—one inch at'a time 'til my pussy gulps it all down. I buck my hips; rock back 'n forth, then start gallopin' up 'n down on the dick.

I got the nigga's eyes rollin' up in his head. Got 'im grippin' my waist. "Oh, fuck…your pussy's tight…gotdamn, you wet… oh, shit…"

"Yeah, nigga…take this pussy, muhfucka…you like how ya fat-ass dick feels in this hot pussy, nigga?"

"Aaah, fuck yeah, yo…aaah, shit…"

I close my eyes. Think of how I split that bitch's shit. See her grill leakin', and before I know it, I'm wildly ridin' down on this nigga's dick, talkin' mad shit. Sayin' shit I shoulda been keepin' to myself. I wrap my hands around his neck. "That bitch fucked wit' the wrong one…Next time I'ma put heat to her forehead… aaah, shit…this fat-ass dick feels good…You want it bloody, muhfucka? Yeah, muhfucka…I'ma kill that bitch…"

"Yo ma…" I hear Tone's voice, but a bitch's in a zone.

"Yeah, bitch…ya shit's leakin'…skank-ass, gutter-trash bitch…"

"Aaah, fuck! Yo, what the fuck!" Tone snaps, grabbin' me by the wrists. He flips me off'a him, jumpin' up outta the bed. "Yo, what the fuck is good wit' you, ma? You wildin' the fuck out, diggin' ya nails in my neck 'n shit like that."

Shit! A bitch was just'a 'bout to coat this nigga's cock. I blink my eyes. Bring him into view. Blink again. Tone brings his hand up to his neck, then looks at his fingas. He's bleedin'. I stare at his clawed neck, shocked. "I-I…ohmyGod, I'm so sorry. I don't know what came over me."

"Yo," he says, pacin' the floor holdin' the side of his neck. "I don't know what kinda shit you into, but I ain't wit' it. The pussy's bangin' but you into some wild, kinky shit, ma, for real. Diggin' ya nails into my neck, tryna choke me out 'n shit. I'm not down with that rough sex shit, ma." I get outta the bed, walk over to him. Try to touch him, but he jerks back.

I feel bad for fuckin' his neck up. "I apologize. I blacked out. I don't know what da fuck I was doin'. But trust me. That's not how I like to get it in."

He raises his brow. "Mmmph. I can't tell," he mumbles under his breath as he walks into his bathroom. He turns on the sink faucet; lets the water run for a few minutes, then comes back out wit' two rags up to his neck. He stares at me; watches me slip into my Vickies. I'm pissed that I didn't get the rest'a my nut off. "So you bouncin'?"

"Well, yeah," I say, snappin' my bra up, "under the circumstances."

"Who said I was ready for you to leave?"

"Oh, you not? Even after clawin' ya neck up."

He shakes his head, smirkin'. "Nah, I want you to chill. I'm good. It's a flesh wound. I've had worse. But I ain't gonna front, you had'a nigga shook for a minute the way you flipped, talkin' all crazy 'n shit." He stares at me, frownin'. "Yo, what popped off in that bathroom with you and ole girl?"

"I beat her ass," I say matter-of-factly. I tell 'im how I brought it to that bitch's face, splittin' her shit wide open.

He shakes his head, rubbin' his chin. "Damn. You all gangsta?"

"I was born and raised in da projects. Sleepin' on a bitch ain't what I do. A bitch come at me slick talkin' 'bout how she gonna bring it, then she better be ready to get it in. Sittin' back waitin' on a bitch to get at me ain't how I get down."

"Oh, shit," he says, shakin' his head, grinnin'. "You sexy *and* ruthless, ma. That's a dangerous combination."

If this nigga only knew. "I bet I got you thinkin' I'ma nut, now."

"I know you fine as hell. And you got some good-ass pussy."

I laugh. "But you still think I'm a nut, don't you?"

He grins. "Are you?"

Am I? I mean, so what if thinkin' 'bout bustin' a bitch's face up and it bein' all bloody had my pussy on fire, that doesn't make me nutty. Does it? "Hell no, muhfucka," I say, laughin'. "I ain't no nut. I'm a real bitch; all day, e'ery day."

I slip into my jeans.

"Oh, word?"

"All day, e'ery day," I repeat.

"Then do what a real bitch does, ma, and take them clothes back off and finish what you started," he says, standin' up. "You ain't finish wettin' my man up." He walks up on me. I stare at his chunky dick. Wit'out thinkin', I lick my lips. "And my man don't like to be cheated outta bein' up in some good pussy."

He pulls me into him.

And instead of steppin' outta his embrace like my mind was tellin' me to, I let the muhfucka scoop me up, carry me over to his bed, pull off my jeans, remove my panties and bra, then bury his face back between my legs eatin' my already soppin' wet pussy. True, I wasn't feelin' this nigga at first, but, right now—the way he's comin' at me, the nigga has me turned the fuck on. On top of the fact a bitch still gotta nut clogged up inside 'er that needs to be plunged out.

"You gonna let me get some more'a this pussy, ma?" he asks, lookin' up at me and dippin' two fingas into my sticky snatch.

I lift my legs, bend at the knees, and part my pussy open wider. "Yeah, nigga…stretch my pussy, muhfucka 'cause this'll be da first and last time you hit this good shit, so you need'a get wit' da program before I decide to change my mind and shut shit down."

"Daaaaamn, ma, it's like that?"

"Like I said," massagin' my clit, eyein' him all sexy like, "you want this pussy, then you betta beat this shit down, *now*, 'cause there ain't gonna be no lata."

"Then I guess I better make it pop," he says hurriedly gettin' up to grab another condom. He rips it open then rolls it down onto his bricked dick. "And this time, I'm on top."

I smirk. "Whatever, muhfucka; fuck all that you talkin'. Feed me da dick, nigga." He laughs, slappin' his cock up against my clit, makin' my pussy twitch. The shit feels real heavy. "Stop teasin' me, nigga," I snap, ready for his dick to stretch me open. I tell 'im to hit it from the back, knowin' he's gonna spit in a matter of minutes as soon as I start makin' my ass clap 'round his cock. A muhfucka can't handle this juicy shit from the back for too long.

He pushes the head in. Tip drills me, then goes all in, grabbin' me by the hips. The nigga ain't hittin' the bottom, but he's damn sure knockin' the sides out. "Oh, fuck…this pussy's good as hell."

I crane my neck, peep the nigga over my shoulder tossin' his head back. I squeeze my muscles, grab at his dick. Make the nigga's body shake. "Yeah, nigga…take this pussy…fuck it wit' that fat-ass dick…" I'm nuttin' but it ain't bringin' down the walls. I close my eyes, replay beatin' that bitch's ass earlier, keep rewindin' her whole grill splittin' open. I start buckin' my hips, throwin' the ass up on the dick.

"Oh, fuck…aaaaah, shit…you not gonna let me hit this pussy again, ma?"

I grunt. "No, muhfucka…" My nut is swellin'; my walls are shakin'. This nigga's dick is stretchin' me, but it ain't guttin' me. I squeeze my eyes tight. Blood splatters. "…uhhhhh…"

My pussy rapidly milks his dick.

"Ohhh, fuck yeah…just like that…squeeze that dick…aaahhh

shit, ma…can I get some more'a this good shit, ma? I wanna keep hittin' this wet pussy…"

More blood splatters.

I'm on the verge of crashin' waves of creamy pussy juice. I urge the nigga to hit it harder; to dig it out faster. I'm almost there. I slide my hand between my legs, take two fingas and work my clit. More blood splatters. "Uhhhh…fuuuucccck me…"

"Can I keep hittin' this pussy, ma?"

"Uhhh…nooooo, nigga…aaaah…"

"Let me keep hittin' this, ma…"

"Uhhhhh…Shut da fuck up and fuuuuuuuck meeeee, muhhh-hhfucka…"

He starts slappin' my ass. I block out his grunts and groans. Concentrate on my fist connectin' to that bitch's face. More blood splatters. But it's not enough to spin'a bitch into a seizure. I need more.

"Bang it harder, muhfucka…is that all you got? What, you scared of da pussy, nigga?"

He grabs me by the waist, rapidly slams himself in 'n outta me. "Oh, you wanna talk shit, ma? You want a muhfucka to beat ya guts in?"

I'm clutchin' the sheets. My eyes are shut tight. I have a 9mm wit' a silencer in my hand. I buck my hips. Moan. "Uhhhhhh… ohhhhh, shiiiiiit…"

I slam my chrome into that booga bear's grill, knockin' her fronts out. More blood splatters. I let out another loud moan.

"Ohhhh, shit, ma, your pussy is soooooo fuckin' wet…God-daaaaamn…"

"Fuccccck me…fuuuuuccccck me…" I chant, wildly windin' my hips 'n bangin' my ass back up on the dick. I raise my gun. "Uhhhhhh…oohhhhh, yesssssss…"

I pull the trigger.

"Yesssssssssssssss...."

I pull the trigger, again.

My pussy muscles squeeze this nigga's dick in sync to me dumpin' my clip into her dome.

CHAPTER FIVE

Gotta nigga wantin' to stroke me wit' his dick…wantin' to feel this pussy heat on his face…beggin' me to drop down on them lips…roll my hips…squeeze his head wit' my thighs… nigga wantin' me to nut in his mouth…yeah, muhfucka… let'a bitch coat ya tongue wit' dis waterfall…open wide, muhfucka…close ya eyes…here comes ya surprise…

My ringin' cell wakes a bitch up outta a deep-ass sleep. I peep the screen, shakin' my head. The word Nut lights up on the screen. It's my nickname for this nigga Alley Cat I met a while back. "Yeah, whaaaat?" I answer wit' 'tude, glancin' at the clock over on the nightstand. It's eleven o'clock in the mornin' I stretch. Can't believe I've slept most of the day away.

"Yo, wassup, ma? How you?"

"Aggravated that you still callin' me. How can I help you?"

He laughs. "Yeah, aiiight. Front if you want, but check this out, beautiful. I'ma keep callin' ya sexy ass 'til you stop playin' games wit' a muhfucka."

"Who said I'm playin' wit' you?"

"Nah, ma, I ain't say nuthin' 'bout you playin' wit' me. I said you playin' games, big difference. If you were playin' wit' me ya hands 'n mouth would be full wit' a buncha dick, feel me?"

"No, I ain't feelin' you," I state, sittin' up.

"Not yet, you ain't. But you will be; real talk."

This cocky muhfucka makes me sick. I hold back a grin, though. No matter how much 'tude I serve this nigga, he stay tryna fuck me. That's the problem. This muhfucka ain't used to a bitch turnin' his ass down. He's the kinda nigga used to bitches droppin' they drawers whenever he wants. Well, he might be lookin' for a fast piece'a ass, but the nigga ain't gonna get it here unless it's on my terms. Hmmph. If you ask me, I think the nigga's borderline crazy. 'Cause if a bitch was always comin' at me sideways 'n all reckless and whatnot I'd be tellin' that ho to eat shit, then be out.

But this nigga right here won't let up. Even when the nigga stood in front of me and blocked my way in the mall down in Phoenix, I thought he was a damn nut. Fine, yes. But, a damn problem, for sure! On some real shit, I wasn't gonna give the nigga the time'a day if Chanel's dumb ass wasn't all up in the mix eggin' me to give the nigga sum air play.

Earlier that day, he was tryna holla as me and Chanel were walkin' outta the hotel we were stayin' in. But we paid the nigga dust. Most niggas just leave it alone, but this muhfucka got up and came up on us like he was really pressed tryna push the issue. Chanel's simple-ass entertained 'im, but I kept it movin'. See, I had already peeped the nigga the day before at the All-Star Jam Session chillin' wit' a buncha niggas.

Then I saw 'im later on that night down in the lobby. And, yes, the nigga was fuckable. And, yes, the nigga was dipped 'n blingin'. But he was sooooo fuckin' arrogant, too! I knew the minute he opened his mouth that he was used to bitches sweatin' his ass and droppin' down 'n wettin' his dick up at his beck 'n call. And I know it fucks wit' 'im that I ain't that kinda chick.

I ain't gonna front. When the nigga walked up on me and

Chanel at the mall, I tried to act like I wasn't beat, but the muhfucka had this kinda confidence that was mad sexy; still, a bitch knows when a muhfucka ain't up to no good. And my gut told me that this nigga right here, mmmph...is a walkin' magnet for drama. But when he stepped up in my space, I kept it cute and gave 'im some rhythm—just a taste, for a hot minute. I had'a laugh when he said I was actin' like he was the muhfucka who had broke my heart. But I quickly checked his ass and let 'im know I ain't the one to let a nigga break shit on me. Little did he know, a bitch was still mournin' the loss of good dick. Shit, I went from gettin' this pussy beat up on'a regular to not gettin' it at all. It had been a minute since I was gettin' served by some dick that wasn't attached to a bullet. Then just like that, it was over. So, my 'tude had nuthin' to do wit' bein' evil. It was 'bout a bitch grievin' 'n needin' a good dickin'.

Annnywaaaayz, for the last year or so, the nigga's been hittin' me up on some let's chill-type shit, and I still ain't rocked wit' 'em. And he still ain't lettin' it go. The shit cracks me up.

"*Whaaa*teva," I tell 'im, gettin' outta bed. My stomach starts growlin', remindin' me that the only thing I had today was that damn blunt. Ohmigod, a bitch could eat three dicks and still have room for a nut or two. That's how hungry I am.

I go downstairs to fix sumthin' to eat. "What, you bored? None'a ya lil' hoes 'round for you to play wit'?" I ask, openin' up the 'fridge. I pull out the carton of eggs, some cheddar cheese, and a green pepper. I decide to fix an omelet.

"Nah, beautiful, never that. I can always find me a broad to get at. But, that's not what I want."

I pull out a skillet. "Oh, really? So, what you want?"

"Yo, I'ma keep it gee wit' you, aiight?"

"Oh, please do."

"I want some pussy, straight up. And I wanna *fuck*."

I laugh, choppin' the green pepper, then peelin' an onion. "Nigga you talkin' like ya nasty ass ain't already gettin' it in. I know betta."

He laughs. "Yeah, my dick stays wet. But I'm tryna get up in some new pussy."

"Nigga you ain't even smooth wit' ya shit. You straight raw wit' it. No kinda finesse. Ain't no classy bitch feelin' that. Save that shit for them boogas."

He laughs. "Check this shit out, ma. I'ma grown-ass man. I ain't got time to be bullshittin' on da pussy."

"Well, that shit might work wit' them bottom of the barrel bitches, but it ain't workin' for me."

He keeps laughin'. "Bottom of da barrel, top of da barrel, it don't matter. As long as da pussy's bangin' 'n I can fuck 'em over da barrel, it's all gravy."

I shred my cheese. "Well, I ain't lookin' to fuck." I crack two eggs. Then beat all the ingredients while the pan heats up. Then I pour e'erything in.

"You ain't sayin' nuthin' but a word, ma. I got you. I know how'ta make love when it calls for it."

"Oh, really? And when does it call for it?"

"When a chick is worthy of bein' treated respectfully. When she ain't beat to know how much dick a nigga's got hangin' between his legs. Or bein' preoccupied wit' the size of a muhfucka's feet, or what kinda whip he's pushin'."

Now I ain't gonna front, a bitch was wonderin' how many inches this black muhfucka was holdin'. Shit, I already done seen da nigga' dick print, so I already know what it is. But I'm damn sure not preoccupied ova it. And a bitch definitely ain't gonna ask 'bout it. I'll leave that shit for them thirsty-ass cluckers he got on his team. Bird-ass hoes. I'll find out what's really good wit' da nigga's dick if and when I decide to rock his top. In da mean time, a bitch's gonna keep it cute, and stay on mute.

I take the spatula and fold my omelet. My stomach growls louder. When my food is finally done, I slide it onto my plate, then sit down at the table.

"Yo what you eatin'?"

"An omelet."

"Oh, you cook? That's wassup."

"Yeah, I can do a lil' sumthin'. But that's not a bitch's purpose in life."

"So you sayin' I can't get my grub on?"

"Not if you lookn' for *me* to cook. My name ain't Aunt Jemima. And I ain't ya mama. So, hell no, muhfucka."

He laughs. "Yeah, aiight. I see you like talkin' real reckless."

"And I can back it up, muhfucka, trust."

"We'll see. Like I said, you talk a lotta shit."

"Whaaaat*eva*. Take it, or leave it."

"Yeah, aiight, yo. I hear you. Right now, I'm tryna take it."

"So you be fuckin' a buncha birds?" I decide to ask, nixin' his last comment. Not that I really care 'cause I already know what it is. Still the nigga has piqued my curiosity.

"On occasion," he says. "And them the ones I *fuck*. And use this big-ass dick as a weapon of destruction to slaughter the hell outta the pussy."

I roll my eyes up in my head. "Whateva nigga. Ya dick game probably whack as hell." I tease, gettin' up to put my plate in the sink. He laughs. I open the 'fridge and grab a bottle of Dasani water, then open it and start guzzlin' it down. "You probably one'a them quick nut type muhfuckas."

It's time for another blunt, I think as I go back upstairs. This time I grab the haze and roll two fatties.

"Yeah, you think that shit if ya want," he says, laughin'. "But I can show ya better than I can tell ya, ma. I ain't that dude who be runnin' his mouth 'bout what he can do to da pussy, then don't deliver. They don't call me Daddy Long Stroke for nuthin'. Believe that, ma."

I suck my teeth, walkin over and sittin' on the bed. I spark the blunt, crossin' my legs. "*Whaaat*eva. You too damn stuck on ya'self." I take a deep pull.

"Nah, baby...I'm tryna be stuck on you."

"Muhfucka, what I tell you 'bout callin' me ya damn *baby*. Ya ass is fuckin' hardheaded. I bet you used to get ya ass beat a lot growin' up."

"Nah, never that," he says, laughin'. "I got my ass beat once. That's it. Other than that, the only thing that was gettin' beat was this dick."

"Hmmph," I grunt, blowin' out smoke.

"Yo, you blazin'?"

"Yeah, muhfucka, why?"

He laughs. "Daaaaaamn, I'm in love. You mad sexy, mean as fuck, and you burn. And you get my dick hard e'erytime you call me *muhfucka*. Where you been hidin' all my life?"

I suck my teeth. "Annnnywayz, why you keep callin' me?"

"'Cause I dig you."

"Nigga, you don't even know me."

"Yeah 'cause you won't let a muhfucka in. You keep frontin' 'n shit. I been tryna holla at you for over a year now—"

"Try almost two," I correct, cuttin' him off.

"Well, shit, that makes it even worse. And you still ain't tryna give a muhfucka no play. Wassup wit' that?"

I take another pull. "'Cause I'm chillin'. Doin' me. And I ain't beat for no drama, or no extra shit from a nigga. And you look like you that nigga wit' a side dish of both. No, thank you. Been there, done that. And I ain't tryna catch'a case."

"Oh, word? Well, I don't know what kinda case you might catch. But if you'd stop frontin' I'll give ya fine ass a case of some good dick."

This muthafucka! I pull at my nipples. A bitch is mad horny. This nigga gotta sexy ass voice. And he's nasty as fuck, but I gotta keep remindin' myself that the muhfucka's trouble. I know this nigga's kind. I get up. Stare at my body in the mirror, turnin' from one side to the other, admirin' my bangin' shape. I tighten and un-tighten my ass muscles and watch my ass cheeks pop.

"Nigga, what makes you think you can come at me all sideways 'n shit?"

"Yo, don't think I forgot that shit you told me in the mall that day. I kept that shit tucked. Now I wanna see you deliver."

"Well, don't hold ya breath," I say, shakin' my head, rememberin' exactly what I said to him when I stepped up in his space and whispered in his ear. "...I bet you a sucka for good pussy, and a bitch who can suck down ya dick and lap at ya balls, too...well, guess what, muhfucka? I'm that bitch, be clear. Fine, fly, fabulous and freaky wit' a pussy 'n throat game so ill it'll make a nigga sick..." And, the minute I stepped back from him, I peeped the nigga's dick stretchin' down his leg. And his nasty ass didn't even try 'n play it off.

"So why you keep answerin' when I call?"

I smile, sittin' at the foot of my bed. I spread open my legs. Lean back on my forearm, then use my free hand to lightly pat my pussy. *'Cause ya sexy, bow-legged ass is thuggish and fine as hell and I might wanna fuck you*, I think. Of course I ain't gonna gas this nigga up. "'Cause you amuse me," I say, laughin'.

"Yeah, aiight. Go 'head wit' that dumb shit. I know better.

Keep shit real, you wanna taste this chocolate, don't you? It's all good. Just say the word, and I'ma serve ya sexy ass all the chocolate you desire. Daddy got enough to satisfy all of ya cravin's."

I suck my teeth. "Next. Nigga, puhleeze. Save that daddy shit for them birds you got cluckin' behind you."

"Yeah, aiight. I'ma have you cluckin' in a minute."

I bust out laughin'. "Oh, neeeeegro, you gotta bitch confused; never that. I'd put a bullet in ya skull, first, before you ever pluck a feather outta me. Trust."

He starts crackin' up. "Yo, ma, you funny as hell, word up. You must gotta thing for guns."

I walk over to my nightstand and open the bottom drawer. I pull out my nickel-plated Colt Python. It's a .357 Magnum wit' the six-inch barrel and nickel finish. It's known for its smooth trigger pull and tight cylinder lock-up. The shit is mad sexy. They stopped makin' 'em in '96, but I was able to cop mine from this white muhfucka who had a '05 special order edition. I slip the barrel between my legs, then slide it over my tight slit. There's sumthin' 'bout holdin' a gun that makes a bitch's pussy come alive.

"Yeah, sumthin' like that," I tell 'im, layin' back on my bed. I lay the gun on my chest. "How many bitches you guttin'?"

"A few."

"I bet you'll fuck anything movin'."

He laughs. "Not wit' the lights on."

"Just what I thought. You fuck them crusty-feet, booga-bear hoes wit' the ashy ankles and chipped toenails, don't you?"

He laughs harder. "Yo, you funny as hell."

"Funny hell. I'm straight-lacin'. You real nasty wit' yours, nigga, ain't you? A bitch like me can't fuck wit' a nigga who's guttin' up a buncha hood crittas."

"Nah, ma, you got me all fucked up," he says, tryna sound serious. "I'ma keep shit a hunnid, though. Yeah, I've fucked a few gorilla-faced bitches in my day. And most of 'em had some good-ass pussy. They were the type to let a muhfucka get it in almost anyway he wanted. From garglin' my balls to lickin' the shit outta my ass, most of them hoes aim to please. But good pussy or not, I fucked 'em from the back and wit' the room pitch black."

I start laughin'. "Ohmigod, nigga, you comical as hell. So what makes you think a bitch like me would wanna fuck wit' a nigga like you?"

"'Cause I'm e'erything ya body needs. And e'erything you crave."

"Oh, yeah, and what's that?"

"A nigga wit' a strong back, strong hands, long dick and a long, wet tongue."

I pinch my left nipple. I decide to fuck wit' 'im. "You eat pussy?"

"Hell yeah, I eat pussy. Eat ass, too. I like it all. Besides beatin' up the guts, pussy eatin' is my thing."

"You suckin' dick, too?"

"Say what?"

"You heard me, nigga. I asked if you takin' dick? You said you liked it all."

"Hell fuckin' no! I ain't that kinda muhfucka. I'm a pussy-lovin' nigga. I like it *all* attached to a *real* woman, wit' titties, ass 'n good, wet pussy. A muhfucka come at me on some sideways shit, and that's grounds to get ya neck snapped, for real for real."

"Yeah, right. You probably one'a them DL, homo-thug muh-fuckas," I say, laughin'. "If you take it in the ass 'n throat, it's all gravy, Miss Hunnneeeee. We can swap stories."

He laughs. "Yo, word up, ma. You funny bad. I'm all man, baby."

I grin. "Ohhhhkaaaay, if you say so."

"Nah, I know so. Don't get shit twisted. But you can think what you want, feel me?"

"Let me stop fuckin' wit' you."

"It's all good."

"So, what's that tongue game like?"

He laughs. "Oh, so now you wanna know how a muhfucka wets the pussy."

"Yup. Tell me how you get down on the pussy to make it pop. Entice me, muhfucka." I pinch both my nipples, then slide my left hand between my legs, while slippin' the tip of my Colt in my mouth wit' my other hand. I slowly suck on the barrel as he speaks.

"First, I'd kiss on the pussy. From soft, gentle kisses to deep, tongue-probin' French-kissin', I love havin' my tongue and lips all up on it, and in it. Next, I'll lay my tongue flat up against it, then flap it up and down, draggin' it along the front and back of ya slit. I'll use my mouth and tongue to stimulate all the sensitive areas of ya pussy and clit, circlin' my tongue all over and 'round it. Suckin' on the sweet pussy lips. See. I listen to what makes a broad moan, and know when to change it up to give her that ultimate tongue experience. Now ya turn."

"*My turn?* My turn for what? I don't eat pussy, nigga."

He laughs. "Damn, that's too bad. But I wasn't talkin' bout that. You throatin'?"

"Nope," I lie, then bust out laughin'. "Yeah, nigga, I suck dick. Who ain't wettin' dick in two-thousand-and-ten? And I'll eat the nut outta it, too, if it's a nigga I'm dealin' wit'. Any bitch who ain't suckin' dick ain't keepin' no man. Not for long, anyway. A bitch can definitely bubble up if her throat game is right, believe that. Have a nigga sellin' his moms 'n shit for another round of that bobble action."

"Oh, shit," he says, laughin'. "I like how you kickin' that shit. That's what it is. So, when we gonna get each other off?"

"Sorry to pop ya bubble," I say, flippin' the script on his ass. "But this pussy ain't on the market. And trust me, nigga, you ain't even gonna sniff my shit 'til you take a bitch out and start spendin' sum'a that paper ya slick-ass collectin'."

He cracks up. "Yo, ma. You think you got'a muhfucka all pegged, don't you?"

"I told you, I know ya kind. And you the type to have a buncha dizzy bitches lacin' ya ass. Now tell me I'm dead-ass and I'll let you skull-fuck me right now. And don't try 'n clown. Keep that shit live."

"You know what," he says, chucklin'. "You gotta lotta shit wit' you, real talk. But I dig it."

"And you still ain't answer the question," I say, laughin'.

"Where you at right now?"

"Yeah, that's right change the subject, muhfucka."

He chuckles. "Nah, I wanna know where you at."

"Why?"

"Maybe a muhfucka's tryna see you," he says, dippin' his voice real low 'n sexy.

"Nigga, puhleeze. You tryna stalk a bitch. That's all that is."

He laughs. "Negative. Never that, baby."

"See, there you go wit' that *baby* shit again.

"My bad, ma. I can't help myself. I wanna make you my baby."

I grunt. Ugh, gag me."

"I wanna do that, too," he says, laughin'.

I suck my teeth. "Nigga, puhleeze."

"So, you gonna tell me where you at, or what?" Why I tell 'em is beyond me. But I do. "Oh, word? That's wassup. So am I. What part?"

"Sausalito," I tell 'im, then ask 'im where in Cali he's at. He says LA. Then I ask 'im what he's doin' there and he tells me he's chillin' wit' his peeps. I laugh. "Unh-huh. I bet. Ya'll fuckin' and she's lacin' you, right?" He laughs. "Just what I thought."

"So where's Salsa-lito at?"

"It's Sau-sa-lee-toe. And it's in the San Francisco area, right on the other side'a the bridge, why? You tryna take a road trip?"

"Don't tempt me."

"Impress me, punk," I tease.

"Yeah, I got ya punk aiight. Yo, you need to stop frontin' and let a muhfucka really get to know you."

Another call beeps through. It's Chanel's ass again. "Maybe I will, maybe I won't. But for now, ya times up. My girl's on the other line, so I'm out."

"Damn, ma. It's like that?"

"Yup, bitches before niggas."

He laughs. "Sounds like we got sumthin' else in common."

"Nigga, peace out." I say as he continues laughin'. I click over, then snap, "Bitch, what the fuck you keep callin' me for?"

CHAPTER SIX

Lonely bitch...dick stuntin'...sac garglin'...lettin' no-good nigga's run all up in 'er back...gotta bitch wildin' out like she's stuck on crack...got 'er chasin' fake muhfuckas who ain't tryna get caught...got da dumb trick countin' all da bitches she fought...forgettin' da tears she done shed...too scared to open 'er eyes...'til one day da bitch ends up stretched out dead...

"Kat, girl, I just got off the phone wit' Tamia—"

I frown. Now she knows damn well I don't get down wit' that bitch anymore. Once I peeped how triflin' her dirty-ass was, it was a wrap. I don't wanna be associated wit'a bitch like her. Especially one who was stuntin' like she was a top-of-the-line bitch, then come to find out that fake-ass trick was rentin' all her handbags and shoppin' in consignment shops. Bitch, please! I don't rock wit' fraudulent bitches, and I damn sure ain't gonna get it in wit' no ho poppin' Valtrex, okay? That bitch is toxic waste! "Umm, sweetie," I snap, cuttin' her off, "why the fuck you callin' me 'bout her ass? You know I don't wanna hear shit 'bout ya convo wit' her."

"Kat, this is serious. You need to come home, *now*."

"Come home for what?"

"Ya moms in the hospital. Patrice tracked down Tamia tryna get ya numbers to call you."

"And?"

"She gave me Patrice's number to give to you."

"Burn it. I'm not callin' 'er."

"Kat, Tamia said ya moms's in I-C-U. It's not lookin' good."

I blink. Does this ho really think I give a fuck 'bout Juanita bein' up in somebody's damn I-C-U ? Nope, I sure don't. And I'm damn sure not about to let myself get dragged into any of that woman's fuckin' man drama. I already know what it is. If her ass is in the hospital, then it's behind a nigga and his dick. When she doesn't have her legs tossed up over a sorry-ass muhfucka's shoulders, bein' pressed down on a hospital mattress is the only other time her ass is layin' flat on her back. So what else is new?

"That's nice," I say.

"Kat," she says, sighin', "all jokes aside. They don't think she's gonna make it."

"Well, then, I guess she'll finally make it to hell."

She gasps. "Ohmiiiiigod, Kat. Now you bein' real messy. Don't you even care 'bout what happened to her?"

"Am I supposed to?"

"Well, why wouldn't you? No matter what, she's still ya moms."

"By whose standards, Sweetie? Definitely not by mine. You put a nigga before ya own child, you pull a knife out on me and get all slick 'n greasy at the mouth in front of a muhfucka, then you ain't shit to me. So please. Don't go there wit' me. Not today."

"Kat, that's fucked up."

"Yep, and so is her life. So what I care? It is what it is. You make ya bed, you lie in it. Bitches need to stop stayin' stuck on stupid, playin' helpless-ass victims all da damn time. There comes a time when a bitch gotta say enough is enough, and pick her dumb ass up, dust shit off and do sumthin' other than what da fuck she's doin'."

"Kat, it ain't always that easy," she says defensively.

"Mmmph. And I ain't sayin' it is. But what I am sayin' is a sick bitch needs to get herself some help and stop havin' muthafuckin' pity parties. You keep doin' stupid shit, fuckin' wit' sorry-ass niggas, then what da fuck you expect you gonna get? A buncha shit, period! At some point these dizzy-ass chicks gotta stop blamin' a muhfucka for her demise 'n misery, and start takin' a look at herself. I'm done. So, movin' on."

"Well, alrighty then. I guess, wit' that said, you don't wanna hear nuthin' else 'bout what's goin' on wit' her, or what hospital she's in?"

"I sure don't. And I'd 'preciate it if you don't waste my time tryna tell me."

"OhmyGod, what a hot mess!"

I feel myself 'bout to snap on her ass. "Well, bitch…whaddaya want me to do? Break down and start yellin' 'n screamin'? You want me to act'a fool over some woman who never gave a fuck 'bout me? Baby, puhleeze. Not gonna happen. I ain't servin' up no sympathy, no tears, and no muthafuckin' love for a ho who has done nuthin' but be da stupid, neglectful bitch she's always been. So, do me a favor. If you really wanna make my day, call me when the bitch is dead." I give her ass the dial tone, then toss the phone over onto the bed.

What the fuck?! I fire up a blunt, then go out onto the balcony to puff 'n chill. Why da fuck can't these muhfuckas leave me da fuck alone. I'm here doin' me and mindin' mine. And these bitches just feel it necessary to get at me tryna disrupt my flow. Two years ago, it was the same shit wit' Rosa callin' me 'bout Juanita bein' in the hospital all beat up 'n shit. Now she's there again. Women like her never learn until a muthafucka stomps their lights out. A bitch like that, weak…needy, is better off dead, if you ask me. I take two deep pulls, hold the shit in my lungs 'til it burns, then slowly blow it out. I sit, starin' out into the view.

For some reason, I find myself thinkin' back to when I was ten. It was late at night and I couldn't sleep. Again, Juanita was at it wit' her headboard bangin' up against my wall, and her nasty-ass holed up in her room, moanin' 'n screamin' out all kinda filthy shit. Words a bitch couldn't wrap her mind 'round back then. But I understood enough. *"Fuck me…Big dick…Good pussy…Don't stop fuckin' me…"* Those were the things that stuck out. I knew enough to know she was in there gettin' gutted, once again.

This one particular night, I remember gettin' outta bed and goin' into the livin' room to watch TV 'cause I didn't have one in my room, and I was fuckin' tired of hearin' her and her fuck of the moment goin' at it. I turned on the Cartoon Network and had the volume down real low. I can't fuckin' remember what the hell was on, but I remember startin' at the screen daydreamin' 'bout someone rescuin' me and gettin' me the fuck outta there, away from her, away from that nasty-ass kitchen, those roaches and all of them on-again-off-again muhfuckas who she kept lettin' come in and outta her bed—and life.

I don't know how long I had been sittin' there starin' at the screen, dazin'. But when I finally took my eyes off'a it and turned my head, Juanita's nigga was standin' in the livin'room butt-ass naked, playin' wit' his sticky-ass dick, grinnin' at me. The only light in the room was comin' from the television, but it was like a spotlight was shinin' on that nasty muhfucka.

I felt like I was 'bout to throw up all over myself. I made a face, twistin' my nose up. "Ewww, that's nasty," I said, shiftin' in my seat and foldin' my arms 'cross my chest. That nigga kept standin' there, peekin' back at Juanita's room door e'ery so often, strokin' his dick.

"You want sum'a this?" I rapidly shook my head. "Yeah, you do. And I'ma give you sum real soon. I'ma tear that lil' tight ass up."

"I'ma tell my mommy," I said, feelin' tears well up in my eyes.

"And if you do," he hushed through clenched teeth, "I'ma kill her and *you*. You hear me?"

What was I 'posed to think? There was this tall, blue-black, burly muhfucka, mean-muggin' and hoverin' over me. A bitch was only ten, and scared. I already saw him yoke her up, once, so if the nigga said he was gonna kill us, then that's the fuck what he was gonna do. So I believed him.

I got up to run into my room, but while I was goin' past him, he yanked me by the arm and covered my mouth with his big hand to keep me from screamin'. I could smell Juanita's pussy on his fingas. The tears I tried holdin' back started pourin' outta my eyes as the nigga threatened, and warned, me to not make a sound.

He put his hot, stank breath up against my ear and reminded me in a whisper, "If you tell, I'm gonna kill you. You understand me?" I quickly nodded. "Besides, who you think she's gonna believe, anyway—me or you?"

He must'a heard sumthin' 'cause he let me go. I raced in my room and shut my door. I buried my face into my pillow, cryin'. A few minutes later, my door swung open, the light switch was flipped up and Juanita was in my room, foamin' at the mouth.

"Bitch, what da fuck you doin' up this time'a night, hunh?"

"I-I-I," I stuttered, wipin' my eyes, "...was watch—"

She cut me off, screamin'. "When it's time for ya ass to be in bed, that's the fuck where I 'pect ya ass to stay 'til it's time for ya ass to wake the fuck up for school! Not sneakin' 'round this muthafuckin' house listenin' to what the fuck I'm doin!"

My eyes widened as I looked up at her. I was shocked at how crazy she looked. Do you think that bitch asked why my eyes were red and swollen, or why the fuck I was cryin'? No! The only thing that cum-hungry ho was worried 'bout was why I was standin' in the bathroom doorway lookin' at her man takin' a piss. Can you believe that shit? That's what that snake-ass nigga told her when he went back into the bedroom, wakin' her up. And the dizzy bitch believed 'im.

"What da fuck you doin' lookin' at my man's dick, hunh?"

"I wasn't, Mommy," I said. "He-he tried…"

"Don't you fuckin' lie to me! I should knock the shit outta ya sneaky, lyin' ass. If you ever do some muthafuckin' shit like that again I'm a beat ya fresh ass 'til it bleeds."

Then that dirty muthafucka had the audacity to walk in my room, smirkin'. "C'mon, baby," he said to her, eyein' me all sly 'n shit, "I think she gets the point."

"Well, she fuckin' better," she snapped, cuttin' her eyes at me. "'Cause the next time it won't be no muthafuckin' talkin'. It's gonna be my fist in her ass." She rolled her eyes at me as he slowly tugged her by the arm, pullin' her outta the room. Then he fuckin' glanced over his shoulder at me and winked, closin' the door behind him.

That stinkin' bitch walked 'round the house for almost three weeks servin' a bitch 'tude like I was tryna steal her muthafuckin' bum-ass nigga. Fuckin' pathetic! So do you really think I'ma break my neck and give a fuck 'bout sum bitch who turned her muthafuckin' back on me, not once…not twice, but all'a my muthafuckin' life?

I ain't 'bout to be stressed over sum shit I can't change. Not today! I take one last, deep toke, then put out the tip, tossin' it over the railin'. I spark up another round, sit for a hot minute wit' my eyes closed, puffin'. *I'm so over that hatin'-ass bitch*, I think, gettin' up and goin' back into the bedroom. I leave the balcony doors open, allow the breeze to sweep through the room as I make plans to get showered and go out and do what I do best. Shop!

CHAPTER SEVEN

Thick nose...thick lips...cocky muhfucka...got dat swagga...
make'a bitch wanna open up da thighs...let 'im push in da
tip...stretch out da hips...nut on da nigga's dick...but'a slick
bitch ain't tryna get played...gotta keep it on da low...move in
slow...give da nigga just enough...'fore he ends up slayed...

"Nigga, you wanna get my pussy's attention, then you gonna need to come a lil' harder than that," I snap at this arrogant fuck talkin' 'bout how he wanna bang my guts up. I swear, this nigga be comin' at me all kinda ways. Mmmph. Fucked up thing, a bitch can't even front like I ain't diggin' the shit 'cause I am. Still, he's the type'a muhfucka a bitch gotta keep on a real short leash. Otherwise his ass'll be shittin' 'n pissin' on me e'ery chance he gets. And I ain't havin' it. "I don't know what kinda bitches you be dickin' wit', but I ain't one of 'em. So come correct when you addressin' me, muhfucka."

He laughs. "Yo, beautiful, I'm only fuckin' wit' you."

"Nigga, I ain't laughin'. And I damn sure ain't fuckin' wit' *you*. I'm dead-ass."

"Yo, ma, my bad."

"My bad, hell. You real extra wit' it, nigga."

"Yo, for real, ma, you need to chill. It ain't that serious. On some real shit, I mean no harm. But, I ain't gonna front. You snappin' makes a muhfucka horny. You got my shit bricked."

I suck my teeth. "What*eva*, muhfucka. Glad I can amuse ya nasty ass."

"Yeah, yeah, yeah; yo, keep it funky wit' a nigga. You diggin' me; just say it."

This time I laugh. "Nigga, puhleeeze. Save that shit for them dumb-ass bitches you got wettin' ya cock. I'm not checkin' for ya conceited ass."

"Yeah, aiight, that's what ya mouth says. But I know better. I'ma have you callin' me Daddy...Daddy Long Stroke, to be exact, in a minute."

I laugh harder. "Muhfucka, understand this: you'll be eatin' ya nut outta my pussy 'n ass 'n beggin' me to finga fuck you in that tight, muscular ass of yours before I *eva* part these dick suckas to call you some shit like that."

He joins in my laughter. "Yo, Kat...word up, you funny as hell, ma. You know I'm only fuckin' wit' you, right?"

"Yeah, yeah, yeah...*whaaaat*eva."

"But I'm sayin', yo...when we gonna chill? This phone shit is gettin' played. A muhfuckas tryna see you in the flesh. I was hopin' we could meet up for a bite to eat, then maybe kick back 'n blaze a bit."

I grin at the idea of burnin'. It dawns on me I haven't smoked since early last night. I glance at the time. Its 11:46 a.m. "Nigga, you ain't ready for a chick like me," I tease.

"Yeah, okay, ma. Think that shit if you want. A nigga like me was born ready."

"Yeah, I've heard that before," I say, headin' downstairs to the kitchen. I decide to fix myself some sautéed spinach wit' sundried tomatoes 'n garlic.

"And it is what it is. All you gotta do is say the word and it's on."

"Hmmmmm, that's what ya mouth says. If you was really tryna get at me you woulda made it pop by now."

"Shiiiiit, how can I when you keep shuttin' a muhfucka down at e'ery turn? A muhfucka comes at you right, you go left. I come at you from the left, you snap to the right. It's like you want me to say 'fuck it' or sumthin'. Yo, is that what you want? I mean, on some real shit, if you want me to stop fuckn' wit' you I will."

The phone goes silent.

I know this muhfucka didn't just hang up on me. "Hello?"

"I'm still here, yo. I'm waitin' on an answer. You keep tryna play a muhfucka like I'm some duck-ass nigga. All bullshit aside, what's good wit' you?"

I sigh. Okay, I ain't gonna sit here 'n front wit' ya'll, there's sumthin' 'bout this nigga that gotta bitch curious. He's so fuckin' rude. He's nasty. He's a womanizer. And he ain't no muthafuckin' good. But, he's oh sooooo damn chocolate and chiseled and muthafuckin' fine that a bitch wanna have a lil' taste. I wanna see the nigga buck-naked; see if he's swingin' one'a them juicy Mandingo cocks. But, fuck that. I ain't 'bout to make shit easy for the nigga, either.

"Look, impress me. You wanna get in these drawers; you wanna taste this pussy, then you gonna need to come hard, or get the fuck on."

He laughs. "Yo, I stay hard and I can fuck hard so all that shit you sayin' ain't nuthin' but a thang, baby."

I huff. "Nigga, what the fuck I tell you 'bout callin' me *baby*?"

"Yo, chill," he says, laughin'. "I'll call you what *the fuck* I want, ya heard?"

"Oh, noooo, nigga, you got the wrong one. Hear this…" I disconnect his ass. A few seconds later, he sends me a text. *LMAO.*

U mad funny, yo. U got that off. But know this, all dat shit did was get my dik hard.

I text back. *Fuuuuuuuuck u!*

Two minutes later, there's another text from this nut. *I'm tryn but u keep runnin' from da dik.* I text back: *lol, whateva*

Once my food is finished cookin', I place e'erything on a plate, then sit at the table, flippin' through the latest issue of *Urban Ink*. I've been givin' some thought to gettin' a cute lil' tattoo on my right hip, but I don't know exactly what I want. I know I *don't* want paw prints or hearts or some other cheesy shit. It's gotta be sexy. I continue thumbin' through the pages, readin' articles on the goings-on in the tat world. Just as I'm 'bout to lift my fork up to my mouth, my cell rings. I glance at the screen and see that it's the nigga Tone, then answer.

"Yo, whaddup, ma?" he asks.

I close my magazine. "Chillin'. Whats good wit' you?"

"I can't call it. Yo, ma, I just wanna give you heads-up."

"Bout what?" I ask, frownin'.

"The chick you slid the other day is all fucked up. You broke ole girl's jaw and nose, and knocked three of her front teeth loose."

"Oh, that's all? Well, shit. She should be countin' her blessin's then."

He chuckles. "They said somethin' about her eye socket, too."

"Oh well. The bitch shoulda kept it movin' instead of tryin' it on my time. She wouldna got lumped up. Next time, the bitch'll get her face dug out."

"Damn, you really go in hard."

"That's the only way to do it," I tell 'im, washin' my dishes. "The bitch brought it on herself. Fuck all that dilly-dallyin'. I'm not that kinda chick."

"I hear you, ma. But, check it. Her peoples been poppin' mad shit about how they gonna get at you when they catch you."

I suck my teeth. "Please, I'm not pressed. I don't give a fuck 'bout that bitch or 'er peoples. Give 'em my number and tell them hoodbooga bitches to call me."

He laughs. "Yo, you wild for real, ma. Got any peoples out here?"

"No," I tell 'im, pickin' at my cuticles. "I do my dirt solo."

"On some real shit, them broads will put that work in on you if they catch up to you."

"You mean they'll *try*. My name ain't pussy. Ain't no bitch gonna just do me and think shit's gonna be all sweet. So let 'em bring it if they want; I got sumthin' for that ass, trust."

"I hear you. I know you can handle ya own, ma. I want you to be safe out there, that's all."

"Well I 'preciate the concern."

"Don't sweat it, though. I got you, ma."

Please, I think, gettin' up from the table, *if them bitches wanna get at me, they betta bring it soon 'cause in two weeks I'ma be back on the east coast. So fuck 'em!* "Awww, how sweet. But, trust, I ain't sweatin' that shit."

"I feel you." He pauses, then busts out laughin'. "Yo, I'm only fuckin' wit' you, ma. Since you whooped that ass, shit's been real quiet. I thought she'd be blowin' up my shit tryna get at me, but nah…nothin'. Obviously it's what she needed 'cause she's always somewhere poppin' shit."

"And that's exactly what she got. But, you was 'bout to get that bitch bodied, for real, callin' here wit' that shit."

He tries to get serious. "My bad, ma. I couldn't resist. But, on some real shit, I meant what I said, I got you if sumthin' pops off. You real cool peoples, Kat."

I smile. "Thanks. You ain't so bad ya'self. But, nigga, you still ain't gettin' no more of this pussy heat."

He laughs. "Nah, I ain't on it like that. But, if you offerin', I'm damn sure takin'."

"Yeah, yeah, yeah, I bet you are. But, not happenin'. And as far as them booga bears go, they pump no fear in me. So it is what it is."

"Ouch, that hurt. You sure know how to shoot a cat in the heart."

I laugh. "Yup, I suuure do; and in his head, too." I dry my hands, then walk into the living room, ploppin' down on the sofa. "So what you gettin' into today?" I ask, changin' the subject.

"Not much; probably study for the exam we got comin' up this week. I need to pass this shit this time. You ready for it?"

Hell no, I think, proppin' my feet up on the table. Shit, I'm tryna keep myself from thinkin' 'bout it 'cause I don't wanna start stressin'. The property management course was some extra shit I took 'til it was time to take the exam. I've already passed the state and federal background checks. Mmmph, as if I didn't think I would. And, as far as they know, a bitch is of good moral character. Now, that shit kinda cracks me up; if they only knew. Annnyway, the only thing standin' between me and gettin' that paper is takin' the exam 'n passin' it. I swear I don't wanna be like this nigga, takin' it over. He mentions how he failed it the first time by four points, then the second time by one. I shake my head. Although the fee is light to take the actual exam, who has another five hours to be sittin' on they ass tryna retake a two hundred multiple question test—twice, no less? Not a bitch like me, that's for sure. All I need is a score of 75 percent, and it's a wrap. I already know what I'ma do the day of. I'ma spark me a blunt to relax my mind, then go in and slay that shit.

"Not really, but I will be." He asks if I wanna meet up to study together. "As long as you plan on not wearin' any of that *Bora, Bora* and you keep ya hands to ya'self, we good," I say, laughin'.

He joins in my laughter. "Nah, I got you, ma. I'ma be on my best behavior. The only thing on my mind right now is acin' that exam on Wednesday. Now, afterward, I might be sayin' somethin' different." I glance at the clock. 2:35 p.m.

"Nigga, the only thing you gonna be sayin' afterward is congrats."

"Yeah, that, too." I tell 'im to hit me up 'round six; that I'd let 'im know then if I'm feelin' it. Shit, I don't know if I want the nigga up in my spot. The last thing I'm beat for is a muhfucka bein' followed, then havin' a buncha bitches kickin' in my doors tryna bring it. We talk a few minutes more, then hang up.

I grab the remotes to both my Sony flat-screen and DVD player, turnin' them on. I press PLAY, then wait for *Dexter*, season three, episode five to come on. However, I change my mind. I mean. As much as Dexter's pyschopathic antics make my pussy moist, right now I need sumthin' a lil more gritty. I scroll through my On Demand, then select what I'm lookin' for.

Spartacus: Blood & Sand comes to life on the screen. I live for the wickedly deliciousness of each episode. Whew, the house of Batiatus…mmmph, a mess! A bitch can't wait 'til September when the series comes out on DVD. Keepin' shit real, I would love to say it's all those sweaty gladiators that make a bitch's pussy hot, but it's not. It's the blood; the splittin' of skulls, decapitatin' of heads that makes my steamy hole sizzle.

I replay episode nine, "Whore," where Ilithyia is fuckin' sexy-ass Spartacus, not knowin' it's him 'cause their faces are hidden behind masks. I lie back on my bed, reach for my clit stroker and spread open my thighs. I smack my pussy, then dip a finga in, stirrin' my slit before layin' the barrel of my gun along the center of my snatch. I stick the tip of it in me, coat it wit' my juice, then suck it clean.

This sex scene is fiiiiyah, but its flame isn't hot enough to make my cunt juices boil. It isn't 'til Ilithyia grabs that other bitch by the head and smashes her skull that my pussy skeets. I slide my hand into my lace panties, press on my clit while usin' my other hand to keep rewindin' back to the part where Ilithyia is on her knees gettin' slayed from da back when Lucretia's messy ass walks in to announce she's fuckin' Spartacus. Ooooh, I love it, love it, love it!

In a matter of minutes, I am moanin' and creamin' all over my fingas. I continue stirrin' my hole while jackin' my clit. Another nut is makin' its way outta me. "Yeah, Ilithyia, you nutty ho, smash that bitch's skull in," I continue moanin', buckin' my hips and grindin' on my fingas and hand. I smack my clit, then explode. "Aaaaah, shiiiit…" *I want sum dick! My pussy needs to be fucked deep*, I think, lickin' 'n suckin' my sticky fingas. I lay my head back on the sofa. And, before I know it, a bitch's knocked out the fuck out.

CHAPTER EIGHT

*Stilettos clickin'...timepiece tickin'...clockin' da niggas all
'bout trickin'...swingin' da hips...lickin' da lips...muhfuckas
ain't ready for a bitch like this...got 'em chasin' a dream...got
'em fucked up in da game...head spinnin'...feelin' all
strange...ain't nuthin' what it seems...wantin' to know who
I am...it's Kat, muhfuckas...repeat my name...ain't shit
change...*

"Attention, passengers. At this time, please turn off all
electronic devices. And place trays and seats in the
upright position as we prepare for our final descent
into Newark-Liberty International Airport. We will be landing
momentarily."

I sigh, starin' outta the window, takin' in the view. A part of me
is mad hyped 'bout bein' back on the east coast, chillin' wit' my
girl and poppin' these hips a bit. Then there's this other part of
me that ain't beat for it. I'm not gonna think 'bout it, though.
I lean my head back. Close my eyes. And for some fucked up
reason, Juanita's voice finds me. *"Kat, what did I ever do to you for
you to be so fucking hateful?...I am still your mother...I promise you,
ya ass is gonna see what it's like to really get it in with a Brooklyn
bitch..."*

I snap my eyes open. Hold the sides'a my head in the palm of my hands, pressin' back a headache. *I'm not goin' there; not today.* I take a deep breath, then slowly blow it out, peepin' the George Washington Bridge. I stare at all the whips, lookin' like miniature toy cars, zippin' up 'n down the Turnpike. I glance at my timepiece. 10:38 a.m.

I make a mental checklist of all the shit I need'a handle once I touch down. *Spark an L…Shoot uptown to get'a doobie 'n nails done… Spark another blunt…hit up da Louis store and Neiman Marcus at Garden State Plaza in Paramus…*

The minute we hit the ground at Newark Airport, I pull my phone outta my bag, then turn it on and wait for it to boot up. I text Chanel to let her know we landed. She hits me back lettin' me know she's already outside'a baggage claim waitin' on me. Before I can hit her back, a call is comin' through. It's from Nut.

"Yes, whaddaya want now?" I ask, grinnin'.

"You already know. Don't front."

I suck my teeth. "Nigga, puhleeze. What can I do for you?"

"You can stop wit' all the extras e'ery time I call you, for starters. Then you—"

I frown, flippin' on his ass. "Muhfucka, *whaaat?!* You callin' me, sweatin' me, muhfucka. I ain't beat for you." The Asian muhfucka in the seat next to me cuts his eye over at me, shiftin' in his seat. Why the fuck he's still sittin' is beyond me. I shoot him a look, raisin' my brow, like "whaaaat, muhfucka?" He quickly gets his monkey-ass the fuck up away from me. I watch as he stretches, then gathers his shit and moves the fuck on. I get up and follow behind.

"Yo, and I'ma keep sweatin' you 'til ya sexy-ass gives a muhfucka some rhythm. So, like I said, take down all that 'tude."

I shake my head, makin' my way toward baggage claim. "Umm, what did you say your name was again?"

He laughs. "Yo, you real funny, ma. Stop frontin'."

"No…seriously. What's ya name?"

"Alley Cat."

I suck my teeth. "No, fool; ya government name."

"Alex," he offers.

"Well, listen—"

"Where you at?" he asks, cuttin' me off.

I suck my teeth. "Nigga, why you checkin' for me like you my man or sumthin'?"

"I will be if you learn how'ta act," he says, laughin'.

"Whateva, Alex, Alley Cat, or whateva other lil' name you got them gutter rats callin' you."

He laughs. "Yo, you can add Daddy Long Stroke to that list."

I grunt. "Mmmph, a mess!"

"And I'm tryna be ya mess."

"Nigga, why you checkin' for me?"

"'Cause I wanna scoop you up tomorrow."

"Is that right? You still in L.A.?"

"Yeah, but it ain't nuthin', yo. I'm tryna see you."

I smile. *I should have his no-good ass fly out to San Francisco. It'll serve his arrogant ass right.* "Well, sorry to piss on ya playground. But, you're a day late and a stack short. I'm back in Jersey. So, no dice; not gonna happen."

"Oh, shit. So how long you gonna be out there?"

"For as long as I want," I tell 'im, snatchin' up my Prada duffel bag. "I ain't punchin' no time clock."

He chuckles. "I heard that, ma. Well, check it. Enough of this back 'n forth shit, Kat, for real-for real. I'ma scoop you up tomorrow night and we goin' out. You been bullshittin' long enough."

I laugh. "Yeah, yeah, yeah; *whaaaaat*eva."

"Nah, I'm dead-ass, yo."

"Oh, so just like that; you gonna hop on a plane and whisk a bitch off into da sunset?"

"Yup, just like that. I told you, I'm checkin' for you—*hard*, ma; real talk. So stop frontin' on a muhfucka. Besides, I need to get home to check on my crib and handle some other shit."

"Oh, so wifey's gonna let you out?"

"Ain't no wifey here, ma. I'm savin' that spot for you."

"Mmmph," I grunt, walkin' outta the slidin' glass doors. I peep Chanel's whip and make my way over to it. "That's what ya mouth says, muhfucka."

"And that's what it is. I'ma hit you up tomorrow to finalize our plans."

I laugh. "Nigga, I ain't say I was goin' nowhere wit' you."

"Aye, yo, you heard what I said. Tomorrow night, you mine. So get ya mind right 'cause big daddy's comin' through to scoop you up."

I suck my teeth and roll my eyes, tryna hold back my laugh. This nigga is funny as hell. "Muhfucka, big daddy on this…" I disconnect his ass, shakin' my head. I open the back door of Chanel's whip and toss my bag on the seat. "What's good, bitch?" I say, hoppin' in the front seat.

"You trick," she says, laughin'. "Glad to see ya ugly ass made it safe and sound. I missed ya stankan-ass." We air kiss. "Smooches, boo."

"What*eva*, ho." I fasten my seatbelt, then recline my seat back, pullin' my Gucci's down over my eyes. I shoot Chanel a look, peerin' at 'er over the rim of my shades. "Umm, bitch, why da fuck you ain't got me a blunt fired up? What da fuck good are you? You know a bitch been travelin' all damn mornin'. The least you could do is have a fatty rolled 'n ready. Damn."

She cracks up, pressin' 'er middle finga up in my face. "Fuck you, boo. You stooopid as hell. Open up da damn glove compartment. I got ya fiend-ass some'a that chocolate goodie-goodie in there."

"Awww, shit, ho, now that's what I'm talkin' 'bout," I say, pullin' out a black python Tumi cosmetic pouch. I unzip it, smilin' the minute the aroma hits my nose. My mouth waters. I wait 'til she pulls off, then spark up. I crack the window and take three pulls, holdin' the shit in my lungs. I blow out a thick cloud of smoke. "Now, this is how you welcome a bitch home."

Four hours later, Chanel and I are back from hittin' up Paramus Mall, sittin' at the table in the kitchen stuffin' our faces wit' jumbo shrimp, blazin', tossin' back a bottle of Ciroc red berry and poppin' mad shit back 'n forth. "Skank-a-dank, why is you sittin' over there hoggin' the damn blunt?" she asks, dippin' a piece'a shrimp in some cocktail sauce, then stuffin' it in her dick sucka. "Ya greedy, fiend-ass is always doin' that shit."

I laugh, chokin' on weed smoke. "Ho, shut ya cum-guzzlin'-ass up. You always whinin'." I take another pull, then hand it to her. "Here, bitch. And pass me that bottle."

She snatches the blunt outta my hand. I take the bottle of Ciroc to the head, guzzlin' it down. "Oooh, this shit is da truth. It tastes like Kool-Aid."

"It suuuuure does," Chanel says, tokin' the blunt. She blows smoke up at the ceilin'. "Now pass me da damn bottle, wit' ya thirsty-ass."

Usher's "OMG" starts playin' in the background.

"Bitch, kiss my ass," I say, laughin'. I take another swig, then slide it back to her. "Ya throat's longer than mine."

She laughs. "Fuck you wit' ya hatin' ass."

"I can't stand this damn song," I say, reachin' for the remote. "It gives me a fuckin' headache."

"Oh-oh-ohmyGod, oh-oh-ohmyGod," she laughs. "I think it's a cute club banga."

I grunt. "Mmmph. Yeah, and I bet ya ho-ass is wishin' he was gut-bangin' ya back out, too." She passes off the blunt, then fires up another. I take two pulls, then put it out.

"Please, Usher can't do shit for me. He lost a buncha cool points when he married and knocked up that man."

I bust out laughin'. "Girl, you wrong for that. That ho ain't no damn man."

She bucks her eyes. "Says who? You ever really look at 'er."

"She's a chick wit' very manly features; that's all." I change the track. Alicia Keyes "Love Is Blind" starts playin'. "Some chicks are just mannish like that."

"Whateva," she says, rollin' her eyes up in her head.

I keep laughin'. "Well, they divorced now, so you can go 'head 'n gargle the nigga's balls."

"Please, I wish da fuck I would. Da nigga still ran his dick up in that; no thank you."

I shake my head. Chanel's simple ass thinks any nigga fuckin' wit' a bitch wit' manly features or mannerisms is fightin' homo tendencies, or is out gettin' his creep on wit' trannies 'n shit. I don't necessarily agree wit' her on it. But what I care. It's her opinion, her choice. I leave it be. She opens her mouth to say sumthin' else, but her iPhone rings. She answers.

"Wassup, Trick? Anyone make you they bitch yet? Mmmph, whateva, ho...yeah, yeah, yeah...well, guess who I'm wit'? No stupid...Kat. Hold on..." she hands me her phone. "Here, some-one wants to speak to you." I ask who. "Don't worry 'bout it."

"Well, I hope it ain't that nasty bitch, Tamia."

"No, it ain't Tamia, ho," she says, suckin' her teeth. "Just take da damn phone."

I snatch it outta her hand. "Hello?"

"Wow," is all she says. And as soon as I hear the voice the hairs on the back of my neck raise up. I shoot Chanel a look. She smirks, poppin' another shrimp into her nasty-ass cum trap.

Nigga, don't play me…did you fuck da bitch or not? I hear the muh-fucka say, *Yeah.* "Oh, wassup, Iris?" I say, nonchalantly. But inside I'm ready to bring it to this ho. Oh, what? I know you didn't think I forgot how this dick garglin' bitch was ridin' down on Naheem's dick while I was fuckin' 'im, too, and never, ever, opened her muthafuckin' nut-coated mouth to let me in on it. Not! Ain't shit change. I'ma still fuck this bitch up when I see 'er. And I don't give a fuck how long I gotta wait.

"Damn, bitch," she says, soundin' disappointed that I ain't all amped to hear her voice. "I ain't talked to you in a minute and that's the best you can do? *Wassup?* A bitch gets locked down and now it's fuck me, right?"

"Looks that way," I say, takin' a swig of Ciroc.

"That's fucked up, Kat. We used to be girls 'n shit. What happened?"

Bitch, you fucked my man, then smiled all up in my muthafuckin' grill. "Sweetie, what you thought it was gonna be? You let ya'self get tricked out and started mulin' for some nigga, so you get what you got. A bitch like me ain't entertainin' no dumb-ass hoes. I told you that from da rip."

"Fuck you, Kat," she snaps. "How da fuck you gonna turn ya back on ya girl 'n shit. I've been locked up for almost two-and-a-half years and not once have you dropped a bitch a card, a letter, nuthin'."

"Bitch, *you* ain't my girl. Be clear. What da fuck I look like jailin' wit' you. I'ma real bitch, ho. And real bitches, ain't doin' no bid wit' a dumb-ass bitch who knew betta."

"No, *bitch*," she yells into the phone, "a real bitch stands by her girls whether she agrees wit' her choices or not! Not turn her back on 'em. I did what I had'a do."

"No, bitch, you did what you *wanted* to do. It's not what you had'a do. Big difference, so don't go there. Save that bullshit for a bitch who don't know betta. I told ya ass before you got knocked what it was. And that's what it is."

"Oh, so you real brand new, I see."

"Bitch, I'm keepin' it a hunnid wit' ya dizzy ass; how da fuck you see that bein' brand new?"

I feel myself 'bout to bring it to this bitch, but I bite the inside of my lip. *Keep it cute, ho*, I think, starin' at Chanel. She has the blunt hangin' from her dick suckas, gawkin' at me. I walk over to her and snatch it outta her mouth. She sucks her teeth, laughin'. I take a pull. I decide to flip the script. "So, how you been?"

She laughs. "Oh, now you wanna know how a bitch's doin'? Mmmph, fuck you, Kat."

"Bitch, fuck it, then."

"You're such a fuckin' evil-ass bitch," she says.

I laugh. "Yup; tell me sumthin' I don't already know."

"Whateva, bitch. When you gonna get ova ya'self and come through? Or is that too much for a real bitch like you? And don't give me no bullshit, either, Kat; we're bigger than that."

I grin. *Oh, bitch, you just made splittin' ya shit that much easier.* "Where they got you?" She tells me she's holed up at a federal correctional facility in Danbury, Connecticut. Tells me they had her down in Tucson, Arizona before movin' up here. "Oh, well, I guess I can squeeze a day trip in. I'll let you know when I'm beat to see ya silly-cock-washin' ass."

The stupid bitch grunts, soundin' agitated. "You know what bitch? I'm done. Put Chanel back on the phone."

"Toodles," I say, laughin'.

I hand Chanel back her phone. "Girl, don't pay her crazy ass no mind," she says to Iris. "You know the bitch is touched." She laughs.

"Bitch, whateva. Both of you slut-boxes can eat shit."

Chanel sucks her teeth, givin' me the finga. "I know, right. But, don't stress that shit. We'll be up there to see you, soon. I know. We got you, ain't that right, Kat?"

Yeah, I got that ho-ass bitch, aiight. "Yup, wit' muthafuckin' bells on."

I sit back in my seat, grinnin'. *Oh, yeah, I'ma serve that ho up a nice dish of whoop ass.* The idea of breakin' Iris's jaw makes my clit twitch. I spark another blunt, takin' it straight to the dome. Chanel finishes up bullshittin' wit' Iris's trick-ass, then lays her phone back on the table.

"Bitch, you was dead wrong for that," she says, tossin' her hair to the side. "Why you do her like that?"

"Fuck that bitch," I say, turnin' the volume up on the stereo when Raheem Devaughn's "Love Drug" plays. "She was fuckin' Naheem, or did you forget that?"

"Bitch," she snaps, takin' the Ciroc to the head. "That ho fucked that nigga years ago. We all were mad young…"

"Yeah, and that bitch was mad nasty; and she still is."

"You need to let that shit go. You ain't fuckin' wit' the nigga, so who gives a fuck if she had his dick in her throat? That's old news."

"Ho, I ain't lettin' shit go. That trick-ass, cum-guzzlin' bitch was grinnin' all up in my muthafuckin' face and suckin' da snot outta my man's dick at the same time. I don't think so. Say what da fuck you want, but that shit ain't sweet."

"Bitch," she huffs, "hand me the fuckin' blunt." I take another pull, then pass it off. She snatches it. "Listen to how da fuck you sound, Kat. That shit popped off, what, almost ten years ago? The bitch is locked da fuck up. And you soundin' extra crazy, for real. Give the ho a pass, damn."

I smirk. "You know what, Trick? You right. I'ma let da ho live. We been through too much to let some dick come between us. Let's make plans to go see her ass, soon."

She grins. "Now that's more like it, Boo. I knew you'd come to ya senses and see shit my way."

Please, you can sit here and think what you want. But I'ma beat the cum outta that bitch, trust!

CHAPTER NINE

*Chocolate muhfucka likin' what he sees...hopin' ta get a fly,
sexy bitch down on 'er knees...gotta keep brushin' da nigga
off...but da nigga stay tryna press...yeah da muhfucka's
fine...but a bitch ain't beat for da stress...this kind'a nigga
cums wit' a buncha bullshit-ass mess...*

"Yo, it's Alley Cat."

"Come again," I ask, fuckin' wit' 'im. "You got da wrong number.
I don't know no nigga named *Alley Cat*."

He laughs. "Well, in another six hours or so, you will. So you
might as well start gettin' ya sexy ass ready."

"Get ready for what?" I ask, sittin' up in bed. "I ain't fuckin'
wit' you."

Yeah, aiight, ma. Front if you want. You already know."

"I don't know nuthin', muhfucka. So what you sayin'?"

He sucks his teeth, sighin'. "Yo, here you go. We already went
through this shit. I told you yesterday I was comin' through to
scoop you. Ain't shit changed, ma. So don't play."

"Who said I was playin'?"

"Gimme ya address, ma."

I smirk. "Oh, so you really here in Jersey?"

"Yeah, I'm on my way to the crib as soon as I stop past my

moms to see wassup wit' her." This is the first time I've ever heard him mention his moms. It dawns on me that all the times we've talked on the phone, I never asked the nigga where at in Jersey he rests; never asked 'im if he had any brothas or sistas. Come to think of it, we never really talked on some real shit. I decide to ask, but the muhfucka shuts it down. "Listen, all that social work shit you tryna get into ain't important, right now; gettin' ya address and snatchin' you up is."

"Nigga, I ain't goin' off wit' a mufucka I don't know shit about."

"Aye, yo, stoppin' makin' 'xcuses; I'll tell you whatever you wanna know tonight, when I see you."

"Yeah, ohhhhkaaay. And don't be thinkin' ya nasty ass is gettin' any of this pussy, either. 'Cause I'ma hate ta shut ya ass down."

"C'mon, ma. Give a muhfucka more credit than that. I mean, yeah…I pop shit to you and whatnot. But, it ain't that serious. Real talk, I might wanna get up in them hips. But, for now…I'm good, yo."

Might? Oh, puhleeze, this nigga is frontin' like hell. I laugh. "Yeah, right; whateva. Don't gas me. If I threw this pussy up in ya face you'd be all up in it, tryna eat my ovaries out."

He laughs. "Yo, you right, I might. But, check this. I get all the pussy, ass 'n throat I want. A muhfucka ain't ever gotta sweat you for no pussy, and that's some real shit."

"Then we good."

"No doubt, so where you rest at?"

"I'm not available," I tell 'im, lyin' back in bed.

"Yo, ma, what the fuck? Why you gotta make e'erything so fuckin' difficult? I wanna see you, *tonight*. Not tomorrow, not next week, or the week after that. *Tonight*, you dig? And I'm not takin' no for an answer. So stop bullshittin' and tell a muhfucka where you rest…*damn*."

Oh no this muhfucka didn't. The nigga got me gaggin'. But I ain't gonna front, either. The muhfucka's aggression got'a bitch's clit to twitch.

"Difficult?"

"Yeah, difficult. Do you need me to spell it for you, too?"

Oh this muhfucka is really pushin' it. "Oh, hell no, nigga. You really tryna get da heat—"

"Yo' hol' up. Take that volume down, ma. All that ain't necessary."

"Muthafucka, you callin' me; you pressin' me. Don't get it twisted, nigga."

"You know what, you right. Fuck it. All a muhfucka's tryna do is chill wit' ya stuck up ass, but you too muthafuckin' retarded…"

What the fuck? Is this muthafucka really tryna get it poppin'? "Muhfucka who is you talkin'—"

"Yo, on some real shit," he snaps, "shut ya fuckin' dick suckas. I'm talkin' now. Dig this. I let you come at me all crazy 'n shit 'cause you mad sexy, and a nigga's diggin' you. But you not gonna keep comin' at my neck anyway you want. All you wanna do is give a muhfucka ya ass to kiss. You got me fucked up, ya dig? You wanna be on some extra shit, then do you. But all that fucked up attitude you got is gonna keep ya ass lonely and miserable."

The line goes dead.

"Hello? Hello?" I say, pullin' the phone from my ear, starin' at it. The screen reads: DISCONNECTED. "Ohmyfuckin'gaaaawd, this nigga hung up on me," I say out loud, still holdin' the phone 'n starin' at it in my hand. "I don't believe this shit." *And the nigga read ya ass for filth!* This muthafucka actually cursed me out, then hung up on me. Now I'm pissed! "Who da fuck that black muthafucka think he is? I will straight take it to his ugly-ass face," I'm snappin' to myself. *Bitch, stop frontin'. You just got finished sayin' how fine da nigga is, now you callin' his ass ugly. It's 'bout time some-body brung it to ya ass.*

Ten minutes later, my cell rings. I glance at the screen. *I should let da shit go into voice mail.* Of course, I don't. "Yeah?" I answer wit' 'tude.

"Yo, ma…let's start this shit over. I apologize for comin' at you like that. But, yo, you really know how'ta make a muhfucka crazy. Ya mouth is real extra, ma; for real."

I ig the apology and the slick-ass comments. "Ummm, did we get disconnected?" I ask already knowin' the answer, but I wanna hear the nigga say it.

"Nah, I hung up on you," he coolly states. He sighs. "You ready to talk like you got some sense?"

"You know what, kiss my ass. You arrogant, egotistical, son-ofa—"

He laughs. "Temper, temper. Why does this gotta be a big-ass production? All I wanna do is chill, blaze, and get to know you; no pressures. No bullshit. Is that too much for a muhfucka to ask for? Shit, I ain't even had the pussy, yet. Don't even know if the shit's worth all the damn drama you be tryna bring."

"Then step, muhfucka. Delete my shit, and make ya way onto da next."

He laughs. "Yo, Kat, stop, aiight? You and I both know if you wasn't beat for a muhfucka you wouldn't be givin' me all this air time. You a grown-ass woman, and I'ma grown-ass man, so wasssup…you givin' me ya address or what?"

Bitch, you know you diggin' the nigga, so get ova ya'self. I blow out a frustrated sigh. "What time you wanna pick me up?" I finally ask, surprisin' myself.

"Aaaah, that's wassup. Finally, we're gettin' somewhere!"

I suck my teeth. "Whaaaaateva."

He laughs. "Yo, you a piece'a work, for real, ma. But check this. The nastier you are, the hornier I get, so how 'bout you try bein' nicer so a muhfucka don't have'ta walk around wit' a hard dick all day."

"Don't press ya luck." I give 'im my address. He tells me he's scoopin' me up at six. I glance at the clock. It's already eleven in the morning. Shit, I'ma need to get my ass in gear if I plan on bein' ready by then. "And don't come up here ringin' my doorbell all late 'n wrong, either. 'Cause a bitch ain't one for waitin' 'round for no nigga."

"Yo, chill. You ain't gotta stress 'bout shit like that; I'ma on time type nigga. The only thing I ever make a chick wait for is this hot, creamy nut, feel me?"

I suck my teeth. "Nigga, you are so full of ya'self."

He laughs. "Yo, I'm keepin' shit real."

"Whateva," I say, dismissin' 'im. "Where you takin' me?"

"Relax. I got this."

"Relax hell. I need'a know how'ta dress."

"All you need to know is you wit' me."

"That's not—"

"See, that's ya problem, ma," he says, cuttin' me off. "You don't know how'ta go wit' da flow."

"Oh, so you think you got me all figured out, hunh?"

"Nah, not really; but I know what I know."

"And what's that?"

"That you like givin' muhfuckas a hard time."

"That's not true," I say defensively. "I'ma cool-ass chick; I'm just not beat to be sweatin' a nigga's balls."

He laughs. "You wanna see a muhfucka beg, that's all. But, check this. I ain't one for beggin', but I've been makin' you an exception, for now."

I raise my brow. "Oh, puhleeeze. And then what?"

"And then I'ma have *you* beggin'. See you at six." The muh-fucka disconnects the call before I can open my mouth to say sumthin' slick. I shake my head in disbelief. I've never had a nigga hang up on *me!* And here this muthafucka comes discon-nectin' me not once, but *twice*, in one damn day! The crazy shit is I feel like the nigga done struck a match on my clit and set my pussy on fire. My insides have gone up in flames, and the nigga got me wantin' some'a that dick!

At exactly six o'clock, my doorbell rings. I purposefully take my time gettin' to the door, not wantin' to come off lookin' all thirsty 'n anxious 'n whatnot. On some real shit, inside I am a nervous fuckin' mess. The last muhfucka who came to my spot to pick me up 'n take me out on a date was Grant. I close my eyes. Picture him standin' at the door. Remember how fine 'n sexy the nigga was; how I straddled up on that muhfucka, foggin' up the windows of his whip, and let 'im slide his thick fingas deep in my pussy 'n fuck me 'til he had me feelin' like I was bein' dug out wit' a dick.

Therrrssp! Therrrsp! Those thoughts become replaced wit' the nigga's skull leakin'; blood splatterin' up against the wall. The sound of the doorbell ringin', followed by bangin', snaps me back to the present. I catch myself starin' at my reflection in the full-length wall mirror. I blink, blink again, shakin' the shit off. I take a deep breath, peepin' my wears; pleased wit' my look. I decided to keep it cute in a red knee-grazin' wrap dress and'a pair of black Manolo Blahnik six-inch, lace-up, cut-out boots. My titties pop just enough to let the nigga know what's what. But, I ain't pressed to be givin' his ass too much sexiness, not all at once; only a taste.

I head downstairs. Take another deep breath, tellin' myself to relax, to keep it cute. *Bitch, get ya mind right, the nigga ain't no-good; all he is is a hot meal and*—maybe, *a good fuck!* I swing open the door. He's leanin' up on the doorframe wit' a huge smile plastered 'cross his face. His fitted hat is dropped down low, coverin' his eyes. *This muhfucka,*" I think, steppin' back and invitin' 'im in, *wit' his sexy ass.*

"Damn, yo," he says, removin' his fitted and lettin' his eyes roam my body. "You lookin' good as hell, baby." I give 'im the evil eye. He throws his hands up, grinnin'. "I know, I know. Quit callin' you *baby.* For once, cut a cat some slack. You sexy, ma."

I don't know why bein' alone wit' this nigga has my nerves so rattled. I need a blunt and a shot'a sum nigga juice—Rèmy, Henny; sumthin' dark and hard! *And a taste of this chocolate nigga's dick milk,* I think, pressin' a grin on my face. "Of course I am; I'm *that* bitch, thought you knew."

He laughs. "Yeah, aiight." His eyes wander 'round the living room. "Nice spot."

"Thanks. Have a seat. I'll be ready in two minutes."

I catch the nigga lickin' his lips. "You look *ready* now," he says wit' sex drippin' from his tone.

"*Whaaaaat*eva," I say, poppin' my hips outta the room goin' into my powder room to put on a coat of lipstick—sumthin' I rarely wear, followed by a coat of lipgloss to give my lips that juicy, I'll-suck-a-dick-all-night-long look.

When I step back into the room, he stands up, smilin'. I scan his wears, peep the ice drippin' from his lobes and the rose gold Brera watch strapped to his wrist. He's rockin' faded True Religion jeans, a thin brown True Religion thermal-type shirt, and a pair of brown Prada lace-ups.

"Why you smilin'?" I ask, grabbin' my Bottega Veneta. I let it drop in the crook of my arm.

He shakes his head. "Same reason you are."

I suck my teeth, grabbin' my keys. "Nigga, I ain't smilin'." I tell 'im to keep still while I set my alarm, then usher 'im out the door.

"Yeah, aiight," he says, openin' the door. He waits for me, then shuts it. "That's what ya mouth says." I roll my eyes, lockin' the top lock.

"Whateva," I say, followin' him to his whip. Truth is the muh-fucka's right. A bitch *was* smilin'.

CHAPTER TEN

> *Puff, puff, pass…Blazin' wit' a sexy nigga…Gotta bitch feelin'*
> *right…got 'er shiftin' in 'er seat…pressin' dem thighs…*
> *roamin' 'er eyes…thinkin' 'bout givin' up da ass…fuckin' 'im*
> *all night…then doin' 'im dirty…like a real bitch should…toss*
> *da nigga out…'cause a bitch know he ain't no fuckin' good…*

"So, where we goin'?" I ask, slidin' into the passenger seat of his Range, then fastenin' my seatbelt.

"You'll see when we get there," he says, flippin' through his CD collection. "Tonight, I'm in charge."

I laugh. "Nigga, trust, you only in charge 'cause I'm lettin' you *think* you are."

He turns his head in my direction, raisin' his brow. "Like I said, *tonight*, I'm in charge. So sit back, relax and enjoy the ride, baby."

I turn my head, lookin' outta the window, actin' like I ain't beat for that shit he's talkin'.

He laughs. "Oh, what? You poutin' now?" He backs outta my driveway, then heads for the highway.

"Nope. I'm chillin'."

"Oh, aiiight. That's more like it, baby. Daddy got you."

I cut my eyes at 'im, sittin' back and foldin' my arms 'cross my chest. "Oh, nigga, puhleeeze. Don't even start. I told you 'bout that *baby* shit."

He laughs. "Yo, chill. I'm tryna make you my baby, but you ain't tryna act right."

"Oh, trust. You can't make me nuthin' I ain't tryna be," I state, shootin' 'im a look.

He grins. *Damn, this sexy muhfucka kinda reminds me of Grant,* I think, shiftin' in my seat. True, he's more aggressive and 'xtra cocky wit' his, still the nigga's swagger is right. "Yeah, aiight. You love talkin' slick 'n shit, but it's all good. I know what you need to get ya mind right, ma."

Yeah, a stiff, thick dick. "Ohhh reallllllly? Do tell," I say, shiftin' in my seat to face 'im.

He pulls out a fat blunt, then sparks it. "Some'a this," he takes two pulls, then passes it off. I take it straight to the head, leanin' my head back on the headrest. I hold the weed smoke in my lungs, then slowly blow it out. "And this," he adds, slidin' a CD into the dashboard CD changer. He cracks the windows and sunroof.

A few seconds later, I hear Erykah Badu's voice comin' through the speakers. "20 Feet Tall" plays.

I turn my head toward 'im, grinnin' as I pass 'im back the blunt. "Oh, shit, let me find out. What you know 'bout Erykah?"

"Don't sleep, ma," he says, glancin' over at me. "I ain't ya average type cat."

"Mmmm, if you say so."

"Nah, it's what I know."

"Well, since you know so much, is there anything else I need?"

He laughs, glancin' over at me. "Yeah, but you ain't gettin' any of it 'til you start actin' right."

I laugh, chokin' back weed smoke. "Keep it, nigga."

"Yeah, aiight," he says, laughin'. "Lucky for you, I'm tryna be a gentleman tonight."

"No, lucky you," I say back.

He keeps laughin'. *Laugh now, muhfuka*, I think, settlin' back in my seat. *But when I'm done wit'cha ya ass I'ma have you grabbin' da sheets like a lil' bitch.*

I hum to the beat. We pass the blunt back 'n forth, vibin' to Erykah. I snap my fingas, and sway a bit when "Window Seat" starts to play, breakin' the silence between us. "Did you see the video to this?" I ask.

"No doubt," he says, keepin' his eyes on the road. "She did her thing."

I smirk, lookin' at 'im. "Was you payin' attention to the video, or to her juicy ass?"

He laughs. "Both." He sparks another blunt. Takes a deep pull, then passes it to me. After a moment of silence, he asks outta the blue, "So what kinda niggas you into?" I choke, shiverin'. Chills go through me when he asks this. He looks over at me. "Yo, you aiight over there?"

I nod, still coughin'. "Yeah, I'm good," I tell 'im, but I'm not. The nigga's question got me shook. That's the exact same question Grant had asked the night he picked me up to take me to Mr. Chow. Right outta the blue, 'exactly like this nigga did.

"Why, you puttin' in an application," I hear myself sayin' as I stare' at 'im; expectin' to see Grant sittin' behind the wheel instead of him. I hear myself repeatin' word for word the same shit I had told Grant. "I'm into niggas who ain't scared of pussy; a nigga who knows how'ta eat it up and beat it up." I blink. See that it's still him sittin' there; that a bitch's startin' to bug. "I'm into real niggas who do real things; niggas who don't cheat, beat or mistreat," I decide to tell 'im. I ain't gonna front. The haze gotta a bitch feelin' mad frisky sittin' next to this nigga. But I'ma keep it cute.

"I feel you."

I stare at 'im. "How many chicks you creepin' wit'?"

"None," he says, smirkin'.

"Whatchu grinnin' for?"

"'Cause I know where this is goin'."

"Oh, really? And where's that?"

"I'm single, ma. So, no…I don't creep. And I don't cheat; and I never have."

"Okay, smart ass, then let me rephrase the question. How many hoes you fuckin'?"

"At the moment?" I suck my teeth, shootin' him a "yeah nigga" look. He laughs. "You really wanna know?"

"Yeah, nigga. And keep it gully. How many bitches you runnin' ya dick in?"

I can see the nigga countin' in his head. "Six, seven, off and on; two on a regular, though." I ask if that's the most he's fucked. He tells me no. Tells me he's fucked up to twenty-seven bitches in a year. Tells me he's had threesomes and foursomes. *OhmyGod, this nigga's real loose wit' da dick; a nasty whore wit' his!*

"Oh, so you slingin' da dick all over da place, huh?"

"Nah, I wouldn't say all that. I'm doin' me; gettin' it in whenever, wherever."

"Raw?" I ask, raisin' my brow.

He takes his eyes off the road, frownin'. "Hell, naw. I ain't that kinda nigga. I wrap it up before I tap it up; no exceptions. The chick who gets this dick naked is gonna be the chick I'm wifin'; real talk. And a muhfucka don't see that happenin' anytime soon, so I'ma keep gettin' it in, one hole, one stroke, one nut, at'a time."

"Mmmm," is the only thing I say, lookin' outta the window bobbin' my head to Erykah's "Love."

He lowers the volume. "So, who you got hittin' that?"

"What?" I question, turnin' to face 'im, frontin' like I don't know what he's talkin' 'bout.

"You heard me the first time. Who you got knockin' them walls?" I tell 'im no one in particular. "Oh, word? So, when's the last time you had some dick in ya life?"

"A few weeks ago."

"Did the nigga dick you right?"

I replay the afternoon of fuckin' Tone out in my head, remember how I dug the nigga's neck out wit' my nails. How I couldn't get my nut wit'out thinkin' 'bout blood. Although it wasn't the greatest fuck, fuckin' the muhfucka definitely made a bitch realize how badly I missed havin' a nigga to crawl up on; how much I've missed havin' this pussy stroked. How I've missed the touch of a real nigga who knows how'ta handle a real bitch. And keepin' shit real, it forced a bitch to realize 'xactly how bad I miss fuckin' a nigga, then snatchin' the muhfucka's last breath right before he nutted.

For some reason, images of Grant's thick dick flash through my head. Flashes of sweaty, knee-bucklin', all-night-long, fuckin' take over and a bitch can almost feel him bangin' this pussy from the back; tip-drillin' and slammin' his thick dick in 'n outta my hot, sticky snatch; slow fuckin' it, deep fuckin' it; runaway train fuckin' it; my hips grindin' 'n windin'; feelin' his warm, gooey cream, slide down into my asshole, drippn' along the back of my pussy. The memory gotta bitch in heat. I cross my legs, try 'n pinch off the stirrin' in my clit.

I clear my throat, take this nigga in. Dark dreamy chocolate muhfucka wit' deep spinnin' waves that can make a bitch sea sick. Dark brown eyes...thick full lips, thick nose, and big-ass hands. *And the nigga's bow-legged! Yeah, but the muhfucka's a dog!*

"Yo," he says, tappin' me on the leg, "you aiight over there? Let me find out that smoke got you zonin'."

"Nigga, puhleeeze...I'm good. This shit you got is a tease."

He laughs. "Yeah, aiight. Well, answer the question. Did the muhfucka beat them walls up?"

"It was aiight. I mean, it wasn't nuthin' to write home about, but the nigga wasn't no slouch, either. I fucked 'im once and knew he wasn't gettin' da pussy again, so I wasn't keepin' a scorecard on his stroke game. He did what I needed 'im to do for that moment, and there you have it."

"Oh, aiight. I feel you. So who you got lined up to hit that the next go round?"

I laugh. "Don't be tryna monitor how I dish out my pussy, muhfucka. But to answer ya question, no one. Why?"

He laughs. "Maybe I'm tryna get next. You gotta problem wit' that?"

I roll my eyes, suckin' my teeth. "Next question."

"Yeah, aiight. Why you don't have a man?"

'Cause da nigga's dead, I think, runnin' my hand through the back of my hair, keepin' my stare locked on 'im. "Nigga, why you think?"

He laughs. "'Cause ya fine-ass is evil as hell."

"Whateva...wrong answer. 'Cause a nigga don't define me; next."

"You lookin' for a man?"

"Nope; now what?"

He hits me wit' a sexy grin, passin' me the blunt. "Aiight, next question. How many niggas have you let run up in you?"

I tilt my head. Tellin' this muhfucka the truth ain't an option. The nigga would think I'ma bona-fide slut-bucket if I did. Fuck what ya heard. I was a cock slayer; and yeah a bitch slutted for the dick. But my name ain't out there in the streets; one'a the advantages of shuttin' a muhfucka's lights out. *Almost e'ery muhfucka I bodied; too many to count.* And plenty more who lapped at this clit and gobbled up this sweet, juicy pussy. I decide to spit a buncha half-truths. "With da exception of the muhfucka I fucked recently, da niggas I let run up in me are the same niggas who I was fuckin' wit' on da regular."

"Okay, so how many?"

Not countin' the young nigga who I let pop this pussy when I needed a burner, I think, count, in my head. *Naheem...B-Love... Grant...Tone.* "Four."

"Daaaaamn, that's wassup. That pussy must be mad tight."

I smirk. "Yup, it'll suck da skin off a dick."

He laughs. "Yeah, aiight. Question is can you handle a dick?"

I stare at 'im for a few seconds. "Who says I'm tryna handle one?"

He keeps laughin'. "It's all in ya eyes, ma."

I roll the window down, take two more pulls off'a what's left of the blunt, then toss the shit out. He frowns. "Yo, ma, why you throw that shit out?"

"Nigga, this shit we smokin' must be laced 'cause yo' ass is seein' shit."

He cracks the fuck up. "Yo, ma, you funny bad. Front if you want."

"And ya narcissistic ass is delusional."

"Yeah, that's what ya mouth says."

"Nigga, that's what I know."

He shakes his head, smilin'. For the rest of the ride up the Turnpike headin' north, we keep it light, smokin', laughin' 'n listenin' to music 'n shit. I stare outta the window, takin' the ride in. It's not 'til after he takes the lower level of the George Washington Bridge, takes the exit for Leonia/Teaneck, then takes the ramp for Route 4 West that I know 'xactly where he's takin' me—Morton's Steakhouse in Hackensack, a high-end, overpriced steak spot. The minute we turn onto Riverside Square, my mouth waters. And it has nuthin' to do wit' the restaurant, and e'erythin' to do wit' The Shops at Riverside Mall. One'a my hot spot fashion stops!

I turn my attention to 'im. "Umm, sweetie," I say, shakin' my head, "You takin' me to Morton's?"

"Yeah, you aiight wit' that?"

I nod. "It's cool. But you really shoulda did ya homework before bringin' me way up here."

"Why?"

I smirk. "'Cause the last nigga who brought me here ended up diggin' in his pockets forty-two hunnid deep."

He laughs. "Yo, if the cat let you do his pockets, then good for you. But, know this, I ain't that nigga."

Nigga, not yet you ain't. "Oh, please be clear. I don't need you to be. I have my own paper."

He smiles. "That's nice to know."

"Yup, it suuuuure is. Now pass da blunt."

CHAPTER ELEVEN

There's sumthin' 'bout da nigga that got'a bitch intrigued...
maybe it's da way he licks them lips...maybe da way da nigga
undresses me wit' his eyes...gotta bitch wantin' to know what
makes 'im tick...pusssy achin' for a quick ride on da dick...still
a bitch gotta keep it on da low...take it slow...not get played
like some dizzy-ass chick...

Once we're inside the restaurant and seated, we place our orders. For appetizers, we share an order of Jumbo Lump Crab Cake and Colossal Shrimp; for dinner, I order the beefsteak tomato salad wit' fresh bleu cheese and red onions. He gets the Chilean sea bass.

Although I ain't wit' all this winery bullshit, I order a glass of Cabernet Sauvignon; sum shit I ain't eva heard of. And shit a bitch ain't feelin'. I wait for the waiter to walk away, then ask, "So, tell me. Is this 'posed to be a date?"

"Nah," he says, smirkin', "it's a cool-ass nigga chillin' wit' a sexy-ass dime-piece, havin' dinner. Why, you want it to be?"

I smirk back, slowly shakin' my head. "Nope, not at all."

"Cool then." The waiter returns to the table wit' my drink, and the appetizers. He waits for 'im to bounce, then says, "So how long you plan on stayin' in Jersey?"

"For as long as I want," I tell 'im, placin' a crab cake on my plate. I shrug, cuttin' into it wit' my knife. "I don't answer to anyone."

"Oh, you don't?"

I tilt my head, raisin' my brow. "No…I don't."

"Good, neither do I; so we straight."

I roll my eyes, twistin' my lips up. "Yeah, right; tell me anything."

"What, you don't believe? A muhfucka ain't latched down to nuthin' or no one."

"It doesn't matter if I believe you or not," I say, placin' a forkful of crab cake into my mouth. "I'm not tryna have you."

"Oh, word. You not?" I tell 'im hell no. "Yeah, aiight; that's what ya mouth says." I roll my eyes. Tell the nigga to kiss my ass. He laughs, then stares at me, shakin' his head. His foot brushes mine. "Well, maybe I'm tryna have you," he says, poppin' a shrimp in his mouth. He licks his thick, titty 'n clit suckas. I shift in my seat, crossin' my legs, then squeezin' my thighs. I feel the pressure buildin' up in my clit. The weed we smoked gotta bitch mad horny. *I wanna feel this nigga's dick in me.* My pussy pulses. I shift in my seat again. "Well, you can't have me," I tell 'im.

He laughs. "Yeah, aiight; we'll see."

"Nigga, are you always so cocky?"

He grins. "Yeah, somethin' like that. I gotta lotta cock, what can I say?"

I suck my teeth. "Oh, so you one'a them niggas whose in love wit' his dick, I see."

"Nah, it's the bitches who are in love wit' this dick. I'm the muhfucka who's in love wit' gettin' it wet." I decide to ig his ass, relieved the waiter comes back to the table wit' our meal. By the time we're halfway finished eatin', I learn he's an only child, like me. That he's close to both his parents, particularly his moms.

That he spent almost two years in college, but dropped out to do nuthin' but hustle bitches off'a they paper. Well, he didn't say it like that, but he might as well had. That he has no children. Burns mad trees. And fucks a string of horny bitches.

"And no baby mommas?" I ask again, half-believin' 'im.

"Nope."

"Okay, so none that you claimin'."

"Nah, none period. I told you, ma, I wrap my shit—all the time. Well, 'cept when I'm gettin' throated." I raise my brow. He laughs. "Word up, I'm dead ass. Unless a broad can get pregnant swallowin' my dick batter it ain't happenin'."

"Alriiiiiighty then. Next."

"What 'bout you; how many baby daddies you got?"

"None. And I ain't tryna have one." I'm kinda shocked when he asks if I've eva been pregnant. Although I coulda told the nigga no, I decide to keep shit real. "Yeah, when I was young and dumb. But I handled that situation real quick, trust."

"I feel you." I'm surprised when he tells me 'bout some nutty-ass bitch who kept claimin' he knocked her up. How she tried'a drag 'im into court for child support; how she kept showin' up at his family's spot wit' a baby that looked nuthin' like 'im.

"Damn. So what you'd do?"

"I got a blood test."

"Okay, and?"

"And it wasn't mine; just like I told the ho from the door. Fuck outta here."

"Mmmph, that triflin' bitch was dead wrong for that," I say, shakin' my head. "Tryna pin a baby on a muhfucka. There's a buncha scandalous bitches doin' grimy shit like that; lettin'a buncha muhfuckas pop off in 'em, then they gotta pull baby daddy names outta hats 'n shit."

"Yeah, that shit was real crazy. She even had my fam comin' at me sideways; 'specially my moms' 'n shit. And I wasn't feelin' that shit at all. I kept tellin' 'em the shit wasn't mine. If it was, I'da manned up and handled my responsiblities."

"Well 'least it worked out for you."

"Oh, no doubt." I decide to ask if he's ever been in a relationship. He shakes his head. "Nah."

"Are you serious? *Neva?*"

"True story."

I twist my lips. "Mmmm, so I guess you one'a them niggas whose gonna spend his whole life runnin' through a buncha bitches, hunh?"

The waiter returns to the table to see if we want dessert, or sumthin' else. We tell 'im no, and send 'im on his way. He waits for dude to walk off, then shifts his attention back to me. He leans up in his seat, rests his forearms on the table. "Yo, check this out. I've smashed a buncha pussy, tore the frame outta a ton of ass, and coated a buncha throats and I have no regrets. So up 'til now I've been cool."

"Okay, so basically you ain't beat for a relationship?"

"Nah, I haven't been. On some real shit, I've always thought relationships were whack, feel me."

Wow, this nigga's head is all fucked up. "Okay and now?"

He shrugs. "The verdict is still out." He winks at me, grinnin'. "But who knows. That might change."

I laugh. "Oh, puhleeze don't let it be on my account 'cause I ain't lookin' for a relationship. And if I were it wouldn't be wit' you."

"Ouch," he says, clutchin' his chest. "You sure know how'ta stab a nigga in the heart."

I laugh. "Oh, you're a big boy. I'm sure you'll get over it. Fact is you ain't built to be wit' one chick. And a bitch like me ain't willin'ly sharin' a nigga wit' another bitch."

"Yeah, you right. At least that's how it's been. But maybe a muhfucka's ready to try sumthin' different."

"Yeah, like some new pussy."

He laughs. "Nah…like tryin' out the whole monogamy thing; you know…see if it works."

"Trust, it works only when two muhfuckas want it to," I tell 'im. "Personally, I rather a muhfucka tell me he wants to fuck other bitches than goin' out there gettin' his creep on tryna play me sideways."

"I feel you." He takes a sip of his water, then studies me. "Do you think muhfuckas can really change, or they just stop doin' shit for the moment?"

I purse my lips, think 'bout my own life. Think 'bout how I stepped outta the killin' game; how I miss it. Still ache 'n crave for it. I slowly nod. "Yeah, I guess they can. It may not be easy. But, if they really wanna, then yeah."

"On some real shit, all my life I've been 'round muhfuckas who didn't give a damn 'bout a relationship. My pops married my moms but kept a string of jumpoffs. He even took me wit' 'im while he went to one'a his hoes' spots to fuck 'em. Then he'd buy me shit to keep quiet. I never told anyone this, but a few of 'em he let top me off when I was mad young." He chuckles. "Damn, a muhfucka must really dig you 'cause I can't believe I'm sittin' here tellin' you all this." He pauses, shakin' his head. "On some real shit, I see a buncha miserable muhfuckas caught up in what they call a relationship and they still out doin' them; lyin' and fuckin' 'round on each other. I ain't beat for that shit."

"I feel you on that. Niggas ain't shit."

"Bitches, either," he adds.

"Mmmph," I grunt, glancin' down at my wrist to peep the time. I can't believe it's almost nine o'clock. The waiter returns wit' the check. Alex looks at the bill, then pulls out his wallet. I pull out mine as well, and toss a hunnid on the table.

"Yo, ma, put that back. I got this."

I smirk. "I thought you said this wasn't a date."

"It's not," he says, handin' me my money back. "But tomorrow night will be."

"Nigga, puhleeeze, who said I wanted to see you again?"

He grins, shakin' his head as he slides two crisp Ben Frankies in wit' the check. "Yeah aiight. Whatever, yo. I ain't tryna hear that shit."

I laugh, followin' behind 'im out the door to his whip. *My Gawd*, I think, peepin' his walk, *this bowlegged muhfucka walks like he got some big-ass cow balls.*

"Yo, I had'a real nice time wit' you tonight," he tells me as he's pullin' up in my driveway.

"Yeah, it was kinda aiight," I say jokin'ly. "You ain't a half bad muhfucka."

He laughs. "Yo, one some real shit, I'ma good dude. I'm glad you came to ya senses and stopped all that frontin' like you wasn't beat for the kid."

"Aiight, muhfucka, you got that. I ain't gonna front, ya conceited ass is fine and all, but you too over ya'self. And I still think ya ass is mad trouble."

"Baby, I'm good trouble. Good dick, good tongue, good fuckin', good nuttin'...I'm all 'round good, ma; true story."

"OhhhhmiiiiiGod, you are so full of ya'self," I say, openin' the car door. "I'm out. Thanks for the meal." He jumps outta his whip comin' ova to me. "Nigga, what you doin'?" I ask, steppin' back, placin' a hand on my hip.

He grins. "Damn, ma. Put the claws in. I'm only walkin' you to the door."

I laugh, reachin' inside my bag to get my keys. "Muhfucka, my door's right here in front of us," I say, pointin' in its direction. "You coulda sat in the car and watched me go in."

He grins, placin' his hand on the small of my back as we walk. "Maybe a muhfucka's really feelin' you and ain't tryna see the night end."

"Well, *maybe*, all good things gotta come to an end."

"Not *all* good things," he says, steppin' into my space. I step back, backin' into my door. He looks down at me, slowly pullin' in his bottom lip. "You sexy as fuck, ma. I don't know what it is 'bout you, but I ain't gonna rest 'til I figure it out." He leans in to kiss me, but a bitch shuts that shit down. *Bitch, keep it cute. You know this muhfucka ain't shit.*

Yeah, but a bitch want some dick.

Then fuck 'im 'n keep it movin'.

No, not tonight!

"Oh, really?" I ask, stoppin' him wit' the palm of my hand up on his chest to hold his ass back from pressin' all up on me. "Well, the only thing you should be tryna figure out is ya way back home; so good night."

He laughs. "Yeah, aiiight. I'ma be findin' my way back to you tomorrow night at six so make sure you're ready."

"I got plans," I tell 'im, openin' my door tryna hide my grin. Truth is I don't have shit planned, but I'm not 'bout to make it easy for this muhfucka to get at me. Bein' at a nigga's beck 'n call ain't what a fly bitch like me does. And, trust. A butter bitch like me *won't* be home.

"Cancel 'em."

"I don't think so; wrong answer."

"Then I'ma be sittin' out this muhfucka waitin' for you to come home."

I shake my head. "And ya ass's gonna be out here lookin' like a damn fool," I tell 'im.

"Yo, you heard what I said. I'ma be here at six."

"Muhfucka, and you heard what I said. Now good night." I shut the door in his face, makin' my way upstairs to get outta these clothes, pull up *Spartacus* on On Demand, and ride the shit outta a dildo 'cause that black muhfucka got'a bitch's pussy boilin'.

SEVEN A.M. MY CELL STARTS GOIN' OFF NONSTOP, AND A BITCH'S pissed she didn't mute the shit. I reach for it off the nightstand, glancin' at the screen. It's a 347 area code number that I don't recognize. I press IGNORE. Three seconds later, the same number calls back. "Yeah?"

"Kat, when the fuck you bringin' ya selfish ass back to Brooklyn to see 'bout your moms?"

The voice catches me off-guard. "Whaat? Who da fuck is this?"

"It's ya aunt Rosa, bitch. Don't play stupid. You know my damn voice. Now why the fuck nobody can get in touch wit' ya disrespectful ass? What da fuck you changin' ya numbers for 'n shit?"

A bitch is too fuckin' through. And not in the muthafuckin' mood, okay?! She's one'a the last bitches I wanna hear from. "How the fuck did you get my number?" I ask, swingin' my comforter off, then sittin' up on the side'a the bed. I realize it's a stupid ass question, knowin' damn well Chanel's stupid ass gave it to 'er. *I'ma fuckin' curse that retarded bitch out for filth!*

She starts spazzin'. "Bitch, ya muthafuckin' mother is in the goddamn hospital on life support and the only fuckin' thing you worryin' 'bout is how the fuck I got ya number, is you fuckin' serious?"

"Yeah, Rosa, I am. And *what*?"

"*Rosa?* Oh, bitch you done ran off and got real glossy callin' me some muthafuckin' Rosa. I'm ya aunt, ho."

"Sweetie, you ain't shit to me. And for da record, I've always been shinin'. So, yeah, I'm real glossy, ho. Now how can I help you? You got three minutes to say what you need'a say and then get da fuck up off my line."

She gasps. "Bitch, I'ma fuck—"

"Two minutes and forty-seven seconds," I warn, cuttin' her off. "Say what da fuck you called to say, and be done wit' it."

The crazy bitch keeps tryna bring it. "Bitch, on e'very-muthafuckin'-thing I love, I'ma beat the dog shit outta you. You ain't shit for turnin' ya back on ya family; especially ya moms. I'ma give you the beatdown she shoulda gave ya ass a long time ago, you stuck up lil' bitch."

I laugh. "*Bitch*, you must be back on crack talkin' that whack ass shit to me. You need to grow da fuck up; for real ho. You got da nerve to be someone's grandmother actin' like a certified trick-ass, gutter-rat bitch. Fuck outta here wit' ya clown ass. Boo-boo, you got da game fucked up if you think I'ma stand 'round and let you or any muthafuckin'-body else do shit to me. You got two minutes, and countin'."

"YOU FUCKIN' SNOTTY-ASS BITCH!" she yells into the phone. "FUCK ALL THAT DUMB SHIT YOU TALKIN'. MY FUCKIN' SISTA IS ON MUTHAFUCKIN' LIFE SUPPORT AND YOU NEED TO GET YA ASS DOWN TO THE GODDAMN HOSPITAL TO SEE HER!"

Interestin'ly, I keep it cute; stay calm. "Thanks for the public service announcement, Sweetie. Time's up," I say, disconnectin' the call. My cell rings, again. This time it's Chanel's ass. "Oh, bitch, you must know you 'bout ta get cursed da fuck out for givin' that crazy bitch my muthafuckin' number after I specifically told ya cock-washin' ass not to give my muthafuckin' number out to none of them bitches."

"Damn," she says, suckin' her teeth. "I was hopin' to get to you before she called you."

"'Damn hell, ho. I hate e'erything ya stankan azz stands for right now. You always doin' dumb shit, bitch." She laughs. "Bitch, ain't shit funny. That ho called here tryna bring da noise. And you know a bitch wasn't feelin' that shit."

"Ooops, my bad," she says, gigglin'.

"Ho, I should slap the shit outta ya ugly-ass face."

"I'm sorry, boo. I knew you was gonna be heated, but Patrice sounded real fucked up when she called me early this mornin'. And I felt bad."

"Bitch, what da fuck you feelin' bad for?"

"'Cause it sounded like she was cryin' 'n shit."

"Boo-hoo," I say, suckin' my teeth. "I don't give a fuck. You still had no muthafuckin' business givin' out my digits. You shoulda called me, *first*, before doin' some corny-ass shit like that."

"I know, I know. But ya ass woulda said hell no, anyway."

"Exactly, ho. But you turn 'round and do what da fuck you want. Fuck it. It's done now. And ya ass done loss diva points for that bullshit, bitch."

She starts laughin'. "Now you goin' too damn far, bitch, snatchin' my diva points 'n shit."

"Whateva. You make me sick. I hate e'erything ya slutty ass stands for."

"Okay, bitch, that shit's all good 'n all, but are we still smokin' today?"

"Hell no, I ain't smokin' wit' ya crusty-ass. Go burn wit' Rosa 'n Patrice since ya no-count ass was so quick to give them bitches my cell number."

"Mmmmm-hmmm. And when ya crazy-ass aunts jump on that ass you make sure you remember that shit 'cause I'ma sit there 'n smoke up all they shit while they peelin' da skin off a that ass."

"Bitch, you sit there and let them hoes jump on me and you don't jump in 'n help set it off on 'em wit' me, I'ma toss acid in ya face 'n set ya hair on fire, okay? Try it if you want. Ya ass'll be laid up at the nearest burn center, okay. Then let's see how many niggas gonna be checkin' for ya bald-headed, crispy-baked, ho-ass." We both bust out laughin'.

"Girl, ya ass is stoopid."

"Yeah, okay." She decides to ask how my phone convo went wit' Rosa. I tell 'er.

"Damn."

"Mmmph, girl, that crazy bitch sounded like she was back on crack."

"So she was wildin' like that?"

"Girl, that ho was blackin' like someone smoked da last rock."

"Daaaamn. That's some shit. I think it's really fucked up ya'll can't get along, though; especially now wit' ya moms bein' brain dead."

"Please, I don't know what da problem is. The bitch calls here poppin' a buncha rah-rah talkin' 'bout I need to get to da hospital to see her sista 'n shit, and the bitch's dead. How stupid is that? The bitch ain't ever gonna know I was there, so what's the fuckin' point? Not that I was goin' up to see 'er ass, any-damn-way. Then they fuckin' wastin' taxpayers' dollars keepin' the bitch chained to a tube. Hello, she's *dead!* What da fuck they tryna keep 'er ass alive for?"

"'Cause she's pregnant, Kat."

"Say, whaaat?!" My muthafuckin' mouth drops open. I am certain I haven't heard 'er right. I ask 'er to repeat what she just said. She does. And a bitch feels like she's 'bout ready to pass the fuck out!

CHAPTER TWELVE

Close my eyes 'n count ta ten...take'a deep breath...blaze'a few trees...then do it again...tryna wrap my mind 'round da dumb shit muhfuckas do...how many times'a bitch gonna keep gettin' burned...'til she wakes da fuck up...takes control of 'er life and sees da lesson to be learned....

It's been two days since Chanel dropped the bomb on me 'bout Juanita's retarded ass bein' pregnant—*again!* Why I'm feelin' some kinda way 'bout 'er ho-ass bein' knocked up is beyond me. But I do! Maybe it's 'cause—once again—the selfish bitch didn't think 'bout no one else but herself. No, scratch that shit. The bitch *was* thinkin'. She was thinkin' 'bout the sorry-ass muhfucka who beat her silly ass. Only a stupid bitch would keep lettin' a nigga pump 'er insides up 'n not be on some kinda birth control. That nigga kicked 'er all up in her stomach the last time he put 'er in the hospital. And she still went back to his ass. Got her dumb-ass knocked again. And now she's brain dead. Shit makes no sense. Now I gotta wonder how many other times the bitch got knocked. How many other babies did she have stomped outta 'er.

For some strange, sick reason, I am consumed wit' wantin' to know what the fuck happened; need to know why her dead ass is still carryin' a baby that she ain't ever gonna be able to take care of. So I wait 'til after midnight—when I know I won't run into any of my nutty-ass aunts; particularly Rosa, then hop into my whip and make my way to the parkway toward the Verrazano Bridge.

As I'm drivin' I start to feel my nerves rattle as images of Juanita's lifeless body shoot through my head. The thought of seein' her after all this time has a bitch all antsy 'n shit. I need a blunt, I think, pushin' in the lighter, then reachin' for my stash. My cell rings. I reach for it, glancin' at the screen. It's Nut.

"Hello?"

"Yo, wassup, ma? How you?"

"Nigga," I snap, sparkin' my blunt, "do you know what time it is?" I take a deep pull.

He laughs. "Yeah, it's time for ya sexy ass to spend some time wit' a muhfucka. You played me the other day when I came through. That was some foul shit, ma."

I laugh. "Nigga, I told you what it was. Nobody told ya dumb-ass to come out tryna check for me."

"Yeah, aiight; whatever. You got that. So when I'ma see you again?"

"Neva," I say, crackin' my window and blowin' out weed smoke.

He sucks his teeth. "Yo, fuck outta here. Where you at?"

"Nigga, what I tell you 'bout tryna check for me?"

He starts laughin'. "Yo, you mad funny; for real for real."

This time, I suck my teeth. "Whateva. I ain't laughin' muh-fucka. Why is you callin' me this time'a night, anyway?"

"'Cause a muhfucka was thinkin' 'bout you; that's why. You gotta problem wit' that?"

"Do you," I state, goin' through the E-Z Pass toll for the Verrazano. "I got more pressin' shit to be concerned wit', than you tryna stalk'a bitch."

"Oh, yeah? Anything you wanna talk about?"

"No, I'm good. Thanks."

"Well, the offer stands. If you change ya mind, I'm all ears."

I laugh. "Yeah right, muhfucka. You just tryna get some pussy."

"Yo, chill wit' that. I'm dead-ass. If you need someone to talk to I got you." On the real, I don't know if the nigga's kickin' some live shit or not, but it sounds good. I thank 'im. "Oh, no doubt, ma. So, what you gettin' into tonight?"

"Not you," I say, speedin' down the Belt Parkway toward Brooklyn.

"Yeah, aiight. That's 'cause you too scared I'ma have you dick whipped. But you need to let me come through and help you take ya mind off shit."

"Nigga, puhleeeeeze, that's what you want'a bitch to be. But, trust. I ain't'a weak bitch, so it's gonna take more than a big, black dick to get me whipped." I take another pull off my blunt. "So take that dumb shit onto the next trick 'cause I ain't the one."

He starts laughin' again. "Let me stop fuckin' wit' you, ma. Like I said, I was thinkin' 'bout you so I wanted to hit you up. If a muhfucka is outta pocket for havin' you on the brain, let me know."

I shake my head. "It's whateva. It's all good."

"I bet it is," he says all low 'n sexy. "What you got on?"

"Clothes, muhfucka," I snap, veerin' off onto Linden Boulevard. "Look, can I hit you back lata? I'm kinda in da middle of handlin' sumthin'."

"Yeah, aiiight. No doubt. Go handle ya business, ma. I'll get at you."

"Cool," I tell 'im as I make a right onto Amboy Street, then pull into the parkin' garage. I find a parkin' space up on the third level, pull in, then sit and finish smokin' my blunt. I check my face 'n hair in the mirror, then get outta my whip, clickin' the alarm.

As I'm makin' my way through the walkway to the hospital, my cell rings again. It's Chanel. "Wasssup, tramp?"

"Shit. What's good wit' you?" For some reason I don't tell 'er I'm in Brooklyn; that I'm en route to see Juanita. I lie and tell 'er I'm out on a date. "Oh, shiiiiiit," she snaps, soundin' all amped 'n shit. "That's wassup. I'm glad you finally are cummin' to ya senses and goin' out to get you some dick."

"Whoa, slow down, cowgirl. It's not that deep. I'm in 'n out; that's it."

"Whateva, ho. Stop neglectin' that pussy of yours and let a nigga bust that dusty-ass hole open. Damn."

"Bitch, please. Ya trick-ass does 'nough fuckin' for the both of us. I ain't beat to have my shit lookin' like da inside of a garbage truck. No thank you, ma'am." She cracks the hell up. "Look, ho, I'm out."

She continues laughin'. "Yeah, aiight. Give me a call when you're finished doin' e'erything else 'cept waxin' a dick. Divine's somewhere doin' what he does and I'm here alone for the week. Come through so we can smoke and you can give me all the details."

"Cool, cool," I tell 'er as I approach the information desk. We talk a few minutes more, then disconnect. The pasty-faced, red-haired chick at the desk—with her splotchy- ass skin—tries to give me feva 'bout the visitin' hours and whatnot, but a bitch like me ain't havin' it. She gives me the info I need and I pop my hips toward the elevator.

"HELLO?" A TALL, DARK-CHOCOLATE MALE NURSE ASKS, STOPPIN' me as I make my way down the hall, passin' the nurse's station.

He has a hint of a Caribbean accent. And the muhfucka got the nerve to be aiight lookin'. "Can I help you?"

"I'm here to see someone," I tell 'im, glancin' his way.

"I'm sorry, but visiting hours are over. You'll have to come back during our regular visiting hours from eleven a.m. to eight p.m."

Nigga, you betta check my credentials, I think, stoppin' in my tracks. "'Scuse me?" I snap, twistin' my lip up. For some reason, I feel myself 'bout to spazz the fuck out on 'im for tryna disrupt my damn flow. But, surprisin'ly, I catch myself and keep it cute; take a deep breath. "Listen," I say, sighin'. "I was told my mother is lyin' up in here on life support. And it's been hard on me."

"I'm really sorry, Miss..." He pauses, waits for me to fill in the blank.

Ohmiiiiiiiiiimuthafuckin'Gaaaawd, this tight-ass muhfucka. "It's Katrina. And I really need to see my mother, *tonight*."

"Okay, Katrina. I really wish I could help you. But you'll have to come back in the morning; sorry, policy."

I blink. Pull in my bottom lip. In a split second I'm 'bout to shred the shit outta this nigga for bein' a goddamn asshole. I take a deep breath; steady my 'tude. "Nooooo, wrong answer. I don't need to come back durin' regular visitin' hours. I *need* to find her room, *now*, so I can see this wit' my own eyes. I flew all the way here from California. I'm stressed and exhausted. All I'm askin' for is a few minutes; that's it. But, obviously that's too much for you to consider. Thanks for nuthin'." I go to step off, but he stops me.

"Hold up," he says, changin' his tone. He reaches for a clipboard, then shifts through the pages. "What's ya mother's name?" he asks. "Oh, Missus Rivera in room six-ten." *Oh, puhleeeeze*, I think, starin' at 'im, *that ho-ass bitch wishes she was somebody's missus.*

"She's not married," I correct. I peep how this horny-ass nigga starts eye-ballin' me and decide to bat my eyes a bit to get what I want. "Listen, umm," I pause, glancin' at his badge, "nurse Lewis"—I lick my lips, lookin' him up 'n down—"I know you're only doin' your job, and I realize it's really late, but if there's anyway you can bend the rules just this once, pleeeeeeease,"—I hit 'im wit' a sexy grin—"I'd 'preciate it. I really need to see her. I've been worried sick." Lies, I know! So the fuck what!

He glances at his watch, lookin' 'round the nurse's station. "Okay, but you'll have to do something for me."

I raise my brow. "And what's that? I know you not 'bout to ask me ta suck ya dick or some other nasty shit like that."

He chokes, coughin' back a laugh. "No, no; nothing like that."

"Oh, 'cause I was 'bout to say," I tell 'im, shiftin' my handbag from one hand to the other. "You tryna get a fist upside ya dome."

He laughs harder. "You a feisty one. But, no, I'd like to get ya number; maybe meet up for dinner sometime; if that's okay with you."

This pussy-hound muhfucka, I think, starin' into his hazel eyes. I decide to play 'im close; keep the nigga on my hip in case I need 'im for sumthin' pressin'."

I grin, fishin' a pen outta my bag. I reach for his hand, then write my number in the palm of his hand. When I am done, I sign KAT underneath it. He smiles. Tells me his name is DeAndre; that he'll hit me up tomorrow.

"I'll be waitin'," I tell 'im, walkin' off. I stop, turnin' back to face 'im. "Ummm, before I go see 'er, do you mind tellin' me exactly what happened to 'er?"

He tells me that she was found unconscious in the bathtub naked and badly beaten. Tells me that she suffered serious injuries to 'er face and head. That whoever did this shit beat 'er in the head numerous times, then bit her face causin' permanent disfig-urement. *Ohmymuthafuckin'Gaaaawd, what kinda muhfucka would bite a bitch in 'er face?* I blink, knowin' the answer. Still, what kinda animal is that no-good muhfucka for doin' some shit like this? He then tells me the police are still lookin' for the muhfucka. Puhleeze, this nigga's still out on the loose 'cause muhfuckas ain't really tryna look for 'im. Juanita may not be shit to me, but ain't no way, a bitch gonna front like she's cool wit' this nigga gettin' away wit' this shit. Once again, I gotta handle another one'a this bitch's battles. That nigga gotta get it. I may not like the bitch, but what this muthafucka did, *this time*, is…unthinkable. I feel my nose flarin'. I ask how long she was unconscious before she went into a coma, then went brain dead.

"She was in critical condition for over a month before she slipped into a coma and stopped breathing," he continues, slowly shakin' his head. He takes me in. I guess he's waitin' for me to respond. I don't. "She basically has no brain function. She's being kept alive on a respirator."

"And ya'll are keepin' her on life support becauuuuuuse?" I ask this already knowin' the answer, but I play stupid. There's a part of me that is hopin' the shit isn't true; that she isn't really knocked up.

"To save her unborn baby."

I take in a deep breath; try to steady my nerves. "Why? The bit…I mean, she's dead. Shouldn't ya'll be givin' her an abortion or sumthin'?"

"That's not our call."

"So whose call was it?"

"Her next of kin," he tells me.

I blink, blink again. "And who was that?"

"There's no living will that the family was aware of, so the decision to keep her on life support was made by her mother." I roll my eyes. "The doctors would have taken her off of life support and declared her dead if it wasn't for her havin' family support and being pregnant. Besides, she's too far along."

What the fuck?! I swallow back my disgust. "'Exactly how far along you talkin'?" I ask, bracin' myself up against the counter.

"She's in her twentieth week."

OhmyGaaaawd, the bitch is five months' pregnanat. "And she's dead," I add for effect. "And probably carrryin' some kinda bubble-head alien with no arms 'n shit."

"On the contrary. From what the sonogram showed three days ago, she's carryin' a healthy baby, kicking and moving about in her womb with all of its limbs."

I feel myself gettin' nauseous. A film of sweat forms over my neatly arched brows and it starts to feel like I'm standin' on balls of fire in these Marc Jacob six-inch pencil-heels. I wipe my forehead. Shift my weight from one foot to the other.

"And how long do you plan on keepin' her tubed up?" I ask, lettin' my handbag drop down from the crook of my arm to my hand.

He tells me for at least another five weeks; that that's the earliest a premature baby can be delivered and survive. Tells me the longer they are able to keep her on life support and the baby inside 'er, the greater its chances of survival. That bringin' it into full-term at thirty-seven weeks would be the preference. But keepin' a fetus in the womb for that long would be a greater risk. That it could expose it to a host of infections. I feel my knees gettin' weak. I don't wanna hear shit else.

"Thanks," I say, walkin' off; my heels angrily stabbin' the white-tiled floor wit' each step. I feel his eyes on my ass so I glance over my shoulder and bust 'im starin'. *Niggas!*

I stop in front of 'er door. Take a deep breath. Steady my nerves. Then step into the dimly-lit room to face my past. A woman I have fuckin' hated for most of my life, but still—like a silly, stupid ass ho—once yearned for something she was incapable of givin'— *love*. The only light in the room is comin' from outta the bathroom. My eyes adjust to its dimness. And there she lay; hooked up to a ventilator and other machines. IV tubes run through her body. Her face and head is wrapped in gauze. The bitch looks a mess!

I step closer to 'er bed. Study e'ery inch of the woman who pushed me outta her pussy, then pushed me outta 'er life. Ignored me; neglected to nurture me and love me. Unexpectedly, starin' down at 'er makes a bitch's heart ache. I block out the hummin' of the machines in the room. My eyes burn wit' hate toward this woman.

As I lean in, I grit my teeth, blink back painful memories of bein' abandoned by this fuckin' heartless bitch. "You no-good, selfish bitch," I hiss in 'er ear. "All my life you've done nuthin' but think 'bout ya'self, bringin' no-count niggas and drama in 'n outta your life, and into mine. When you were gettin' ya ass beat, you neva gave'a fuck 'bout how that shit affected me. E'ry nigga you let disrespect you, you let disrespect me. But you was too dick-whipped to see that shit. When two'a ya muhfuckas was comin' into my room and I told you how da niggas were creepin' in my room, you had da muthafuckin' audacity to blame me for da shit, or act like I was makin' da shit up. And 'cause of you, you dick-dumb-ho, I had'a take matters into my own hands…"

I take a deep breath. I'm fifteen, again; back in that darkened, piss-stained stairwell holdin' a gun. It's cocked and aimed at the nigga who constantly beat Juanita's ass and snuck in my room suckin' on my titties and diggin' his nasty-ass fingas all up in my pussy. I pull the trigger, empty the clip. Blood and brains and chunks of skull are splattered against the cement wall. I squeeze my eyes shut, then reopen them, bringin' my attention back to Juanita.

I clench my teeth. "…Not once, bitch, did you eva consider how your fucked up ways and choices hurt me; that my own mother turned 'er muthafuckin' back on me; chose 'er niggas ova me. I fuckin' hate you for that shit, bitch. All my life you've hurt me one way or another wit' your neglect and bullshit. And, now, even in death you fuckin' come wit' drama. All I want is to be free from you, once and for all."

I glance down at her protrudin' belly beneath the white sheet. *Another fuckin' life ruined.* "I hope you rot in hell. I feel like punchin' you in your fuckin' stomach. You couldn't be a mother to me, and now your stupid ass is lyin' here dead, carryin' anotha child you'll never be a mother to. Another child you're 'bout to abandon 'cause your stupid, trick-ass couldn't stay da fuck away from fucked up muhfuckas. You're a fuckin' bitch," I say, fightin' back tears. "Do you really think I'ma let you bring an orphan into this world?" I ask, pausin' as if she can hear me. "Oh no, sweetie, I will have that thing that grows inside of you gutted out, first, before I let that happen. I'd rather see it dead along wit' you."

I have the urge to slap the shit outta 'er bandaged face and spit on 'er. I clench my hand shut. Glance 'round the room, then bring my eyes to the machine that pumps air into 'er lungs. I stare at the cord that connects the ventilator. Follow its length to the outlet. Wit'out a doubt, I know 'xactly what'a bitch has'ta do. "Sweet dreams, bitch," I say, walkin' out the door.

CHAPTER THIRTEEN

Lights out...da party's ova...nuthin' to be confused 'bout...no use in sheddin' tears...bankrupt ho had 'er run...wasted 'er years...lettin' niggas steal 'er worth...drain 'er senses...empty out 'er heart...now she's laid up on 'er deathbed...poor thing...bitch died a long time ago...walked among the livin' dead...no use hangin' on...I already know why da caged bird sings...

"Pull da plug," I tell the doctor. It's nine o'clock in the mornin', and I made it my business to get back to the hospital to let 'em know what it is. I can tell I've shocked 'im. But I don't give a fuck. I want Juanita's ass put to rest so I can get on wit' my life. He stares at me; pushes his rimmed glasses up over the bridge of his stumpy nose.

"Excuse me?" he asks, blinkin' his wide brown eyes.

"You heard me. It's time to put that bit...my mother, outta her misery."

"It's not that simple; she's with child," he tells me like I don't already know this shit. He tries to convince me to reconsider; to think on it a few more days. He tells me she's carryin' a healthy baby that can be safely delivered in another five to six weeks.

"I know all that," I tell 'im. "Still doesn't change my mind."

"Miss Rivera, if you'd just hold off for a few more weeks. Then the fetus will be viable outside of the womb."

After seein' her last night, then talkin' to that nigga DeAndre afterward, I'm well aware of my options as her daughter, and next of kin. I let 'im know this. If I wait too long, like 'er hittin' her third trimester, then it's a wrap. A judge can step in 'n block shit. "I'm not interested," I say, gettin' up. "I want the plug pulled today."

He calls for a social worker who tries to talk me out of it, then in comes the on duty charge nurse and the hospital administrator. All three, white bitches wit' a buncha pressed powder on they faces. They are all lookin' at me like I'm fucked up for wantin' to shut shit down.

"And what about the unborn fetus?" the skinny social worker bitch asks.

"What about it? It has no rights."

"But it'a life," the nurse states.

"Wit' no rights," I repeat. "And no damn say."

The administrator threatens to get a court order to protect its rights. I laugh in the bitch's face. Little do they know I sat up and kicked it wit' that nigga DeAndre for almost two hours last night and got put onto what's what.

"Bitch, I don't give'a fuck 'bout no court order. Like I said, it has no rights. As long as Jua...my mother is not in her third trimester; no judge can tell me what da fuck to do. There is no livin' will. And there is no other parent to step up to speak on its behalf. And if there was, his ass would be en route to prison for doin' what he did. So da only one in this matter who has rights would be Juanita Rivera, but since she's incapable of makin' any decisions that leaves *me*. I'm her daughter. And that makes *me* her next of kin *and* guardian, no?"

"Yes. But, Miss Rivera, please. Take some time to think about what you are asking us to do. All we ask is that you reconsider and think this through."

"I've thought it through, and I've made my decision. So, this discussion is ova. Pull the goddamn plug." I get up to walk out, then turn to face them. "If you won't, I will. So go get the priest, pastor or whoever so we can get this done. I'll be—"

I'm interrupted by a buncha commotion comin' from outside the door. The door swings open. "Where da fuck is that, bitch, hunh?! Where is she?!" It's Rosa, wide-eyed and wild. My aunt Elise is right behind 'er. Obviously one'a these cream-puff bitches in the room called 'em. "Bitch, who da fuck is you wantin' to pull the plug on my sista, hunh? How dare you wanna kill her and her baby. You crazy-ass bitch!"

I laugh. "Which one'a you called this clown-ass ho, like that's gonna stop shit?"

"I can't believe you are tryna kill ya own goddamn blood. Ya mother, Kat. Who da fuck are you to do some shit like that wit'out talkin' to da rest of her family?"

"You stupid bitch," I snap, "The nigga her dumb ass was wit' killed 'er. I'm just shuttin' shit down. And for da record, ho, I'm 'er daughter. *That's* who da fuck I am, trick-ass bitch. And I have more say than you."

She looks over at Elise. "Oh, now this ho-ass bitch wants ta play daughter 'n shit. Well, where da fuck was you when we were callin' ya ass. You ain't been tryna be no goddam daughter—"

"Ladies, please," the administrator says, cuttin' in. She looks frightened outta her lil' Cracker Jack mind. "I'm sure we can talk this through rationally."

"Bitch," we both snap, eyein' the shit outta 'er, "shut da fuck up!" Her face turns beet red.

"Had you not called this crazy bitch," I say, pointin' at Cracker

Jack, "shit wouldn't be—" The next thing I know, Rosa bum rushes me, and she and I are tossin' up the office, swingin' each other into tables and walls 'n shit. She's hookin' off on me, and I'm hookin' off on 'er.

"I told ya ass I was gonna bring it to ya fresh-ass for talkin' all greasy 'n shit." She slaps and punches me. "Welcome home, bitch!"

I'm not gonna front, this ho caught me off guard. But, I'm rockin' wit' the bitch. I don't wanna slice 'er wit' my blade, and I know she don't wanna slice me wit' hers. So we straight duke it out. Somehow we end up fallin' and we are on the floor rollin' 'round like two crazy bitches. I dig my nails in 'er face. Punch the bitch in the mouth.

"Bitch, I'ma fuck you up!" she screams.

"Then let's go, ho!" I scream back, punchin' her upside the head. I have my knee in 'er throat. Now I'm tryna crush the bitch's windpipe. "I will fuckin' shut ya lights out, bitch, puttin' ya mutha-fuckin' hands on me." She claws and wildly swings her arms to get me offa 'er. I punch 'er in 'er socket, shut one'a 'er lights out.

Elise jumps on me from behind, wrappin' her hands in my hair and yankin' me off'a Rosa. "Oh, so you wanna fight ya aunt like she's a bitch on da street, hunh? Oh, no bitch it ain't goin' down like that." I start kickin' and stompin' on Rosa. Then dig my nails into Elise's hands, tryna get Elise off'a me. But the bitch has my hair tightly wrapped 'round her hands and she's pullin' the shit outta it.

"Bitch, let go of my goddamn hair and fight me like a real bitch!" I snap, rammin' 'er back into a wall. I ram 'er again. Rosa comes chargin' me and I lift my legs up and kick 'er backward. By the time security comes through the door, we've tore the office up and all of the buttons on my thousand dollar shirt are ripped open. My sleeve is torn. And the heel of my left shoe is broken off. I'm too goddamn through!

ALL THREE OF US HAVE BEEN ARRESTED, AND TAKEN DOWN TO the seventy-third precinct. The stupid rookie pig has all three of us sittin' in the same area, handcuffed. What a dumb fuck! I glance down at my shirt, then feet. I'm 'xtra pissed that this crack-ho bitch tore my fuckin' blouse and I'm even more heated 'bout my muthafuckin' heel bein' broke off. On top'a that, I have a bangin'-ass headache from Elise tryna rip my scalp off.

Although Elise jumped in the shit, I don't really have beef wit' 'er. Yeah, the bitch was outta pocket, but she was only doin' what they do—fight together, so it is what it is. She gotta few shots off. But, a bitch like me is still standin'. I lean forward on the bench, look over at Rosa. "Bitch, be clear," I say, lowerin' my voice to almost a whisper, glarin' at 'er. She's sittin' here wit' a busted lip 'n swollen left eye. "This shit ain't ova, trust. You swung off on da wrong ho."

This stupid bitch ain't swift enough to keep it cute, instead she starts spazzin' the fuck out, loud talkin' 'n poppin' mad shit 'bout how she's gonna slice my face 'n shit. "Bitch, you right. This shit ain't ova. I'ma fuck you up. I'm ya muthafuckin' aunt, and you disrespected me. Oh, hell no, ho. From now on you like any bitch out on da streets and that's how I'ma handle you."

This is where a bitch goes into 'er Academy Award-winnin' performance. I wait 'til the officer comes to take me to the back, then bust out in tears; sobbin' 'n slobberin' 'bout the bitch threatenin' me; 'bout flyin' in from California, 'bout bein' distraught ova findin' out 'bout Juanita's situation. 'Bout bein' attacked at the hospital by Rosa and how a bitch's fearful for 'er safety.

"All I'm tryna do is deal wit' my mother bein' brain dead and plan for her funeral, and them nuts attack me 'cause we got beef."

"And those two ladies are your aunts?" the detective asks, raisin' his brow and givin' me a what-kinda-crazy-ass-shit-is-this look.

I nod, allowin' tears to streak my face. "Unfortunately," I say, sobbin' harder. "It's a hot damn mess. I don't need this shit right now, you know?"

He hands me a box of tissue and tries to console me by sayin' a buncha shit I ain't really hearin'. I blow my nose and continue sobbin'. By the time I finish draggin' them hoes, I'm bein' released; charges are bein' pressed against both of them bitches for puttin' they muthafuckin' hands on me. And I'm granted a temporary restrainin' order. I pop my hips outta there, smirkin'. Fuck wit' me if you want, biiiiotches!

"BITCH, YOU DID WHAAAAAAAAAAAT?!?" CHANEL SCREAMS IN MY ear. I'm on the phone wit' 'er dishin' the juice 'bout how Rosa and Elise tried to bring it to me. And this bitch ain't listenin' to shit I'm sayin'. "Ohmiiiigaaaawd, Kat, I can't believe you wanna pull da plug on ya moms like that. And the baby...omiiiifuckin' gaaaawd. Kat, you've gone too fuckin' far now."

"Bitch," I snap. "I ain't call you for no muthafuckin' sermon. I'm tellin' you 'bout them two nut-ass bitches tryna bring da noise and you talkin' 'bout some other shit. What da fuck, ho?! Them bitches jumped me."

"Well, what da fuck you 'xpect? You tryna pull plugs 'n shit on their sista. And...the baby! That's ya lil' brotha or sista inside of 'er, Kat. Why da fuck would you wanna do some cruel shit like that? Is the baby deformed or sumthin'?"

"Bitch, how da fuck I know what it is. All I know is, Juanita's dead ass shouldn't be layin' up there wastin' hospital space. The bitch is dead and there ain't no sense in draggin' da shit out. And, as far as that lil' thing inside of 'er, I'm doin' it for its own good. Why da fuck would I wanna see that thing come into this world all fucked up?"

"Ohhhh, puhleeeeeze. Give. Me. A. Fuckin'. Break. You ain't doin' shit for nobody but ya'self. And it's not a thing or a it, Kat. You talk like it's an object. It's a *baby*. Wit' hands and feet and a mouth and nose. And you wanna take its life."

I sigh. "Oh, well. There's 'nough motherless and fatherless babies in this world. No sense in lettin' *it* suffer, too."

"Bitch, it's murder!"

"How da fuck is it murder? Do ya homework, Sweetie. As long as that plug gets pulled while that thing is under twenty-four weeks, it's all good."

"Bitch, on some real shit, you've done and *said* some fucked-up shit before, but this right here goes waaaaay beyond fucked up. It's some vicious, nasty, psycho bullshit."

"Ho, please. Spare me. Since when da fuck you find a set'a morals?"

"Ohhhh no, trick, don't try 'n flip this shit on me. You're a real fucked-up, selfish bitch for this shit. And if you ask me, you ain't no different from ya moms."

"Excuuuuuuuuuuuuse you?! What da fuck you say?"

"You heard me, ho. For years you been callin' ya moms all kinda heartless, selfish-ass neglectful bitches. And here you soundin' just like 'er."

"Bitch, fuuuuuuck you," I say, gettin' up off'a my bed. "I ain't nuthin' like that woman."

"No, fuuuuck *you*. And yes, you are. You just too damn blind to see it."

"Uhhhhhh, noooooooooooo, sweetness. You got it fucked up."

"Yeah, okay. Denial looks real fucked-up on you, boo."

"Whateva," I say, pacin' the floor.

"Annnnnyway, if I was Rosa 'n 'em, I woulda jumped on ya ass, too. Keep shit real, boo. Is this about *you* or ya fuckin' hate for ya moms? And da only bitch you need to be real wit' 'bout it is you."

The bitch bangs on me, but I'm not fazed 'cause my mind is made up. And there ain't shit she or anyone else is gonna say to me to change it.

I take off my bra 'n panties, then head to the bathroom to fill the tub. A bitch need's a real Calgon moment. I pour in bath crystals, let the water fill to the rim, then step into the steamy water. Chanel's voice rings in my head. *Bitch, on some real shit, you've done and said some fucked up shit before, but this right here goes waaaaay beyond fucked up. It's some vicious, nasty, psycho bullshit.*

"Ho, that bitch read ya ass for filth," I say, layin' my head back. I close my eyes, inhalin'. *Am I bein' selfish? Is this really 'bout me, or my hate for Juanita? Why da fuck should I let 'er baby live? Who's gonna care for the thing? Rosa…Elise…ho-ass Patrice?*

Before I start slippin' down memory lane gettin' all depressed 'n shit 'bout shit a bitch can't change, I open my eyes, decide there's nuthin' to think 'bout. It is what it is. Right now, I need sumthin' to relax me; to take my mind off'a all this craziness. I play wit' my nipples, slide my right hand down into the water, and massage the front of my pussy. *I need to be fucked nice 'n deep*, I think, reachin' for my cell. I scroll through the call log, then press TALK. As soon as it rings, I hang up, punkin' out.

What da fuck is you doin', ho?

Tryna get this pussy rocked?

Then why da fuck ya silly-ass hang up?

'Cause I don't need da drama."

Yeah, but ya dumb-ass needs sum dick.

My ringin' cell disrupts the mini conversation in my head. I glance at the screen. *Fuck!* "Hello."

"Yo, you call me?"

"Yeah, but it was a mistake. I dialed da wrong number."

He laughs. "Yeah right. Stop frontin'. You know you was thinkin' 'bout me. It's cool, ma. You can say it."

I suck my teeth. "Nigga, get real."

Bitch, fuck all this back 'n forth shit. Tell da nigga ta cum rock ya box. "Whatchu doin'?"

"Chillin'. Why, wasssup? You tryna get into sumthin'?"

I take a deep breath. "Yeah, come fuck me."

I hear the nigga chokin' on the other end of the phone. "Hol' up...what you just say?"

"Muhfucka, don't play stupid, you heard me. Come. Fuck. Me."

"Oh, shiiiit...now?"

"Yeah, *now*, nigga," I huff, steppin' outta the tub, then dryin' myself off. "And you need'a hurry up 'fore I change my mind."

"Nah, fuck that," he says, soundin' real amped. "Change ya mind hell. I'm on my way. I'll be there in twenty minutes."

"Oh, and be clear. The offer expires if you're not here in 'xactly twenty minutes." I disconnect the call, swingin' my naked hips into the bedroom to slip on sumthin' sexy in case the nigga shows up before his time's up. I go into my walk-in closet and open up my cedar chest filled wit' toys. *If he doesn't, then I'ma have'ta take matters into my own hands*, I think, pullin' out my my vibratin' Long Dong and Zing vibratin' butt plug. Let the nigga not get here, I'ma slip this plug in my ass, then slide down on the dildo and put 'em both on high speed, then make this nut pop. Fightin' them roaches today really got a bitch horny!

FOUR HOURS LATER, I WAKE UP WIT' MY PANTIES DOWN 'ROUND my ankles and the scent of my sweet pussy dried up on my fingas. I get up, grabbin' my toys and head to the bathroom to wash my hands and my lil' fuck buddies, then strut back into the bedroom, dryin' 'em off before puttin' 'em back in my chest. I glance at the clock. It's already eleven o'clock, and *noooooo*…Nut didn't come through…okay, scratch that. The nigga didn't get in. He pulled up late, so I let the nigga keep ringin' the bell 'n blowin' up my cell 'til he got the hint. You ain't gettin' no pussy; you ain't get-tin' no brain. So take ya late ass on.

I scoop my cell up off'a da dresser, checkin' my missed calls 'n text messages. There's two missed calls and'a text from Alex; one missed call from Chanel; and three calls from a three-four seven area code. Right off the bat, I already know it's from one'a my nutty-ass aunts. I text Alex back; tell the nigga next time to get his ass here on time, then retrieve my voice messages. There's three.

"Bitch, I'ma fuck you up! You hear me, trick?! Don't let me catch ya ass anywhere in Brooklyn, ho. *Capiche*? Don't! I'ma bring it to ya muthafuckin' face for puttin' out a restrainin' order on me and have me banned from da goddamn hospital…" *Save.*

I laugh. *This bitch is outta muthafuckin' control, but I promise you this. Let da bitch try 'n serve me again, and they gonna be dumpin' 'er ass in a box next to 'er sista. And I mean that shit.* I listen to the next message.

"*Puta, que me de mi hermana. Tienes un asno ferina con su nombre para ello, está bien?*" *OhhhhhmiGaaawd,* now this crazy bitch is poppin' shit in Spanish talkin' 'bout how she gotta ass whippin' wit' my name on it for keepin' her from 'er sista. Bitch, *puuuhleeeze! Save.* The third message I don't even listen to. I delete the shit.

Alex texts back. *It's all good. Pussy ain't ever gonna be sumthin' I can't get.*

I text back. *Good for u, muhfucka!*

CHAPTER FOURTEEN

*Bitches stay tryna talk slick…but they don't really want it…
junkie-ass tricks…gulpin' a buncha dicks…eatin' asses…
smellin' like shit…maggots stuck to them sheets…e'erytime
bitches open they mouths…flies flyin' outta they grills…but I
ain't pressed…a bitch's ready to step outta da heels…and take
it to da streets…*

Three days later, I'm at Chanel's spot in Brooklyn, like
e'erything's e'erything. She and I 'posed to be chillin' 'n
gettin' lifted, then doin' some shoppin' today, but her
fat-ass, big-faced cousin Peaches—who looks more like a muthafuckin' pumkin than some goddamn peach—done tossed shit up
in the game by showin' up. So instead of Chanel's ass tellin' me
she was expectin' this bitch, before I drove all the way over here
'cause she knows I don't like the ho, she waits 'til I walk through
the door to mention the shit. Now I'm sittin' here at the dinin'
room table—disgusted, lookin' at this fat, Hungry-Jack bitch
practically chew the ends off a the goddamn blunt. And you know
a bitch ain't diggin' this bitch wastin' no smoke.

I glare at her. "Bitch, is you gonna smoke da shit, or eat it?" I
shoot a look over at Chanel. "Bitch, where da fuck you find Fiona?
Someone needs to teach her ass how'ta hit a blunt."

Chanel bursts out laughin' 'n chokin' at the same time. "Ooooh, bitch, you wrong for that. Be nice."

"'Be nice', hell."

"Who da fuck is you callin' *Fiona*, bitch?" Hungry Jack snaps.

"You, Booga," I snap back, slidin' my hand down into my Hermès bag in case she wants to bring it. I feel for my ice pick. See a big bitch gotta get gutted. Ain't no time for puttin' a razor to slice 'n dice a pork roll ho. You gotta poke her ass up. "Ya ass sittin' here fuckin' up good smoke wit' ya bullshit. Who da fuck wanna be smokin' behind some bitch wettin' da shit up like it's a dick. This shit ain't no damn snack, ho."

Chanel cracks the fuck up. "Bitch, you is dead wrong. Leave my fam alone."

"Dead wrong, my ass. Next time, leave this Booga bitch outside where you found 'er."

Hungry Jack gives me the finga. "Bitch, fuck you; you can suck my dick!"

I laugh. "Sweetie, you look like the kinda chick wit' them black, nasty fat burns between ya stumpy-ass legs, okay. And there ain't'a 'nough smoke in this muthafuckin' world to entice me to wanna eva get between them hamhocks to suck on ya lil' piggy dick. So you can save that for them Chunky-Monkey bitches you roll wit'."

"Bitch, I don't know who da fuck you think you is, you've been comin' at me all sideways 'n shit since ya stuck-up ass got up in here. And I'm about ready to jump on that ass. You don't know shit about me, bitch."

"Booga, all you gotta do is jump, and we can make it bounce up in this muthafucka, trust."

"Ohhhhhhmiiiigaaaaawd," Chanel says, slappin' the table wit' her hand, "will you stupid bitches pleeeease shut da fuck up! I wish you bitches learn to get along. Both of you hoes are tryna fuck up my high. Damn."

"Ho, you need to be talkin' that shit to ya girl," Hungry Jack says, glaring at me. "You know it's whatever for a bitch like me. I ain't one to keep lettin' no skinny, stuck-up bitch talk greasy. Yeah, I'ma big bitch. But I hit hard, okay?"

I raise my brow, tilt my head. "Bitch, yabba-dabba-doo. You don't really want it wit' me, Barney, so shut da fuck up wit' ya double-necked ass and finish eatin' ya blunt."

She stares me down, openin' and closin' 'er fists like she's ready to bring da noise. I smirk, waitin'. The bitch rolls 'er eyes, but she keeps 'er ass planted in her seat. Once I see this ho ain't really tryna bring it, I take my hand off the ice pick and pull out my emergency stash—three blunts packed 'n ready to go—I keep in a Louie eyeglass case. I take one out as I tell Chanel to hand me the lighter, then spark up. I take a deep pull. Hold it in for a few, then blow smoke out over in Hungry Jack's face. I can't stand this bitch, so now I'ma fuck wit' 'er.

Lucky for 'er my cell rings. I fish it outta my bag, then glance at the screen. It's Nut. "Hey," I say, shiftin' in my seat.

"Yo, what's good, beautiful?" For some reason, a bitch starts grill-cheesin' it up. "Yo, that was fucked up how you played me the other day."

I laugh. "Oh, well. I told you what it was; shoulda got there on time."

"Yo, whatever. I was five minutes late."

"And now it's ya loss."

"Yeah, aiight. I see how you doin' it. It's ballgame, baby. The first chance I get to get at you, I'ma bust that ass up; real talk."

"There won't be a next time."

"Fuck outta here wit' that. Yo, where you now?"

"Nigga, don't be checkin' for me," I snap, takin' another pull off a my blunt. "The last time I checked I wasn't da one ridin' ya dick. You were five minutes too late, remember. And you damn sure wasn't ridin' mine."

He laughs. "Here you go," he says, lettin' the shit go ova his head. "Whatever, yo. I wanna see you tonight."

"Umm, don't you have some dick hungry hoes to chase down?"

"Yeah, but I ain't beat for 'em. I'd rather be chasin' you. But I see you still wanna be on ya bullshit. You dissed a muhfucka, and you stood me up the night before that. You just keep playin' a nigga to the left. But it's all good."

"Nigga, puhleeze."

"Yo, stop fuckin' 'round, Kat. A muhfucka's tryna see you, so what's good?"

I suck my teeth, rollin' my eyes at Chanel for bein' all down my throat. "Bitch, what da fuck," I say to 'er, shiftin' in my seat.

She gives me da finga. "Ohhh no, bitch, don't try 'n get cute. Let me find out you got some nigga on da low I ain't heard about."

"Yo, who's that in the background?" Alex asks.

"Nobody," I tell 'em, takin' another toke, then blowin' out the smoke. "Just sum nosey bitch tryna be all up in mine." Chanel gives me da finga again.

"Oh, word? What, you smokin'?"

"Yeah, sumthin' like that."

"So, what's up for later? I told you I'm tryna see you. So what's good? You think you can squeeze a muhfuck into ya life, or do I gotta keep beggin'?"

I grin. "Let me think on it. And I'll hit you back."

"Yeah, aiight. I heard that shit already. Don't front on me."

"Nigga, whateva." We go back 'n forth a few minutes more wit' me tellin' him I'll hit 'im back later tonight, then disconnect.

Chanel points 'n wags a finga at me. "Oh noooooo, Miss Bitch, who's this nigga you all goo-goo, ga-ga ova?"

I laugh. "Bitch, ain't nobody goo-goo, ga-ga-in' nuthin'."

"Mmmph, sounds like it to me," Hungry Jack says, rollin' another blunt to eat.

"Bitch, who asked yo' ass?" I snap, shootin' 'er a look.

She laughs. "Slut, you'se a real funny-style bitch, but I ain't sweatin' it."

"Unh-uh, ho," Chanel says to 'er, puttin' her hand up, "not now. Save the dumb shit for later. Right now"—she turns 'er gaze on me—"back to yo' ass, you sneaky ho. I wanna know who this nigga is you all grin 'n giggles wit'."

I roll my eyes, flickin' my hand at 'er. "What-da-fuck-*eva*. I ain't grinnin' shit."

"Yeah, whatever, tramp; just tell me who da nigga is and why I ain't heard 'bout his ass." I tell 'er it's the nigga from All-Star Weekend. "As funny style as ya ass is, I didn't think you was even fuckin' wit' that nigga like that." I tell 'er nosey ass 'bout the lil' outin' he took me on. "Get out! *And* you went out wit' his ass? Oh, shit. Let me find out you diggin' 'im."

I shrug, takin' another pull. "He's aiight. It ain't nuthin' serious, trust."

"Okay, skip all the silly shit. A bitch wanna know did you fuck 'im, yet?"

I frown, knowin' damn well I wanna fuck the skin off that nigga's dick. "Hell, no."

She sucks her teeth. "Bitch, yo' ass is always tryna play like you Miss Goodie Two Shoes. You act like you don't like dick, boo."

Hungry Jack grunts. I shoot 'er a look. The bitch blows smoke in my direction. But I ain't mad at 'er 'cause it's the same shit I've been doin' to 'er. I decide to make 'er invisible.

"Annnnnyway…Bitch, puhleeeze. Just 'cause a bitch ain't suckin' 'n fuckin' e'ery thing movin' that don't mean she ain't lovin' da dick. It means she ain't beat for havin' a beat up snatch, okay? So don't get ya fronts knocked."

Chanel flicks 'er hand at me. "Whateva; it sounds good. But that Virgin Mary shit you talkin' is gettin' real old, boo. It's time for you to let ya freak flag fly."

I give 'er the finga. "Fly on this, trick."

Hungry Jack rolls her eyes up in her big snow globe head. "Bitch, get real," she says, lookin' at Chanel, then shootin' a look at me. "I know this ho's kind. Her ass is an undercover freak, okay. So she can spare us the okey-doke."

"Bitch, why is you all up in mine?"

"Like I said, I know ya kind," she repeats, splittin' open another blunt, then packin' it wit' Kush. "Sneaky, freak-nasty hoes."

"And I know ya kind, too, sweetie. You the kinda bitch who lets a nigga come through after the clubs close—all sweaty and drunk da fuck up—when he can't get his dick wet nowhere else. Niggas call on yo' ass 'cause they know you a sloppy-ass, man-eatin' dick gobbler who'll let 'em fuck you in ya crater ass e'ery-which-way."

Jabba Jaws licks the blunt, seals it. Then slides it in and outta her mouth, like it's a damn toothpick. She sits it on the table. This bitch is outta control.

I frown.

Chanel bucks her eyes. "Bitch, what da fuck is you doin'?"

I get up from the table, shootin' a look over at Chanel. "Bitch, I'm out. Call me when Orca goes back out to sea, then we can get it in like real bitches do." Hungry Jack says sumthin' slick back, but I laugh it off, throwin' up the finga.

"Don't forget the party is in two weeks," she yells out. "So don't go makin' no plans wit' that nigga who you say you ain't fuckin, but got you all ga-ga-googly."

"Whateva," I yell back, walkin' out the door. I click the alarm to my whip, slide in, then make my way back over to the hospital for what I hope will be my last visit.

CHAPTER FIFTEEN

*Ready or not…da ho gotta go…bitch won't eva rest in peace…
Grim Reaper done came to take 'er…now it's time for 'er to
meet 'er maker…but da dead bitch has a baby inside 'er
womb…wrapped 'round doom 'n gloom…what's a bitch to
do…do I take one life, or take two?*

The minute I reach the nurse's station I spot the nigga
DeAndre. But, before I can speak, I peep the pasty-faced
charge nurse from the other day, sittin' on the other side
of 'im behind a computer. She glances in my direction and looks
shook. I grin and keep it cute, puttin' 'er mind at ease. "Bitch,
ain't nobody thinkin' 'bout you. I'm here to see my mother." She
quickly shifts her eyes back to what she was doin'. DeAndre bucks
his eyes, surprised. "How you doin', Nurse Lewis?" I ask, turnin'
my attention to 'im. I smile.

He smiles back. "Missus Rivera. Good morning. I'm good, thanks.
I was on my way to your mother's room so I will walk with you,
if you don't mind."

I shake my head. "Fine wit' me. I'll be glad when all this is ova."
I peep Pasty-Face pick up the phone. "Sweetie, if you're callin'
for security, there's no need for that," I tell 'er. "But I would like
to speak to the doctor."

"I'm calling him now," she says, lookin' over at me.

I roll my eyes at 'er. "Oh, goodie. You do that." *Stupid bitch!*

She hangs up. "He'll be down momentarily to speak with you."

I lean up against the counter. "Good. Send 'im to my mother's room." I walk off wit' DeAndre. And of course the nigga's tryna get his rap on on the sly. It'd be real cute to fuck wit' a nurse if I was a junkie-bitch. I could fuck the nigga into snatchin' me up a few of them 'script pads to keep a bitch lifted. But I ain't the one. Still, I keep it cute and let the nigga try 'n spit his game; no matter how wack.

"I get off at three today. You wanna go grab something to eat?"

"Maybe sum other time," I tell 'em as we approach Juanita's room. "I need to do—" I stop myself when I see a brown-skinned chick and some tall, blond-haired, Ken-doll-lookin' muhfucka in the room who's movin' a wand slowly ova Juanita's swollen belly. "What's goin' on in here?"

"We're completin' an ultrasound," the chick says. She glances ova at DeAndre, who tells 'em who I am. The brown chick is introduced as Doctor Larsons; the white dude as Doctor Peters, both ob-gyn specialists for high-risk pregnancies. Fuck all the formalities! A bitch wants to know what the fuck they doin' another sonogram for when I'm here to shut this sideshow down.

"We want to make sure the pregnancy is…" Ken Doll's mouth is movin' but I don't hear shit he's sayin'. My eyes lock on the image on the screen. A bitch is frozen. *It's a baby. Wit' hands and feet and a mouth and nose. And you wanna take its life; murder it.… You a real selfish bitch for this shit…*

I blink, try 'n shake Chanel's voice outta my head. *Is this about you or ya fuckin' hate for ya moms? And da only bitch you need to be real wit' 'bout it is you.*

I feel myself startin' to hyperventilate. "Turn that shit off!" I hear myself screamin' in my head. My mouth opens. But a bitch can't get the words out. *It's a baby…And you wanna take its life…*

"…Missus Rivera? Are you okay?"

"I-I-I," I stutter, slowly backin' outta the room. *Pull da goddamn plug!* I have'ta get the fuck outta here—away from the image on the screen; away from Juanita; away from this fuckin' hospital. I turn to walk out. Race outta the room and down the hall 'til I get to the bathroom.

As soon as I get into the stall, I throw my guts up. I am mad siiiiiick! Do you hear me? Sick…sick…sick! Sick wit' disgust! Sick wit' knowin' that there's really a baby inside'a Juanita! Sick knowin' that no matter how fucked up a bitch *might* be—no matter how cold-hearted; no matter how bad I wanna see the plug yanked outta the wall—I can't do it. Not to that lil' helpless thing growin' inside'a that bitch's belly. No matter how many times I say I'm done wit' 'er ass, somehow, someway, this bitch finds a way back in my space—fuckin' up my world 'cause I keep lettin' 'er. And *that* has a bitch siiiiiiiiiick!! I throw up again, flush the toilet, then walk outta the stall.

I run the water, splashin' my face wit' it, then pat dry my face wit' sum'a their hard-ass paper towels, starin' at myself in the mirror. *Bitch, you shoulda pulled that plug ya damn self when you had da chance. Now you done seen that fuckin' sonogram, and now you gotta wait 'til it can be cut outta 'er.*

I stare at myself in the mirror. I might have'ta wait 'til I'm finally free of Juanita, but a bitch damn sure doesn't have'ta wait for shit else. I pull out my makeup case. Apply a fresh coat of eyeliner and lip gloss, then pull out my Kat line. Although, I still carry it, and keep it charged, it's a phone I haven't had'a use in two years. One I hoped I wouldn't have'ta eva use again. Still, I held onto it.

I turn it on. Wait for it to boot up, then scroll through the address book. I press the CALL button, then wait.

"Ohhh, shit. Let me find out my baby girl ready to come home to Daddy. I been waitin' to hear from ya sexy ass. Took you long 'nough. Maybe now I can finally get sum'a that good-ass pussy you been holdin' out on me."

I cringe. Hearin' his voice takes me back to the last thing this fat muhfucka said to me when I decided to shut down the *Kat Trap*. "It's twisted muhfuckas like you and me who can do this shit in our sleep. It takes a cold, vengeful, mean-streaked muhfucka to look a nigga dead in his eyes, then smoke his ass and never blink. Somewhere in our twisted minds, we think ain't shit wrong with takin' a muhfucka out. And what keeps us doin' this sick shit is the fact that we like takin' chances, livin' on the edge, thinkin' we'll never get caught. Killin' is ya callin', baby. You'll be back. And when you ready, I'ma be here waitin' for ya."

I roll my eyes. "Nigga, puhleeze. Annnnnnnywaaaaaay, I need you to track someone down for me."

"I got you, ma. Is it someone you need me to send the goons out on?"

"No," I tell 'im, runnin' my hand through my hair, "this is a muhfucka I need'a handle myself."

"Personal?"

"Very."

"Aiight, I got you. You gotta descript?"

Kat, this is Jawan, my fiancé. I close my eyes. Picture the nigga in my head; him standin' in Juanita's kitchen, grabbin' 'er ass— tall and prison-sculpted and bare-chested wit' a long dick swingin' in a pair'a flimsy gray sweats. I keep this part to myself.

"Yeah. He's like six-two wit' a caramel-colored complexion, curly hair and a chipped tooth." I tell 'im the nigga's from somewhere over in Brownsville; that he did a bid, then tell 'im his name.

"Oh, aiight. Anything else?"

I think; try 'n remember. The tattoo on his arm pops into my head. "Yeah, he has a tatt of a panther wit' green eyes on his foream."

"Bet. Give me a few weeks to see what I can find out 'bout this cat." He lowers his voice. "Whatchu tryna give a muhfucka for findin' 'im? You know I been wantin' to run this big-ass dick up in you for a minute."

I laugh. "Nigga, da only thing ya ugly, black-ass will eva get is a bullet to da head, trust. You'll neva feel da inside of my pussy."

"Ouch," he says, laughin'. "Yo, Kat, I see ya ass is still fuckin' crazy; still poppin' mad shit."

"That's right, muhfucka. Ain't shit changed, nigga. Hit me up when you find that nigga." I disconnect, shut the phone off, tossin' it back in my bag.

The bathroom door swings open, almost knockin' the shit outta me. My mouth drops open. "*Abuela*," I say, steppin' back. I'm not sure if I should be shocked or happy to see my grandmother since I haven't physically seen 'er in over three years.

"*Puta, por qué you wanna take mi hija y nieto de mí? Why?*"

Ohmiimuthafuckin'gaaaawd! I can't believe she has come outta her face and called me a *bitch*. She's standin' in front of me ice-grillin' me. I know chickie has a right to be pissed knowin' I wanna shut shit down, but comin' at me sideways…uh, I don't think so.

"I'm not takin' anyone away from you. She's already dead. And, as far as that grandchild you're talkin' 'bout, who's 'posed to raise it?"

"Who else," she huffs, indignantly like I done asked a retarded-ass question, "*su familia.*"

I laugh. *"Her family?* Who, you?" I swing my bag up over my shoulder. I have'ta get away from 'er ass before I really go off on 'er. "Oh, puuuhleeze. You have...well, *had* four daughters, and all four of 'em are fucked up. Now one of 'em is out there on a respirator, dead 'n pregnant. So, if you didn't get it right wit' any of them trick-ass bitches, what makes you think you gonna get it right now?"

She slaps me. I squeeze my hand into a fist. Catch myself from knockin' the shit outta 'er. Grandmother or not, this bitch has crossed the line. I stare at the bathroom door, wonderin' if anyone else is gonna walk in. Hopin' I'd have time to slip on my knuckles and bring it to granny's head.

I touch the side of my face. Glare at 'er. A bitch is blazin' mad right 'bout now. And, although I have neva, eva, disrespected this woman, today she might get it if I don't get the fuck away from 'er—now!

"Vergüenza me!"

I still can't get past the fact that she hit me in my face. Now she's standin' here talkin' 'bout I've shamed her. *What da fuck?!* "How, grandmother? How have I shamed *you?* Please explain that to me."

"Su espalda en su familia. Why? You weren't raised like this; hateful."

"Ohmiifuckin'gawd, do you really wanna do this, *here?"* I slam my hand up on my hip. Point my finga in 'er face. And straight disrespect the shit outta 'er. She steps back, clutchin' her chest. Her eyes widen. *"Bitch,* I don't have no family. They turned their backs on me a long time ago, includin' you. So how da fuck you know how I was raised, hunh? Were you there? No! Ya ass was too busy lettin' Patrice's niggas run drugs 'n guns in and outta ya spot. And too muthafuckin' busy makin' excuses for Rosa stealin' from ya ass when you knew da bitch was gettin' high. Did you eva give a fuck 'bout whether or not I ate 'cause Juanita's dick-junkie ass was too damn fucked up over niggas to make sure I had food to eat? No, ho, you weren't. You were too muthafuckin' busy worryin' 'bout Elise's kids while her ass was munchin' on pussy in prison. So don't *eva* talk to me 'bout how da fuck I was raised."

She raises 'er hand to slap me again. But I grab it. Clench my teeth. "Let me make myself very clear. I don't give. A. *Fuck*. If you eva put ya muthafuckin' hands on me again, I will forget you're my grandmother and beat ya old-ass down." I let go of 'er wrist. "You know what, forget it. Get da fuck outta my face. I want you, and your cracked-out, whore-ass daughters to stay da fuck away from me. All you bitches have fucked my life up enough."

"Oh *mi Dios*! You talk to me like this? Curse me? Su *abuela?* I will pray for your soul. You're nothing but *hijo del Diablo*!"

She tells me I'm the devil's child. I laugh. "You need'a pray for ya own soul, sweetie. The Devil's been fuckin' you and your daughter's your whole life. So, I guess that makes ya'll bitches his whores!"

I brush past 'er, angrily swingin' the bathroom door open, leavin' 'er standin' in the middle of the bathroom lookin' stupid 'n fucked up.

I stop back ova to the nurse's station. Tell 'em I've changed my mind; that they can do whateva they need to do keep Juanita's baby alive. The doctor and head nurse look relieved. He goes to say sumthin', but I put a finga up to stop 'im. I'm not in the mood to hear shit he or anyone else has to say. I tell 'em this. Tell 'em I'll be back in a few days to talk. Then I pop my hips to the eleva-tors one foot in front of the other, holdin' back a flood of tears as I make my way back to my whip. I disarm it, then slide behind the wheel. My face is streaked wit' tears, but a bitch refuses to break down. For what? It's not gonna change a muthafuckin' thing.

Maybe it won't, but you're doin' da right thing, Kat.

For who?

For you.

How da fuck is keepin' a brain-dead bitch who ain't neva gave a fuck 'bout me alive da right thing to do for me? *She's not even aware of what's goin' on 'round 'er; that's not livin'.*

Before I can cum up wit' an answer that makes fuckin' sense, my cell rings, snappin' me outta my thoughts. I swipe tears from my face, pullin' my phone outta my bag.

"Yeah?"

"Yo, wassup? You want sum company? I'm tryna see you."

I stare at myself in my rearview mirror. I feel so fuckin' numb. And a bitch really ain't beat for bein' alone today…or tonight. I know this muhfucka ain't nuthin' but trouble for a bitch like me. But, right now. I don't give'a fuck. I wanna get lost in a nigga's arms; wanna feel a hard, chiseled body pressed up against mine; feel a heavy, bricked dick pressin' up against my ass, then stretchin' out my pussy. This muhfucka is it.

"I'm on my way home," I tell 'em, startin' my engine, then slowly backin' outta my parkin' space. "Be at my spot in an hour."

"Aiight, bet."

"And, muhfucka, you already know what it is if ya ass ain't there on time."

He laughs. "Yeah, aiight. Not this time, baby. I'm already in ya driveway."

CHAPTER SIXTEEN

I'm cummin'...nuttin' all over ya dick...freak-nasty bitch 'bout to make you spit...wit' one tongue lap on my clit...'bout to make you forget...bitch so fly...pussy so tight...got ya thinkin' you can touch da sky...

"Aaaaah, yesssss...eat my pussy, muhfucka...yeah...ohhhh, shit... get ya tongue all up in there..."

I'm dropped down low on Alex's face wit' my thighs clamped 'round his head. He has my fluffy ass cheeks pulled wide open, lickin' my pussy, suckin' on my clit, dartin' his tongue in 'n outta my slippery slit. A bitch can't front. The nigga's tongue game is siiiick! "You like how that pussy taste, nigga?" I ask, grindin' my pelvis down on his face. His long tongue feels soooooooooooo fuckin' good inside'a me.

He moans. "Yeah, ma...ya pussy taste good...you gonna let me put my dick in this pussy?"

I moan. "Shut...aaaah...da...oooh, shit...fuck...mmmm...up... and eat my pussy, nigga."

When I finish bustin' all in his mouth, I let go of the head-board, slide my body down his and grind my hot, steamy pussy on his long, black dick. Nigga gotta thick dick like a tree trunk.

He's runnin' his hands up 'n down my body, then stops on my ass. He palms it. "Daaaaamn, ma...you gotta fat ass. I love da way you feel on me. Ya body feels like silk." He kisses me, then slides his tongue deep in my mouth. I taste my pussy all over his lips and tongue. And the shit makes a bitch go wild. I suck 'em. Feel my insides start to pop like a firecracker. I wanna feel the nigga's dick in me.

I reach down for his dick. Stroke it. It's bricked the fuck up. Hot and heavy and feels like it could fuck a bitch into 'er grave. The nigga's dick is bigger than Grant's was. And it kinda reminds me of Naheem's—black and thick, but a few inches longer. "You think this lil'-ass dick can handle this pussy heat, muhfucka?" I tease him.

He grins. "Yeah, aiiight. I got ya lil'-ass dick aiiight. I'ma 'bout to bust that pretty pussy wide open wit' it, too."

I roll off of 'em. Lie on my back, throw my legs up in'a V, then bend my knees back. I pull open my wet pussy. "Then cum bust it open, muhfucka. I hear a buncha yip-yappin', nigga, but you ain't puttin' in no work." I slap my clit, wind my hips. "Cum fuck me, muhfucka."

He jumps outta the bed, runs ova to the other side of the room, snatches up his pants, then digs into his pocket, pullin' out a box'a condoms. Magnum XLs. "You talkin' a buncha shit, ma. Let me see how much shit you gonna be talkin' when I finish stuffin' ya fine-ass wit' a buncha this dick and start pushin' ya guts in."

I grin, watchin' 'im tear off da wrapper, then roll it down on his shiny black pole. I take the nigga in. Mymuthafuckin'gaaawd... this nigga is built like a black stallion. Muscles for days, wit' a porn-star, super-size dick and big-ass balls.

I hope this muhfucka knows how'ta use all that dick. 'Cause if he doesn't, I'ma toss da nigga out. I tell 'im to run his tongue back up on my clit; to dip it back in this slit to scoop outta 'nother nut I feel buildin' up inside'a me. I tell 'im to keep eatin' my pussy 'til I bust'a 'nother nut in his mouth.

"Stick ya tongue out…mmmm, yeah…stick it all da way out, muhfucka…tickle my pussy…there you go…you want that nut, muhfucka…"

"Mmmmm-hmm…"

"Work for it, nigga."

I lean up on my forearms while he looks up at me. "You like that?"

"Fuck yeah…" he starts suckin' 'n lickin' 'n slurpin' the fuck outta my fat, juicy-ass pussy. The muhfucka rapidly wiggles his tongue from side to side, then flaps it up and down against my clit before slidin' it back into my slit. He gotta bitch archin' 'er back, clutchin' the sheets. "Yo, tell Daddy how nasty he is? You like Daddy's tongue on that pussy, baby?"

Daddy? This nigga's crazy if he thinks I'm gonna acknowledge 'im as some muthafuckin' *Daddy. Nigga, get real!* But, his tongue work…*Ohmiiiiigawd, ohmiiiigawd, ohhhhhhhmiiiiiiiigaaaawd! This nigga's makin' my walls shake.*

I moan.

He changes the pressure of his tongue on my clit. The nigga goes from light, feathery tongue strokes to heavy, deep tongue strokes; alternates from short tongue strokes to long, fast licks. The nigga uses the front of his tongue, then the backside of it. Slurps me, swallows me, then sucks my pussy in his mouth. I'm on the verge of crackin' a nut. He zig-zags his tongue, lickin' back 'n forth, then swirlin' it all 'round my pussy. His left hand wanders over my body, squeezin' and kneadin' my titties and nipples. He takes his right hand and slips two fingas into my bubblin' snatch, searchin' for my hot spot. This nigga has a bitch on fiiiiiiiiiiyah!

"Aaaaaaaaaaaah, oooooooooh, fuck…gobble my pussy up, muhfucka…uhhhhhhh…I'm gettin' ready to cum…mmmm-hmmm…" I palm his head, press his face and tongue deeper into me. "…Catch my nut, nigga…"

He gulps down my pussy cream, then climbs up ova me and slowly works his dick in me. My tight pussy grips da shit outta his dick. I hold back a scream. He takes his time, works da dick in. I watch his facial expressions. Smirk when he closes his eyes and bites down on his cum-stained lips.

"Yeaaah…uhhhh…ohhhh, fuuuuck…

My pussy is sooooo wet 'n creamy 'n muthafuckin' on fire. I keep spurtin' 'n buckin' my hips. He's strokin' my insides so damn good. But a bitch ain't 'bout to tell his conceited ass this. "When you gonna stop teasin' a bitch, and put da dick in, nigga, unh?"

"Oh, you don't feel this big-ass dick in you, hunh?" He plunges his dick deep in me, then slowly pulls it out to the tip. He tip-drills my hole, teases it wit' the head, then slowly winds his hips, pushin' the dick in one inch at'a time. He puts half'a it in, then pulls it back out to the tip. The nigga is teasin' me. He slams it all the way. My eyes widen, I gulp in air, but I refuse to give this nigga what he wants. "You still don't feel it? You still don't feel this dick?"

"No, muhfucka," I snap, holdin' back a scream. I grab his ass. Pull 'im into me, diggin' my nails into his skin. "Uhhh…mmm…"

"Then why ya eyes rollin' all up in ya head, hunh, baby? Talkin' 'bout you can't feel this dick…"—the nigga starts poundin' away, pushin' my legs all the way back over my shoulders—"Yeah, aii-ight…you know this big dick's beatin' this good-ass pussy up…

you feel that shit all up in ya stomach…uhhh, fuuuuck…tight-ass pussy…mmmph, shit…" He raises up on his arms, drippin' sweat down on me. "Hold them legs back…yeah, that's right…let me see that pretty pussy grab this dick…yeah, yeah, yeah…you still don't feel that shit?"

"Uhhh…nooooooo, muhfucka…"

"Yeah, aiiigtht…"—slam, pull out—"Then why…"—slam, slam, slam—"you"—pull out. Tip drill—"makin' faces?"

"Uhhhhhh…oooohhh, shit…'cause ya breath…aaaaah…mm-mmm…stinks, muhfucka…"

He busts out laughin' and I can't help but to start laughin' wit' 'im. "Yo, you mad funny…you just fucked up my rhythm."

He slow grinds into me. "Uhhh…whateva, muhfucka…"

He leans in and starts kissin' me, then pulls his dick outta me, and starts eatin' my pussy again, lickin' 'n lappin' all over it. I can't front, this muhfucka eats pussy like it's supposed to be eaten—non-stop lickin', slurpin', kissin', flickin', and tonguin' every nook and cranny.

He raises up on his arms. My juice coats his lips as he hovers back ova me. He presses his dick up against my clit, slaps it, runs it along the center of my pussy, pushes it back in, then leans in and offers me his lips 'n tongue, again, so I can suck up my cream.

We finally change positions. And the only thing you hear is my pussy slurpin' his dick and his balls slappin' da back of it as he fucks me from da back, fucks me from da side, fucks me on the edge of the bed, fucks me standin' up, fucks me bendin' ova the chair, fucks me on top'a the dresser. Basically, he fucks me all ova da damn place. And I'm fuckin' 'im back. I got da nigga moanin'. He got me moanin'. I'm goin' for mine. He's goin' for his.

"Aaaaaah, shiiiiiiit, baby…aaahh fuck, the pussy so goooood… gotdaaaamn…"

I'm buckin' my hips. He's buckin' his. "Mmmmm...fill my pussy up, muhfucka...that's right, stroke that shit, muhfucka..."

"Daaaaamn, baby...aaaaaah, fuck...aaaaah, shit..."

Eventually we end up fucking missionary wit' me lyin' top, then I sit up and ride 'em rodeo-style, leanin' in and puttin' a titty in his mouth. He sucks my nipple, twirls his tongue 'round it, while lightly pinchin' 'rollin' my other nipple between his fingas.

I close my eyes and milk da nigga's dick, liftin' my hips up, then rockin' his top wit' da mouth of my pussy.

"Aaaaah, shit..."

"You like that, muhfucka?"

"Fuck yeah..." He grips my ass, slaps it 'n makes it jiggle. "I been waitin' for too muhfuckin' long to get up in this shit...aaaah fuck..."

"You wanna see this pussy gobble up ya dick?" I ask, slowly turnin' my body 'round on his shaft. I keep turnin', twistin' my pussy 'round on his cock 'til I'm facin' his feet. I lean forward and brace myself on his shins, givin' 'im a backshot view of my pussy suckin' down his dick.

"Aaaaaah, shit...oooh...that's wassup, baby...pussy so damn tight...hmmmm...mmmmm..." I show da nigga how a real bitch rides a dick. Show how 'em a freak-nasty bitch can handle a dick. I bring my pussy all the way down on the nigga's dick, bounce my ass up on it. "Aaaaah, fuck, yeah...aaah, shit this pussy's good..."

I cup his hairy balls, lightly squeeze 'n pull 'em. I speed ride the cock. Gallop up 'n down on the shit while playin' wit' my clit.

I glance ova my shoulder. "Stick ya finga in my asshole." He does, and my pussy grips his dick tighter.

"Daaaamn, girl, you grabbin' that shit!"

"You wanna see my nut splash all up ova it?

"Yeah, baby...give me that nut...ohhh, shit...dirty Daddy's dick up...aaaah, fuck...you gonna let me get some more of this pussy?"

"Uhhh, ooooh..."—I slam down on his dick—"...hell noo-ooooooo, muhfucka...this is all da pussy you gonna get...mmm-mmm..."

He lifts up and, somehow, in one swift move the muhfucka has me lifted up off'a the bed and he's standin' up, fuckin' a bitch for filth. He dips at the knees, thrusts his dick up in me while slammin' me down on it. Long strokin' my pussy; feedin' my cat deliciously. I lay back on his chest, reach down 'n play wit' my clit, and let the muhfucka rock my pussy 'til my cream shoots out and runs down the shaft of his thick dick, and along his balls.

"Daaaaamn, I need'a blunt," he says, catchin' his breath. "That shit was good as hell. You gotta muhfucka hooked, wit' that fat, juicy pussy."

I laugh, reachin' for a blunt. I spark it, then take two pulls, slowly blowin' smoke. "Nigga, puhleeze. Picture that." But, a bitch already knows she got that bomb-ass pussy.

I hand 'im the blunt. He shifts his body, raises up on his forearm, and takes it from me. I watch 'im pull it up to his thick lips, and puff. He looks at me. He strokes my hair, then rubs the side of my face. "Look, ma, I don't know what it is 'bout you, but a muhfucka's really diggin' you." I raise my brow. "What?"

I shake my head.

"Yo, you think I'm bullshittin', don't you?"

"I think you'll say whateva you think I wanna hear at da moment." I take the blunt from 'im.

"Nah," he leans in, kisses me on the lips, then stares me in the eyes. "True story, baby. You gotta muhfucka open."

I blink, blink again. Shake my head. "Don't."

"Don't what?"

"Don't say shit you don't mean."

"I tell you what. You don't believe me. Let me introduce you to da only woman whose ever meant anything to me. She'll keep da shit funky and tell you what it is."

"Oh, really? And who is that?" He takes another pull off'a the blunt, leans ova me, puttin' it out in the ashtray, then blows weed smoke up at the ceilin'. "Well, muhfucka, who is it?"

He grins. "My moms. E'ery Sunday I have dinner wit' 'er. I want you to meet 'er. She's as real as they get, and she's a good cook. She ain't gonna front on you."

I twist my lips up. "And you want me to meet 'er?"

"No doubt." He gets outta bed. I watch 'im as he walks ova to his pile of clothes. He pulls out his cell. "I'ma put it on speaker so you can hear it for ya'self since you think a muhfucka's frontin' on you." I sit up in bed, proppin' a pillow up in back'a me. He shakes his dick at me while the phone rings. I roll my eyes. "And when I'm done wit' this, I want some more'a that pussy, too."

"Whateva."

"Oh, you finally decide to call," a woman says, soundin' like she gotta taste of the streets in 'er.

He smiles. "You know I was gonna be hittin' you up, sooner or later."

"Mmmph, so who you whorin' wit' now, and where?"

I give 'im a look, shakin' my head. "He laughs, starin' at me. "No one, ma. I'm chillin'."

"Yeah, right. And I'm goin' blind."

"Nah, real talk, ma. I'm good. But there is someone I want you to meet."

It sounds like she's chokin' on sumthin'. "Say, whaaat? You want me to meet who, a woman?"

He laughs. "Yeah, ma."

"Who is she?"

He looks at me. "This beauty I'm diggin'." I suck my teeth, rollin' my eyes up in my head.

"Who?" she asks, soundin' shocked. He repeats himself. "I thought that's what I heard you say. Are you alright? Have you banged ya head on something?"

"Yeah, ma, I'm good. And no I ain't banged my head. Why?"

"Boy, something must be wrong 'cause you ain't never called here wantin' *me* to meet any of your lil' girlfriends."

He keeps his eyes on me. Okay, so the nigga ain't neva brought any of his hoes ova to meet his moms. I can't front. I'm caught off guard wit' this. I've neva met any nigga's moms before. Still, I'm smart enough to know that that shit still don't mean nuthin'.

"Yo, ma, they weren't girlfriends."

"I know them lil' hot-ass hoes weren't. I'm tryna be nice today. Does this *beauty* you want me to meet have a name?"

"Yeah, Kat."

"Kat? What kinda damn name is that?"

He looks ova at me. I raise my brow, twistin' my lips up. "Yo, ma, chill. That's her nickname. It's Katrina."

"Mmmph. That's more like it. Does Katrina know 'bout all them nasty-ass hoes you..." I grin, startin' to like' 'er already. He takes 'er off'a speaker.

"Yo, ma, chill, aiight. I gotta bounce. I'ma be thru Sunday... yes, I'm bringin' 'er wit' me...Aiight, aiight, I got you...See you Sunday...love you, too." He turns his phone off, walkin' back ova to the bed, holdin' his dick 'n grinnin'. "Now what?"

I smirk, spreadin' my legs 'n pullin' open my pussy. "You tell me, muhfucka."

CHAPTER SEVENTEEN

Family is overrated…hoes been hatin'…dislikin' da facts a bitch been statin'…bringin' it raw…gotta bitch wantin' ta throw up da hands…fuck bein' related…step outta pocket…a bitch knockin' sockets…breakin' jaws…ain't shit to understand…

"Ohmiiiiiiiifuckin'gaawd, Kat, you are really outta fuckin' control cursin' ya grandmoms out like that. That shit is straight disrespectful 'n nasty."

Me and Chanel are chillin' at my spot, doin' what we do best. Blazin' 'n poppin' mad shit 'n cursin' each otha out. I finally decided to fill 'er in on the rest of the hospital drama wit' my nutty-ass family. As you already know, Chanel's my *only* true friend. And I got mad love for the ho 'cause, on e'ery thing, she ain't gonna tell me what the fuck she thinks I wanna hear; she's gonna serve it to me just how I dish it to 'er—raw. Still, a bitch ain't always tryna hear the shit. And today happens to be one'a those days.

I roll my eyes, flickin' my hand. "Oh, well. Life's a bitch, boo. She had no business comin' at me da way she did."

"It doesn't make a difference how she came at you, bitch. That's still ya grandmother."

"Bitch, be clear. I'ma grown-ass woman; I don't give a fuck

who it is. You bring it to me wrong, you gonna get handled. You act like I come at these hoes tryna bring da noise. No, sweetie. A bitch stays mindin' 'er own business. But these bitches stay tryna serve me. Sorry, boo-boo, I ain't da fuckin' one." I take another puff of the blunt, then pass it back to 'er.

"Kat, c'mon, ya *grandmoms*? It's one thing you dissin' ya moms and ya aunts, but ya grandmoms. That's some foul shit. No matter what, she's da one person you 'posed to always respect."

"Says who?" I get up from table to check on the lasagna I have in the oven. Yeah, believe it or not, a bitch cooked. I remove the foil so it can brown on top, then start choppin' up da lettuce, then slicin' cucumbers for our salad. "Tell me what handbook that shit's written in so I can smack da shit outta da bitch who wrote it."

She huffs. "Bitch, there ain't no damn handbook. You 'posed to respect ya elders; period, point-blank."

I tilt my head. "Again, says who?" When she can't give me an answer that makes sense to me, I add, "News flash, Sugah: It's kinda hard ta respect a bitch who ain't neva did shit for you. When a bitch ran away from home 'cause I couldn't take all da bullshit Juanita was into anymore, that old-ass ho told me I couldn't stay wit' 'er. Da bitch told me she didn't have any room for me. But she had room for all'a Elise's kids when 'er ass was in prison. I came to that bitch cryin' 'n she flat out told me ta take my ass back home. Didn't say I could stay for da night, then go home; nuthin'. She straight out told me I couldn't stay there; that a bitch wasn't welcomed there. And you expect me to respect 'er. Fuck outta here. Grandmother or not, she can lick da inside'a my asshole. And I'll leave it filled wit' a buncha shit for 'er."

Chanel coughs, chokin' on weed smoke. "Ugh, that's some nasty shit right there."

"Oh well."

"Bitch, I still think ya ass is crazy as fuck. I'm glad ya ass at least came to ya senses where da baby's concerned."

"Mmmph. That lil' muhfucka is lucky. 'Cause trust, had I not walked in on them bitches doin' that sonogram, it woulda been scraped out 'n tossed in da toilet." Chanel stares at me, then blinks 'er eyes. I shrug. "Whaaat? I'm keepin' shit real."

"Whateva. All that matters is that you didn't. We gotta lotta shit to get done before da baby comes home. I'm kinda excited 'bout bein' an auntie."

I stop choppin', snappin' my head in 'er direction. "Whoa, whoa...pump ya brakes, boo. What da fuck is you talkin' 'bout?"

"I'm talkin' 'bout da baby. After it's born, aren't you takin' it?"

I buck my eyes, shakin' my head. "Bitch, I *said* I changed my mind 'bout pullin' da damn plug. I ain' say nuthin' 'bout bringin' no baby up in here. Where da fuck you get me takin' a baby outta that?"

She tilts 'er head, frownin'. "Ummm, it's ya lil' brotha or sista, so why da fuck wouldn't you?"

I look at 'er ass like she's one'a the dizziest hoes alive. "Ho, I gotta life, that's why."

"So you mean to tell me you're gonna abandon ya own blood; is that what da fuck you tellin' me?"

"*Abandon?* Ho, I ain' abandonin' shit. It doesn't know me. And I don't know it. So how is that me abandonin' it?"

"It's ya blood. It's a baby you know exists, and instead of steppin' up to da plate you turnin' ya back on that innocent baby."

"Sweetie, that baby can go into foster care. I'm sure some family will adopt it, and hopefully do right by it. But, this bitch ain't da one."

"Let's see. Abandonment, neglect, self-centeredness...hmmmm, once again, here you go soundin' more 'n more like ya moms."

Hearin' this shit for the second time from 'er makes my skin crawl. And she shuts me the hell up wit' that. The only comeback I can think to say is, "Like I said, I gotta life."

She laughs. "A life doin' what?"

"Doin' me."

She shakes her head, tightly rollin' another blunt. She seals it. "Oh, puhleeze." She sparks up, then takes it to the dome.

I stop slicin' tomatoes. "And what is that 'posed to mean?"

She gets up and walks ova to me wit' the blunt danglin' from 'er dick suckas. She takes another pull, then hands it to me. "Bitch, it means, yeah you gotta life, but ya ass ain't really livin' it. You fuckin' existin', that's it."

I stare at 'er. Raise a brow. "Oh, so I guess you're livin' life, but a bitch like me is only existin', right? Bitch, puhleeze."

"I neva said I was livin' shit. I know I could do betta, but I'm good. The difference between me and you is I'm not goin' through life pissed off at da world."

I take two pulls from the blunt, then pass it back to 'er. I go back to finishin' up the salad. "Sweetie, I ain't pissed at da world. I'm pissed at bitches who keep tryin' it on my time; simple as that."

"Yeah, okay, boo. If you say so."

"Think what you like, but I ain't takin' on another bitch's problem. As far as I'm concerned my good deed is lettin' da lil' thing live, not raisin' it."

"Ohmiiiifuckin'gawd, I done heard it all. See, that's ya fuckin' problem. You so busy lovin' ya'self that you don't know how to love anyone else."

"Bitch, get real. I love ya ho-ass."

"I know you love me. And I love you, too. But I ain't talkin' 'bout me. I'm talkin' 'bout you bein' so damn closed to lettin' anyone else in ya space. Bitch, I love you like a sista, but I swear ya ass is too damn selfish."

Is this slut serious? "Ho, since when you become da expert on love? Love don't come easy, and it ain't guaranteed. So, a bitch like me ain't givin' any out unless it's earned and deserved."

She goes back to 'er seat. "Kat, it ain't always 'bout you. That baby needs you. And if you ask me, I think you need it, too."

I roll my eyes. "Girl, you sound fuckin' crazy."

"And, bitch, you crazier than I am."

I laugh, dismissin' e'erything she's said. "You know what, ho, pass me da damn blunt. And instead of playin' Oprah, make ya'self useful and take the lasagna outta da damn oven. Trick-bitch tryna lecture me. Not!"

"Fuck you, slut-bucket." We go back 'n forth callin' each otha a buncha names, laughin' 'til it's time to get our grub on.

TWENTY MINUTES LATER, WE'RE SITTIN' AT THE TABLE EATIN' 'N tossin' back Jose Cuervo mix margaritas. Our convo has changed up and I'm glad 'cause I really didn't wanna have'ta go off on my girl 'bout shit she'll neva understand. "Mmm, this shit is bangin', Boo. I had no idea you could throw down in the kitchen." She licks 'er fingas, takin' a sip of 'er drink.

"Well, Sweetie, a butta bitch like me can do more than be fly 'n fabulous."

"Hmmmph, so I see, boo. So I muthafuckin' see. Annnnyways, what's good wit' you and Allstar?"

"Shit. But interestin'ly da nigga took me to meet his moms."

Her mouth drops open. "Say what?"

"You heard me. It fucked a bitch up, too."

She smiles. "That nigga must really dig you. You know ain't no nigga takin' a ho he ain't really diggin' home to meet his moms; period." I agree. "So how was she?"

"On some real shit, she was mad cool. She checks da nigga left 'n right, and was puttin' 'im out on front street da whole time, draggin' 'im for filth." I start laughin'. "Ohmigod, girlfriend was airin' his drawers all da way out."

"What was she sayin'?"

Ohhhhkay…this is my girl and all. But, on some real shit, a bitch ain't really up for tellin' 'er too much 'bout this nigga. So I tell 'er just enough to let 'er know the nigga has real doggish ways.

She wets 'er throat, tossin' back the rest of 'er drink, then refills 'er glass. "I guess you were shocked when she told you all that."

"Kinda. I mean, not by what she was sayin' 'cause I already knew da nigga had a buncha whores on his squad." She sparks an after dinner blunt, takes a pull, then hands it to me. "I wasn't expectin' 'er to put 'im on blast in front of me. And da funny thing is, he didn't try 'n stop 'er. It was like da nigga wanted 'er to spill his dirt."

"Yeah, that nigga's diggin' you, Kat."

I shrug. "Maybe."

She rolls 'er eyes up in 'er head. "Bitch, whaddaya mean, *maybe?* You already know what it is."

I put the blunt to my lips, thinkin' back on my convo with his moms while I was in the kitchen helpin' her wit' the dishes. Yes, believe it or not, a bitch rolled up 'er sleeves and helped his moms out. For me, that was a first. But it gave me a chance to get to know 'er some.

"Let me tell you something 'bout my son," she said, eyein' me. "Alex is my only child. And I know him like I know the back of my hand. That man has never brought any woman to my home to meet me. And believe me, he has been through multiple women. Even when he was a teenager, sneaking them fast-assed girls into my house, he wasn't tryna have me meet 'em.

"But, for some reason, he wanted me to meet you. Now I don't know what it is about you, but whatever it is, it has my son open. And, between you and me, I have been prayin' every day that he'd meet someone he can settle down with. I don't know enough about you to say if I think you're the one. But I know enough to know that my son thinks you're the one good enough for me to meet. So, that says a lot." She paused, then added, "You seem like you on point. You classy, beautiful and I can tell a feisty one. And that's what my son needs—someone who won't put up with any shit. But I'ma tell you like this, don't fuck him over, or you and I will have to take it to the streets."

Believe it or not, a bitch was taken aback when she said that. But I kept it cute. The only thing I could do was smile 'cause on some real shit she brought it to me how a real bitch should—straight to the damn point.

"So, all that said, you tryna make it pop wit' da nigga or what?"

I shake my head. "No. I'm chillin'."

"You *chillin'*? Bitch, ya ass need'a man."

"I don't need shit. And I definitely don't need 'im. Not for anything serious; that's for sure. The nigga is too extra for me."

"Mmmph, if you say so. Well, have you at least fucked 'im?"

I smirk. "Sumthin' like that."

She drops 'er fork in 'er plate. "Ohmiiiigod, you dirty whore. Since when you start holdin' out on'a bitch? That's da first thing that shoulda been cumin' outta ya cock washas. Fuck goin' to meet his mammy. Spill it. Is the nigga's stroke game right?"

I laugh. "No comment."

She sucks 'er teeth, rollin' 'er eyes. "Well, answer me this. How many times you fuck 'im?"

"Twice," I tell 'er, liftin' my glass in toast.

She laughs. "Say no more. Da dick's good, and you diggin' his ass."

I grin. "What makes you say that?"

"'Cause I know ya kind, boo."

I chuckle. "Oh, bitch, puhleeze. You think you know so damn much."

"Well, am I wrong?"

"Ho, finish eatin' ya damn food."

"Tramp; just what I thought."

"Fuck you, Booga," I say, gettin' up from the table to get another bottle of Cuervo.

She bursts out laughin'. We spend the rest of the afternoon, blazin' and drinkin' 'til we're both so damn lit we can't see straight. And as usual, Chanel's drunk-ass ends up stayin' the night.

Bang, bang, bang! Ding-dong, ding-dong! I OPEN MY EYES NOT sure if it's a dream or if someone is really bangin' on my damn door and ringin' my doorbell like they two steps from crazy. The bangin' and ringin' continues. I glance ova at the clock. 8:47 a.m.

"Who da fuck's bangin' on ya door like that?" Chanel asks, standin' in my doorway in 'er bra and panties wit' 'er hair all ova her head. She pops 'er hips in my room, walkin' into my closet to get a robe. I glance at 'er. The bitch's body is bangin'.

"Beats da hell outta me," I say, rollin' ova on my left side and pullin' da covers up ova my head. "Go down and see."

She walks outta the room, goes downstairs. I hear the alarm chirp when she finally opens the door, then wonder what the fuck is takin' 'er so long to come back upstairs.

A few minutes later she comes up and says, "Kat, girrrrrl, you gotta real problem."

There's more bangin'. Then pressin' down on my doorbell. I snap up in bed. "What? Who da fuck is on my doorbell like that?"

She shakes her head. "Baaaaaaby, you might wanna boot up. It's ya Aunt Rosa."

My eyes buck in surprise. "Whaaaat?! Rosa's at my mutha-fuckin' door?"

"In da damn flesh. And girlfriend looks like she's ready to make shit pop."

Bang, bang, bang, bang! I swing the covers off, then jump outta bed. "You gotta be fuckin' kiddin' me. That bitch brought 'er ass to my muthafuckin' home tryna bring da noise? Oh, hell no. I'ma fuck this bitch up once 'n for all."

I run into my closet, snatch'a Baby Phat sweatsuit off'a hanga, then hurriedly put it on. I boot up; tie my laces tight. "I'ma break this bitch's face," I say, brushin' past Chanel. She follows behind me as I race down the stairs, then peek outta the livin' room window to see what kinda work I gotta put in. *Ohmigod, this crazy bitch came here solo,* I think when I don't see anyone else outside wit' 'er.

"Kat, maybe you should call da police," Chanel says, slippin' into a pair'a sweats. She pulls 'er hair into a ponytail. "You said there's a restrainin' order, right?"

"Oh, I'ma call da police alright. *After* I finish rockin' 'er sockets 'n knockin' 'er grill out. I'ma need you to be on watch in case some 'xtra shit pops off."

"I got you."

Bang, bang, bang! "Kat, I know you're in there, bitch! Open up this fuckin' door and take ya ass-whoopin' like a real bitch. Fuckin' no-good bitch!"

Bang, bang, bang!

I decide to go out the back door and run 'round to the front to catch this ho by surprise. I tell Chanel to open the front door to distract 'er. I grab two bricks from off'a the patio table, then race 'round to the front. I hit the bitch in the back of the head wit' one brick and throw the otha through my front window to make it look like the bitch was the one who tossed it.

She grabs 'er head. "Aaaaaah! Pussy bitch! You wanna sneak a bitch?! You wanna fight dirty?!" She charges me, but I got the ho dazed.

I grab 'er by the hair. "Bitch!" I snap, swingin' 'er onto the ground, then draggin' 'er by her scalp. "You come to my mutha-fuckin' home like you wanna get it in, then let's."

"Bitch!" she yells, tryna pry my hands outta 'er hair. "Let my muthafuckin' hair go and fight me like a real bitch." I don't let go 'til I yank'a handful of 'er hair out.

"Get da fuck up, bitch. You wanna rock wit' da hands, then let's." I wait for the bitch to get up; hands balled in tight fists. Give 'er a moment to get 'er thoughts in check, then we bang it out. We go at it like two bitches who have hated each other for years. She's punchin'. I'm punchin'. My fist connects wit' the side'a 'er face. Hers connects wit' the side'a mine. We go blow for blow. I hit 'er dead in 'er grill. She stumbles backward. "I'm so fuckin' sick of you. I wish you'd die, bitch!" I punch 'er again. "I want you dead!"

She runs toward me, and kicks me in the stomach. I stumble back. "I'ma fuck you up, Kat, for all da pain ya ungrateful ass caused my sista, for disrespectin' ya grandmutha, and for comin' at me like I'm some gutter bitch."

"Suck'a crack pipe, slut," I snap, punchin' 'er in 'er throat, then kickin' the bitch in 'er bad knee—the one I'm sure she thought I forgot 'bout—wit' my steel toes. "You are a gutter rat." She falls to 'er knees. "Get up, bitch! Let's finish this shit once 'n for all."

She gets up and, then in one swift motion, the bitch whips out 'er blade and swings it, slashin' into the air. I jump back. She swings 'er blade again. Slashes the air again; attempts to bring it to my face. But I am smart enough to know not to get too close to 'er crazy ass.

Right now, I am too fuckin' mad to be concerned if the bitch cuts me or not, I want 'er ass dropped. I charge 'er. "Biiiiiiiiiiiiiiiiitch, I hate you!" I knock 'er backward into a tree, grabbin' her by the wrist, then twistin' 'er arm 'til she drops the blade. I flip 'er onto the ground, then jump on top'a 'er. We roll 'round in the grass, slappin', punchin' and clawin' each other 'til I reach for the brick that's beside me and start rockin' the front of 'er face wit' it. Blood gushes out. And it only entices me; gets a bitch's juices flowin' and makes me wanna crack this ho's skull open. Right now, I wanna smash 'er brains in. I bang in 'er mouth, again.

I hear Chanel scream. "Ohmiiigaaaawd, nooooo, Kat!"

Someone must have called the police. I can hear the sirens in the background, but I don't give'a fuck. I let go of the brick, drop it on the ground, then get up, leavin' Rosa lyin' on the ground busted 'n bloody.

CHAPTER EIGHTEEN

Crazy bitch shoulda stayed in 'er lane...tryna set it off wit' a bitch like me...ho shoulda opened 'er eyes...she woulda known a bitch don't take lightly to threats...don't live wit' a buncha regrets...trick bitch...welcome to ya demise...

"Detective Samuels, speaking."

I clear my throat. "Detective Samuels, this is Katrina Rivera. I'm callin' regardin' my mother, Juanita Rivera. She's the pregnant woman who was beaten up, and is on life support."

"Yes, I know who she is," he says wit' a lil' too much 'tude for my likin'. But I let it slide. "How can I help you?"

"Well, it's my understandin' you're one'a the detectives assigned to the case."

"Yes, I am."

"Well, I was wonderin' if you have any leads yet."

"Not at the moment. However, there is the boyfriend that we are still trying to locate."

"Is he a suspsect?"

"No, but he is definitely someone of interest we'd like to bring in for questioning."

"Well, have you at least been able to track down his where-abouts?"

There's a moment of silence, then rustlin' of papers or some other shit. "We're still search—"

"So basically that means ya'll muhfuckas ain't doin' shit, but sittin' on ya asses," I interrupt, lookin' outta my bedroom window. I peep a big-ass U-Haul truck 'cross the street, movin' someone in.

"Miss Rivera, I understand your—"

I disconnect the call, hopin' I get at that snake-ass muhfucka before they locate his ass. I see someone called and left a message while I was on the phone. I check the voicemail, shakin' my head.

"Watch ya back, bitch. I'm outta jail, ho. You knock my fuckin' teeth out. Break my nose. Lie to them muhfuckas talkin' 'bout I threw a brick through ya window. Bitch, you know you did that shit. Then you have *me* arrested. Bitch, I'm gonna gut ya face. You think I give'a fuck 'bout a muthafuckin' restrainin' order, or goin' to jail. Bitch, I'm from da streets. You really crossed da goddamn line this time, ho, disrespectin' 'n threatenin' my mutha and comin' at me all reckless. So watch ya face 'cause when I'm finished wit' ya ass, da only thing you gonna be good for is da circus." I save the message, decidin' to be finished wit' this bitch for good. *I'm done fuckin' 'round wit' this crack-head bitch.*

I walk ova to my handbag and pull out my other phone. I turn it on, then press open the call history. I place the call. Wait for the nigga to answer. "Yo."

"I need'a hire a crew," I tell 'im, wishin' I didn't have'ta call this fat-nasty muhfucka, again. But'a bitch done worked my last nerve, and—aunt or no fuckin' aunt, I need 'er ass handled. I know I promised myself I would never body a muhfucka for personal reasons unless they were tryna play me. And I definitely said I would neva body children or chicks. But, I ain't the one pullin' the trigga, so it's whateva. Rosa has got ta go. I need this bitch outta 'er misery and outta my damn space. The sooner, the betta. She's the type'a bitch who'll try 'n bring it e'ery chance she gets. One or two times, cool. But that ho will fight to the death. So I need'a take 'er down, and keep 'er down—swiftly.

"Damn, you really know how'ta make a nigga's dick brick. Two calls in da same week, I think I'ma nut on myself."

I suck my teeth. "Muhfucka, get a grip. Ain't nobody tryna hear that dumb shit. I got more pressin' shit ta do."

"Yo, chill out. I'm only fuckin' wit' you, ma."

"Well, take that shit ova to da next bitch. I need sum work put in."

The nigga changes his tone. "Aiight, what kinda work order you need done?"

"I need'a jack gone bad," I tell 'im, sittin' on the edge of my bed. It's the code for makin' a murder look like a robbery gone wrong.

"Aiight, cool-cool."

"How much?"

"It'll be on da house," he says.

This crusty muhfucka thinks he's slick, tellin' me some shit like that. He'd be turnin' 'round tryna stress a bitch for some extra shit. And I ain't havin' it. "Nah, nigga, I know you. How much?"

He starts laughin'. "Nah, baby girl, I got you. No extras. You my peoples. So if sumthin's gotta be mopped up, then it's done; no questions asked. That's on e'erything I love, ma."

"Mmmph. And you ain't gonna be pressin' me for some pussy?"

He keeps laughin'. "Yo, I'ma always wanna get in them drawers. You keep a muhfucka's dick bricked. So what's good? You finally gonna let a muhfucka stretch ya seams?"

I frown. "You still fat?"

"Yo, a muhfucka ain't fat. Just gotta lotta meat to go wit' all this bone."

"Mmmph…I'll take that as a *yes*. You still black?"

"All muthafuckin' day 'n night, baby."

"You still ugly?"

"As eva."

"Then ain't shit changed, nigga. Ya fat, black, ugly ass will neva stretch shit on me, muhfucka."

He laughs. "Yo, you real funny, ma. But, damn…I'm sayin'. Can a muhfucka at least smell them drawers? Let me bust this nut in them panties. Help a nigga out, ma. You already know what it is."

"Nigga, I know you can kiss my fat ass, so get da fuck ova ya'self. Now can you handle this shit for me or not?"

"Aye, yo, slow ya flow, fam. I told you I got you."

"Then let's wrap this shit up, and get back down to basics. I want this shit done, like now. It's been a messy situation for longer than a bitch can stand. I need it cleaned up quickly."

"Say no more. Any birdies need'a go down with this mess?

"No. They can keep flyin', for now. I'll deal wit' 'em as needed."

"Cool. You remember da spot?"

"Yeah; when you wanna meet?"

"When you free?"

I glance at the digital clock. It reads: 11:47 a.m. "I can be there at two."

"Bet. See you then. Oh, and that other situation. I'm still researchin'. My squad should have a location in a few more days."

I smile. "Perfect." We disconnect.

Threaten me, *bitch*, I think, walkin' into my walk-in closet. *I don't think so. You just sealed ya fate.* I press a button hidden under the right side corner of the mahogany island that sits in the middle of my closet. A wall panel opens up. I step in, then press in the code, then place my two fingas on the finga print recognition panel to my Paragon safe. It unlocks itself. I pull the door open, inhalin' rows of paper. I count out a twenty-five pack, packin' the stacks into my Michael Kors python satchel. I decide I ain't beat for a free ride. So I'ma hit Cash wit' twenty-five gees, then be on my merry way. I don't want that nigga eva thinkin' I owe 'im shit. I shut the safe door, then step outta my panties and remove my bra.

I grab my titties and start squeezin' 'n tweakin' 'em. The idea of Rosa's lights bein' shut, gotta bitch's clit twitchin'. *Bitch, you ain't shit to me...after tonight, ya ass'll be a long gone memory.*

I pull out an eight-inch vibratin' dildo and harness, then strap it to my stool. My pussy is on fire, knowin' a bullet is gonna pop Rosa's skull open. *Oh yes, bitch,* I think climbin' up on the stool. *Ya muthafuckin' ass is gonna be eatin' dirt before the sun rises.* I pull my ass cheeks open, lower my hips down on the tip of the dildo, then slowly wind down on it. *Oh, yes...they gonna blow that bitch's head off...* I slam my pussy all the way down on the base, grind my pelvis, press on my clit and moan. "Ohhhhhhh, yesssss, bitch...they 'bout to take it to ya muthafuckin' dome...uhhhhh...aaaaaaah..."

I toss my head back, close my eyes. See blood and brains and skull splattered on the concrete, splashed up against the wall. E'erything in me starts to shake. My pussy tightens "...ohhhhh-hhhhh...yesssssss, biiiiiiiitch...you 'bout to go down..."

I cum.

I scream.

I cum again.

And again.

And again. In rushin' waves, a bitch's pussy explodes and crashes and gushes and floods the space between my legs. I keep grindin' 'n windin' 'n buckin' my hips 'til the room starts to spin, 'til e'ey last nut spurts outta me, and a bitch's ready to collapse.

AT EXACTLY TWO P.M. I AM WALKIN' INTO THE SPOT I HAD HOPED I'd neva have'ta see again. I keep it real cute in a black Stella McCartney mini and a pair of black Christian Louboutin flannel, over-the-knee boots wit' gold military buttons runnin' all'a way to the knee. I have my bubble-gum pink lambskin Balenciaga work bag wit' the chunky gold studs hangin' in the crook of my arm, holdin' the satchel filled wit' the fetti for the job in my right hand. Muhfuckas do double-takes as I walk through.

On the surface the shit looks like a reputable auto body 'n detail spot. And on the real, it *is*. Cash owns two shops and has clients from all ova comin' through to get their cars piped out 'n customized. So anyone comin' from off the streets walkin' in would have no idea that down in the basement, or the dungeon— as it's called, the real dirty work pops off. This is where Cash manages his hire-to-kill organization. This is where a bitch has collected stacks of paper, literally hundreds 'n thousands of dollas for bodyin' muhfuckas. Yeah, blood money.

I take a deep breath, walkin' through an office that has a reception area. The yella-crayon lookin' bitch sittin' at the desk, looks up from the book she's readin' 'n eyes me.

"Ummm, 'scuse me, can I help you?"

"No, I'm here to see Cash," I tell 'er, walkin' by the desk. "He's expectin' me."

She jumps up. "Well, you can't just walk into—"

"Sweetie, beat it. I do what da fuck I want." I push open the door to Cash's office, shuttin' it in 'er face. This nasty muhfucka has porn playin' on the 46-inch flat-screen hangin' on the wall. And he's stretched back in his leather chair wit' his big-ass feet stuffed in a pair of white Gucci sneakers propped up on his desk. It looks like the nigga has his hands down his sweats. I suck my teeth. "Nigga, you nasty. Turn that shit off."

He laughs, sittin' up in his chair. "Only you will walk up in a muhfucka's office wit'out knockin'."

"Nigga, whateva. You knew what time I was comin' through." He eyes me, lickin' his lips. I roll my eyes. "For real; turn that shit off, nigga."

He grabs the remote and puts the shit on mute. "Yo, check this shit out, ma…you still fine 'n shit, and a muhfucka missed ya evil ass. But, on some real shit, da only reason I haven't broken ya fuckin' jaw for slick-talkin' a muhfucka is 'cause I dig ya mean ass. And you da only bitch that keeps a nigga's dick hard e'ery time he sees ya sexy-ass. But don't get da shit twisted. You ain't runnin' shit, ya heard? This is my muhfuckin' office. You don't wanna see da shit I'm watchin', don't look at it."

"Nigga, that shit you talkin' don't move me. It's whateva, muh-fucka. And you know this."

He smiles, shakin' his head. "Yo, you still a crazy-ass bitch." He smirks. "But you got my shit hard as hell, poppin' that extra shit."

"Nigga, yuck. You so fuckin' nasty."

He laughs. "Yo, a muhfucka missed fuckin' wit' you on some real shit, Kat."

"Well, I ain't missed fuckin' wit' ya ass."

"Yeah, aiight. What you got for me?" I slide 'im the info, along wit' a pic of Rosa. I tell 'em I want this shit handled the minute that ho bails outta jail. Yeah, her ass is locked the fuck up for comin' up to my spot tryna bring the noise. I got that bitch for trespassin' 'n smashin' in my window. And for a bonus, I got to knock that ho's fronts out. He stares at the photo, then looks up at me. "Yo, what's good wit' this? I thought you weren't down wit' hits out on bitches 'n shit."

"No, I'm not down wit' bodyin' 'em myself. But I ain't eva say shit 'bout not havin' a bitch bodied if da ho tries to serve me. So this particular bitch needs ta go." I open up my satchel and dump out the money onto his desk. "And here's payment for da service."

He looks at the stacks, then back at me, shakin' his head. "I told you, it's on da house." I tell the nigga no thank you. Tell 'im I ain't eva gonna be a bitch that owes his ass shit, or be made to feel like I do. He stands up, straightenin' out his wears. Looks like he's lost some pounds. I peep the Gucci emblem on the nigga's sweats, *and* the thick-ass lump in the front of his pants. *Ohmiiiiiigod, this nigga gotta big-ass dick.* I shift my eyes, actin' like I ain't peep the shit. *Nasty muhfucka probably stood up on purpose so I can can get'a eyeful of cock.* This nigga's dipped 'n paid 'n got dick for days, but that damn face...ugh! It hurts a bitch's eyes.

I blink.

He grins, shiftin' his dick in his sweats. I frown. He starts laughin'. "Yo, cut that shit out, ma. I see you lookin' at all this dick."

I ain't gonna front. A bitch wants to see the shit live and direct. The freak nasty me wants to fuck wit' the nigga. Watch 'im beat his shit off. I decide to keep the shit a hunnid. If the opportunity presents itself, I'm get the muhfucka to pull the shit out.

"So what if I was? Nigga, I'm sittin' down. And you standin' up wit' ya crotch all in my face, of course I'ma look. *And?*"

He smirks. "Yo, don't play. You already know what it is wit' this big-ass dick."

"Yeah, that a big dick don't mean shit, muhfucka."

He walks 'round his desk and goes ova to the door and locks it. A bitch ain't stressin' it. Although I don't think the nigga would actually try 'n rape me up in this bitch, I slide my hand down in handbag; just in case.

"Yo, you a real problem for muhfuckas," he says, walkin' back ova to his desk. He sits on the edge of it. "You know that, right?"

I tilt my head, raisin' my brow. "Why you say that?"

"C'mon, ma. You da muthafuckin' truth. You fine as fuck, mad sexy, and ruthless as hell. That shit is a problem. You could have a muhfucka's head all twisted up in da game."

I shrug. "Then I guess muhfuckas should stay away from me."

"Nah, that only makes a muhfucka wanna get at you more."

"Well, that shit's on his dumb-ass."

"Yo, Kat, so what's good, ma? You lookin' mad sexy. Wassup?"

I frown. "Whaddaya mean 'wassup'? Wassup is you handlin' that job for me, muhfucka."

"Yo, fuck all that, baby girl." He grabs at his dick. "Real talk, ma, a muhfucka's mad horny. I wanna—"

I jump up outta my seat. "Nigga, I know you ain't tryna get no pussy."

He rubs his dick. "Nah. I ain't on it like that. I ain't takin' shit you ain't tryna give freely. I'm just sayin'…"

"You ain't sayin' shit, nigga. So what da fuck you really sayin'?"

He glances ova at the paper on his desk, then cuts his eyes at the TV screen. The muhfucka lowers his voice. "Yo, take that money back. I don't want that shit. I want them panties you got on; real talk, ma. I wanna wrap my dick up in 'em, then bust off. That's all the payment I want."

"That's it?" I stare the nigga down. He nods. "Muhfucka, you crazy as hell."

"True story, ma; let me get them panties."

Bitch, you need'a get ya ass up outta here. Leave well 'nough alone.

Fuck that. Ya nasty ass been wantin' see the nigga's cock, so get it ova wit'. Besides this muhfucka's been comin' at you sideways for years.

You, nasty bitch, you know you wanna feel that muhfucka's snake in ya hand.

I smirk. I stand up, plop my bag up on his desk, then pull up my dress and slowly slide my panties down. I keep my eyes locked on this nigga, imaginin' myself puttin' a bullet in his dome. Instantly, my pussy starts to moisten. I step outta my panties, rub my pussy wit' 'em, then sniff 'em.

"Mmmm, this pussy smells good, nigga."

The muhfucka licks his lips. "Yo, that's wassup." He leans back on his desk. The gigantic lump in the muhfucka's sweats is sick. Yeah, a bitch needs to see this nigga's dick once and for all.

I twirl my panties 'round on my finga. "You want these panties, muhfucka? You wanna sniff this sweet pussy?"

"C'mon, ma. You already know what it is." He grabs at his dick.

"Pull ya dick out. Let'a bitch see how you hangin'." He unties the drawstring, then stands up and pulls the front of his sweats down and pulls his dick outta his Polo boxer briefs. It's black as coal, long 'n thick. I fight to keep my mouth from waterin'. Keep remindin' myself of how ugly this muhfucka is. *Bitch, you know you wanna touch da shit.*

Fuck all'a his ugliness, seein' this nigga's monster cock has a bitch on fire. I toss 'im my panties. "Nigga, I wanna watch." I sit my ass back in my seat, cross my legs, pinchin' the swellin' in my clit. And wait for the freak show to begin. "Stroke that shit, muh-fucka…"

CHAPTER NINETEEN

Pussy steamin'…asshole sizzlin'…gotta nigga's dick drizzlin'… ooey, gooey…nut, nut…muhfucka moanin' 'n groanin'…long tongue gotta bitch creamin'…turnin' it up like a dick-hungry slut…

"Lay back, muhfucka," I snap, pushin' Alex back on the bed, then rollin' a condom down on his dick wit' my mouth. I climb up on top of 'im, then reach under and guide his dick into my wet slit. A bitch's pussy's been on fire from watchin' Cash's ugly-ass stroke his long, black donkey-kong cock in my silk panties. I had always heard the nigga's dick was outta control, but to see it up close 'n personal…mmmph. That muhfucka's dick is siiiiiick! And the thought of crackin' his skull while he beat his dick made a bitch's hole pop. I left up outta there wit' my pussy lips stickin' to my clit. A bitch wanted some dick. So I hit this nigga up.

I gallop up 'n down on his dick, then sit all the way down on it, rockin' back 'n forth, grindin' my clit against his pubic hairs.

He looks up at me; his eyes half-slits. I know a bitch got this nigga's head spinnin'. "Damn, ma…you throwin' the pussy on me. What's up wit' that?"

I grunt. "Nigga, don't be askin' a buncha questions…" I grunt, again, coverin' his mouth. "Keep ya mouth shut and let me fuck this dick."

He looks at me shocked, thrustin' his hips upward, jabbin' my pussy wit' his chocolate cock. I toss my head back, shut my eyes. Cash's face pops in my head.

Black muhfucka…you wanna fuck this pussy?

I let out a moan. Cash's cock flashes in my head.

You wanna pump ya dick down in this wet throat?

I moan again, creamin' all ova Alex's dick.

"Daaaaam, baby…fuck…aaaah, shit…ya pussy's so fuckin' wet, ma…ohhhhh, shiiiit…aaaah, fuck…"

Alex grabs me by the ass, pulls open my cheeks. I lean forward, stop movin' and let 'im punch my pussy up wit' his dick as he rapidly thrusts upward.

"Ohhh, yes…beat my pussy up, muhfucka…yeah, yeah, yeah… right there…right there…I'm gettin' ready to nut all ova that dick…"

A bitch's in a sexual zone. My steamy pussy's grabbin' the nigga's dick.

Cash's face flashes through my thoughts. I buck 'n bounce up 'n down. Pull a titty into my mouth, lickin' my nipple.

Cash's is swingin' his dick at me; strokin' it and grinnin' at me. I can feel my nut buildin'; feel it bubblin' up from my asshole to my clit.

"I'll slice ya muthafuckin' dick off 'n ram it in ya ass…fuck you rough 'n hard deep in that fat, black ass of yours, nigga…a bitch'll put a bullet in ya dome, muhfucka…"

I don't hear or see shit. Just Cash and his fat anaconda-cock spurtin' out a buncha dick milk. "Yeah, black, crusty muhfucka… bust that nut, nigga…I'ma split ya shit, muhfucka…"

It's not 'til Alex flips me off'a 'im that I realize my hands have been 'round his throat, and my nails into his skin. "Yo, what da fuck was you doin'? You was on some real extra shit tryna choke a muhfucka out 'n shit. What da fuck you into, ma?"

"Oh shit…I-I-I'm so sorry. I got caught up in a role-play fantasy," I lie.

He frowns. "Role play? That shit sounded like you was tryna take a muhfucka's manhood, talkin' 'bout cuttin' off a nigga's shit 'n rammin' it in his ass and all kinda crazy shit like that. What's really good wit' you, ma? A muhfucka needs to know what kinda shit you in to?"

Fuck, shit…goddamn it! Bitch you gotta be more aware what comes outta ya mouth, I think, tryna explain my way outta the situation. I apologize again. Tell 'im that I got so caught up in how good his dick was feelin' that I got lost in a zone; that his stroke game has a bitch comin' outta character.

I kiss the fresh scars on his neck caused by my nails. Lucky for 'im his scratches aren't as deep or as long as the ones I put on Tone. On some real shit, I feel bad for clawin' this nigga up.

"I really apologize," I say again, rollin' back on top of 'im. His dick is still hard, stretchin' the condom to full capacity. I can tell the muhfucka's ready to explode; ready to spurt out a bucket of hot creamy nut. I reach underneath me, grab it and squeeze. "How can I make it up to you?" I kiss 'im lightly on the lips, then his neck, again. "Tell me how I can make it all betta."

He grins. "You really wanna make it up to me?"

This sexy muhfucka, I think, noddin'. *Bitch, keep it cute. You already know what it is wit' this nigga.*

He pulls off the condom, tosses it ova onto the floor.

I raise up, frownin'. "Muhfucka, I know you don't think I'ma 'bout to let you run ya dick in me raw."

He laughs, pullin' me into his arms. "Nah, chill, ma. Ain't nobody tryna go naked in you. I want you to lay in my arms; that's it. Let a muhfucka hold you, aiight?"

He wraps his arms 'round me, and I lay my head on his chest, closin' my eyes. I inhale his manly scent. It's a mixture of sweat and cologne. He strokes my hair. And on some real shit, a bitch's surprised at how good it feels to be in his arms, listenin' to his heartbeat. Sumthin' 'bout its rhythmic beat is calmin'.

Bitch, how da fuck you get here, goin' from iggin' this nigga to lyin' in his arms?

Why da fuck you keep fuckin' wit' his ass when you know he ain't no fuckin' good?

"Yo, tell me 'bout ya life," Alex says, disruptin' the questions runnin' through my head.

I look up at 'im. "'Scuse me?"

He repeats himself. "I wanna know how you grew up. Tell me 'bout ya fam."

"There's nuthin' much to tell. Born in Brooklyn, raised in da projects, bred in da streets; pops in prison, moms dead. No brothas, no sistas. A bitch is solo."

"I can dig it. Damn, sorry to hear 'bout ya moms, though."

"Don't be. She was already dead a long time ago."

He strokes my hair. "Drugs?"

I shake my head, sighin'. "No-good niggas." I'm relieved he doesn't ask me to elaborate. He keeps strokin' my hair. And it relaxes me. *Bitch, keep it cute. Cut this nigga off now 'fore ya ass gets too caught up in his shit.*

He holds me tighter, kisses me on the side of my head. The nigga is showin' me the kinda affection a bitch craves. I swallow back emotions I ain't tryna deal wit'. I lift my head from off'a his chest. Stare at 'im. He smiles. "Wassup, ma? You good?"

"Why you insist on fuckin' wit' me?"

"I ain't tryna fuck wit' you. I dig you; real talk."

"How many otha bitches you diggin'? And keep shit a hunnid."

"At this moment...only you."

I smirk, rollin' my eyes up in my head. "Yeah, right. Tell me anything."

"Nah, true story. You got my full attention"—he grabs his hard dick—"and as you can see in more ways than one." I suck my teeth, playfully swattin' at 'im. I can't front, a bitch's feelin' real comfortable wit' this muhfucka. "I'm dead-ass. You got me wide open, baby. I've fucked wit' mad bitches and plenty of 'em been bad as fuck. But there was always sumthin' missin'."

"Oh yeah? And what's that?"

"You."

I blink, blink again. Surprised by this nigga's answer. *Don't let this muhfucka gee you, ho. This nigga's a master manipulator.*

Ho, get ova ya'self. Let da nigga live. E'ryone has a past. You of all people should know this. "How 'bout you tell me 'bout all'a these hoes you been dickin'."

"All of 'em?"

"Yeah...*all* of 'em from da last five years to now. You can start wit' da most recent, then work ya way backward." He laughs. I don't.

"Damn, aiight." He glances at the clock. It's almost eleven at night. "Yo, we better blaze a fatty for this." I laugh as he slips outta bed. Watch his naked, muscular body go 'cross the room. He takes a blunt from off the dresser, then sparks it. I sit up in bed, starin' at his swingin' dick as he comes back to bed. He lays 'cross it, takes two deep pulls, then passes it to me. "Da only reason I'm gonna spit shit raw to you is 'cause like I said, I'm big on you, so I'ma tell you shit I ain't ever told anyone else."

As we pass the blunt back 'n forth, he starts off tellin' me how he got the name Daddy Long Stroke; tells me 'bout his days as a stripper, then starts rattlin' off'a buncha states he's had hoes in. And the ones he still does, fourteen. *Fourteen?! Ohmiiiiigod this nigga is a travelin' whore.* He tells me e'ery way he's fucked 'em; tells me 'bout the threesomes and trains he's got down on; how bitches have paid for the dick; how they lace 'im wit' wears 'n jewelry 'n shit. How he's had 'em thinkin' he was broke and homeless. He tells me 'bout some rich bitch he fucks wit' out in LA who asked 'im to bust his nuts up in 'er so she can have'a baby; how she hits 'im wit' five gees a month and keeps 'im on-call for when she wants the dick. He tells me 'bout some midget chick from Georgia he was fuckin', then fucked 'er cousin in 'er own bed. Tells me how most of the chicks he's met are either Myspace or Blackplanet hoes searchin' for dick and companion-ship. Tells me 'bout all the psychos and stalkers he's had. Tells me 'bout the restrainin' orders; and e'erything else in between.

By the time this nigga finishes tellin' me 'bout all'a his sex-capades wit' these stupid ass bitches, we're puffin' our second blunt and my head is spinnin' from tryna keep up. On some real shit, I'm surprised he tells me all this shit. I hit the blunt, then pass it back to 'im, lettin' e'erything he's said wrap 'round my brain.

I fall back on the bed laughin' my ass off, imaginin' this thick muhfucka bangin' up a midget. "Ohmiiiigod, I still can't believe you actually fucked a midget. You'se a real nasty fucka."

"They're called lil' people," he says, laughin' wit' me. "But, yeah, I ain't gonna front. I've been a wild cat when it comes to da pussy. Always prowlin' 'n shit. But, I always keep it real wit' them broads."

"Mmmph. If them birds were stupid 'nough to catch feelin's

and get all caught up in you, then they got what da fuck they deserved. But, don't eva think you gonna have a bitch like me stalkin' or huntin' ya ass down; not gonna happen."

"I don't plan on givin' you a reason to," he says, climbin' back into bed. He kisses me on the lips. "Yo, I wanna stay da night."

I stare at 'im. Sumthin' tells me to tell 'im, "Hell no!" But I don't. "And do what?"

"Make love to you, hold you in my arms 'n wake up to ya sexy ass in da mornin'."

Ohhhhkay, yes, a bitch is grinnin'. But, I keep it cute. "You can stay, tonight. But don't think this is gonna become a habit. And, puhleeze don't think you're gonna eva get a fuckin' dime outta me."

He shakes his head, sittin' up in the bed 'n proppin' two pillows in back of 'im. "Yo, I don't want ya paper, ma."

"Well, good 'cause a bitch ain't givin' none out. So there should be no confusion. Now, tell me. What is it a muhfucka like you really want? And don't playground me."

He stares at me. "Nah, no playgroundin' you; I'm dead-up." The way the nigga is lookin' at me is makin' me uncomfortable. He's lookin' at me in a way I can't remember another muhfucka eva lookin' at me. He pulls me into his arms. "All I want is you, ma."

I look up at 'im, squint my eyes. "I'm not on da menu."

He leans in, kisses me on the lips. "Maybe not tonight you're not. But, you will be."

"Wrong answer, muhfucka."

He laughs. "Yeah, aiiight; that's what's ya mouth says. But I'ma wait on you. And when you ready to serve it up to me, I'm scoopin' ya ass up. And that's on e'erything."

He wets his fingas wit' spit, then slides his hand between my thighs and starts playin' wit' my clit. I spread my legs wide, bendin' at the knees. Give 'im full access to my wet pussy. The muhfucka slips two fingas in 'n slow strokes my hole 'n clit. I reach ova and start strokin' his dick. Then lean ova into his lap and kiss the head of his rock-hard cock. I take 'im into my warm mouth, then suck the skin off the muhfucka 'til we both are moanin'.

When I've givin' 'im all the throat work he's gonna get, I pull up off'a his dick, and lay all the way back. Let the muhfucka finish stirrin' my pussy. Let 'im strum along my clit 'til I buck my hips and cream all ova the nigga's fingas.

THE FOLLOWIN' MORNIN' I WAKE UP WONDERIN' WHY I'M NOT stickin' to the script and feedin' this nigga wit' a long-handled spoon. I know his ass had no muthafuckin' business stayin' the night, but a bitch can't front. It felt good havin' a muhfucka in my bed, and it felt even betta bein' wrapped up in a muhfucka's arms.

"Yo, check it. I'ma be hangin' wit' my mans 'n 'em tomorrow night, but I wanna get at you on Sunday. Maybe we can go into da city 'n chill 'n shit."

"I'll let you know," I tell 'em, eyein' 'im as he goes in 'n outta the bathroom. "I have plans wit' my girl, so it all depends."

"Oh, word? What ya'll gettin' into?"

"Nigga, I gave you some pussy; that's it. Not permission to be all up in mine."

He laughs, comin' outta the bathroom brushin' his teeth. "Yeah, aiight. You talkin' that shit now, but you already know."

The nigga drops his towel. I ain't gonna front. He's lookin' real comfy standin' here butt-ass naked. And I'm not sure how I should feel 'bout it.

Keep shit real. You dig da nigga.

Yeah, I do. Still—

Bitch, take da shit for what it is. Da nigga got good dick 'n good tongue. *Let 'im keep eatin' ya ass 'n lickin' ya pussy, then dismiss da muhfucka when you've had'a 'nough.*

I'm sittin' at the foot of my bed, watchin' the nigga lotion his naked body, then step into his boxers. Droplets of water are still on his back. I wanna get up 'n lick the shit off'a the muhfucka. But I don't. I glance at the clock. 8:47 a.m.

"All I know is it's time for you to hurry up 'n bounce. I've had'a 'nough of ya cocky ass."

He laughs, slippin' his wife beater ova his head, then puttin' on his jeans. He pulls out his cell. It dawns on me that I don't eva hear it ring when I'm wit' 'im. I contemplate askin' the muhfucka why, but decide I don't really give'a fuck. He walks up on me and pulls me up off'a the bed.

"Listen, I wasn't poppin' a buncha BS last night. I meant e'erything I said to you. On e'erything, yo, I'm feelin' you."

I keep my eyes locked on his. "Enough to give up all ya bitches?" I ask, raisin' a brow.

"Yo, I don't have'a buncha bitches. I gave 'em all up a minute ago. The only one I'm still fuckin' wit' is my peeps in LA."

"Ohhhhkay. Isn't that da chick who wanted you to give 'er a baby?"

He nods. "Yeah, but I deaded that. Ain't nuthin' happenin' wit' that. I'm still wrappin' it up."

"Let me tell you this. And be clear. If I was eva to decide to fuck wit' you on some solo type shit, *that* lil' situation wit' chickie would need to be shut down wit' e'erything else. I don't cheat. And I *don't* share. So, understand this. If you know you ain't ready to stop slingin' da dick, then you need'a let shit play out da way it is."

I step outta his embrace. "Yo, you think I ever wanted to be on some settle down type shit? I didn't think I had it in me. Shit, maybe I still don't. But I wanna try, if you let me. Look, this is comin' from a cat who always thought relationships were overrated and monogamy was extinct. So for me to be comin' at you thinkin' differently is some major shit for me. That's on some real shit."

"Nigga, I ain't tryna be ya experiment. Go get some practice playin' boyfriend somewhere else before comin' at me."

"Yo, go 'head wit' that silly shit. I don't need to practice shit. I already know what it is."

"Muhfucka, when you come to me, you betta come correct. And be ready to man up. Don't come pushin' up on me tryna bag a bitch, knowin' you still stuntin'." I walk ova to my nightstand. Open up the bottom drawer, pullin' out two guns, my Colt Python and a Beretta Storm 9mm. "'Cause trust 'n believe"—I turn, aimin' 'em at 'im—"I will take ya face off."

He jumps back. "Oh, shit. You wildin'; for real, yo. Put that shit up." I keep 'em aimed at 'im. I don't blink. And neither does he. "Yo, Kat for real, yo. Put that shit up."

"Alex, Alley Cat, Daddy Long Stroke and whateva else they call you on da bricks. This gun right here"—I raise the Python—"I use to play in my pussy so it ain't da one I'd use to splatter ya skull. But make no mistake, this one right here"—I raise the Kel-Tec chrome—"is da one I will use to light fire in ya skull if you play me." I drop 'em on the bed, walkin' back ova to 'im. I can tell I done spooked the nigga, but he keeps it cool.

"Yo, that was some foul shit, pullin' guns out on a muhfucka like that."

"And I hope I don't eva have'ta again. Soooooo, before you start comin' at me any more 'bout tryna wife me up 'n shit, you need'a think long 'n hard 'bout what you sayin'. Now hurry up get ya boots on 'n bounce."

The nigga steps up in my space. "I ain't no pussy, yo. And I ain't no confused muhfucka. I know what I want. And it's you." He snatches me up and starts tonguin' me down. And I ain't gonna front. A bitch's pussy starts to pop. We kiss for a few minutes, 'til he unlocks his lips from mine and backs away. "Save ya bullets, baby, 'cause you ain't usin' 'em on me."

I smirk, followin' 'im down the stairs. "We'll see, muhfucka."

"Yeah aiight." He leans in and gives me some more tongue, grabbin' a chunkful of ass wit' his hands. "You really think I'm bullshittin' don't you?"

"Nigga, what I *think* is you wanna get me wrapped 'round ya finga, but you see I ain't lettin' it go down."

He laughs. "Yo, you funny bad. You know what, let me get somethin' to write wit' 'n some paper." I walk off through the dinin' room and he follows behind me to the kitchen. I hand 'em a notepad and pen. He writes sumthin' down, tears the sheet of paper off'a the pad, then hands it to me.

I glance at it. It's a buncha numbers 'n passwords. "What's this?"

"It's my passwords to e'erything." My mouth drops open. This nigga done gave me the codes to his cell, Myspace, Blackplanet and Facebook accounts. "You don't trust a muhfucka. You don't think a muhfucka can be all 'bout you. You think a muhfucka still gonna be on some extra shit. Cool. Check da shit for ya'self, whenever you want."

"Mmmph. I don't need this." I hand it back to 'im. "You givin' me this shit means nuthin'."

He sits the paper on the table, then opens the door. "Well, guess what, ma. For a muhfucka like me, you da first, so it means e'erything. If you can't see that, then shame on you."

He blows me a kiss as he walks out, beboppin' it toward his whip. I stand in the doorway and watch 'im get in, backin' outta the driveway before closin' the door.

I scoop up the paper wit' all his passwords, then take the steps two at'a time to log into the nigga's shit to see what's really good.

CHAPTER TWENTY

Music poppin'…mad sexy bitches dressed in da ill wears… battin' da mink lashes…got da niggas havin' hot flashes… stacked in da stilettos…jewels got da bitches shittin' in they draws…gotta 'em shook…thinkin' we gonna snatch they mans… gotta 'em rollin' them eyes…we iggin' da glares…keepin' shit cute…Brooklyn bitches ain't fuckin' wit' no boys…but got no problem slidin' a bitch we despise…if she wanna bring da noise…

I t's Saturday night, and I'm speedin' up the Turnpike on my way to scoop Chanel up so we can get it in tonight. I gotta blunt fired up and Rihanna's "Rude Boy" knockin' outta the speakers to get me in the mood. It's been a minute since a bitch popped 'er hips on the dance floor, so hopefully I can twirl these hips a bit and get it sweaty. I'm hopin' they ain't featurin' a buncha low-budget booga bitches up in that piece. My cell rings. I glance at the screen, then answer. It's the nigga Tone out in Cali.

"Hello."

"What's good, Beautiful, how you?"

"Chillin'. And you?"

"I can't call it, ma. I had'a call you and let you know I got them papers."

"Ohhh, shit," I say all amped, knowin' he passed the real estate exam. "Get da fuck out. Congrats, muhfucka. That's wassup."

"Yeah, ma. Thanks. It's on now. Yo, you get yours?" I tell 'im no. "Well, when you do we gonna have'ta celebrate."

"And you know this."

"Yo, on some real shit, I been thinkin' 'bout you, ma."

"Uh-oh."

He starts laughin'. "Nah, nah, nuthin' major. I mean, yeah, you been on the brain. Shit, you mad cool, Kat. And I ain't gonna front, you fine as fuck."

"And da pussy's good."

He keeps laughin'. "Yo, ma, you mad funny."

"But am I lyin'? Keep shit real, nigga."

"Oh, no doubt, ma. I'ma real-type nigga. Hell yeah, you got that bomb-ass pussy. I ain't even gonna front on it."

"Nigga, you can't front on it even if you wanted to," I say, laughin'. My cell beeps lettin' me know there's another call. It's Chanel. "But, look, my girl is on the other line. Let me hit you up lata."

"Oh, aiight. No doubt. I'll holla."

I click ova. "I'm like five minutes away."

"Shit, well, hurry da fuck up. Divine's horny-ass tryna get some pussy and a bitch ain't tryna sweat out 'er hair."

I laugh. "Then suck da nigga off."

"I already did. Now he tryna fuck."

"Poor thing. I'm turnin' down ya street now."

"I'm on my way out now. No need to stop, just swing da door open and I'll jump in, then speed da fuck off."

I crack the fuck up. "Bitch, you stoopid."

By the time we hit club Eden, Chanel and I are smoked out 'n feelin' right. The line is mad thick and there's a ton of hoes and niggas fussin' 'n stressin' 'bout standin' on line for over forty-five minutes. The bouncers are poppin' mad shit to some'a the females, manhandlin' them 'n shit. But I ain't pressed. This bitch ain't the one.

I cut my eye over at Chanel. "Bitch, I know you not expectin' *me* to stand up in this shit. And you know I ain't beat for no muhfucka feelin' all up on me like how that nigga's doin' her."

"Girl, don't sweat that shit. You already know," She says, flippin' open her cell. "I got it covered." She lets whoever she's talkin' to know we're outside. Five minutes later, this tall, brown-skinned muhfucka waves us over to him. Chanel gives him a hug. Dude eyes me over her shoulder, givin' me a nod. I turn my head. Act like the nigga don't exist. Two minutes later, we are breezin' right up to the front of the line.

"Mmmph," I whisper, smirkin'. "Let me find out ya ho-ish ass done broke that nigga off wit' a dose of throat action."

She laughs. "Fuck you, ho. He's one'a Divine's cousins."

"Ain't that special. Now let's see if them juicy dick suckas of yours get us free drinks for the night."

She continues laughin'. "Bitch, let me find out ya high-post ass finally wit' the program lettin' muhfuckas buy you drinks."

I suck my teeth, usherin' her toward the stairs. "Ho, walk."

As we make our way up the steps, Juelz Santana's joint "Back to the Crib" is knockin' through the speakers. The idea of grindin' up on a nigga's cock on the dance floor makes my pussy twitch. *I swear I hope they got some fine, sexy muhfuckas up in this biiiotch!*

Chanel and I keep it real sexy in bangin'-ass brown Gucci slip dresses that wrap 'round our dangerous curves like a windin' road. She rocks her wears wit' a pair of chocolate brown Chanel pumps and a beaded clutch. While I kill it in a pair of orange Jimmy Choo strappy stilettos and Judith Lieber clutch. Niggas peep our swag and do double-takes as we make our way through the crowd. I peep a few hoes tossin' haterade in the air, which makes me pop 'n shake my hips real extra. Just enough to let 'em know what a bitch is workin' wit under these wears.

I scan the club and peep a few muhfuckas over by the bar who look like they might be worthy of a dance, or two, posted up bullshittin' wit' they boys. The club is mad packed and the beats are sick.

"I need a drink," Chanel yells ova the music. I agree, followin' 'er to the bar. Niggas step back, eye-fuckin' us—lettin' us get through, but we pays 'em dust. I hand 'er a fifty. Tell 'er the first two rounds are on me. Of course this lush bitch orders a double shot of Rèmy and a Corona to chase it. I frown at the combo. But let 'er do 'er.

"Bitch, ya ass get drunk, you crawlin' home." I order the same thing, but I ain't chasin' shit. I'm takin' the shit straight.

She laughs, givin' me the finga. "Crawl on this." We take our drinks, clink our shot glasses, then toss 'em back. She guzzles down the Corona. Muhfuckas got they eyes on us, grinnin' as Chanel orders 'nother 'round. We take it to the head, again.

"Damn, ya'll pretty ladies know how to get it in," this golden brown nigga wit' light brown eyes says, smilin'. For some reason the nigga looks familiar, like I seen 'im somewhere before, but I don't put no energy into tryna figure the shit out.

"That's how we doin' it," Chanel says, lookin' the muhfucka ova.

He laughs, starin' at me. He puts his finga up. "Yo, I know ya'll."

Chanel and I frown. "Nigga, you don't know us. You buggin'."

He smiles. "Nah, ma, I never forget a face. The Forty-Forty

club. Ya'll the two beauties who housed me 'n my man on the pool table."

Chanel blinks at 'im. Of course her ass don't remember the nigga. But I do. "Oh, yeah, that's right. We spanked that ass, and walked off wit' ya paper. Let me find out you ready to get that ass beat again."

He laughs. "Ouch. Kat, right?"

"Yeah."

He turns to Chanel. "I'm Bronze. And you?"

"Bored," she says, turnin' 'er head.

"Oh, shit. I got you, ma."

I laugh. "Don't pay 'er cranky-ass no mind. It's Chanel. She gets crazy when she don't take 'er medicine." He laughs. "Damn, you gotta good memory. How da hell you remember my name? We mopped ya'll asses up on that table 'bout two years ago."

"Yo, a muhfucka never forgets gettin' his ass spanked by a beauty who likes to talk a buncha shit on the table. Me 'n my man, Leo, still laugh 'bout that shit. Yo, we still wanna rematch."

I eye 'im. "Well, anytime you wanna bitch to run ya pockets 'n give you 'nother round of whoop ass, let me know." He laughs. Asks for my number, but I tell 'im to give me his. We bullshit a few more minutes 'til Chanel's had 'nough'a standin' in one spot.

"Bitch, it's hot in here. Let's go outside." I tell the nigga I'll hit 'im up for that rematch, then dip. As soon as I get outta his view, I toss the nigga's number on the floor and pop my ass out onto the rooftop.

I GLANCE AT MY TIMEPIECE. IT'S ALMOST ONE-THIRTY A.M. Chanel and I are still out on the rooftop, standin' at the bar, talkin' to these cats from Uptown. She's already on her third Red

Bull vodka. And we've already tossed back two shots of soco—uh, Southern Comfort. Something told me to keep it light, after we tossed back those two shots of Rémy earlier so I'm slow slippin' this shit.

Cypress Hill's "Bang Bang" is blarin' through the speakers. I finga pop and wind it a bit, but ain't really beat to drop it on the floor. "Girl, I'll be back," Chanel says, rudely spinnin' off on the nigga she was talkin' to. I watch her poppin' her hips back inside.

I continue half-listenin' to this nigga wit' the curly 'fro, bobbin' my head to the beat while tryna figure out why he's out here rockin' dark-ass shades.

"I had'a feelin' I was gonna run into this bitch," I hear someone say in back of me. As soon as I hear the voice, I already know it's 'bout to be a situation. "Oh, you fly wit' it, hunh? You can be all up in da club shakin' 'n poppin' ya ass 'n shit, but a bitch too good for her family 'n shit, talkin' real slick 'n greasy to my mutha like you got it like that. Is that how you doin' it, bitch?"

I take a deep breath. Ignore the bitch standin' in back'a me. Look over at the nigga I was talkin' to and say, "Do me a favor and tell that bird in back'a me to shoo."

"Ho, *shoo* hell! You disrespect ya grandmutha, sign complaints on ya aunts 'n get restrainin' orders 'n shit on 'em. Bitch, that shit ain't cute."

I keep my back to 'er. Let the bitch keep poppin' shit, but in a minute I'ma 'bout to take my glass to 'er face. I keep sippin' my drink. "How da fuck was you gonna pull da plug on ya mutha and kill 'er baby, hunh, ho?"

I take a deep breath. Finish up my drink, then turn to face Patrice, tuckin' my clutch under my arm. She's standin' in a black sequined Donna Karan scoop-neck tunic dress. Her neck, lobes 'n wrists are lit the fuck up. I can't front. The ho looks fabulous. But I still can't stand her snake ass!

I eye her. She's cut off all'a 'er hair for a short tapered do wit' a sweepin' bang. In another life, me and this bitch coulda been a real problem together. "Bitch," I snap, twistin' my lips, "step da fuck away from me 'fore you end up pickin' ya face up off da floor."

"Bitch, hol' da fuck up," she snaps, handin' her bag to one'a 'er girls. A shapely brown-skinned chick dipped in low-end jewels, wearin' a one-shoulder, black draped Jersey getup that clings to her body. I can't figure out the designer so I decide it must be a low-end piece. I peep her burgundy Marc Jacobs leather satchel. *Cute*, I think, bringin' my attention back to Patrice.

"Girl, don't," Miss Low End says, grabbin' 'er arm. "This ain't the time. We ain't come out for all the extras tonight; let it go. You can get at this ho some other time."

"*Ho?* Bitch, I will rock ya eye sockets," I say to her, layin' my clutch on the bar 'cause in a minute I'ma 'bout to knock this bitch in both 'er eyes. Of course Chanel's somewhere wit' 'er juicy ass pressed up against some nigga's cock on the dance floor.

Muhfuckas peep the ruckus goin' on between this bitch and me. But I know she don't really want it. Not out here for all to see.

"You know what. You right, girl," Patrice says to Miss Low End. "Let's do what we came out do; fuck this bitch."

I laugh. "You get a pass tonight, Sweetie," I warn. "But, trust. There won't be no othas."

"Bitch, you wish." She starts walkin' back ova to me. I close my fist, ready to bring it to 'er face. She peeps this, keepin' her distance. "You know what. You need to get ya mind right. All ya selfish-ass eva cares about is ya'self. You're one hateful-ass bitch."

"Whaaaateva, bitch. Back da fuck up from outta my mutha-fuckin' face."

"I ain't in ya face, yet, bitch. But—"

"But nuthin', Trick." I flick my fingas at her. "Poof, bitch, be gone!"

"You know what, ho. I'm real sick of you thinkin' you can dis-respect me. Bitch, I ain't them hoes on da street you fuck wit'."

"And bitch, what you gonna do?" I ask, walkin' up on 'er. "I ain't one for all this yippity-yap. If you wanna make it rock up in this muthafucka, then let's rock, ho!"

Before I can hook off on 'er ass, someone grabs me from behind, wrappin' they arms 'round my waist. I spin 'round to see who the fuck is puttin' their hands on me. And forget 'bout takin' it to Patrice's head. "Yo, baby, you too fine to be out here fightin'."

"Nigga, don't be grabbin' up on me like that. You was 'bout to catch it, too."

He laughs. "Yeah, aiight, beautiful. Fuck fightin'," he says, pullin' me by the arm. "Come dance wit' me."

I bring my attention back to Patrice. "Bitch, thank this nigga for savin' you from an ass whoopin'."

"Whateva, bitch," she huffs. "I'ma see you; trust."

I laugh, lettin' Alex pull me toward the dance floor. "Yeah, see da back of my ass, ho."

Fabolous's "Money Goes, Honey Stay" remix is playin'. Alex pulls me into 'im. "Yo, what was all that shit out there 'bout?"

"Nuthin' serious; just sum lightweight bitch tryna bring it, that's all."

He wraps his arms 'round my waist. "Damn, ma, you look sexy as fuck."

I spin outta his embrace. "Nigga, just 'cause I gave you sum pussy, don't start thinkin' you can be grabbin' all up on'a bitch like you got it like that."

"Oh, I don't?" he says, laughin' ova the music. "Yeah, aiight; not yet. Yo, why you ain't tell me this is where you were gonna be."

I eye 'im. The nigga's all dipped in jewels, rockin' a black Versace silk shirt and a pair of smoke-gray slacks wit' a black Louis belt.

I step back, peep his footwork—black Louis loafers. I'm impressed. "Not eva, muhfucka," I say, laughin wit' 'im.

He pulls me back into 'im. "Yeah, aiight; whatever. You still ain't answer my question."

"And I'm not."

The nigga keeps his eyes locked on me, lickin' his lips. "Yeah, aiight. Who you here wit'?"

"Damn, nigga. You tryna dance or interview a bitch? I'm out wit' my girl, why?"

"I'm doin' both. So fall back. I don't wanna have'ta go in no nigga's mouth, that's why."

"Oh, yeah, cocky muhfucka. You feelin' real ova ya'self."

I peep Chanel's drunk-ass ova at the bar, talkin' to two choco-late muhfuckas. I can't really see what they look like. Knowin' 'er thirsty-ass, she's gonna run they pockets all night if they let 'er. She catches my eye, and gives me the finga. I laugh.

When Twista's "Wetter" starts playin', I decide to fuck wit' 'im. I twirl my hips real slow 'n sexy, then press my ass up on his crotch. I grind up on his dick, drop down low. He leans into my ear, places his hands on my hips. "Damn, you feel good, ma. Yo chill, 'fore you get my dick hard." I keep grindin' into 'im. Feel his dick start to thicken. "Yo, aiight, keep it up. You gonna have me pin ya lil' ass up in a corner and run this dick up in ya."

I turn to face 'im. Throw my pussy up at 'im. "Nigga, a bitch like me'll fuck 'round and have you nuttin' in ya pants."

He smiles. "Yo, you a real trip."

Some oriental lookin' bitch walks up on us, cuttin' in on our lil' convo. I ain't gonna front, the bitch is servin' it in'a sexy lil' low-cut black one-piece. And 'er titty game is sick. Still, the bitch cuttin' in is rude as fuck. And I tell 'er that. She apologizes, sayin' how she only wanted to say hello to Alex. I tilt my head. Tell the bitch she shoulda waited to speak to 'im after I was done wit' 'im. Alex says sumthin' to 'er, then introduces me to 'er as *his* girl. Tells me 'er name is Akina. I keep it cute, but decide to check 'im on tryna claim me as soon as chick bounces. But before I can, sum other ho walks up and starts dancin' behind 'im. She slips 'er hands 'round his waist, lays her face on his back, and starts muthafuckin' swayin' and droppin' it like it's hot. The bitch is clearly drunk. And straight playin' it like a real live clucker.

I keep on dancin' like I ain't fazed by the bitch 'cause the truth is, I ain't. He pulls the chick's arms from 'round 'im, then turns 'round to see who it is.

He frowns. Next thing I know he straight snaps. "Bitch, what da fuck is you doin'? I gotta a restrainin' order on ya stupid ass."

"Fuck that restrainin' order. I miss you, baby. Our baby misses you, too."

"Bitch," he snaps, frownin'. "That baby ain't mine. Take ya drunk-ass on."

I blink, blink again. *Restrainin' order? Baby? Oh, hell no!* I know the music is loud 'n shit, but I know 'xactly what the fuck I heard. I walk off, leavin' them two goin' at it on the dance floor.

I make my way ova to Chanel. She tries to introduce me to the niggas she ova here bullshittin' wit', but a bitch ain't beat. "Ho, let's get da fuck up outta here. I done had 'nough drama for one damn night."

"Drama? When? Where? Girl, what da hell happened?"

I throw a hand up on my hip. "Well, bitch, while you were in here trickin' for drinks 'n shit, Patrice tried steppin' to me like she was ready to make it pop up in here. I was 'bout to really take it to 'er grill 'til Alex snatched me up…"

"Alex? Who da fuck is Alex?"

"The nigga from Allstar," I tell 'er, glancin' ova to where he is.

I see two security niggas talkin' to chick. She's goin' the hell off. The bitch looks half-crazed if you ask me. I see Alex pullin' sumthin' outta his wallet, they look at it, then a few minutes later, they draggin' chick's ass off the dance floor.

Two minutes later, I peep Alex walkin' ova toward Chanel and me. I turn my back on 'im. He says wassup to the niggas, then says wassup to Chanel.

"Wasssup, Allstar?" she says, grill-cheesin' all up in the nigga's face. "So you da nigga who got my girl all goo-goo-ga-ga 'n shit. It's 'bout damn time you stepped up. Took you long 'nough."

He laughs. "Oh, word? I got ya girl open like that? It's Chanel, right?"

"Oh, you remember?"

"No, doubt." He laughs. "The way ya'll were throwin' shade at muhfuckas who could forget ya'll two."

I suck my teeth. "Whateva." I shoot Chanel a look. "Ho, puhleeze. I ain't goo-goo-ga-ga'in shit. Don't gas this nigga's head."

She flicks 'er hand in my face. "Whateva, ho."

He grabs my hand. "Yo, why you walk off on me like that?"

I pull my hand back. "Nigga, you didn't need me out there. Ya lil' girlfriend was more than 'nough."

"Yo, that's one'a da broads I was tellin' you 'bout. She's da ho that got all nutty on a muhfucka, tryna pin that baby shit on a muhfucka." He tells me the bitch's name is Ramona, then pulls out a restrainin' order and shows it to me. Tells me he carries it 'round wit' 'im just in case the ho shows up somewhere. "And Akina is someone I used to fuck wit' 'til she put 'er hands on me, and I had'a choke 'er up."

I blink, blink again. I shake my head. "Nigga, you got too many extras in ya life for me. I'm out." I toss up the deuces, and spin off. "Chanel, let's go, ho."

CHAPTER TWENTY-ONE

> *Bitch tryna keep it on cruise control...low profilin'it...ain't beat for a buncha shit...ain't tryna get hood...fake bitch wanna be stylin'...talkin' 'bout she a nigga's baby mamma... neck-rollin' it...tryna crank da heat...bitch wanna serve drama...it's all good...she 'bout to get that ass beat...*

A week later, me and Chanel are at this hair salon, Nappy No More, ova in South Orange. A high-end spot plastered in all the hair magazines that she's been pressin' me to check out for a minute. So here we are. I won't front. The place is real cute. I peep the mix of chicks sittin' up in here. There's a mixture of hoodbooga, ghetto-fab, 'n celebrity wife bitches up in this piece waitin' to get they wigs done. Erykah Badu's "I Want You" is playin' low through the Bose speakers up on the walls.

Chanel's sittin' next to me, checkin' 'er emails 'n textin' back 'n forth wit' Devine, and a few other muhfuckas. I'm flippin' through the latest issue of *Vibe* magazine, bobbin' my head to the music. A bitch's chillin'. Mindin' 'er own business, gettin' lost in the beat when I feel someone burnin' a hole through me.

I look up and catch the bitch. From the look she's givin' me

I'm not sure if she wants to cut or *fuck* me. I tilt my head. She shifts 'er eyes. I go back to readin'. A few minutes later the bitch is starin' me down, *again*. I close the magazine, leanin' ova toward Chanel.

"Ummm, why is da Spanish-lookin' ho ova at da counter starin' at me like she's tryna get beat da fuck up?"

Chanel cuts 'er eye ova in 'er direction. "Mmmmmph, looks like she wants ta bite ya ass wit' them big-ass teeth." I chuckle. "Da bitch probably wants to be you when she grows up."

"Puhhhleeeeze, that bitch could neva be me," I state, starin' at Trey Songz on the cover. A bitch can't front. The muhfucka is lookin' kinda sexy all bare-chested 'n wet. But, since he's not my flava, I don't spend too much time or energy into it. I go back to flippin' through the articles in the magazine instead.

A few minutes lata, the Spanish bitch is walkin' toward me, but I act like I don't see 'er.

"Excuse me."

I take my time lookin' up at 'er. "How can I help you?"

"Were you at club Eden last week?"

I look 'er up 'n down. Of course a bitch like me's gonna answer this ho's question wit' a question. "Why, who wants to know?"

"I do."

"And you are?"

"*Ramona*," she says wit' a buncha stank in 'er voice.

As soon as she says 'er name. It clicks. *She's the nut that was all up on Alex, then got dragged outta da club.* "Ohhhhkay, so you want my autograph or sumthin'?"

"Your autograph? Nooooo, Sweetie. I wanna know how you know Alley Cat. I kept staring at you because you looked familiar. Then it dawned on me. I saw you grinding all up on him at the club like you two were real familiar."

I frown. Take a deep breath. This bitch had'a be hawkin' me the whole muthafuckin' night to remember me from a week ago in a damn packed club. Then, again, a fly bitch ain't eva hard to forget. Chanel cuts 'er eye ova at me, shiftin' in 'er seat. I shift in mine as well, crossin' my legs. I have my body turned in chickie's direction in case I gotta leap up on 'er ass. "Ohhhkaaaay. And if we were?"

"Then you need to watch your back because he's a real scam artist. He'll use you until he can't get anything else out of you, then toss you to the side for the next."

I laugh. "Sugah, I don't know why you tellin' me all that. That shit sounds real personal."

"I'm basically advising you, that's all." The bitch still has a buncha stank in 'er tone, but I'm tryna overlook the shit. Still tryna keep it cute.

"You ain't advisin' me 'bout nuthin', Sugah. Only stupid bitches get caught up in lettin' a muhfucka use 'em. I ain't da one, so move along."

She puts a hand on 'er hip. "Move along, hell. I wanna know how long you've known him."

Ohmiiiiiiiifuckin'gawd! Let me find out this bitch's retarded. "Look, chick. What's up wit' all these damn questions? Do I know you? 'Cause if not, then you need to bounce up outta my space."

"Like I said, I saw you up at the club with Alley...uh, I mean, Alex."

"And?"

"*And?* I'm his baby's mother."

Chanel toots 'er dick sucka's up, eyein' me. 'Cause she knows in a minute I'ma bring it to this bitch. I tilt my head. Play the bitch like I'm stupid. "Ohhhhhkay, *and?* Why didn't you say that shit from da rip instead cummin' at me wit' a buncha extras?"

She igs the question, foldin' 'er arms 'cross 'er chest. "Are you *fuck*ing him?"

I count in my head. *Keep it cute, ho. See what this bitch gotta say.* "Why?"

"'Cause we're tryna work some things out, and he doesn't need to have any outside distractions altering his judgment."

I laugh. "Sweetie, you have two seconds to get to ya mutha-fuckin' point."

The bitch plants a hand up on 'er hip, and starts neck-rollin' it. "Well, the point is this: He's my man. And I don't know if you're sleeping with him or not, but if you are—from one woman to another, *stay* the fuck away from him."

Ohhhhkay...see. This is the part where I should really get up and smack this stupid, silly-ass bitch in 'er face. But, I feel like fuckin' wit' the dizzy bitch, so I won't.

"Is that a threat, Sweetie?"

"It's a warning, but you can take it however you want."

"Uh-oh," Chanel says, pullin' my handbag from me, "sounds like sumbody tryna make it pop up in this piece."

"Girl, I don't know what da fuck this chick tryna do, but I know she betta get movin' real quick."

"I know that's right, 'cause da bitch is startin' to get on *my* nerves."

She laughs, glancin' ova at Chanel. "Mind ya manners, Boo. Mind ya motherfucking manners. This is between me"—she points 'er finga at me—"and her."

"Bitch," Chanel snaps, "I know you ain't talkin' to me. I will—"

I put my hand up, cuttin' her off. "Don't. Let me handle this." I scoot up in my seat. Place a hand up on my hip. "Bitch, there ain't shit between you and me. I don't know you, and I don't give a fuck 'bout you."

"Yeah, well maybe you don't know me. But you *obviously* know my man."

I laugh. "Ya man? The nigga gotta restrainin' order against ya dumb-ass, so how da fuck is that ya man? Define that for me?"

"Bitch," she snaps, raisin' the volume, "I don't have to define shit for you. Stay the fuck away from him or we gonna have some problems."

Chanel gasps, coverin' 'er mouth wit' 'er hand.

I keep laughin'. "Sugah, you'se a real clown thinkin' you standin' here pumpin' fear in a bitch like me wit' that yip-yap. What you betta do is go do ya homework. Or end up flatlined."

"No, you better go do yours. That nigga is usin' you. You don't know the first thing about loving a man like Alex. I'm the only woman he'll ever love. He's never going to love you, like he loves me."

I laugh. "Med check, med check. Bitch, did you just escape from da Looney bin or sum shit? Get da fuck away from me. That nigga don't give a fuck 'bout ya trick-ass."

A cute brown-skinned chick wit' shoulder-length locks hurries ova to us from the back area. "Ramona, you need to take that mess on up outta here. You know Pasha ain't playin' this shit up in here. If you got beef, take that shit outside."

"Oh, no, we cool, Felecia. She and I were just having a friendly chat. I've finished schooling her so I'm out."

"*Bitch*," I snap, tossin' the magazine ova at Chanel, "don't get it fucked up." I stand up. "You ain't schooled me on shit. I don't know how you Jersey bitches do it, but be clear. I will rock ya muthafuckin' sockets, so don't let the wears 'n the pretty face fool you. I asked you nicely to bounce up outta my space da first time. And you still wanna stand here yippty-yappin'. So, now I'm fuckin' tellin' you, step da fuck on. Or step outside to get ya ass beat. Take ya pick. You know what."—I pull out my phone, then press open my call history—"Since you wanna school a bitch, let me call *ya man*, right now, and school 'em on how'ta eat my pussy 'n ass out. 'Cause guess what, bitch? I'ma fuck da muhfucka tonight and tomorrow night, too. Stupid bitch!"

As soon as Alex picks up, I put 'im on speaker. "Yo, what's good, Beautiful?"

"Shit. Chillin'. I'm at this hair spot ova in Orange wit' Chanel and ya BM's up in here poppin' a buncha ying-yang?"

"My *BM?* Yo, what you talkin' 'bout? I told you, I ain't got no baby momma."

I cut my eye ova at this Ramona bitch. "Well, obviously this bitch here didn't get da memo. So you need'a remind this ho—"

"Yo, ma, who you talkin' 'bout?"

"This silly-ass Spanish ho who's 'bout to get beat da fuck up."

"Bitch," she says, walkin' up on me. "You ain't gonna beat shit. But, if I catch you near my man again—"

Before she can get the rest of her words out, I run up on 'er and bash the bitch in 'er muthafuckin' face.

"OHMIIIIIGOD," CHANEL SAYS, PASSIN' ME THE BLUNT, CRUISIN' down Old Short Hills Road toward the Mall at Short Hills. After that incident back at the salon, a bitch needs to do a lil' shoppin', then get home and play in my pussy. Poppin' that ho in 'er snot box got my snatch hot. "I'm so glad you shut that ho up. Took ya ass long enough. I was 'bout ready to bring it to 'er bubble head my damn self. But you delivered, boo. Broke that ho's nose lovely."

I open 'n close my swollen hand. "I think I sprained my hand fuckin' wit' that silly bitch."

"Well, da ho got what she deserved."

"I swear I didn't wanna have'ta go there, but that ho kept tryna serve it up. So I had'a take 'er down." After I hit that bitch in 'er mouth, she fell backward onto the counter and I pounced on that ass, splittin' the side'a 'er face wit' my 18-karat gold 'n platinum diamond and emerald Jean Schlumberger Pave X ring. It took Chanel and two other chicks to pull me off'a 'er. And the bitch was still poppin' shit. Talkin' 'bout how shit ain't ova; that she's gonna fuck me up the next time she sees me; just talkin' a buncha off the wall shit that don't mean me no neva mind. "I don't know what da fuck is in da air. Seems like e'erywhere I turn some bitch is tryna serve me da extras."

"Sounds like you a walkin' magnet for drama these days."

"Well'a bitch is tired. All I wanna do is fuckin' chill; that's it."

"I hear you. So what da fuck was her deal?"

"Fuck if I know. Some disgruntled bitch Allstar"—Chanel's nickname for Alex—"used to fuck wit'. He dumped 'er. Then da trick-nasty ho got all desperate and tried pinnin' a brat on 'im. But da shit backfired on 'er ass, and came back not his."

She cuts 'er eye ova at me. "You sure it ain't his?"

"He said it's not. Da nigga has no reason to lie to me. But, on some real shit, I don't give'a fuck if it is or not. He's not my man."

"Mmmph, not yet," she mumbles.

"Ho, I heard that. You actually think I'm tryna fuck wit' a nigga who has hoes tryna get at me on some dumb shit? When you know me to be fightin' a bitch ova some dick?"

She shakes 'er head. "I haven't."

"Exaaactly. And I'm tryna keep it like that."

"I hear you. So how da fuck da bitch connect you to AllStar?" I tell 'er how she came up on 'im at the club, grindin' 'er pussy all up on the back of 'im; how they went at it, and I walked off. "Mmmph. So, what's up now, you axin' da nigga?"

"Shit, after this, I need to." I take another hit off the blunt, then pass it back to 'er. I pull out my cell as soon as it starts to ring. "Hol' up...speakin' of da nigga, this's 'im now. Wassup?"

"Yo, what da fuck happened? All I heard was a buncha screamin' 'n scufflin' 'n shit, then ya phone went dead. Then, when I tried callin' you back, it kept goin' into ya voicemail."

"What happened was ya bitch—"

"Yo, that's not my bitch, so stop sayin' that shit."

"Whateva. I don't give a fuck who she was to you. All I know is da bitch stepped to me tryin' it on my time, poppin' a buncha shit and I cracked 'er muthafuckin' nose open."

"How da fuck she know who you was?"

"From da club."

"*Da club?* From last week?"

I suck my teeth, feelin' myself gettin' aggravated wit' this nigga. "Yeah, muhfucka, what otha club were we eva at together?"

"Yo, why you snappin' on me?"

"Muhfucka, let me tell you sumthin'. I'm not wit' bitches comin' at me 'bout no muthafuckin' nigga; especially one I ain't fuckin' on a regular, okay? And, right now, that whole situation gotta bitch real hot."

"I feel you. But you actin' like I caused da shit. I haven't fucked wit' that crazy bitch or seen 'er in over a year."

"Whateva. All I know, I betta not catch that bitch again."

"Yo, listen, fuck that bird. You aiight?"

"Yeah, I'm good, nigga. A bitch like me is gonna always be aiight. All that lil' shit did is get my pussy wet."

"Oh, word? You want me to come through and handle that for you?"

"Unless you comin' through wit' that bitch's address, no thank you."

"Damn, you'd rather have that crazy ho's address instead of gettin' a dose'a Daddy's dick?"

"Nigga, fuck all that daddy shit. I want that bitch's address."

He lowers his voice. "And Daddy want some more'a that juicy pussy."

"Nigga, get real. You ain't my fuckin' daddy." Chanel cuts 'er eyes ova at me. I ig the ho.

"Yeah, aiight. Not yet."

"Not eva, muhfucka."

He laughs. "Yo, I can tell you fired up. And I ain't tryna beef wit' you, ma. I'm gettin' ready to scoop my moms up and take 'er out to eat, so I'm hit you up later."

"Bye, nigga. Have fun," I tell 'em, takin' the blunt from Chanel. I take two long pulls, then toss it outta the window. "And I still want that ho's address."

He laughs, but I'm dead-ass. I'm ready to stomp that bitch's skull in for even thinkin' she could step to me and bring it.

CHAPTER TWENTY-TWO

*Silly of me…silly of you…gotta muhfucka all up in my space…
talkin' 'bout he wanna change…bitch knows what she gotta
do…but still lettin' da nigga hit da drawz…ain't tryna catch
feelin's though…nigga don't know…fuck me ova…bitch'll blow
off ya muthafuckin' ballz…*

This nigga Alex and me are layin' in bed; both starin' up at the ceilin' sweaty and breathin' heavy, passin' a blunt 'n back forth. We've been kinda in this zone for almost thirty minutes or so. I told myself I wasn't gonna fuck 'im again, but I haven't been able to keep the muhfucka outta my dome, so when he showed up here lookin' 'n smellin' all good, a bitch decided to fuck 'im, again—this time for the last time.

You can't get all caught up in this nigga, Kat.

Trust, I'm not. I already know what it is.

Bitch, it ain't like you gotta line of dick beatin' down ya door or pussy.

Meshell Ndegeocello's playin'. I turn my head toward the nightstand, glance at the clock. This nigga's been here laid up in my bed for over four hours, and we've fucked at least six different times. I can't front. A bitch's well-fucked.

I can't lie. Lyin' here wit' this muhfucka feels…different. He's the first nigga since Grant who I've actually chilled wit'. But I ain't dumb wit' it. I already know what it is. I'm usin' the nigga, and I'm sure the nigga's usin' me. I take another pull from the blunt, then pass it back to 'im. I shift my body to face 'im. Take in his smooth, chiseled body, gaze at his dark nipples, then allow my eyes to travel down to the ripples of muscle that become his stomach. "This nigga's trouble," I keep tellin' myself. "You have no business fuckin' wit' his ass."

But e'ery bitch needs a bad boy rockin' 'er bed e'ery now 'n then.

Bitch, fuck this nigga...get yours, and go!

You said you already know what it is, so what da fuck you pressin' it for. Keep it cute, ho...fuck 'n go!

And while ya at it...you might as well taste da nigga's dick; spin da muhfuckas top. Let 'im know how a real bitch does it!

Meshell's "Loyalty" starts playin'. I close my eyes. Slowly bob my head to the lyrics....*Told her daughter to beware...both secrets and dreams you should never share...*

"Yo," he says, disruptin' my private moment, "what you over there thinkin' 'bout?" He hands me the blunt.

I take it, hit it hard; hold the shit in my lungs, then blow out a gush of smoke. I turn to look at 'im. "I'm tryna decide," I tell 'im, raisin' up and takin' his dick in my hand, "if a bitch wanna suck down on this black dick, or not."

He grins. "Oh word? That's wassup. I was wonderin' when you were gonna bless a nigga wit' some'a that headwork."

I smirk. "You ain't ready for me," I tease.

He laughs. "Yeah, aiight. Try me."

My eyes hungrily rove e'ery inch of this nigga's sculpted body again. My mouth waters. This nigga has a bitch's inside still shakin'. My pussy aches, still wet from all the fuckin' we did. Still I wanna fuck 'im sum more, before I toss his ass out.

Bitch, you need'a dead this shit. You'd end up killin' a muhfucka like this!

I scoot down some, then take 'his soft dick in my hand and gently stroke it, placin' gentle kisses all over it. I glance up at 'im. He's starin' down at me all hazy-eyed 'n shit. His dick starts to thicken.

"What, you wanna bitch to tell you how much she loves this strong, black dick?" I lick it.

"Yeah, baby…you love this dick?"

I don't answer. "You wanna bitch to tell you how she loves the way this big black dick tastes; the way it feels in a bitch's hands 'n throat?" I twirl my tongue 'round the head, flickin' my tongue ova it. It starts to stretch and thicken.

He moans, pulls in his bottom lips. "Yeah, baby…"

I lick the head, again, like an ice cream cone; along the shaft, 'round the sides, then ova the top. "Give me sum'a that sticky dick juice, muhfucka…you wanna nut in a bitch's mouth?"

"Yeah, baby…suck Daddy's long, black dick…you know you been wantin' this big dick…why you been frontin' on me, ma… aaah shiiiit…"

I ignore the nigga, increasin' the suction 'round the head. *Cocky muhfucka!* I massage his balls, remove his cock from my mouth, then spit on it.

"Damn, nice, big, pretty lips…"—I continue slurping and sucking and gulping him—"…slap them lips with it, baby…yeah, like that…bounce that shit on ya wet tongue…suck that cock…take it all the way down in ya throat…suck on that muthafucka…"

I slide my right hand between my thighs and massage the front of my pussy, lightly brushin' my clit while gobblin' up this muhfucka's cock. I spit on it. Suck it real nasty-like, smackin' my face, lips and tongue wit' it; jackin' it while nibblin' 'n lickin' and suckin' on his balls. Then bury his dick in my warm mouth and slow suck the muhfucka, balls deep.

"Aaaaaaah, fuck man...aaaaaah, shit...gotdaaaamn..."

I spit on it again, stroke it, squeeze his balls, then run his dick back down in my throat, lappin' at his balls. Hold the head in my throat, workin' this fat, juicy muhfucka ova wit' my long tongue while strokin' my pussy.

"Oh, daaaamn...I like that...shiiiiiiit...ooooh, ooooh....that's right, baby...spit all over that shit. You can do whatever u want wit' it... this is your dick, baby...Suck on them balls for me."

This is your dick, baby...I roll my eyes up in my head. *Yeah, right, nigga! How many otha bitches you run that shit to?*

When I've given this nigga all I'm gonna give 'em, I pull his dick from outta my throat, then get outta bed.

He looks up, all wide-eyed 'n crazy. "Yo, why you stop?"

I open up a drawer, pull out a silk purple teddy, then shimmy into it. "It's time for you to go," I tell 'em ova my shoulder as I'm slippin' its straps over my shoulders.

"Say what? You fuckin' wit' me, right?"

I stare at 'im, tilt my head. "Hell, no, I ain't fuckin' wit' you, muhfucka. Get ya shit on and bounce."

He blinks. I walk ova to his clothes piled up in the middle of the floor, tossin' 'im his boxers. "Let's go, nigga."

He's still sittin' here, starin' at me. I stare back, placin' my hands up on my hips. He sucks his teeth, snatches 'em from off the bed, then gets outta the bed. His dick is on rock. I can tell the nigga's heated. But I don't give a fuck. He slips on his boxers. His dick is pokin' outta the slit. I almost laugh.

"Yo, you really gonna put me out wit' this hard-ass dick?"

"Yup."

He shakes his head. "Yo, that's fucked up; word up."

"I'm sure you gotta 'nother line'a hoes you can hit up to feed da dick to."

He walks up on me. "Yeah, aiight, if you say so. But, you already know what it is. You know I ain't tryna fuck wit' no one else so why you trippin' 'n shit." I ig his ass. Tell ''im to hurry up 'n step. He snatches me up; manhandles me. And the shit makes my pussy pop. "Yo, you really gonna do this." He grinds himself into me. "You feel all this hard-ass dick?"

I ain't gonna front. I wanna drop down low and finish this muhfucka off. *Bitch, stick to da script...put da nigga out.* I push 'im back wit' my hand, then step outta his way.

I pop my hips toward the door. "I'll meet you downstairs. And don't take too long puttin' ya shit on, either."

He laughs, shakin' his head. "Yo, I don't believe this shit."

"Believe it," I say, walkin' outta the room and down the stairs.

Five minutes later, he comes down fully dressed. I can see how a weak bitch could get caught up in the matrix and get strung the fuck out on this chocolate muhfucka. The nigga ain't lie. He got good dick, good tongue, and a buncha good damn game.

He steps up in my space, smirkin'. "Yo, you got that off, ma. Real fucked up. But, it's all good. I got you, though. I'ma be back thru."

I grin. "Yeah, if you say so."

He pulls me back into 'im. And I let 'im. "I know you think I ain't shit. But I told you, a muhfucka's ready to change." He grabs me by the ass, squeezes. "I want you, Kat; real talk. All I'm askin' is for you to give a muhfucka a chance. Damn."

"Muhfucka, you don't want *me*. You wanna have me wrapped 'round ya finga, sweatin' ya ass, that's all."

The way the nigga's gazin' at me is makin' a bitch's knees wobble. "Nah, you wrong, baby."

"I'm not ya baby. I keep tellin' you that."

"Yo, check this shit out," he unzips his jeans, fishin' out his dick. "You see this dick"—he shakes it in front'a me—"it's yours. I'm yours. Yeah, I've fucked mad bitches, aiight. I told you this. And, yeah I can fuck 'em anytime I want, and I got 'em sweatin' a muhfucka for this dick. You know that shit, too. And you already know I gotta buncha bitches who hit a nigga up wit' that paper. All that shit's been established already. So what? I ain't feelin' 'em like that. I done put da shit out there for you; straight up. No secrets. No bullshit. And that's what it is."

I shrug. "So what you tellin' me for?"

He stares at me. Shakes his head. "Do you even have'ta ask? Yo, have you heard anything I said?"

I eye 'im. "Nigga, I don't wanna play games wit' you. I'm really not that kinda bitch. So before you put me through it, we need'a peace this."

"Yo, I ain't peacin' shit, ma. I told you what it is. And I ain't playin' no games, either. A muhfucka's diggin' you. And I wanna see where this shit takes us."

I fold my arms. "*This* ain't takin' *us* nowhere."

He smiles, then leans in and kisses me. Against my better judgment, I let the muhfucka slide his tongue in my mouth and run his hand up under my teddy. I part my thighs and let the nigga finga my pussy. And a bitch lets out a moan. *Damn, this nasty muhfucka!*

He pulls his fingas out, then sucks on 'em. "All bullshit out da window, Kat. You gonna be mine; ya heard?"

"Get out," I tell 'im, openin' the door.

"I'ma call you tonight. Make sure you pick up."

I slam the door in his face. And hear 'im laughin' to his car. *Cocky muhfucka!*

CHAPTER TWENTY-THREE

Tossin' 'n turnin'...buncha shit spinnin' on da brain...stirrin' up emotions...long gone 'n forgotten...gotta bitch's heart burnin'...tryna ig da pain...pissed...been dismissed...knowin' there ain't gonna be no apologies...'cause da neglectful bitch ain't returnin'...

A bitch couldn't sleep last night. I stayed tossin' 'n turnin' all fuckin' night. I wasn't beat to get lifted, and I didn't wanna toss'a bottle back. I needed to be sober; needed to have my mind clear. So I laid on my back, starin' up at the ceilin', tryna remember if I ever saw Juanita smile; if I had any recollection of her kissin' me or wrappin' 'er arms 'round me. I stared up into space, tryna count. Count the number of niggas Juanita had in 'n outta 'er life; the number of times she'd shut her bedroom door and lock herself in; the number of times I heard 'er headboard slappin' up against the wall or 'er balled up in a corner or curled up on 'er bed bawlin' her eyes out. It was all too much to remember 'n count; it required too much thought for a bitch. So I focused on sumthin' that didn't require much thought; sumthin' where countin' wasn't a difficult task. How many times did the bitch tell me she loved me? I closed my eyes. Searched my damn brain, then opened my eyes. None.

So why I'm sittin' up at this hospital at two in the muthafuckin' mornin' beats the hell outta me. But I am. The nigga DeAndre is on duty, so he let me come thru. I'm sittin' here lookin' at Juanita, shakin' my head. I don't know this woman. Never have. Even if the bitch didn't wanna be a mother, I wish she woulda been the kinda chick who woulda at least had my back. A bitch I coulda vibed wit'. I'd wanna know what made the bitch tick. I'd wanna know what made 'er so damn needy; why she felt like she needed a man. I'd really wanna know why this bitch was so damn dick hungry 'n stupid.

"You are such a stupid bitch," I say, rollin' my eyes at 'er. "I'm so fuckin' mad at you for not knowin' how'ta be a gotdamn mother. Shit, ho, a big sista woulda worked. But, you couldn't even be that. Mmmph...I always thought you were jealous of me. I still think that shit. I think you hated da fact that I was e'erything you wanted to be. Truth is I think you secretly hated me. But you wasn't no real bitch, so you woulda neva admitted to da shit. Still, I know you did. 'Cause on some real shit, I hated me, too. I hated myself for bein' so fuckin' stupid thinkin' you would eva be a mother to me. I hated myself for thinkin' shit woulda gotten betta between us; that you would one day wake da fuck up and finally see...*me*."

I stand up, and look 'er ova as if I'm gonna see sumthin' different from da last time I stared at 'er. But I don't. She's still dead; still pregnant. Still a bitch who I'll neva know. And I'm still wonderin' why the fuck I'm really here.

I stare at 'er stomach. *It's a baby, Kat!*

I pull back the sheets. *It's a fuckin' baby, bitch!*

Sumthin' comes ova me, and I place my hand on 'er stomach. I keep it there for a few minutes, then quickly snatch it off when I think I feel sumthin' move. I wait a few seconds, then place my hand back on 'er stomach. This time I rub it. It's the first time I've eva touched 'er, that I can recall. I try to remember the last time—hell, the first time—*she* touched me. I can't. There are no memories of bein' touched by this woman. No hugs. No kisses on the forehead or cheek. Not one muthafuckin' lovin' gesture. I feel myself gettin' angry lookin' at 'er ass and feel like bangin' the bitch in 'er stomach. I fold my arms, glarin' at 'er.

"That little guy inside of your mother is a fighter." I snap my neck 'round to see who's standin' in the doorway. It's DeAndre. He walks in the room and stands beside me. His arm brushes against me. "The longer he stays inside of the womb, the stronger he gets and the greater his chances are for survival."

Nigga, you think I care? I move ova. "How do you know it's a boy?"

"From the last ultrasound."

I keep my eyes locked on 'er stomach. "Hmmm."

"He's going to need a lot of love and support when he gets into this world."

Good luck, I think, shiftin' my weight from one foot to the other.

"Children are such an amazing gift." *Why da fuck is this nigga tellin' me this shit?* I peel my eyes from Juanita and turn to look at 'im. "I have three of my own."

"And you're tellin' me this because?"

He shrugs. "I felt like sharing."

"That's nice," I say, turnin' my attention back to Juanita.

"She hurt you." He says knowin'ly; maybe the shit's accusin'ly. Still, hearin' it come from outta his tit sucka makes the hair on the back of my neck raise.

I don't look at 'im. I stare straight ahead. "What makes you say that?"

"It's in your eyes. The way you look at her. It's in your tone.

The way you speak about her. Your energy is filled with hate toward her."

I turn to look at 'im. "So what'a you, sum kinda psychic witch doctor?"

He laughs. "No. But I am a man who knows hurt and pain and disappointment when I see it. I can spot it and feel it a mile away. Besides, we've all had our share."

"So is this where you offer me a buncha self-help tips? 'Cause if so, I'm not interested."

"No, but I would like to offer you some advice if I can."

"You can't. Not interested in that, either. So do me a favor. Let it go."

He smiles, puttin' his hands up in the air in mock surrender. "I didn't mean to upset you."

"Oh, trust. I'm not upset; just not interested." I glance at my watch. It's already three in the mornin'. The thought of drivin' back to Jersey gives me a headache. I decide I'ma wake Chanel's ass up and stay the night at 'er spot. I shift my attention back to Juanita. "If you don't mind, I'd like to finish havin' my private moment wit' my mother before I leave."

He smiles. "Miss Rivera, you're a very beautiful woman, but this hate you have in you is eating away at your soul. Let it go."

I take a deep breath. Slowly turn my head in his direction. "Oh, trust. I will." I turn my head back to Juanita. "As soon as I pull da plug."

TWO DAYS LATER, I PULL OUT THE KAT LINE TO SEE IF THERE ARE any updates, but before I can turn it on, my otha cell starts ringin'. It's another 347 area code. I sigh. *This crazy bitch!*

"Bitch, why da fuck is you still callin' me? Didn't I stomp ya ass once already?"

"Bitch, this ain't Rosa. It's Patrice. And you ain't shit for how you been movin' ho." Sounds like she's cryin', but I don't pay it no mind.

"Ohhhhhkay, thanks for ya kind words. Now why is you callin' me?"

"Bitch, not that you give'a fuck, but I thought you should know Rosa was killed last night."

Good. One less bitch I gotta deal wit', I think sittin' on the edge of my bed. *I was wonderin' when Cash was gonna put that work in for me and put that bitch down.* My mouth starts to water wit' anticipation wantin' to know all the details of how she got put down. The freaky bitch in me wants to slip 'er hands down in 'er panties in play in my pussy as Patrice gives me the details. "What happened to 'er?"

"She was on 'er way home. They think somebody tried to rob 'er, but when she didn't have shit, they shot 'er in da head."

"Did she suffer?"

"No, police found 'er dead at the scene."

That's it?! That's all you gotta say? I wanna know if there was blood and brain splattered e'erywhere. Was the bitch sprawled out on the concrete? Were 'er eyes rolled up in 'er head?

I keep my morbid thoughts to myself. "Anything else?"

"No," she pauses, soundin' like she's snifflin' 'n gettin' all emotional 'n shit.

"Poor thing," I say, all nonchalant. "Well, thanks for that news bulletin. Now if you'll 'scuse me, I have more pressin' things to deal wit'."

She screams into the phone. "Bitch! I've lost two fuckin' sistas back to back. Ya moms and aunt, and that's all you have'ta say. 'Thanks for da news bulletin'? Bitch, are you fuckin' serious? They are ya blood!"

"Sweetie, be clear. Those are your losses; not mine. So I ain't sheddin' no tears, and I ain't passin' out no sympathy cards. So if that's what da fuck you lookin' for you betta call Hallmark."

"Bitch, ain't nobody call ya ass for no muthafuckin' sympathy. I don't even know why da fuck I called ya fucked-up ass, anyway."

"And neither do I. But I tell you what. You might wanna hol' off on buryin' 'er 'til after I pull da plug on Juanita. This way you can dump both trash bags down in da same ditch. No sense in havin' to go through all that shit twice."

I disconnect the call, then check my messages on the Kat line. There are two.

"Yo, I wanna 'nother pair of them panties, ma. I swear, Kat, I wanna beat that ass up one good time wit' this dick." I shake my head, laughin'. *Nigga, puhleeze. You'll get a bullet to da head 'fore I eva let you stretch these walls.* I delete the message, then listen to the next one.

"Yo, that clean up job you needed is done. It was swift and straight to da point. You should have no further problems." Swift and straight to the point is code for a sharp shooter poppin' 'er dome 'n droppin' 'er in one shot. *Good,* I think, tossin' the phone ova on the bed, grinnin'. *That's what da bitch gets. Bitch shoulda stayed in 'er lane and left me da fuck alone. One down, and one more to go. You can run, but you can't hide nigga. The Kat Trap is comin' for ya.*

"Yeah, muhfucka, you betta hope da police find you before I do," I say out loud, walkin' into my closet to pull out a dildo and one'a my vibratin' butt plugs. A bitch wanna celebrate Rosa gettin' bodied wit' two holes stuffed. Knowin' she's on ice got my pussy steamin'.

I step outta the closet wit' my gadgets in hand, makin' my way into the bathroom. I squeeze my ass, alternately slappin' my ass cheeks, makin' 'em pop 'n bounce wit' each smack. I am so fuckin' horny. I bend at the knees, squat down low, then lean ova the sink. I slap my ass harder; got the shit stingin', causin' my pussy to snap open and shut. It needs to be feed and stretched and worked over by sumthin' long, black and thick.

I slide my right hand between my thighs 'n massage the front of my pussy, lightly brushin' my clit. "Bitch got dropped...skull got popped...ooooh, yes, slumped that ho..."

I work myself into a frenzy, turnin' on the vibratin' butt plug, then slidin' it into my ass. I keep playin' wit' my clit. The vibrations in my asshole gotta bitch's pussy creamin'. I shift gears. My murderous thoughts go to the nigga, Jawan.

"Yeah, muhfucka...you like beatin' on women?" I ask, starin' at myself in the mirror, pretendin' I'm talkin' to Juanita's nigga. "You wanna stomp baby's outta bitches? Well, I'ma stomp ya nut out, muhfucka. Open wide, bitch-ass muhfucka. I'ma 'bout to shut ya lights."

The thought of havin' that nigga butt naked, then pullin' off my disguise 'n lettin' the nigga look me in the eyes makes me moan. I wanna see shock 'n fear in the nigga's face when I cock back my piece. "Mmmmmm...aaaaaaah..."

I slip my dildo into my gushy hole. *Pop, pop, pop!* "Uhhhhh, welcome to da Kat Trap, muhfucka," I grunt, pumpin' 'n windin' my hips. I grind down on my dildo, squeeze my ass cheeks together, then lift my left leg up onto the counter and fuck myself into a delicious trance, yellin' 'n screamin' 'n moanin' out shit I can't even remember 'til my cream squirts outta me, and coats my dildo. I pull it out, then greedily suck on it while still workin' the butt plug in my ass. I push the dildo back into my pussy, then nut all ova again.

CHAPTER TWENTY-FOUR

> *Don't wanna hate 'im...ain't tryna date 'im...nigga still pressin'...spendin' time...chillin'...winin' 'n dinin'...definitely diggin' da nigga's swagga...still...a bitch don't know if she wanna let 'im bag 'er...*

I'm standin' in the middle of the bedroom naked in a pair of red Jimmy Choo stilettos. My body is oiled. Candles are lit 'round the room. And a bitch is feelin' real sexy. I wait for Tamia's "Can't Get Enough of You" to start playin', then go into a slow-sexy hip wind. I run my hands through my hair, then twirl my hips. I wind it down low, then bring it back up, bend ova and grab my ankles. Shake 'n pop my ass; one cheek at'a time. Pull open my ass. Let the muhfucka see what he's 'bout to get.

Alex is sittin' at the foot of the bed, butt-naked, rubbin' his balls and strokin' his hard-ass dick. I got the nigga droolin'. I been teasin' 'im—and teasin' myself, for the last thirty minutes. My pussy juices are already runnin' down the inside'a my thighs. I'm ready to fuck this nigga. But I'ma make 'im wait for it. I want the nigga to beg for it.

I haven't seen 'im in three days, but he sent me flowers two days in a row—pink roses the first day, and birds-of-paradise the second. I ain't gonna front. A bitch was surprised and grill-cheesin' it extra hard. No nigga has eva sent me flowers. So when he called to get at me I told 'im to come through. Told 'im I wanted my pussy eaten 'n beatin'. Told 'im tonight, I was gonna give 'im sumthin' he might neva get again. Thirty minutes later, he was at my door.

So here we are.

I gyrate and shake my hips. Lift my titties up to my mouth and start lickin' each nipple slow 'n seductive. "You wanna suck on these titties, muhfucka?"

"Word up," he says, tryna reach for me.

"Look. Don't touch," I playfully warn, pushin' his hands down. I let my titties go. Then slowly run my hands all ova my body. I drop down in front'a 'im, start playin' wit' my clit, pat the front'a my pussy, then stick a finga in. I keep my eyes locked on Alex. I stick anotha finga in. Finga-fuck myself as he strokes his dick. "You wanna put ya dick up in this? You wanna feel this pussy heat, muhfucka?"

"Hell yeah, baby. You see how fuckin' hard this dick is? Stop fuckin' 'round, yo, and let me taste that pussy." He stands up. I tell 'im to sit his ass back down. Tell 'im if he gets up again, I'ma shut shit down. I let 'im know I'm in control tonight. He sits his ass back on the bed. "Yeah, aiight, you got that off. But be ready to take it when I get ya ass pinned down in these sheets."

I pull my finga outta my hole, standin' up. I slip my fingas in my mouth. I moan. "Mmmm, this pussy's soooo good." I greedily suck 'em dry.

"Damn, yo…I'ma fuck da shit outta you. I'ma beat them muthafuckin' walls up, ya heard?" He's grabbin' and shakin' his dick side to side, then strokin' it. "Fuck. I'ma wear ya lil' ass out, girl."

I ignore the nigga. Stick two fingas back into my pussy, finga fuck myself some more, then scoop out some'a this pussy cream, walkin' on 'im. "Open ya mouth, muhfucka." He does. I stick my fingas in. His horny ass slurps my fingas up. "Keep poppin' shit, muhfucka, and you ain't gonna get none'a this kitty-kitty, bang-bang. You wanna bang up this wet kitty?"

"Yo, you fuckin' wit' me, girl. You 'bout to make this dick spit."

"Yeah, muhfucka...bust that dick." I push my titties up. "You wanna shoot that nut all ova these pretty titties?"

He rapidly strokes his dick. "Aaaah...ohhh yeah, baby. Fuck..."

I tell 'im to stop jackin' his shit. Tell 'im not to nut yet. Tell 'im I wanna coat it wit' my spit. Tell 'im I wanna milk the nut out wit' my mouth. I walk up on 'im. Tell the nigga to stand up, then I drop down low. I take his dick in my mouth; start suckin' it off all slow 'n sweet, then start gulpin' the shit. I got the nigga dippin' at the knees. Got 'em moanin'.

"You like that shit, muhfucka?"

"Ohhhhh fuck yeah."

Then a bitch starts gettin' real nasty wit' it, spittin' and slobberin' all over his cock, makin' a lotta smackin' and poppin' sounds wit' my lips and mouth, then lickin' up the spit from 'round his balls.

"Gotdaaaaamn, you nasty, baby. You suckin' da fuck outta this dick. Fuck, yo." His leg starts shakin'. I reach up and start squeezin' his smooth muscular ass wit' my hands, swallowin' his dick balls deep, like only a true dick suckin' bitch can. This muh-fucka's big-ass dick got my eyes waterin', but I keep on rockin' his top. My clit throbs for his tongue on it.

"Damn, nice, big, pretty lips..."—I continue slurping and suck-ing and gulping him—"...slap them lips with it, baby..." I give the muhfucka the throat work just how he wants it. Let the nigga beat up the tonsils. "...aaaaah fuck...bounce that shit on ya wet tongue...yeah, ohhh, shiiiit...suck that shit, baby...take it all the way down in ya throat...suck on that muthafucka..."

I increase the suction, rapidly bobbin' my head. All this cock washin' has my pussy achin' and wet and horny for a dose of dick rammed deep in it. His knees start to buckle as he lets out a loud moan and grunt.

I pull up off'a his dick and start jackin' it, lappin' at his balls. Yeah, muhfucka...I'ma fuck the shit outta this big-ass dick, nigga. You gotta bitch's pussy blazin'...you wanna sink ya dick in da fire, nigga?"

"Yeah, baby...ohhh, fuck..." I slip his dick back into my mouth and let 'im knock my throat back. I breathe in, extend my tongue, then let the nigga stretch my neck out. A few minutes later, the nigga starts shakin' as his nut gushes outta his dick. I smile, knowin' a bitch's throat skills are mad crazy and can put any porn-star bitch to shame. Say what you want. Bottom line, I'm *that bitch!*

TWO DAYS LATER, WE'RE IN THE CITY WALKIN' THROUGH TIMES Square. As usual, it's mad packed out here. The energy and all the niggas in the streets makes my pussy hot. I feel like tossin' my hair in the breeze and poppin' these ass cheeks real extra while I strut. But I don't. Alex is all up on'a bitch like he owns 'er. He grabs my hand, slippin' his fingas through mine. I ain't gonna front. I'm diggin' the attention.

We just finished seein' the musical *Fela!* on Broadway. And the shit was fiiiyah. Crazy thing, this was my first time eva goin' to a show. Concerts, yeah; but a musical...who woulda thought a bitch would enjoy some shit like that. But I did.

"Yo, ma...lookin' good," some young nigga hustlin' a CD says as we walk by. I grin at 'im. A few minutes later, anotha muh-fucka says the same thing. I grin again.

"Damn, my man, you gotta real beauty right there. She's defi-nitely a keeper," a dark-skinned muhfucka says to Alex. He smiles and nods at the nigga like he's all proud 'n shit to have me on his arm. I act like I don't peep the shit. But the nigga's walkin' wit' his chest all puffed out like he's the muthafuckin' man.

As we walk down the blocks toward 44th and Broadway, most of the niggas cut they eyes at me, or make it obvious they tryna get my attention, but I don't pay the shit no mind. Of course Alex peeps the shit tryna act like he feelin' some kinda way 'bout all the attention muhfuckas givin' a bitch. Shit, ain't my fault I'm so damn fine. Hell, I ain't payin' the hoes who are snappin' they necks peepin' his ass no mind. I already know the nigga looks good. He wraps his arm 'round me like he's my man. I let 'im get it, though. The nigga can front if he want. I can tell his ass is diggin' the attention, too.

"Damn, these muhfuckas all over my baby," he says as he kisses me on the side of my head. "I need to get ya fine-ass up outta here."

I smirk, teasin' 'im. "Maybe you shoulda been walkin' wit' a booga bitch instead of a buttery bitch like me."

"Nah, it's all good. I don't wanna have'ta go in anyone's mouth; that's all."

"Oh, puhleeze. Let me find out you jealous," I say, laughin'.

"Nah, ain't nuthin', yo. I'm sayin', though. Niggas real extra tryna holla at you, that's all."

"Boy, stop...you don't hear me sayin' shit 'bout them hoes I peeped eye-fuckin' you."

"I ain't beat for none'a them. But you know what. I want muh-fuckas to see what they can't have."

I laugh. "Oh Lawwd. Here you go. And what makes you think *you* can have me?"

"Yo, don't front. I already got you. You just need to admit it."

"Wrong answer. You only *fuckin'* me. You don't have me."

"Yeah, whatever. Go 'head wit' that dumb shit. You already know what it is."

I smirk, shakin' my head. "What I know is when you walkin' the strip wit' a fine-ass bitch like me on ya arm, you gotta 'xpect muhfuckas gonna look and say what they say. Now if that's gonna be too much for you to handle, then maybe you might need'a downgrade."

"Downgrade hell. Fuck outta here." He pulls me into 'im tighter. "I already know my baby's a problem."

I suck my teeth. "See, here we go wit' this 'baby' shit, again."

When we finally get to Virgil's restaurant, he holds open the door for me. "Yup-yup; so get used to it."

I walk in. "Whateva. I ain't tryna hear that shit. You need'a hurry up and feed me. I'm hungry."

"Yo, I got you. This here's only da appetizers, so it should hold you over 'til we get back to da crib."

I look up at 'im, smirkin'. "Oh really? And then what?"

He grins, leanin' into my ear. "I'ma feed you this big-ass dick."

I roll my eyes, followin' behind 'im and the maitre d' to our table. But, trust and believe. Him whisperin' that shit in my ear done got a bitch's pussy poppin'. Nasty muhfucka!

CHAPTER TWENTY-FIVE

Ice on my neck, wrists and hands...Hermès Birkin bag draped on my arm...diamond stilettos on my feet...don't be mislead... I'm from the hood, baby...shit ain't sweet...do me wrong... end up dead...

For some reason, a nervous energy fills me as I walk through the funeral home's doors. I have no intentions of sittin' through this bitch's funeral service, but I thought it only right to make an appearance at 'er viewin'. I peep the ivory casket up at the front of the room and the few flower arrangements, then glance 'round the room to see who's here. Not many. Most of my cousins are here; some I'm cool wit', othas I don't give'a fuck 'bout. My grandmother is sittin' up in the first pew, Patrice is on one side'a 'er and Rosa's oldest son, Arturo, is on the otha side. They are both huggin' 'er, tryna console 'er. Elise is standin' up at the casket wit' Rosa's youngest son, Javier. They are all cryin'.

I take a deep breath. Oversized black Dior glasses on my face and chunky diamonds in my lobes, a bitch struts down the aisle toward Rosa's casket in a sexy black, long-sleeved Diane von Furstenberg silk beaded wrap dress wit' plungin' neckline and a

slick-ass pair of Jimmy Choo double-banded, five-inch shim-
merin' booties. My Hermès bag hangs in the crook of my arm.
Yeah, a bitch is bringin' it high-fashion—*and* overdressed. So da
fuck what! Any chance I get, I'm servin' it to these hoes. Besides,
the only ho who I knew would be tryna bring it is Patrice, so a
bitch had'a be two steps flyer than 'er even if I was only makin' a
brief appearance.

The closer I get to the casket, the louder e'eryone's cryin' gets.
Elise reaches into the casket and lays 'er hand on top of Rosa's,
then grips it. She kisses Rosa on the forehead, then starts hollerin'
and grippin' the side of the caskets all broken up. *Poor thing*, I
think, makin' my way to the front of the room. I watch as Javier
helps 'er back to 'er seat. Arturo scoots down so she can sit on the
otha side'a 'er mother.

All eyes are on me as I stand at the casket, starin' down at Rosa.
I lift my shades up ova my head. *Oh well. It didn't have'ta be like
this, Sweetie. All you had'a do was stay in ya lane. But noooooooooo, ya
crackhead ass wanted to get funky wit' it and try 'n bring it to a bitch.
Now look at you. All boxed 'n ready to go. I feel like spittin' in ya face,
ho, and knockin' you otta that casket for havin' me have'ta body ya
dumb-ass. All you had'a do was fall da fuck back. Oh well. Rest in
peace, ho.*

As I turn to walk off, Arturo comes up to me and gives me a big
hug. "Hey, cuz, glad you came."

I hug 'im back. I haven't seen 'im in over four years. I take 'im
in. He's ova six-feet tall wit' bronze-colored skin wit' jet-black
curly hair and almond-shaped eyes. The nigga's all grown up and
fine as fuck. "Sorry 'bout what happened to ya moms," I say,
tryna sound as sincere as I possibly can.

"Yeah, it's all fucked up. If I ever find out who did this to 'er
it's on, feel me?"

I nod, peepin' my grandmother starin' me down. The old ho is burnin' a hole through me. I roll my eyes. *Bitch, you can get it, too,* I think, shiftin' my attention back to Arturo. His eyes start to water. "I can't believe she's gone." He wipes tears as they fall.

Bitch, keep it cute. Don't say anything reckless. "You gotta stay strong" is the best I can say to 'im. "Ya moms wouldn't want you gettin' caught up in no extras. You gotta keep 'er memory alive by stayin' focused."

"Yeah, you right, cuz. Still, the shit's hard. She's been in this neighborhood for years, ain't never had no issues. And all'a sudden some punk-ass muhfucka pops up 'n just snuffs 'er out. Shits crazy, man."

"You keep ya head, cuz. It was good seein' you."

"No doubt. You bouncin'?"

"Yeah, you know I ain't got no real love in this room."

He shakes his head, smilin'. "I can't believe ya'll still beefin' like this. Kat, life is too short, ma. Look at us. We all scattered 'round. This half ain't fuckin' wit' this one. The other half and fuckin' wit' the others. Shit's crazy. We 'posed to be a family."

I take a deep breath. *Bitch, hurry up 'n get da fuck outta here 'fore he says sumthin' and you gotta crank it up in here.* "The only ones I eva had beef wit' is Patrice 'n Juanita. But ya moms 'n 'em had'a make they beef, too, instead'a stayin' outta it and let us handle it how we were gonna handle it."

"I hear you, cuz, but you gotta let that shit go. I miss seein' you 'round when we have family functions 'n shit."

"Trust me. I'm lettin' it go," I say, givin' 'im anotha hug. "I'm not a part'a this family; neva was, neva will be. And I'm cool wit' that. I came to pay my respects, but I'm so ova all'a them."

"Yo, I'm sorry 'bout what popped off wit' ya moms."

I shrug. "She brought it on 'erself."

"That nigga gotta get it, yo."

"Oh, trust. He will."

"You gonna take da baby?"

"I'm thinkin' 'bout it. I'm not sure, yet."

"I know Abuela was talkin' to my moms 'bout 'em takin' da baby and raisin' it."

I frown, feelin' myself 'bout to kick it up a notch. I wanna walk ova to them hoes and snap on 'em. But I don't. Javier comes ova and gives me a hug. He looks almost like his brotha; a few inches shorter, and stockier. His hair is freshly braided in cornrows that zig-zag and criss-cross.

"I almost didn't know who you was," he says, eyein' me. "Aunt Pat had'a tell me it was you. You lookin' real good, cuz. Still keepin' it on ten; fly as ever."

I smile. "That's da only way I know how'ta do it. You lookin' good ya'self."

He smiles back at me. "Where you been?"

"I've been 'round; just keepin' it real low-key."

"I feel you. You know some'a us do miss you, Kat."

I glance ova at Elise, Patrice and my grandmotha, then back at 'im. "I wish I could say da same. This family neva cared 'bout me."

"That's not true, cuz," Arturo says. "I care."

"No doubt," Javier adds.

"Well, that's how I've always felt."

Arturo takes me by the hand. "You need'a come through so we can chill. We fam, Kat. Wit' my moms and ya moms gone. We all we got, feel me?"

I nod. "I hear you. I'll think 'bout it." We spend a few more minutes talkin' and catchin' up and exchangin' phone numbers. I stay up 'til it's almost time for the funeral to begin, then give 'im both hugs. I dip out, neva lookin' back.

LATER IN THE AFTERNOON, I'M SPEEDIN' DOWN THE GARDEN State, headin' southbound to the shore. Outside of drivin' to Atlantic City to put in gun work, this is the first time a bitch has driven down this way durin' the day to chill. It's my first time goin' to Allstar's spot. And on some real shit, I'm surprised the nigga actually wanted me to come. And I'm more surprised that a bitch is in 'er whip goin'.

It's mad nice out. I got the windows down and the beats knockin'. Drake's "Light Up" is playin' as I fire up a blunt. By the time I pull up in Alex's condo development, I'm lit the fuck up, feelin' mad sexy 'n real 'xtra.

I park my whip, then flip down the visor to make sure shits on point. Hair 'n face still in place. *You'a sexy bitch*, I think, grinnin' at my reflection. I step out of my car, peepin' the area. The nigga's spot is surrounded by all kinda restaurants, boutiques and clubs. I see the ocean 'cross the street and find myself walkin' ova toward it to get a closer look. Beaches here have neva impressed, or interested me, so why I'm leanin' on the rail starin' at the water is beyond me. I take in a deep breath. Hold back my head and enjoy the ocean's breeze. I have a lotta shit on my mind. A bitch needs change. But I don't know if a baby is what's gonna get it. And I don't know if this nigga is the kinda change I need, or want, eitha. I can't front. He's been on my mind heavy. The last couple'a weeks we been kickin' it almost e'ery damn day. And a lotta the time we ain't even fuckin'. He be on some "let me hold you"-type shit. And I be wit' it. I don't know what's really good wit' this nigga, and I ain't really tryna spend too much time tryna figure it out. I already know what it is for me. I'ma keep it real cute, and keep doin' the nigga 'til he fucks up, then its bubble-wrap for his ass. Still, a bitch gotta wonder if I'm gettin' in too deep wit' his ass.

My cell rings, disruptin' my moment. I pull it outta my bag. It's NUT. *It's time to change up his nickname.* I decide to start change it to Allstar. "Hey," I say, turnin' to head toward his place.

"Where you at, yo? I thought you woulda been here by now."

"I'm outside," I tell 'im crossin' the street, "on my way up to ya buildin'." I peep this salon-tanned white muhfucka gettin' out'a black Maserati and anotha steppin' outta a Bentley, headin' to the Gold's Gym on the corner. I see a slew of otha high-end whips in parkin' spaces as well, grinnin'. *These muhfuckas out here gotta be paid out da ass, pushin' them big boyz.*

"Cool-cool. You aiight?"

"Yeah, I'm good." I tell 'im I'm impressed wit' his neighborhood. That it reminds me of a quaint village filled wit' a bunch'a rich muhfuckas.

He laughs. "That's 'cause it is."

When I get up to the eleventh floor, he's already standin' in the hallway waitin' on me. He's grinnin' from ear to ear. And I can't help but to smile back at 'im. He's in a pair of dark-blue True Religions and a wife beater, showin' off his chiseled arms and lookin' sexy as fuck. I swear I don't wanna catch feelin's for this nigga, but e'erytime I'm 'round 'im it gets harder and harder to keep that from happenin'.

He pulls me into his arms the minute I walk up on 'im. He kisses me wit' them sexy-ass lips and my pussy starts juicin'. "Damn, you lookin' good," he says, shuttin' the door behind me. I step outta my heels. "Let me show you 'round."

I glance 'round his spot, impressed. The nigga's shit is piped in buttery-soft Italian leather. My feet sink into the plush carpet. I peep the fifty-two-inch Sony Bravia flat-screen up on the wall wit' its surround sound. His spot is nicely decorated in all earth tone colors. I shake my head at all'a his man toys: the Xbox, PS3, and Wii games and tons of games for each. I follow 'im into the master bedroom. He has a huge mahogany king-size sleigh bed, and matchin' nightstands. There's an oil paintin' of a naked woman's profile wit' a big juicy ass and titties hangin' on the wall ova his bed.

"Nice. I'm really impressed," I tell 'im, walkin' back out into the livin' room. He shows me the kitchen, which is piped out wit' granite countertops and stainless steel appliances.

He laughs. "What, you thought I was livin' foul or sumthin'?"

"Truthfully, I didn't know what to think. So is this ya crib or some chick's you done scammed?"

He frowns. "Nah, ma. I ain't scam shit. E'erything up in this muhfucka is all me. Yeah, I been gifted up 'n shit, but don't get it fucked up. I ain't no bum-ass nigga, baby."

I smirk. "That's good to know."

"That ain't all you 'bout to know,' he says, scoopin' me up into his big arms.

"Oh yeah; what else am I gonna know?"

He licks his lips and eyes me all sexy-like, then slips his tongue in my mouth. His hands land on my ass, then squeeze it. He grinds himself into me. "Take them clothes off and let me show."

TWO HOURS LATER, WE'RE IN THE LIVIN' ROOM LOUNGIN' ON THE sofa. Alex's lyin' 'cross my lap, sparkin' a blunt. He's in his boxer briefs, bare-chested. And I'm wearin' one'a his button ups wit' nuthin' else underneath. The nigga slayed my pussy like no otha, but I ain't gonna play myself short eitha—a bitch fucked the nigga down, lovely. Had 'im moanin' like a bitch e'ery time I lifted up on his dick and rode the head, milkin' that shit wit' my pussy muscles.

"Yo, you really got a nigga goin' through it, Kat," he says, takin' two puffs on the blunt, then handin' it to me. "Real talk; I'm really feelin' you, ma. You know that, right?"

I hold the blunt wit' one hand and rub his head wit' the otha, lettin' my fingas move ova the pattern of his waves. I nod, blowin' smoke outta the side of my lips. "That's what ya mouth says."

He looks up at me. "Yo, that's what it is." I hand 'im back the blunt. "I ain't tryna get all fucked up in this shit, yo."

I lay my head back on the sofa, thinkin' 'bout Juanita and all the otha bitches who lost their damn minds and souls to a nigga. Bitches who couldn't think straight wit'out a nigga in they lives. I don't care how good the nigga's dick and tongue game is, I can't eva let that shit happen to me. "Me either," I say, shakin' the shit outta my head. *'Cause muhfucka it ain't gonna pretty if I do.*

He lifts up off'a me, takin' anotha pull from the blunt. He hands it to me, but I tell 'im I'm good. For the last few days a bitch ain't really been beat to burn it up like normal. Shit, I ain't even really tossin' back the drinks like I used to eitha.

He looks at me. "I'm a hunnid wit' you 'cross the board. No games."

"Okay. And I'm real wit' you."

"Aiight, then we cool. Don't play me, Kat."

"Nigga, don't *you* play me."

He leans ova and tries to kiss me. I yank my head back. "Oh what, now I can't get no lips?"

"Nope," I say, smirkin'.

"Yeah right." He hovers ova me, presses me back on the sofa. "Stop, playin', girl, give me some'a that tongue."

I stick my tongue out, then pull it back into my mouth. "You want it, nigga. You gotta take it." He pulls me into him, kisses my lips. I press my lips tight to keep 'im from slippin' his tongue in. "You gonna have'ta come betta than that."

"Oh, aiight. I see how you doin' it. I got you." He starts nibblin' on my neck, unbuttons the buttons on the shirt I'm wearin', then takes my left nipple in his mouth. His tongue swirls 'round it while he reaches ova and lightly pinches my right nipple. I fight to keep myself from moanin'. *Oh, gaawd, this muhfucka is gonna have'a bitch all fucked up*, I think, closin' my eyes. *Keep it cute, ho.* He looks up at me. "Can I get some'a that tongue, ma?"

I grunt. Moan. Shake my head from side to side. "No."

He starts kissin' down the middle of my chest to my stomach, then dips his tongue into my belly button. Wit'out thinkin', a bitch spreads open 'er legs anticipatin' the next spot his tongue makes. The nigga got me in heat. Got my pussy lips stickin'. He grabs me by the waist, pulls my legs up ova his shoulders, then wraps his arms 'round the back of me and lifts me up, standin' up. He lifts my hips up in the air and begins suckin' 'n lickin' on my clit. "Oooooooh…aaaaaaah…" *Ohhhhmiiigaawd, this nigga's tongue is deadly.* I grab the back of his head, fuck his face. "Ohhhhh, yes, muhfucka…make my pussy skeet, nigga…" I let go of his head and lay backward, lettin' the nigga have his way wit' my pussy. His dick stabs me in my back. I twist my body so I can get at it, then start strokin' it ova his boxers. I'm not sure how or when, 'cause the muhfucka has a bitch in a zone, but the next thing I know the nigga turns me around wit' his mouth still mounted on my kat-box and I'm face-to-face wit' his dick. He alternates from lickin' my asshole to the back of my pussy. I pull his boxers down ova his waist, takin' his dick in my hands. I lick the precum leakin' from its tip, then start suckin' on it—slow and sexy at first, then fast and nasty. I take my hands off the dick, grab the back of his thighs and give the nigga all throat and neck action. He's moanin'. I'm moanin'. Then, a few minutes later, we are both nuttin', gulpin' and slurpin' each otha's nut.

The nigga lets me down, then collapses back onto the sofa.

"Fuck," he says, lickin' the rest of my cream from 'round his lips. "You da truth, baby—word up." I grin, lickin' my lips as well. I drop down in front of 'im and finish milkin' the rest of his nut out.

When I'm done, I climb up on top of 'im and look 'im in the eyes. "Now you can have some tongue," I tell 'im, slippin' it deep into his mouth. Our tongues twirl and flick up against the othas. We kiss and stare into each otha's eyes. I'm feedin' the nigga a taste of his nut and he's feedin' me a taste of mine. I grind down on his dick, let my pussy coat it wit' juice. And, for the first time in a long time, I wanna feel this nigga bust his dick up in me raw.

CHAPTER TWENTY-SIX

Where there is life...there is death...pullin' in da final breath...one life traded for anotha...mixed emotions slicin'a bitch like a knife...da birth of a tiny lil' brotha...gotta ho rethinkin' some things...should a bitch play 'er position...be his sista, or play his motha?...

Three weeks later, on Saturday, June 26, 2010 at 6:36 p.m., after bein' pumped up wit' a buncha steroids to help the baby inside'a 'er lungs develop, the plug is finally pulled on my mother. And the truth is, I feel nuthin'; just like I knew I would. Watchin' 'er life support machine bein' shut off is like liftin' a switch and turnin' on bright lights to a dark, lonely past.

I am in the labor 'n delivery room, relieved that this is my last time lookin' at 'er. I've been comin' back 'n forth up to this hospital practically e'ery damn night, starin' at Juanita. Cursin' 'er out, sayin' a buncha shit I kept bottled up for what I knew would be the last time, knowin' she couldn't hear shit I had'a say. But, I realize she didn't need to. I needed it for me. And like I've said, there will be no tears, not ova 'er. And a bitch ain't livin' wit' no regrets.

Patrice, Elise 'n my grandmother are here—lookin' through the glass window, bawlin' they eyes out. This is the first time I'm 'round all'a these hoes and we ain't goin' at it. Still, the tension is thick as shit, but we keep the drama at bay—*for now*.

I keep my back to them bitches. We are all consumed wit' tears. Theirs are for the loss of another daughter 'n sister. Mine for seein' this tiny lil' baby brought into this world by C-section, then laid on my mother's shoulder for a brief moment. Neither aware of the otha's presence. Then havin' the doctor hand the baby to *me*. I am nervous at first, takin' it. It is the first time I've held a baby—a tiny life; a baby boy brought into this world at twenty-six weeks, weighing' only 3 lbs. 8 oz. A bitch bursts into tears, so fuckin' distraught knowin' I woulda killed 'im.

Chanel is here wit' me—my real family. Masked and suited up, she is cryin' wit' me. She's the only bitch who knows and understands me. "Ohmiiiigod, Kat, look at 'im. He is soooo tiny."

I don't speak. I can't. There are no fuckin' words in me. E'erything 'round me is one big blurry mess from tears. And when the nurse finally takes 'im from me, I feel myself 'bout to collapse. I am shocked at myself. Surprised that I am feelin' the way I do—overwhelmed. That I have all'a these emotions wrapped up in me. That I am a snotty-nosed mess behind all'a this. He will be placed in an incubator, and be under ultraviolet light. I watch 'em place a lil' mask ova his eyes. Watch 'em place a trach tube down into his lil' lungs, then connect it to a machine so he can breathe. I watch 'em stick a catheter into his umbilical cord so they can pump 'im wit' fluids and drugs. He is pinched 'n pricked 'n probed and it tears a bitch's heart to see this. I'm exhausted and emotionally drained. But I can't stop cryin'. The doctor is sayin' shit to me, but I ain't hearin' it all.

"...He will be in the NICU...the next few weeks are the most critical..."

I tell 'em I gotta leave. Tell 'em I can't deal wit' this right now. Tell 'em I'll be back later. Chanel follows behind me, wrappin' 'er arm 'round me. She swipes tears from 'er own face wit' 'er other hand.

"I'm here for you, girl."

"I know you are," I tell 'er, squeezin' 'round 'er waist.

"Kat, you can't let them take 'im; you gotta step up and take that lil' baby. He's so precious and tiny. Ohmiiiigod, you gotta, girl." I don't say shit; just break down, sobbin'. She hugs me, rubbin' my back. "It's gonna be aiiiight. I know you scared, girl. But I got ya back. We can do this. It's whateva, ho. You know how we do. You hear me?"

I nod. Hold onto 'er tighter, catchin' Elise lookin' ova in our direction. She says sumthin' to Patrice 'n my grandmother, then walks ova toward us. "This bitch," I mumble.

Chanel whispers in my ear, "Be nice, Kat. Keep it cute."

Elise reaches out to console me, but I pull away. I don't want the bitch touchin' me. And I ain't beat to hear what comes outta 'er cunt muncha. I look ova to the left of me and peep Patrice huggin' my grandmother. The poor thing is all broken up. And so she should be.

"Kat, we're family. Whateva shit you think we've done to you, right now we gotta let that shit go. We gotta work it through. I know you're hurt. We're all hurt. But this shit, this bullshit-ass feud, has gotta stop. I lost two sistas, back to back. And now there's a baby that's gonna need all of us."

I blink. Finally look the ho in the face.

"I know you're angry at ya moms, but she loved you. And she did the best she could wit' what she had."

"Please. Get. Away from me."

The bitch keeps standin' here. "I know you're hurtin' that the two of you couldn't rebuild ya relationship, but—"

I tilt my head. I catch Chanel's eye. She raises 'er brow. Gives me a "girl-don't-do-it look." *Ohmiiiiigod...this dizzy bitch thinks these tears are 'cause I'm grievin'.*

"But nuthin'. Me and Juanita neva had a relationship, so there wasn't one to try 'n repair. Get ya facts straight."

She clenches 'er teeth. "You know what, Kat, I'm really tryna be civil wit' ya ass. But, you really pushin' it. I know you goin' through a buncha shit so I'm givin' you a pass."

Chanel starts pullin' me by the arm. "C'mon, girl, keep this shit cute; let's go."

For once, I think before I speak. I don't call 'er a buncha bitches and low-budget hoes like I want. "Elise, be clear. You ain't givin' me a pass to shit. So hop, lil' froggy, and get dropped. 'Cause you can get it just like ya crackhead sista did; trust."

"Elise, c'mon, girl," Patrice calls out. "Don't get into no situations wit' that crazy-ass chick, not tonight. We need'a get Momma outta here. Don't worry; she got it comin' to 'er."

I snap my neck in 'er direction. "And who's gonna bring it to me? You? 'Cause I know you ain't crazy enough to think that this"— I flick my thumb over at Elise—"this chick is gonna serve it."

Elise turns 'er attention back to me. "Bitch, don't sleep. As soon as we bury my sista, I'ma see you."

I eye the bitch. "Oh, really. Well, let me tell you this. You betta keep a 'xtra hole dug 'cause da day you raise up on me will be da day ya mammy will be tossin' ya ass in it next to ya dead-ass sistas."

She raises a hand to swing off but I catch it, pushin' 'er back into the window. "Biiiitch!" she yells, causin' a bigga scene than necessary. Fuck tryna keep it cute. A bitch is ready bring it to this ho's head.

"Stop it! Both of you," my grandmother snaps. "I will not have this. Elise, leave that hateful devil child alone."

I raise my hands up and pointin' at 'er like their guns. "Granny, boom," I say, makin' poppin' gestures at the air as if I'ma shoot 'er the fuck up.

She stops in 'er tracks. "Elise, let's go," she says. "*Esta puta es loco.*"

I force myself to laugh. "Yeah, I'ma crazy bitch. And *whaaaat?* Stay da fuck away from me. All'a you."

I'm surprised Patrice isn't tryna set it off. I guess the bitch is too distraught to bring it. Elise says some extra shit still tryna make it pop 'bout not lettin' me get away wit' disrespectin' 'er mother. My grandmother yanks 'er by arm, and the bitch still keeps poppin' shit.

"You lucky ya grandmother's here. She saved you from a beat-down. But, bitch, be clear, I'ma jump on that ass so fast you won't know what da fuck hit you."

Instead of escalatin' the shit, I straight spin-off on them bitches. Bottom line, my mind is made up. If the bitch comes at me on any kinda shit, I'ma push 'er fronts all the way to the back, then I'ma be makin' that call for anotha clean-up crew. And a bitch don't have'a problem tossin' Cash's freak-nasty ass another pair'a panties to make this ho go away—permanently.

LATER THAT NIGHT, ME AND CHANEL ARE SITTIN' UP AT 'ER SPOT, blazin' 'n tossin' back a bottle of Moscato while listenin' to Eric Roberson. As usual Devine is out grindin' and Chanel is sittin' here schemin' on how she can get 'er creep on. "Do you know if Allstar got any niggas on his squad I might wanna chill wit'?"

I shrug, frownin'. "Bitch, how da fuck I know?"

"Well, da next time you talk to 'im, ask."

"Ho, I ain't askin' 'im shit. You already gotta man. So be happy wit' what you got."

She rolls 'er eyes. "Bitch, pass me da damn blunt." I laugh. "Annnnway, wassup up wit' ya'll any-damn-way?"

"Trick, why is you always askin' me wassup wit' me 'n that nigga? Ain't shit up. I keep tellin' you we chillin'; that's it."

"Does he know 'bout the baby?"

This bitch has had'a 'nough smoke for one night, I think, starin' 'er ass down. I kick my shoes off, then curl up on 'er sofa. "What's there for his ass to know? I keep tellin' you da nigga ain't my man, ho."

She flicks 'er wrist, dismissin' me. "Yeah, whateva. I don't know why you keep frontin'; you know you diggin' da nigga. Face it."

"Okay, ho, you got me…busted. Guilty as charged. And?"

"And give da nigga some rhythm."

"That nigga gets all the rhythm I'ma give."

She pours us both 'nother round. "Kat, be real. What da fuck you afraid of?"

I buck my eyes open. "Afraid? Who said anything 'bout bein' afraid?"

She stares at me. "Aren't you?"

"Hell no." *Bitch, shut ya lyin' ass up. Keep shit real.* I toss back my glass, gulp down my nerves.

"Bitch, you lyin'."

I huff. "Aiight, damn, ho. I hate ya ass; for real, for real. Real shit. I don't eva wanna end up like Juanita. All fucked up ova a muhfucka. I saw what that ho went through. Saw what she was. All broke down 'n pitiful 'n desperate. I don't wanna be that kinda bitch, you know. Cryin' 'n fightin' ova a nigga."

"Girl, not you. That's not even ya steelo. You too damn strong-willed to let a nigga do you sideways."

"Yeah, you right. But some'a the strongest bitches have been broken down gettin' too caught up wit' a muhfucka."

"Kat, that ain't you."

"Still, the shit haunts a bitch."

"Girl, puhleeze. Don't let that keep you from gettin' close to a nigga you feelin'. Shake that shit off." She looks at me. "You eva think 'bout how you mighta turned out if ya moms was a different kinda woman, or if ya pops was in ya life?"

I shake my head. "No, what for? Fantasizin' 'bout shit that is already done can't change shit for me. Juanita was a dick junkie, and my pops is a career criminal. I'm kinda thinkin' that's how shit was 'posed to be. But, it's not shit I'm tryna live. It's not how I wanna be. And it's damn sure not what I wanna become."

She twists 'er lips. "I feel you. Do you think they gonna eva find that nigga who did that shit to ya moms?" she asks, fillin' our glasses to the rim wit' more wine.

Hopefully not before I do. "Who knows. All I know, that nigga needs to get served, lovely. I want that muthafucka's head on'a platter wit' his dick stuffed in his mouth."

"I feel you, girl. I know you don't wanna hear it. But what that nigga did to ya moms is mad crazy. And now there's a beautiful lil' baby wit' no parents."

What that nigga did is a blessin' in disguise, I think, gulpin' down the last drop of wine in my glass. Chanel asks if I want more. I tell 'er no. Tell 'er I ain't for beat any more'a that fruity-tooty shit. Tell 'er to spark up 'notha blunt. We change up the subject and start talkin' 'bout takin' a trip to either Italy or France."

"Shit," I say, takin' the blunt from 'er. "We can do both. We young, fly, butta bitches who can do whateva da fuck we want."

She laughs. "Hell yeah, Boo. We two siiiiick bitches doin' it up. Oh, wait...you sponsorin' me, right?"

I bust out laughin'. "Ho, I can't stand nuthin' yo broke ass stands for. You know Divine got you."

She laughs wit' me. "Bitch, you know Divine ain't gonna give me 'nough paper to live it up. His cheap ass'll only give me few bullshit gees, then 'pect me to stretch it out for da whole time we gone."

"Well, if ya cheatin' ass started suckin' 'n fuckin' top-dolla niggas instead of them nickel 'n dime muhfuckas you be chasin', you'd have ya paper up."

She rolls 'er eyes. "Whateva, tramp. Pass me da damn blunt."

We go back 'n forth for a few rounds, draggin' each otha for filth, laughin' and whatnot 'til Eric Roberson's joint "Dealing" starts playin'. Wit'out any thought, we shut the fuck up and go into our own lil' zones, bobbin' and puffin'. I'm sure 'er horny ass is imaginin' 'im wit' them big, juicy lips swallowin' up 'er titties. I'm stuck in mine, wonderin' if I should give the nigga Alex a go, or cut the nigga off now 'fore shit gets too hectic.

TWO DAYS LATER, CHANEL IS BACK UP AT THE HOSPITAL WIT' ME. I just finished talkin' to the doctor 'bout the baby's progress. And so far he's doin' good. The doctor is optimistic he'll make it through this. But, for now, he is still in ICU. And on some real shit, a bitch can't stand seein' 'im and all them otha lil' babies in incubators wit' all kinda tubes comin' outta 'im. They are so tiny 'n fragile. The shit is really fuckin' my nerves. I stare at 'im. Feel myself gettin' all choked up.

What am I gonna do?

Bitch, you was poppin' mad shit 'bout 'im goin' into foster care. 'Bout you not bein' beat. Now ya confused-ass standin' here switchin' it up. Ho, make ya mind up.

My mind is made up. I can't let these muhfuckas take 'im. I can't do it.

"Oh, bitch, puhleeze. And you think you can raise 'im? Get real.

"Do you have any idea what you wanna name 'im?" Chanel asks, cuttin' through my thoughts.

"Huh?

"Hello, hello? Anybody home? I asked whadaya gonna name 'im?"

"Fuck if I know. All this shit is new to me." On some real shit, I really haven't thought the shit all the way through. It feels like shit is movin' type-fast for a bitch. I'm torn...okay, okay, and fuckin' scared to death. I don't know the first thing 'bout carin' for a baby. Shit, who knows if it's sumthin' I even got in me. All I know is, from the moment I laid eyes on that lil' boy, he's been on my brain, heavy. And I can't turn my back on 'im.

"Well, you need to think of sumthin', soon. We can't keep callin' 'im 'baby'. Our lil' man needs a name. I'm gonna start lookin' through some baby books for a name."

I grin. "Oh, he's *our* lil' man, huh?"

"Damn straight 'cause you know I ain't tryna stretch my snatch all outta shape tryna pump no babies outta it. So we gotta share 'im."

I laugh. "Girlfriend, as much mileage that kat-box of yours got on it, it really ain't gonna be that much stretchin' goin' on. You real loosey-goosey wit' yours, boo. All you gotta do is squat down low and a baby'll drop right out wit' ya big-pussy self."

She laughs. "Whateva, tramp. Shut ya cum-trap and come up wit' a name for our baby. And da shit gotta be fly."

I laugh wit' 'er. "Yeah, you right. I don't—"

"Umm, 'scuse me. Are you Miss Rivera?" I turn in the direction of the voice. There are two chicks—one black, the otha white—standin' wit' notepads. The black chick is the one talkin' to me. She has a real strong face, mannish-like. And 'er short blonde 'fro ain't helpin' matters. I look 'er up 'n down. Take in 'er cheesy makeup job. The ho got on foundation that is two shades lighter than 'er neck wit' a buncha eyeliner 'round 'er eyes. She's a makeup artist's nightmare. I glance down at 'er footwear. *Cheesy patent-leather heels; mmmph, a Payless booga.*

"Who wants to know?"

"I'm Samantha Hillinger-Brown, and this is my colleague, Dana Movella." I glance at the white chick. The first thing I peep are a pair of white seashell earrings danglin' from 'er lobes. She's all dolled up in 'er Sunday best; a purple dress wit' large white polka dots. All the bitch needs is a pair of white gloves and a Bible. "We're with Child Protective Services." She extends 'er hand. I glance at it, raisin' my brow. She quickly puts it down.

"And?"

"We're here on the matter of Baby Rivera."

Okay, now a bitch's radar kicks up a notch. "What'a 'bout 'im?"

"We understand your mother had been on life support until he was delivered. And we understand the father is a person of interest in her death."

"Yeah, that's right. What does that have to do wit' me, or you?"

"Well, now that he's born we need to begin planning for—"

"Oh, no, Sweetie," Chanel cuts in, shiftin' 'er handbag from one hand to the otha. "We don't need no plannin' committee. We got this. So thanks for ya interest. But you can go hop scotch on back ova to ACS. He's in good hands."

"And you are?" Sam the Man asks.

"I'm his aunt."

"Can we have your name?"

"It's Aunt," Chanel says fuckin' wit' 'em. "A-U-N-T."

I tilt my head. "So the only plannin' there's gonna be is what color I'm gonna paint his room."

"Well, here's the thing, Miss Rivera," Miss Sunday's Best says.

"We're here in the interest of the child. We've received several calls from concerned parties on behalf of the infant."

"Concerned parties like who?" I ask, lookin' 'er dead in 'er blue eyes.

"Well, I'm not at liberty to disclose who the parties are. However, we'd like to discuss with you some concerns…"

Right at this moment, I ain't tryna hear shit this ho is sayin'. And although I wanna drag this bitch for filth, I know I gotta keep it cute. So I force myself to keep my mouth shut and pay attention. The bitch starts talkin' 'bout allegations. Someone called in and told 'em that a bitch sells drugs and sits 'round blazin' all day; that a bitch is aggressive and violent; that I assaulted my grandmother and attacked my aunts; that I get drunk and fuck a buncha men.

I blink, blink again.

"You wait one damn minute," Chanel snaps, pointin' 'er finga at 'em. "That's a buncha bullshit."

"And that may be so," Sam the Man says. "But we still have to follow up with every call received. Our priority is for the safety and well-being of the child."

"Hmmm," I say, twistin' my lips up. "And so it should be. So know this. I don't have shit to hide. So you can ask me whateva you want. Bottom line, I have my own money, and my own home. I don't sell drugs; neva have, neva will. And I don't do 'em." Okay, yeah a bitch blazes, but that ain't none'a these hoes' business. Besides, Kush ain't no damn drug any-damn-way. I continue wit' my story. "And in terms of bein' aggressive or assaultive. I neva slapped my grandmother. I grabbed her arm. So what? The bitch slapped *me*."

"Well, did you threaten her?"

"Ho," I snap, puttin' a hand on my hip. "What that gotta do

wit' da baby? If I threatened 'er, then it should be the police standin' here, not you. But since you asked. No, I ain't threaten 'er. I warned 'er. I told 'er the next time she put 'er hands on me, I'ma forget she's my grandmother and beat 'er old ass up. I don't care who you are. Don't put ya hands on me. Otha than that, I like to keep it real simple. Don't fuck wit' me, and I won't fuck wit' you. But if you bring, then I'ma sling it. And there you have it. Now go back and tell whomeva called you that I said ta fall da fuck back or get knocked da fuck back. Anything else?"

They both blink. I guess they shocked that a bitch brought it to 'em like that. These bitches got the wrong one.

Miss Sunday's Best says, "We're gonna have to follow up and do an investigation and background check on you."

"That's fine by me. Do whateva you need ta do ta rest ya minds." I give 'em my contact info, then spin-off on 'em. As soon as me and Chanel get into the elevator and the doors shut, I snap. "Can you believe this shit?! They send out sum muthafuckin' low-budget booga bitches to try 'n eye scan me. Bitch, puhleeze. They can investigate all da fuck they want."

"Who da fuck you think called them hoes?"

"Who you think? Them whore-ass trick bitches Elise and Patrice. Shit, they old, crusty-ass mammy probably called 'em too; dusty bitch!"

"I know you gonna keep it cute, though?"

"Sweetie and you know this. First things first, a bitch gotta flush out these insides in case they try 'n get crafty wantin' me to do piss tests 'n shit. Then I'ma invite them trashbag hoes into my home and serve 'em wit' grace, okay?!"

"I know that's right. So, I guess we ain't rollin' today?"

My cell rings. I fish it outta my bag, then glance at the screen. It's Alex. I press IGNORE. The elevator doors open. "Bitch, puhleeze, ain't shit changed for today. We gonna burn down da muthafuckin' forest all day. But come tomorrow, a bitch gotta shut shit down 'til after lil' man is released from da hospital and I'm bringin' 'im home."

"That's right. Right where da fuck he belongs."

Bitch, how da fuck you get ya'self into this shit?

Ho, you doin' da right thing.

Bitch, puhleeze, ya ass ain't tryna be nobody's mammy.

"I swear I hope a bitch can handle this shit," I say as we exit the glass doors. "The last thing I wanna do is fuck his life up da way Juanita fucked up mine."

"Girl, trust me. You won't." Chanel loops 'er arm 'round mine and we walk arm 'n arm.

I sigh, lookin' up at the sky. For what, who knows; maybe for a sign. "Let's hope so."

CHAPTER TWENTY-SEVEN

> *Ain't gonna front...bitch loves ridin' down on da nigga's dick...nigga wanna be my daaaaddy...wanna eat it up 'n beat it up...pussy like crack...one hit...got da nigga cummin' back...got 'im wantin' this sticky nut-nut...got 'im whisperin' my name...fly, buttery bitch got 'em all fucked up in da game...nigga, what?*

"Aye, yo, what's good wit' you?" Allstar asks, soundin' kinda tight. Truth is the muhfucka probably is since I've been playin' 'im to the left for the last two weeks. On some real shit, I just ain't been feelin' it. This whole baby situation gotta ho's cage rattled. I'm startin' to feel like I'm gettin' into some shit way ova my head. And a bitch don't like feelin' like she ain't in control of shit. Still, I don't wanna see 'im in the system. And damn sure don't want 'im bein' placed wit' Elise or Patrice. But I keep askin' myself ova and ova, "what da fuck am *I* gonna do wit' a baby? One voice in my head says: "Love it." The otha is tellin' me: "Fuck up its life."

Real shit, that's the last thing I eva wanna do. Give 'im a fucked up life, or mistreat 'im. Still, I don't know if I really got it in me to love—someone else, that is. I thought I did. Howeva, now a bitch gotta wonder. Not blazin' the last two weeks hasn't helped shit, either. It gotta ho on edge. And it has me thinkin' 'bout shit. Like love and life and niggas. I'ma young, fly, beautiful bitch, got paper for days, good pussy, a sick throat game and muhfuckas tryna get at'a chick, hard. Muhfuckas sweatin' to rock a bitch on their arms, but I ain't beat.

When I was fuckin' Naheem, I thought he was the muhfucka I was in love wit'. He wasn't. I cared for that nigga, true. But I realize it wasn't shit more than a crush, and me lovin' the fact that the nigga helped a bitch get outta a fucked up situation. When the nigga got knocked, I really thought the achin' I felt was from a broken heart. It wasn't. All it was was a bitch stressed 'bout how she was gonna keep from endin' up back in the projects—stuck and miserable.

But a bitch was able to snatch up the nigga B-Love and bubble-up lovely. But I know I neva gave a fuck 'bout his ass. I only cared 'bout makin' sure I didn't end up eva bein' one'a them bottom of the barrel bitches. All I cared 'bout was that nigga's paper. And, keepin' shit real, I know the nigga didn't really care 'bout me, either. The only thing he cared 'bout was havin' me as his. Catchin' that nigga wit' his naked dick up in Patrice's fuck-box, then offin' his ass, was the best thing I coulda did. And it gave me all the fetti I needed to get on top, and stay on top.

And Grant. Well, Grant was the nigga I thought was gonna be my savin' grace from myself. 'Cause I knew I was gettin' too caught up and comfortable poppin' a muhfuckas cork. But the truth is, the only muhfucka who could really save me, is *me*. Grant was only anotha escape, maybe an excuse, for me.

"Shit," I tell 'im, walkin' into the kitchen, openin' up a bag of Ranch Doritos. I start crunchin' in his ear. I know, rude; whateva.

"Oh, word? I can dig it. You home?"

"Yeah, why?"

"I see you ain't really been feelin' a muhfucka. I've called and text you and you couldn't even hit a muhfucka back. That's some pussy-ass bullshit, Kat. And you know it."

"Shit happens," I say, nonchalantly.

"So, it's like that, right?" It sounds like this muhfucka is strugglin' to keep it together.

"I've been busy. Nuthin' personal." I place a handful of chips on a napkin, then fold the bag closed.

"*Nuthin' personal?* Oh, aiight. So, you play a muhfucka to da left like I'm sum kinda duck muhfucka and I'm not 'posed to take that shit personal. On some real shit, I thought we was vibin'."

"Nigga, we was. But, shit. I got otha pressin' shit goin' on. So I don't really have no time for niggas."

"Oh, so that's what I am, just some nigga, yo?"

"Well...uh, yeah. You ain't my man."

"Yo, ain't nobody sayin' I am. But I've kept shit a hunnid wit' you; told you what it is, and what I want."

"And I told you what it is, too. I'm not beat."

"So fuck me, right?"

The doorbell rings. I ignore the shit since I don't remember sendin' out no invitations for guests. I sigh. "You know what I mean."

"Nah, I don't. Why don't you tell me."

I feel myself 'bout to spazz out on this muhfucka. But it really has nuthin' to do wit' 'im. A bitch is aggravated that she missed hearin' this nigga's voice; that his smooth baritone voice is makin' my clit pulse. I need a fuckin' blunt! *And a dose'a some dick, bitch!*

"Look, nigga. Don't try 'n make this out to be no more than what it's been. We been fuck buddies; that's it. I ain't gonna sit here 'n front like a bitch don't dig you 'cause I do. But at da end of da day, we both know that shit ain't gonna be no more than what it's been—us fuckin'. You ain't ready for nuthin' more. And I don't know if I am either. So before shit gets too hectic, it's best if we squash this."

"Yo, it's best for who?"

The doorbell rings again. This time whoeva's ringin' it, keeps pressin' down on my shit like they fuckin' crazy. I glance ova at the clock on the time. 7:41 P.M. I suck my teeth, pissed. *What da fuck! Who da fuck is comin' here unannounced—and fuckin' uninvited!* I think gettin' up from the kitchen table.

"For both of us."

"Oh, so basically you punkin' out on me, right? You not even gonna take a chance on a muhfucka, right?"

I roll my eyes up in my head, makin' my way to the door. "Nigga, you ain't ready to roll da dice wit' a chick like me, aiight? So, let's leave it be. Go get ya gamble on sumwhere else. I told you I ain't beat for da bullshit." I'm so caught up in gettin' ready to bring it to this nigga that I swing open the door wit'out checkin' the peephole.

This muhfucka's leanin' up against my doorframe wit' his cell pressed up to his ear. "And I told you, I ain't tryna let you go that easy. So wrong answer." I don't know if I should be happy to see this nigga or heated that his ass popped up at my spot wit'out permission. He smiles at me, disconnectin' our call. "Yo, you gonna let me in, or what?"

I stare 'im down, slowly shakin' my head. "Nigga, you know you crazy, right?" I step back, openin' the door so he can come inside. He brushes past me. "What are doin' here?"

He lays his phone down on the coffee table. "Well, I figured since I can't get you by phone, and you ain't respondin' to any of my text, I thought I should come by to make sure you aiight."

"Nigga, you can't be poppin' up ova here like you King Ding Dong 'n shit. You real outta pocket now."

He starts removin' his chain and watch, then takes off his AF Ones. "Then I guess I might as well get outta these clothes, too." He pulls off his Ed Hardy tee shirt, then his wife beater.

I stare at 'im. "What da fuck is you doin'?"

"What it look like? You said I'm outta pocket, so now I'm 'bout to be outta my clothes. I'm strippin' butt-ass naked and I ain't leavin' this muhfucka 'til we air shit out; real talk." He unbuckles his belt, unsnaps his jeans, then pulls 'em off.

I fold my arms, starin' at 'im standin' here bare-chested and in his Polo boxers. *This muthafucka is too fuckin' extra.* "Nigga, you need to put ya shit back on."

He steps outta his drawers. Then has the muthfuckin' audacity to throw 'em at me. "Whatchu gonna do, throw a muhfucka out?"

I try not to glance down at his shiny black dick. Try to act like a bitch ain't tryna slurp his chocolate ass up. He licks his lips. "Muhfucka, I ain't playin' wit' you." *Bitch, but you know ya horny ass want this muhfucka playin' wit' you. So shut ya ho-ass up 'n get wit' da damn program.*

He walks up on me. "Yo, some real shit. You gotta muhfucka feelin' 'n actin' like a real bitch right'a 'bout now." He pulls me into 'im, and kisses me on the forehead, then on the tip of my nose. "You wanna know the one thing that has always annoyed da shit outta me?"

This muhfucka smells so damn good. My pussy lips 'n clit are startin' to swell. I look up at 'im. "What's that?"

"A whinin', needy-ass bitch. And here you gotta muhfucka doin' da same shit, yo."

I smirk. "Is that what I'm doin'?"

He looks me in the eyes. "I don't know what da fuck it is 'bout you. I ain't never been a sucka for good pussy. But you got a nigga's head all fucked up, yo; true story. I keep you on da brain, heavy." I wanna tell 'im that the shit's mutual, but I don't. Pride won't let me. He kisses me on the lips. "I dogged a lotta bitches 'cause they let me, Kat. Not 'cause I was lyin' to 'em or misleadin' 'em. I always kept shit a hunnid. I would tell 'em from da rip what it was. That a muhfucka wasn't lookin' for love; that a muhfucka wasn't beat for no extras other than good pussy, throat 'n ass. And if they caught feelin's then that shit was on them. Not me." He strokes the side of my face. "And a muhfucka knows I hurt a few—hell, a lot—of 'em real bad, but they opened da door to that shit, feel me?"

I nod my head, knowin'ly. His hands travel up and down my back. His dick is already brick and I'm tryin' my damndest to act like I don't peep this big-ass stick gaugin' me. I try to step outta his embrace, but he doesn't let me. And my achin' pussy won't, eitha.

"Nah, stand here and let a muhfucka hold you, and finish tellin' you this shit. "Wit' da exception of maybe two or three, I had no respect for none'a them bitches, Kat. And that's on e'erything. I would tell 'em all, 'fuck wit' a nigga like me at ya own risk'. I'd warn 'em to not come at me lookin' for love 'cause a muhfucka wasn't givin' none of da shit out. And when they didn't stick to da script, I'd dismiss 'em from their dick wettin' duties. Now here I am, and you hittin' me with da exact same shit I used to tell e'very broad who was tryna bag me." He shakes his head, smilin'.

"What, why you grinnin'?"

"It's funny how shit turns out, that's all. I was really feelin' some kinda way when you wasn't pickin' up my calls or respondin' to my text, but it's da same shit I used to do to chicks who were startin' to get nutty on me. Then when they'd finally get at me whinin' 'bout why I didn't hit 'em back, I'd tell 'em if a muhfucka doesn't get back at 'em, then it meant a muhfucka ain't interested. I guess I should start listenin' to my own shit."

Mmmph, maybe you should. I shift my weight from one foot to the otha. "Look, muhfucka, if you stayin', we need to sit da fuck down sumwhere." He takes me by the hand, pullin' me to the sofa. "Uhhh, nigga, I *know* you ain't gonna plop ya bare ass down on my sofa."

"Nah, yo. C'mon wit' that. I'ma put my jeans back on."

"Mmmph. I don't know why you took them shits off in da first place." I watch 'im slip back into his pants. He leaves 'em unfastened, sittin' next to me.

He takes my hand back into his, then brings it up to his lips and kisses it. "Kat, real shit, you know more 'bout me than anyone else besides my moms. Them bitches I was out there fuckin' were nuthin' more than a buncha pussy attached to low-self esteem, a ton of insecurities and mad loneliness. What da fuck I want wit' that shit?"

I shrug. "I don't know, you tell me."

"Like I said, I didn't respect 'em, Kat. And da fucked up thing is most of 'em didn't respect themselves. A muhfucka like me ain't never been da type'a cat to reassure some emotionally bankrupt ho 'bout shit she should already know." He pauses, shakin' his head. Then starts laughin'. "Yo, my moms told *me* I had betta proceed wit' caution, fuckin' wit' you. She said you da kinda chick that would fuck a nigga up for tryna play 'er. And she didn't wanna have'ta bury my ass. Yo, I couldn't believe she told me that shit. Then she told me to leave you alone unless I was serious."

"Well, she's right," I say, raisin' a brow. "And you might wanna take heed, nigga."

"Yo, and that's da shit that's funny 'cause I know this. And a muhfucka still wanna rock wit' you. I know ya fine-ass is crazy. But I also know that underneath all that tough shit, is a woman wit' a heart full of love. A woman who wants a muhfucka she can be real wit', who she can chill wit' and be in love wit'. A woman who wants a muhfucka she can count on; a muhfucka who can hold shit down."

I shift in my seat. Let go of his hand. "You don't know that."

"Yeah, aiight, Kat. Keep frontin'. I see it in ya eyes. You scared."

"Nigga, I ain't scared of shit," I lie.

"Well, I am. Look. I'ma do shit that ain't always gonna be right. But if you worried 'bout a muhfucka creepin' on you, don't be. That's not what I do."

"Nigga, you ain't neva been in a relationship, so you don't know what you will or won't do."

"True. Da only thing I ever had on my mind was pussy and brain. 'Til now. On some real shit, this is da first time in my life where a muhfucka is thinkin' 'bout da future. This ain't me, ma."

I squint at 'im. "What ain't you?"

He opens his arms. "This. Sittin' here, feelin' what I feel. I ain't never felt 'bout no female da way I feel 'bout you, yo. And I damn sure wasn't tryna have any of 'em meet my moms or be all up in my personal space. For me to bring you to my crib; let you know how a muhfucka's livin' is major. So I know I'm not 'bout to fuck up da chance to make this work."

*Yeah, yeah, yeah...womp, womp, womp...*a bitch ain't tryna hear all this shit. This muhfucka has me all off my square. Gotta bitch feelin'...unsure. Then this nigga sittin' here barefoot and bare-chested is a fuckin' distraction. A bitch can't think straight. If I was still pumpin' heat in muhfuckas' skulls, I wouldn't be all twisted up. But a bitch wit' a horny, wet pussy ain't always gonna think straight, like right now. I'm ready to Amtrak this nigga and ride the tracks off'a his dick.

I stare at his chest, then lean ova and lick his nipple. He puts his head back. My mouth covers it and I lightly suck it, 'til he lets out a moan. I grab at his crotch, massage his dick ova his jeans 'til it starts to get long 'n thick.

"Right now, all I care 'bout you makin' work is this dick."

He opens and shuts his legs. The lump in his pants swells and stretches. "Damn, you gotta nigga's head spinnin', Kat."

Don't let me have'ta put a bullet in it.

I glance up at 'im. Look 'im in his eyes. "You want some'a this juicy pussy, muhfucka?"

"Hell, yeah. But I wanna finish talkin', first."

"Listen, fuck talkin'. We can finish all this chit chat. But, for right now, we need to take it to da sheets. A bitch's pussy needs some tongue 'n dick action. Fuck this pussy, then we can get back to me dismissin' ya ass."

I stand up. "Yo, fuck that. I ain't lettin' you dismiss shit. So we need'a finish talkin' this shit out, first."

I tilt my head. "Nigga, you betta get ya ass up and take care of this pussy. Fuck all that 'xtra shit you talkin, or get put da fuck out."

He grins, jumpin' up like his ass caught fire. "Yeah, I thought so."

I turn to spin-off on 'im, but he pulls me by the arm, spinnin' me into 'im, then scoopin' me up in his arms. I quickly throw my arms 'round his neck, holdin' on tight.

"Nigga, you crazy. Put me down 'fore you drop me," I say, tryin' not to laugh. But a bitch is lookin' forward to bein' dropped down on this muhfucka's dick.

"Yo, I got you, baby," he says, takin' the stairs two at a time. "I can't wait to get lost up in them walls. Daddy wanna long stroke you to sleep, ma."

"Yeah, right, muhfucka. We'll see. I bet this pussy'll milk ya ass to sleep first."

He laughs, pushin' open the bedroom door. He lays me on the bed. "That's all good. I gotta lotta nut, baby, so it is what it is. We can go round for round up in this muhfucka. Yo, I don't give a fuck what you say. I know you diggin' me. And I'ma keep pressin' ya fine-ass 'til you admit it."

I suck my teeth, untyin' my robe, then layin' back on the bed. I bend my legs all the way back. "Nigga, da only thing I'ma admit to is wantin' ya tongue on my clit."

"Shiiiit, you ain't said nuthin' but a word, baby. A muhfucka's face loves bein' pressed up in between them highs."

"Then clock in, nigga, and get ta work."

He kisses all ova the front of my pussy, then slowly licks the right side of my lips, then the left side. He flicks my clit wit' his tongue, then dips his tongue in my slit.

I arch my back. Palm both sides of his head. "Oooooh, yes… ohhhhh, yessss, muhfucka…mmmm…eat that pussy, nigga…"

On some real shit a bitch can see why this muhfucka has a buncha hoes ready to jump offa bridges 'n shit ova 'im. This nigga's tongue work is siiiick. *Yeah, muhfucka*, I think, moanin', *it ain't no use in denyin' it. You gotta bitch diggin' ya no-good ass, hard!*

TWO HOURS LATER, WE'RE LAYIN' IN BED. ALEX IS ON HIS BACK, lightly snorin'. I am on my side, propped up on my forearm, gazin' at 'im in the dark. *Yeah, muhfucka, pussy heat done knocked ya ass out.* I lift up the sheet and stare at his nakedness. The muhfucka has a body sculpted to perfection. Smooth chocolate wrapped 'round neva-endin' muscles. *This shit makes no damn sense*, I think as I lick my lips. *A muhfucka bein' this damn fine.*

Yeah, bitch, and no damn good. Leave this nigga alone.

But he sounds like he's really tryna make it pop with a bitch.

Ho, you know this nigga ain't doin' nuthin' but spittin' game at you.

Yeah, but muhfuckas can change, too. The nigga done introduced me to his moms, and took me to his crib. Sumthin' he's neva done wit' any otha bitch.

Ho, that shit don't mean nuthin'.

But he seems like he's kickin' truths; like da nigga's really feelin' me.

Bitch, don't fall for the okey-doke. Delete his ass.

He stirs in his sleep, then reaches ova and pulls me into his arms. I lay my head on his chest, close my eyes and listen to the nigga's heartbeat 'til I drift off to sleep.

CHAPTER TWENTY-EIGHT

Mad hot...'bout to bring da heat...gotta bitch spittin'fire...
can't change what a muhfucka's done...fuckin' wit' a buncha
birds...but a bitch bringin' drama to my door...I ain't da
one...I guess I'ma haveta bring it to this whore...

The next mornin', this muhfucka starts beatin' a bitch in the head again, tryna convince me to give 'im a try. Truth is, the minute he pulled me into his arms last night, my mind was already made up. Of course, I don't tell 'im this. I decide to let the nigga sweat. Besides, I still need'a be sure 'bout it.

"Yo, you aiight?" he asks, circlin' my nipple wit' the tip of his finga. I nod, closin' my eyes. His finga feels good teasin' my nipple. He stops, leans in, then wets it wit' his tongue. I moan as grabs my otha titty and starts squeezin'. He pinches my nipple.

"Ooooh..."

His hand slowly roams down my stomach 'til his fingas find my clit. He presses, starts massagin' it.

"Aaaaah..."

"You like that?" He slips two fingas in my pussy, strokes my clit wit' his thumb.

My pussy grabs his fingas. He finga fucks me knuckles deep,

pushin' his two long, thick fingas in 'n out. The nigga's workin' my nipple wit' his mouth and my box wit' his fingas. I spread my legs, bend at the knees. Let out another moan.

"I want some breakfast," he says, lookin' up at me.

Whaaat? Is this nigga serious? I know he don't think I'ma be flippin' up no muthafuckin' waffles 'n shit up in here. I snap my eyes open.

He's grinnin' at me. "You ready to feed Daddy?"

"You ain't my daddy, nigga. And I ain't feedin' you." He speeds up his finga work, cups his two fingas upward inside'a me.

I moan again.

"Yeah, you nuttin' on Daddy's fingers. Daaaamn, baby, ya shit's so fuckin' wet…you ready to feed me?"

He shifts his body, scoots down toward the foot of the bed. It dawns on me the muhfucka is talkin' 'bout eatin' up this pussy. *Meep, meep, follow da script, ho*, I think, holdin' back a chuckle. I smile. "Yeah, nigga…gobble up this pussy…"

He gets between my legs, kisses the center of my pussy, then pulls my lips apart and slowly starts lickin' up 'n down and all 'round 'em. He sticks his tongue up under my clit, rapidly flickin' it. I moan, restin' my legs over his shoulder. He pushes 'em all the way back wit' his hands, buries his face deeper between my thighs.

"Yeah, baby, make that pussy skeet…bust ya nut all over my tongue…give ya Daddy that sweet cream…" The nigga wraps his whole mouth ''round my pussy and sucks 'n slurps. Five minutes later, a bitch is shakin' and squirtin' a nut into his mouth and onto his tongue. He swallows, licks up the rest of my juices, then says, "Gotdaaaamn, you gotta sweet, creamy pussy."

I can't front. The muhfucka gotta bitch lightheaded and seein' stars 'n shit. I lay still for a minute to catch my breath and get my mind right. After that nut, I really wanna blaze, but a bitch's tryna keep it cute 'til I get custody of the baby. On some real shit, I'm glad Alex doesn't say nuthin' 'bout sparkin' up 'cause I don't know how cute a kush-lovin' bitch like me could keep it.

He strokes his dick, pullin' in his bottom lip. "Yo, feel like suckin' some dick?" Little does the nigga know, I had already planned on spinnin' his top lovely. Show the nigga how a real bitch does it. I lean ova and stick my tongue out, lettin' 'im brush the head of his dick up against it as he jacks off.

I shift my body. Press my lips to the tip of his dick and start plantin' soft, wet kisses all over it. I swirl my tongue 'round the head, then wrap my mouth 'round it. The nigga tells me he gotta thing for havin' his balls grabbed, then yanked—well, okay, lightly pulled is what he says—while a bitch is spinnin' his top.

"If it's done right, it'll have a muhfucka shoot rockets in the air, word up...yank them shits for me...you got my muhfuckin' dick achin'...oooh, shit...a muhfucka's ready nut..."

"That's what you want, muhfucka? You wanna feel these pretty-ass lips wrapped 'round ya dick while I work them balls?"

"Straight up, baby."

"Stop callin' me that, nigga."

"Yo, c'mon, you killin' da mood." He cups his balls. "You know I'ma keep callin' you the shit, so chill."

"Whateva, muhfucka."

"C'mon, stop fuckin' 'round, Kat...yank on these muhfuckas and let me feel ya mouth heat up on this dick, baby."

Let me stop fuckin' wit' this nigga, I think, grinnin'. I slowly stroke the lower part of his shaft. "Yeah, just like that. Oh, fuck...keep doin' that shit, baby."

"Mmm," I moan, lookin' up at him, speed jackin' his dick while suckin' and lickin' his balls.

"Aaaah, fuck..."

"I want that nut, muhfucka. You gonna give me that nut?"

"Yeah, baby…Daddy 'bout to let you get that nut. What you gonna do wit' it?"

Daddy? This muhfucka is so ova himself. I let the shit go, keep milkin' the nigga's dick. "I'm gonna use it as a face moisturizer… it's good for da skin."

He chuckles. "Damn, baby…oh, shit…you nasty, you know that, right?"

I nod my head, spittin' on his dick. "Yeah, muhfucka, you like it when a bitch gives it to you nasty." I flick the head of it wit' my tongue, then plant soft kisses all over it. I slather it wit' my spit. Suck the shit real nasty like. Get that thick, juicy cock nice and wet and shiny.

"You gonna haveta work for that load, baby," he tells me, holdin' the back of my head.

I slowly slurp 'im, then pick up the pace, decidin' to stop fuckin' 'round and show this muhfucka how'a real bitch handles a big-ass dick. I swallow his dick down one inch at'a time, slowly ease 'im down into my throat. When the head hits the back'a my throat, I stop, take a deep breath, ease up on the dick a bit, then gulp and push my face up against the base of his dick.

"Ohhhh, shiiiiit, baby…aaaah…that's wassup…you 'bout to make me spit…"

I pull his dick from outta my throat, then spit on it and start jackin' him off. "Give me that milk, muhfucka."

I start deep throating him again. Take him deep into my neck for ten minutes, nonstop. A bitch's in neck 'n gulp mode, tryna spin this nigga's top to the roof. I glance up every so often, watchin' him fluctuate from moanin' and pantin' to tossin' his head back and groanin' to bitin' down on his bottom lip to peerin' down at me amazed at how his whole dick disappears down in my throat.

He reaches 'round wit' his free hand and starts playin' wit' my pussy 'til it starts to drip down his hand. I slurp and moan and wiggle my fluffy ass to match the thrust of his fingas movin' in and outta my fat, tight pussy. He palms the back of my head like a basketball and bounces it up and down on his dick. I suck the shit harder. I guess the nigga thought a bitch was gonna start gaggin'. Not. My eyes start to bulge and get watery, but I keep the pace, speed slurpin' the dick nonstop. *I'm that bitch, muhfucka; thought you knew*, I think, squeezin' 'n yankin' his balls.

"Oh, yes…aaaah, fuck…ohmigod…ohmigod…aaah, shit…you 'bout to make me spit, baby….here it comes…uhhhh…aaaaaah… aaaaah…fuuuuuuuuuk…"

Forty minutes later, I'm at the bathroom sink brushin' my teeth while Alex takes a shower. I peep 'im through the glass shower doors.

"You sure you don't wanna come in?" he asks, turnin' to give me a full view of his soapy body. Soap suds cova his dick and balls.

I laugh, sittin' up on the sink counter. "Nigga, ya greedy ass ain't gettin' no more of this pussy." He starts strokin' his dick. "And you ain't gonna be standin' there wastin' my water playin' wit' ya dick, eitha."

He laughs wit' me. "Yo, why you always tryna put a muhfucka out?"

"'Cause I don't want ya ass gettin' all comfortable 'n shit."

He opens the glass door, then steps out. Beads of water roll down his chest. The mouth of my pussy opens 'n closes. *Bitch, you know you wanna 'notha round of that cock.* I watch 'im as he dries off, then wraps the towel 'round his body.

"Too late. I already am."

"Well, that's too bad."

He walks up on me, leans in and kisses me on the lips. "Yo, I want you to spend da weekend wit' me down at my crib."

I grin. "I ain't stayin' no whole weekend wit' you so you can try runnin' ya dick up in me da whole time. I don't think so. I'll stay da night."

"Nah, I want you"—he kisses me again—"to myself da whole"—more kisses—"weekend." He slips his tongue in my mouth. *Ho, get this nigga up outta here 'fore you end up fuckin' 'im again.*

"I'll think 'bout it," I tell 'im, jumpin' off'a the counter, then poppin' my hips back into the bedroom. He follows behind me, grabbin' at my ass. "Nigga, will you stop."

"Daaaaamn, you gotta bangin'-booty. All fat 'n juicy and whatnot; I want sum'a that."

I snap my neck ova at 'im. "Nigga, puhleeze. You jokin', right?"

"Nah, I'm dead-ass. I been meanin' to ask you when you gonna let me hit that."

I walk into my walk-in, then open up my trunk. "So, let me get this straight. A muhfucka who ain't my man and ain't put no ring on it thinks a bitch should let 'im run his dick all up in 'er ass, right?"

"Baby, I'm tryna be ya man, but you keep frontin'."

I keep searchin' for what I'm lookin' for. "Yeah, well, I want da ring muhfucka."

He laughs. "How 'bout you let me test run it, first. Then we can talk 'bout it."

When I find what I need, I walk back out into the bedroom. "Well, I tell you what. Since you ain't tryna put no ring on it, how 'bout you let a bitch run this"—I swing a twelve-inch dildo at 'im—"up in you, then you tell me if you still wanna hit this ass."

He laughs. "Hahahaha; you got jokes, right?"

I smirk. "Nah, nigga. I'm dead-ass. Let me fuck ya asshole out da frame wit' my lil' friend, then we can talk 'bout you gettin' up in this juicy ass."

He shakes his head, slippin' on his underwear. "Whatever, yo. You can cancel that shit. It ain't happenin'."

I shrug, tossin' the dildo onto the bed. "Oh well, then I guess you don't get none'a this."

He slips on his jeans. "Yeah, aiight. I need to leave a change of clothes here."

I tilt my head and look at his ass like he's crazy. "Oh no da hell you don't. You ain't leavin' shit up in here. When you go, e'erything else goes, includin' that toothbrush I gave you."

I walk outta the room and head downstairs. He follows me.

"Yo, you real extra; you know that, right?"

"I know it's time for you to go. I got things to do."

"Like what?"

I shoot 'im a look ova my shoulder, suckin' my teeth. "Nigga, like none'a damn business." I watch 'im pull out his phone, then turn it on. I decide to ask 'im why e'erytime he's wit' me he turns the shit off. He tells me e'erything shuts down when he's wit' me 'cause he ain't tryna have a buncha distractions. That there's no one else he needs to talk to. "Hmmmm," is the only thing I say.

"What, you think I'm bullshittin'?"

I eye 'im, puttin' a hand on my hip. "I think it's time for you to be gone."

He walks up on me. "Yo, check this shit out. You da the first chick I ever turned my phone off for. I don't even check da shit when I'm wit' you. No other broad ever got that. So all that 'hmmm'-in' you doin', save it." He eyes me. "Stop tryna look for shit. I'm keepin' e'erything on board wit' you."

"Nigga, I ain't lookin' for shit. Whateva you do is what you do."

He leans down and kisses me. The muhfucka's lips are soft 'n juicy. "Yo, I'ma call you later, aiight."

"If you want," I say nonchalantly, walkin' ova to the door.

"Yo, Kat, real shit…stop fuckin' frontin' on a muhfucka. You know you feelin' me, so let's see if we can make this shit pop."

"You right. But know this. I'm not da kinda bitch who lives wit' regrets, so, do not have me regret fuckin' wit' you."

He grins. "Yeaah, baaaaby; that's what I'm talkin' 'bout."

He tries to kiss me again, but I push 'im back wit' my hand. "Whoa, slow down, Playboy. Let me give you da ground rules. You not my man. We chillin' to see what kicks off. I tilt my head. "We clear."

"Yo, fuck outta here wit' all that 'you not my man' shit."

"Aiiight, muhfucka. Be stupid if you want. You get three strikes; nuthin' more, nuthin' less. You fuck me ova, you get fucked up."

"Whatever, yo. Am I gonna be ya man or not?"

"Like I said, three strikes, muhfucka."

"I ain't strikin' out, shit. So go 'head wit' that. Now stop all ya bullshittin' and give ya man a kiss."

Ohmigod, this muhfucka is a piece'a work, I think, lookin' up at 'im, smirkin'. I keep my mouth shut. Let 'im press his lips up to mine. We kiss for a few minutes wit' this nasty nigga tryna play wit' my clit and run his fingas up in my pussy. But I shut it down, openin' the front door. My eyes 'n mouth pop open.

His whip is kissin' the ground; somebody done slayed all four of the nigga's tires. He races out the door, snappin'. "What da Fuck?! Who da fuck got at me like this?"

The bitch who did 'im in wrote PUSSY-ASS NIGGA in big red letters across his windshield. And YOU AIN'T SHIT is written on the back window. The nigga looks wrecked.

I fold my arms, leanin' up against the doorframe wit' my lips twisted, watchin' 'im walk 'round his whip, lookin' like he's ready to flip his lid. I don't say shit. Shit, ain't shit to say. A bitch's mind is already made up. *Nigga, strike one!*

CHAPTER TWENTY-NINE

Decisions, decisions, decisions…what'a bitch gonna do?…Tell da nigga it's a wrap…that a bitch is thru…dead it 'fore he gotta get jacked 'n slapped…nigga poppin' sum good shit, though…still…a bitch ain't tryna be played like she type-slow…

"Yo, why you actin' all funny 'n shit? You actin' like I did some shit to you. What's good, yo?" Alex asks two days after that shit went down wit' his whip. Today's the first time I'm fuckin' wit' 'im since the shit happened. And the nigga sound mad tight, too.

"Muhfucka, I'm still tryna figure out why ya shit got housed on my muthafuckin' property and what bitch you done pissed off and got tailin' ya ass to my muthafuckin' spot. That shit ain't it, nigga."

"Yo, you act like I know who da fuck did it. I ain't fuckin' wit' no one. I told you. I cut all them birds off a minute ago; true story."

"Well, maybe you did; maybe you didn't. I don't know what da fuck you've done. But I do know this: whoeva da fuck it is, the bitch fucked up, bringin' that shit here. So 'til you find out who da fuck it is, ya black ass ain't comin' here."

"Aiight, cool. Then you can come down and chill at my spot."

I frown. "Nigga, you done got the shit twisted. I ain't 'bout to be ridin' up 'n down da parkway for a muhfucka who gotta buncha shit wit' 'im. You need ta handle them bitches you been fuckin' first."

"Yo, stop sayin' that shit. I told you, I ain't fuckin' no one. Damn."

"Then one'a them needy bitches ain't tryna let go. Either way, I ain't feelin' da shit; especially since you done brought the shit up to my doorstep."

"Yo, I ain't bring it to ya door."

"Nigga, puhleeze. Obviously da bitch followed you here. So, as far as I'm concerned, *you* brought da shit here. Say what da fuck you want."

"Yo, you actin' like I got control over what da fuck some nutty-ass bitch does. What you want me to do?"

"Muhfucka, you know what, don't do shit. Just keep on doin' what you do, but leave me outta it. A bitch got more pressin' things to deal wit' than to be wrapped up in a muhfucka wit' a buncha drama."

He lowers his voice. "Yo, c'mon wit' that bullshit. I ain't beat for da drama, either."

I huff. "Nigga, I can't tell."

"Yo, I'm tellin' you."

"Yeah, and what you tellin' me don't mean shit. All of a sudden out da blue ya shit sittin' on da ground and all tatted up wit' paint. Nigga, puhleeze. That's the handiwork of some ho you done pissed off. You need'a handle that. And I ain't fuckin' wit' you 'til you do."

"I ain't tryna hear that shit, yo."

"Well, too bad. It is what it is. So get ova it."

"Nah, fuck that. I don't have nuthin' to hide from you. I gave you all my passwords and shit, so you can see for ya'self. What da fuck I gotta lie for? Why da hell would a muhfucka give you access to all of his shit if da nigga wasn't tryna be on the up 'n up wit' you? C'mon, Kat, give a muhfucka some credit, damn, yo. Have you checked the shit?"

Mmmm, da nigga gotta point. Still..."Yeah, I checked da shit once," I admit, steppin' outta my panties, then walkin' into the bathroom. I turn the shower on. The same day he gave me the shit I went upstairs and ran all through his shit. Read his messages, emails and the shit on his Blackplanet guestbook. The nigga has thousands of naked-ass hoes up on his shit, throwin' the pussy at 'im. It was mad extra. I even read notes and emails he sent. But, nuthin' really popped out to make me think the nigga was tryna be on some playground shit.

"And?"

"And, there wasn't shit to see."

"Aiight, then. That should tell you sumthin'."

"Nigga, that don't tell me shit. All it says is that day there wasn't shit to see—*that* time. That doesn't mean that next week or week after that that some extra shit ain't gonna pop off."

"Yo, then keep checkin' da shit anytime you want."

"Nigga, my name ain't Inspector Gadget. I ain't da kinda bitch whose gonna keep investigatin' shit. Only dumb-ass, dick-whipped bitches do that stupid bullshit. I'm good."

Me and this nigga go back 'n forth for anotha ten minutes wit' 'im tryna convince me that ain't shit extra goin' on on his end. That he's kept it funky wit' me from the rip. I wanna believe the nigga, but I know how crafty and slick muhfuckas can be. I start zonin' out on the nigga 'cause the shit's startin' to cramp my asshole. "Look, I ain't beat for this convo. So you either change it, or hang up," I tell 'em, puttin' the phone on speaker. I step into the shower.

"Yo, what…you in da shower?"

"Yeah."

"Oh, word? What you gettin' ready to get into?" I tell 'im I got business to handle. The fact that I got these child welfare hoes comin' up to my spot to complete their background investigation ain't really none'a his concern. Nor is tellin' 'im that I'm goin' up to the hospital to sit wit' a baby that I'ma be raisin'. I get knots in my stomach just thinkin' 'bout it. If I decide to keep this nigga in my space, then I'll eventually tell 'im what's really good. I know it's not sumthin' I'ma be able to keep from 'im. But for now, he only needs to know the basics. Not much. Shit, takin' on a baby is gonna be mad responsibility. Shit, I don't even know if I'ma be beat for. So the last thing I need is to be fuckin' wit' a nigga who's gonna come wit' a buncha distractions. "What time you gonna be done?" I tell 'im not 'til late. Tell 'im I might be stayin' in Brooklyn. "Wit' who?"

I suck my teeth. "Damn, nigga, wit' Chanel."

"Yeah, aiight, yo." The nigga gets quiet. "Dig, if you ain't beat to fuck wit' a nigga, let me know so I can fall back before a muh-fucka's head gets all fucked up."

"Nigga, puhleeze. Ya head's already fucked up. You know you ain't ready to let go'a this pussy heat."

"Whatever, yo. Who else you lettin' hit that?"

I shake my head, steppin' outta the shower. "No one at da moment. But, trust. That can change at any time. Right now a bitch is chillin'."

"Yeah, aiight. Let me find out ya biscuit head givin' out Daddy's goods."

I laugh. "Ohhhhhhhmigod, you so fuckin' ova ya'self."

"And I'm tryna be all over you, but you wanna be on some ole other shit."

I walk into my closet, pullin' out a red long-sleeve Gucci tee and a pair of pencil jeans. "Mmmph; if you say so." I decide to pick the nigga's brain to see how he feels 'bout kids. "Would you eva deal wit' a chick wit' kids?"

"I don't know. I've fucked chicks wit' kids, but I ain't neva wanna wife any of 'em. I'm not sure if I would wanna be dealin' wit' a chick wit' 'em on some exclusive shit unless she doesn't have a buncha baby daddy issues. A muhfucka ain't beat for that. Why, you got some kids you ain't tellin' me 'bout?"

"Maybe; maybe not."

"Yeah, aiight."

"Well, what if I did?"

"Well, *hypothetically*, if you did. How many you talkin' 'bout? One, two?"

"One," I tell 'im, slippin' a pair of socks on my feet. He tells me one is cool. But since it's me, two is aiight, too. Then he tells me as fine as I am I could have twenty and he'd still wanna rock wit' me on some solo-type shit as long as my pussy stayed right.

"Then again, that shit could be wide as an ocean and I'd still wanna wife you. You'd just have'ta let me beat that asshole up e'ery night."

I laugh. "Nigga, you a real fool, you know that, right? You know damn well you ain't runnin' that big ass dick in my ass e'ery damn night."

"Then we'll rotate that shit," he says, laughin' wit' me. "One night in ya throat, the next night in ya ass."

My doorbell rings. *It's showtime*, I think, peekin' outta the bedroom window. I peep the state car in the driveway. *Let's get this shit ova wit'*. "Yeah, whateva. Listen, I gotta go. Call me lata."

"I got you, baby."

I suck my teeth. "Muhfucka, what I tell you 'bout callin' me that?"

"Yo, chill out wit' that dumb shit. I call you what I want. You know you Daddy's baby."

"Nigga, suck my ass and daddy on this," I say, disconnectin' the call and headin' down the stairs to greet these state hoes.

Alex sends me a text: *Yo, u got my dik hard wit' that shit.*

I text back: *Whateva.*

I hope these bitches don't say nuthin' slick and have me flippin' da fuck out. I swing the front door open, pastin' a phony-ass smile up on my grill. "Hi, glad you made it. Come on in."

CHAPTER THIRTY

Shoot 'em up...bang-bang...Glock cocked...ready to pop... muhfucka thought he could run 'n hide...nigga done ran outta time...thought he was gonna get away way wit' da crime... ain't got no clout...justice 'bout to be dished out...gonna show 'im what revenge's 'bout...bum-ass nigga...and it's a ruthless bitch who's 'bout ta pull da trigga....

"Yo, pretty baby, wasssup? We found da muhfucka you were lookin' for. Holla back. Oh, yeah, and a muhfucka's still waitin' for you to come through wit' anotha pair of them panties. A muhfucka's tryna get his sniff on. Take care of that, pronto." He laughs into the phone. I delete the shit, rollin' my eyes. *This fat muhfucka*, I think, hittin' 'im back.

"Yo, you get my message?"

I suck my teeth. "Nigga, why else would I be callin' ya black ass? Geesh, you dumber than you look."

"Yeah, aiiight. Keep talkin'shit, and get ya fronts knocked, Kat."

"Cash, listen carefully..." I pause. Wait 'til it gets quiet on the otha end. "You listenin'?"

"Yeah, wassup?"

"Nigga, kiss my ass. That's wassup. Now, what you got for me?"

He laughs. "Yo, ma, you funny as fuck. You betta be glad a muhfucka fucks wit' you."

"Yeah, yeah, yeah. Now let's cut da shit. Where's this bum-ass nigga at?"

"The muhfucka's been hidin' out down south in some small-ass country town in North Carolina called Como."

What da fuck kinda place is that, I think, twistin' my lips up. *Do they even gotta airport?* "Where?" he repeats the name. "Mmmph. Corny-ass nigga had to run off to some backward-ass part'a the country. Do you know how he's livin'? Is he down there wit' someone?"

"Yeah, he's there wit' some chick stayin' up in one'a them trailer homes."

Probably some country-coon trash he done bagged on da run. Now I gotta think how I'ma get at this nigga wit'out drawin' heat to myself. "Listen. I need'a fava."

"I got you, wassup up?" I tell 'im I need 'im to handle the arrangements. Set up the hotel shit and have my items I need to dust this nigga's top sent down like old times. I tell 'im I need'a report of how the nigga moves, a list of his comin's and goin's.

"You got that. You need anything else? A disposal crew?"

A part of me wants the nigga to be found wit' his eyes rolled back up in his head and his brains splattered. Then anotha part wants it to look like the nigga done got ghost all together. I decide I want the nigga to disappear, for good.

"Aiight, bet. I'll have a crew on standby. When you tryna get it in?"

Shit, I gotta go up to da hospital. And I got these ACS and court bitches I gotta deal wit'. I tell 'im to give me a few days to handle some things, then disconnect.

I stare at myself in the mirror hangin' on the wall in my foyer.

"Bitch, after you put a bullet in this nigga's head, this gotta be da last time you pull da trigga on another muhfucka." *Ho, you gotta get ya mind right, quick. There's a baby you gotta start thinkin' 'bout.*

E'vry since his birth, he's been on my brain, heavy. Sittin' up at the hospital e'ery day, watchin' 'im cling on to life, fightin' to get stronger, has been wrackin' my nerves. It hurts me. A bitch's heart fills wit' guilt e'erytime I look at 'im. I am so fuckin' scared, but I gotta do right by 'im. I gotta try to give 'im what Juanita was neva able to give to me—*love*. Doin' that nigga has to be it for me.

I take a deep breath, glancin' at my watch. It's eleven o'clock. I grab my keys and pink Gucci clutch bag, then race out the door to make my way to the Family Courthouse in Brooklyn. I am finally gonna handle the paperwork to get legal custody and guardianship of Juanita's baby, and make this shit legit.

When I'm done filin' all the necessary paperwork, I drive ova to the hospital to see the baby. The last few days I've been tryna come up wit' a name for 'im. I wanna give 'im a name otha muhfuckas ain't pushin' heavy. For some reason, the names that I'm really diggin' are Zion and Zaire.

I take the elevator up to the neo-natal unit. As I'm walkin' down the hall, a bitch's 'tude shoots from zero to a hunnid when I see Patrice's ho-ass standin' at the window lookin' into the unit, wipin' tears. I wanna snap and tell the bitch to bounce, but I decide to let shit play out. I swallow my 'tude, walkin' up on 'er.

She snaps 'er neck in my direction. "Before you stop poppin' shit, I ain't here to beef wit' you," she warns, turnin' 'er attention back to the baby. "I'm here to see my lil' nephew, then I'm out."

"Good," I say, shiftin' my handbag from one hand to the otha. "No need for you to linger any longer than you have'ta."

She turns and stares at me. "Kat, answer me this. Why do you have so much hate in you? What happened to us?"

"You fucked my man; that's what happened to us. I trusted you. And you shitted on me."

"Ohmiimuthafuckin'god, let that shit go, Kat. That shit happened years ago. And da nigga's dead. When you gonna get ova it? We done fought ova his ass twice and—"

"No, boo, we didn't fight ova that nigga. We fought ova you tryna play a bitch. Big difference; don't get it twisted."

She shakes her head. "And you let some dick come between us. I can understand if you wanted to be pissed for a few weeks, even a few months, but to be draggin' this shit out for *years*, Kat; that's some real 'xtra shit. That nigga didn't give'a fuck 'bout you, or me. All da nigga saw was some young, hot pussy."

"Well, guess what. Maybe da nigga didn't care 'bout me, but *I* cared 'bout ya trick-ass. I loved you like a fuckin' sista, bitch. And you hurt me."

"I watched my moms bury two of my sistas in da same month, Kat," this bitch says, changin' the subject. "And you didn't even have da decency to show up to ya own moms' funeral. Why?"

I tilt my head. "I had my funeral for that bitch a long time ago, so that shit ya'll had for 'er was only a formality."

She frowns at me. "I feel sorry for you."

"Oh, no, Boo. Don't feel sorry for me. Betta yet, don't feel nuthin' for me. I'm good; trust."

"Okay, if you say so. I know I'm not."

"Well, that sounds personal," I say, surprised that I'm still standin' here entertainin' this ho. After all these years, this is the first time we've talked wit'out the otha snappin' off.

"Life is too fuckin' short for da bullshit," she says, turnin' 'er attention back to the nursery. "In da grand scheme of things, this corny-ass beef you got wit' me is a fuckin' waste of energy. So, trust, sweetie. On e'erything I love, I'm done beefin' wit' you.

Movin' forward I'm not gonna get into it wit' you ova dumb shit. I have a beautiful lil' nephew my sista left behind. You and 'im are da only links I have left to 'er. You wanna stay hurt, stay hurt. You don't wanna have shit to do wit' ya family, then don't. But…"

Okay, now a bitch is ready to bring it to this ho and tell 'er to suck the shit outta my ass 'cause she ain't gonna eva get 'er hands on that baby. But I know a real bitch gotta know when to play it smart. She gotta know when to keep 'er mouth shut and let'a bitch keep flappin' 'er cum trap. And, in listenin' to this ho rattle on, the one thing a bitch is finally certain of is that that baby layin' up in there wit' all them tubes in 'im, ain't goin' no-muth-afuckin-where but wit' me. And if I gotta make sure e'ery last one'a them hoes gets bodied to make that happen, I will.

"…that baby in there is gonna be surrounded by his family. And we will raise 'im and love 'im, no matter what."

Okay, bitch, it's time to spin-off on this ho, I think, glancin' at my watch. *You've heard'a 'nough of this shit.* "Well, listen. You do what-eva you feel you gotta do."

"I plan to," she says, glancin' ova at me.

I smirk. "Bitch, you're delusional. But good luck."

A WEEK LATER, I'VE LANDED AT NORFOLK INTERNATIONAL AIRPORT, and now I'm pickin' up my rental to take the hour-and-a-half drive to Ahoskie, North Carolina. It's where Cash booked my hotel room. It's also a few miles away from the town Como. A bitch is amped to get at this nigga swiftly, then be on the next thing smokin' back to Jersey. But shuttin' his lights is gonna pose a problem since the nigga only leaves his spot at night. So a bitch gotta lay low and work the area for a few days 'til I can run up on 'im. Cash hipped me to these spots called Shot Houses—homes of muhfuckas who sell drinks 'n shit. Where they play music, cards and shoot pool and whatnot.

I get into my rental, pullin' out my Tom-Tom GPS system, typin' in my destination. *Ahoskie? I can only imagine what kinda shit I'ma see when I get there.* I pull outta the airport, and turn onto Azalea Garden, then Military Highway.

My cell rings. It's Chanel.

"What's good, hooker?"

"Shit. A bitch is bored as fuck."

"Poor thing," I say, mergin' onto US 13 South toward I-264 West. Then outta nowhere a bitch has this crazy idea to bring Chanel down here to help me work these country coon-muh-fuckas ova. I quickly shake the shit outta my head. *This ho ain't built for puttin' in this kinda work*, I think, glancin' at my reflection in the rearview mirror. "Sounds like you need some dick?"

She laughs. "Fuck you."

"Where's Divine?"

"He's on his way home."

"Then let that nigga be da one fuckin' *you*. Wit'cha freak-ass."

"Whateva. I'm comin' to Jersey to chill for a few days. You home."

"Sorry, sweetie, I'm outta town."

She sucks 'er teeth. "Figures. When ya ass comin' back?" I tell 'er in a few days. She grunts. "Mmmph, you always dippin' on a bitch."

"Awww, let me find out you feelin' all salty 'n shit," I tease. "You know I love you, Sugah. But get ova ya'self. I need you to do me a fava."

"Wassup?"

I tell 'er I need 'er to go up to the hospital to spend time wit' the baby 'til I get back. I tell 'er I finally came up wit' a name for 'im. "Girl, you know I got you. What you gonna name 'im?" I tell 'er I decided to go wit' Zaire. "Ohhhhkaaaaay now. I like."

"Me too," I say, smilin'.

"So who you outta town wit', Allstar?"

It dawns on me that I haven't heard from the muhfucka in'a couple'a days. I've been so sidetracked wit' my own shit that I hardly noticed 'til now. *Mmmmm, that's strange. Da nigga must be real busy.* "No, I ain't heard from da nigga."

"Reallllllly? Ya'll still cool, right?"

"I guess. Like I said, I ain't heard from 'im."

"Hmmm, da nigga must be preoccupied."

"Whateva. Da nigga ain't my man."

"I feel you, boo. Da only man you gonna need in ya life is Zaire. Fuck'a Allstar or any otha muhfucka."

"And you know this, trick," I say, laughin'. She asks how my visit went wit' them CPS bitches. "You know I kept it real cute wit' them hoes. They gonna do a corny-ass background check on'a bitch, but I ain't sweatin' it."

"I know that's right. Then what?"

Then a bitch gonna eitha sink, or swim, or die muthafuckin' tryin'. I swear I don't wanna be one'a them hoes you read 'bout in the news who tosses 'er baby outta a window, or leaves it locked up in a closet. I start feelin' fucked up knowin' a bitch ain't have a mother to show—or teach—'er how to *be* a mother.

"Then a bitch gonna be sittin' up in somebody's parentin' class," I tell 'er.

"And I'ma be right there wit' ya, boo." I smile. Tell 'er how much I love 'er freak-ass. Tell 'er how much 'er friendship means to me. "Ho, let me find out ya ass gettin' all sappy on a bitch."

I suck my teeth. "Bitch, puhleeze."

"Well, I know ya stank-ass ain't tryna get no pussy. Or are you?"

"Bitch, you must be tryna get ya fronts knocked." She starts laughin'. "Hahahaha hell, tramp. You done said this a few times. So keep shit real. You a twat muncha?" She tells me no. Tells me she's fantasized 'bout it, but hasn't done it—yet. Tells me Divine wants to have a threesome wit' 'er and anotha chick. I frown at the thought of that nigga rabbit-fuckin' two bitches. But, keep my trap shut. A bitch ain't tryna get reeled into any of their sex fantasies, so I cut the shit short. "Mmmph, do you, boo. Look. Let me get up off this line. I'ma hit you up when I touch Jersey." We go back and forth poppin' shit a few more minutes, then disconnect. I decide to hit up Allstar up to see what's good wit' his ass. He answers on the fifth ring.

"Hey wassup?" he says, soundin' all nonchalant 'n shit.

I frown. *Wassup? Is this nigga serious? I ain't heard from this muhfucka in almost four days and 'wassup' is all the muhfucka can say?*

I can't front. A bitch is feelin' some kinda way. I grunt. "Mmmmph. You aiight?"

"Yeah, I'm cool. Kinda goin' through some shit right now, but it's all good."

"Anything you wanna talk 'bout?" I ask, mergin' onto I-664 headin' north.

"Nah, I'm cool; gotta handle a few things."

"Oh, aiight, then. Well, I haven't heard from you in a few days, so I thought I'd check in on you." There's silence. "Hello?"

"Yeah, I'm here," he says, soundin' all down 'n shit. "I 'preciate you checkin' in on me."

"You sure you aiight?"

I sigh. "Yeah. Got some family shit I gotta handle."

Mmmph. Fuck this nigga. You already know what it is. Put da muhfucka on ignore 'n keep it movin'. "Look, go do you. Hit me up when you beat to talk."

"Nah, baby, it's not like that. I'm just really goin' through it right now. But a muhfucka keeps you on da brain real heavy, ma."

Then why da fuck you ain't been callin' me? "Is that so?"

"True story, baby. As soon as I can handle this shit, I'ma make it up to you, aiight?"

"That's on you. Look, let me go. I'm in da middle of some shit myself."

"Oh, word? You home?"

"No, outta town," I tell 'im, mergin' onto US-58. It gets quiet on the otha end. I can tell the muhfucka wants to know more, but I don't give 'im shit 'xtra.

"Yo, all shit real, ma. A muhfucka's been stressin' hard, but I'ma handle it. Then I wanna take ya fine-ass away somewhere, aiight?"

"That's what ya mouth says."

"That's what it is, baby. Give me a minute to tie up this shit. And I'm all yours; real talk."

"Mmmph, we'll see." We talk a few more minutes, then end our call. *Fuck that nigga. He wanna be on some funny-style shit, cool. His dog-ass is probably somewhere laid up wit' some dusty-ass bitch, any-fuckin'-way.* I dismiss the nigga outta mind. *Strike two, muhfucka!*

CHAPTER THIRTY-ONE

Hotter than fiiiyah…da object of a nigga's desires…usin' this pussy for bait…nigga wanna knock it from da back…wanna test out da dick ridin' skills…'bout to have 'im poppin' Viagra like Tic-Tacs…nigga betta run 'fore it's too late…dumb muhfucka 'bout to get had by a bitch who kills…

After two muthafuckin' days stuck down in this dusty-ass town, my mark has finally come out to play. My pussy snaps, 'crackles 'n pops at knowin' this muhfucka is finally gonna get it to the dome. I'm in one'a the local shot houses tucked up in the cut way back in the woods, shootin' pool and poppin' shit wit' one'a the muhfuckas up in this piece. I'm keepin' it cute in a white five-pocket Gucci mini-skirt and sexy silk jersey halter top. I'm standin' in a pair of four-inch high-heeled ankle strap clogs, posin' for all the admirers. I'm surrounded by a buncha thick, hamhock 'n biscuit-eatin'muhfuckas buzzin' all 'round a bitch. And they all look like they got some big-ass country cock.

That's right, muhfuckas…all eyes on me! The booga bitches up in here roll they eyes or suck they teeth, but you know a top-dolla bitch ain't pressed 'bout no shit like that. This is my third round on the table housin' muhfuckas. Although a bitch is ready to get outta this costume—the curly bob wig, green contacts, and wire-framed glasses—I'm enjoyin' the fact of knowin' I'ma finally be able to get at this nigga.

"Eight ball, corner pocket," I say, bendin' ova the table just a taste to give 'em all a sneak peek of my fluffy ass cheeks. I hear a few niggas mumble shit when I stand or bend in front of 'em as I go 'round the pool table.

"Ooooh-weee. Looka-here, looka-here, that purty young thang got some sweet cakes on her."

"I'd sop her up with a biscuit any day."

I ig the comments, let 'em talk what they talk as I pop my hips up in they faces. My eyes sweep 'cross the room, takin' in all the stares and sideway glances. I grin, lovin' the attention. I chalk my pool stick, then sink the ball into the pocket. Muhfuckas start clappin' 'n shit.

"Aiight, who wanna get whipped next?" I say, lookin' directly at my target 'cross the room. He's at'a table playin' cards wit' three otha muhfuckas. A bitch is feelin' frisky and ready to earn a lil' lunch money in the process. I look 'round the room, knowin' aint' nobody in here ready to bring it. I turn it up a notch when I peep my mark eyein' me on the otha side of the room. He's kept his eyes on me practically the whole night, which is exactly how it's 'posed to be. I can tell the nigga is likin' what he's seein'. *Dumb muhfucka, too bad I gotta take you outta ya misery.* "I gotta gee for da baddest muhfucka up in here who thinks they can handle me on da table." I open my bag, pullin' out a wad'a bills, wavin' it in the air, then tossin' ten Ben Frankies on the pool table. A few niggas shift in they seats; some move away from the table 'cause they pockets are on low. "Goin' once, goin' twice..."

"Rack 'em up, shorty," this deep, boomin' voice says behind

me. I glance ova my shoulder. There's a big, black greasy-ass muhfucka walkin' up on me, grinnin'. And the muhfucka gotta nerve to have a nice smile. I turn to face 'im. I cringe when I spot two brown-skinned boogas wit' 'im. *Mygaaawd, they some big linebacka bitches.* One of 'em is a real live amazon. She's 'bout five-eleven, and a good two hundred-and fifty-plus pounds wit' humongous-ass titties bustin' outta some kinda blouse that criss-crosses in the front. And she has a set'a 'xtra juicy dick sukas. The bitch kinda reminds me of a moose. It looks like all she does is sit on her fat ass stuffin' her big face wit' muthafuckin' Ho Ho's and Ring Dings. The other ho is tall, too; but not as hefty. She looks like a chipmunk, though, wit' er chubby cheeks and two big front teeth. I peep the booga has more stomach than titties. And the bitch is rockin' a black dress wit' some kinda powder blue sash— a fuckin' *sash?!*—wrapped 'round what I guess is supposed to be her waist. *Mmmph, straight country coon-trash*, I think, shiftin' my eyes. *I gotta hurry da fuck up outta this hick-ass town wit' they back-ward-ass fashion.*

I smirk. "Oh, you ain't said nuthin' but a word, Big Man. Show ya paper, and let's get it poppin'.'"

He snaps his finga at the Chipmunk wit' the sash. She digs into her blouse pullin' out money. She counts out ten Ben Frankies, then stuffs the rest back down in 'er titties. I take his money, count it, then scoop up my paper and hand it all to the amazon. Why I choose 'er ova the Chipmunk is beyond me.

I eye 'er, walkin' ova to 'er. "Here, Boo, you hol' this. But don't hol' on to it too tight 'cause I'ma be takin' it back in a minute." Big Man laughs. Tells me he digs my cockiness. Tells me is gonna beat me softly. I roll my eyes. Tell the nigga instead'a yappin' his trap to break the balls and let the games begin.

The first round I fuck wit' the muhfucka, give 'em all'a good show and let 'im win. Then I dare the nigga for anotha round; double or nuthin'. At first he wants no parts of it; pussy muhfucka wants to run wit' his change. But muhfuckas start eggin' 'im on, gassin' the nigga up that it's an easy win. The nigga starts feelin' himself, gettin' all caught up in the hype. Fifteen minutes later, I rock the nigga's socks off, moppin' 'im up off the table. Niggas start high-fivin', and poppin' mad shit. Big Man runs me my paper, then I step, walkin' right into my mark.

"Hey, beautiful, I see you know how'ta handle a stick," he says, grinnin'.

I look 'im up and down. He has on a V-neck Polo tee and a pair of faded blue jeans. His curly hair is tucked under a blue Yankee fitted. Seein' this no-good, women beatin' muhfucka makes my guts churn. But my clit jumps, anticipatin' finally spinnin' the nigga's clock back. "That's not da only thing I can handle."

He stares at me as if he's tryna remember me from somewhere. But the nigga's only seen me once, and Juanita wasn't the kinda ho to have a buncha flicks of me all round 'er spot, so I ain't beat.

"Oh, is that so?" I nod. "Where you from? I can tell you ain't from around here." I tell 'im I rest in Cali; that I'm here for a family reunion. "Oh word? That's wassup. How long you in town for?"

"'Til Sunday," I lie, glancin' 'round the room for a spot to sit. I peep two empty seats ova in the corner. "How 'bout we finish our talk ova a drink, then see what else pops off; if you know what I mean."

"I got you. How 'bout you go grab them seats, and I'll go get us some drinks." He tells me they only servin' moonshine and brandy up in this muhfucka. Oh, and beers. I tell 'im to hit me wit' some brandy, then walk off, feelin' the muhfucka starin' at my ass as I spin off.

"Here you go," he says, five minutes later when he comes ova, handin' me a plastic cup. He grabs the chair next to me and sits it in front of me. He sits so he can face me. "Damn, ma, you look real familiar. You got people in New York?"

Yeah, muhfucka, the bitch you beat into a coma. I shake my head, shiftin' in my seat. "Not that I know of."

"Oh, aiight. For some reason it feels like I've met you before."

I stare at the nigga, then shake my head. "I doubt it. A bitch like me would definitely remember a sexy-ass muhfucka like you," I say, baitin' the nigga in.

He smiles, flashin' his chipped tooth. *Muthafucka, I'ma be knockin' ya fronts out in a minute.* "Oh word? You think I'm sexy?"

I slowly nod my head. "You made my pussy pop da minute I peeped you walk through da door," I tell 'im, reachin' ova and lightly touchin' his hand.

"That's wassup. You get on?"

I frown. *No this no-good muhfucka ain't cokin' it up, too.* I shake my head. "No. I ain't wit' that shit."

"Oh aiight. What you wit' then?"

I lean into his ear real-sexy like, then say, "I'm wit' a fine muhfucka wit' a big-ass dick fuckin' my pussy deep."

"Daaaaamn, it's like that? You real bold, ma. I like that shit."

"It is what it is. I'm on vacay, and a bitch tryna have a good time, you feel me?"

He licks his lips. "I got you." I ask the muhfucka if he gotta girl. "Nah, I'm chillin'."

"Good. 'Cause I'm lookin' for good dick, not drama. You got good dick, daddy?" Of course the muhfucka starts suckin' his own dick, talkin' 'bout how good the shit is; 'bout how he brings it in the sheets, makin' bitches breakdown. Juanita pops into my head.

"Yo, you got my dick hard as hell right now. I wanna freak you, real talk. I wanna eat it up, heat it up, then beat it up. Nonstop fuckin', feel me?"

I keep myself from rollin' my eyes up in my head. I laugh in his face. "Nigga, that kinda talk might work wit' these country boogas, but you wanna impress me, you gonna have'ta pull ya dick out and show a bitch; not tell 'er."

He flashes his crooked smile. "I dig you." I shrug. "I'm sayin'… what's good, ma?"

I sit back in my seat, open and close my legs real slow and sexy. Let the nigga see a bitch ain't wearin' no drawers. "What's good is this hot-ass pussy, muhfucka." I cross my legs, then put the tip of the straw back up to my lips and sip on my drink.

His eyes scan my smooth cocoa-brown thighs. "Daaaamn, you got some pretty-ass legs. I'd definitely like to slide up in them hips."

"Nigga, you couldn't handle this pussy," I say, twirlin' my tongue 'round the straw, "so you might wanna stick to these dusty bama-freaks you got eyein' you." I slide the tip of the straw in and outta my mouth as if I'm suckin' a dick. I'm done wit' drinkin' the shit since I know a bitch can't spend too much time wettin' 'er throat. Gettin' lit ain't on the menu, but lightin' this muhfucka's dome up is. So I gotta keep it cute. A drunk bitch, can become a messy bitch. And I ain't the one.

I stare at the panther on his forearm. Juanita's face flashes in my head, again. *Kat, this is Jawan, my fiancé…*

I hear his voice in my head. *Baby, you didn't tell me she was this fine.* He stares at me. "Damn, ma, you remind me of this chick I met a while back. What part of Cali did you say you were from?"

Bitch, you need'a hurry up 'n wrap this lil' party up. I lean in and slowly lick my lips. "I didn't. I told you I was lookin' for some dick, so how 'bout we take this party someplace more private so I can show you where I'm from." He looks 'round the room. "What, you scared? Let me find out you scared'a pussy."

"Nah, ma. Never that."

"That's what ya mouth says. Now let a bitch feel what da dick says."

"You gotta spot?" I shake my head. Tell 'im I'm sharin' a room wit' my moms and sista. Tell 'im we gotta move on the low. The muhfucka tells me his papers low. *Broke ass nigga*, I think while tellin' 'im I'll front the money. I tell 'im he'll have'ta get the room in his name. Tell 'im to wait five minutes after I slide out, then dip out and meet me at my rental—a red Mini Cooper.

I toss back the rest of my drink, then lean in his ear and whisper, "I'ma fuck ya brains out tonight. I hope you can deliver."

He grins. "My dick game is right, ma. I ain't ever had no complaints."

"We'll see," I say, gettin' up. "I'll be outside waitin'." I walk off. The minute I get to the car, I pull out my Kat line and hit Cash up to make sure he got his crew on standby.

"No doubt, pretty-baby. We just waitin' on you."

"Good. I got da nigga hooked, now I'ma 'bout to reel 'im in. Here he comes now. I'll text you all'a da info as soon as I know where he's gonna get da room."

"Aiiight bet." I get ready to disconnect when he says sumthin' else. "Aye, yo, Kat...how you feel? Ya pussy wet, yet, knowin' you 'bout to body this muhfucka?"

I laugh. "Nigga, what you think? Look, I gotta bounce."

"Aiight, save me them drawz." I hang up on his ass, rollin' my eyes an suckin' my teeth as my mark opens the passenger door and hops in my whip.

"Yo, ma, I ain't get ya name."

I look at 'im and reach ova and rub his crotch. "And I ain't get yours, but that ain't gonna stop me from fuckin' this dick. Now u wanna name, or you wanna fuck?"

"Fuck," he says, openin' and closin' his legs.

"Good, then let's get to a hotel quick so I can rock ya cock."

And welcome you to da Kat Trap, muhfucka!

CHAPTER THIRTY-TWO

Lights out, muhfucka…don't you weep…ya moment in life is comin' to an end…ruthless bitch done reeled you in…silencer cocked and ready to go…now it's time ta rock you ta sleep…

"**D**aaaaaamn, baby, you fine…you gotta fat ass…make that shit pop for me…" I got the nigga sprawled out in the middle of the bed in this cheesy-ass, low budget hotel—the Ahoskie Inn—butt-ass naked. As sick and twisted as the shit is, a bitch can't front. Lookin' at this muhfucka's body gotta bitch's pussy weepin' for a ride on his dick. The shit is siiick; thick, veiny and a beautiful golden brown. I wanna feel the dick inside'a me. Wanna see what it is 'bout this nigga that had my mother so muthafuckin' dizzy and dick-dumb. But I don't want this nigga puttin' his hands on me; don't want him touchin' any part'a my body. I can feel a nut slowly buildin' up inside'a me as I think 'bout ridin' his cock, then poppin' his top.

I stick my hands up my skirt, play in my wet pussy, dippin' one finga, then two, into my hole, scoopin' out my juices. I slowly suck on my fingas. "You wanna taste this pussy, nigga?"

He sits up on his forearms. "Yeah, ma. Stop fuckin' 'round and take them fuckin' clothes off so I get up in that pussy."

I frown, but keep it cute. *Pussy muhfucka, who da fuck you think you rushin'*, I think, tellin' the muhfucka to be easy. I tell the nigga to lay back and enjoy the show. Tell 'im I'ma give 'im sumthin' he'll neva forget. He scoots up toward the headboard, proppin' pillows in back of 'im.

I slowly pull my skirt up ova my hips, turnin' 'round. "You wanna fuck this pussy, nigga?" I ask ova my shoulder, bendin' ova and pullin' open my ass cheeks to give the muhfucka a backshot view of my goodness.

He strokes his dick. "Fuck yeah, baby…look how hard you got my shit…"

Think, bitch. How you gonna get up on that nigga's cock wit'out him puttin' his muthafuckin' hands on you?

Bitch, get ya mind right. You don't need'a be tryna fuck Juanita's trash. Shoot this nigga and bounce the fuck on.

Fuck that; squat ova da muhfucka's face and smear ya pussy all ova it. Then pop his top.

This nigga ain't worthy ta taste ya pussy, ho. Body his ass and go!

I decide to do 'im the way I had'a take Grant out, one bullet at a time. I walk ova to my bag, lettin' da nigga think I'm gettin' a condom. The whole time I'm in this piece I'm mindful not to touch shit. I open my bag and pull out my nickel-plated nine-millimeter wit' the silencer attached. The irony in it all is it's the exact type'a gun I used when I bodied Grant and his brotha. For some reason, Grant's face pops in my head. I shut my eyes, tryna will 'im outta my head.

"You ready for this heat, muhfucka?" I ask, slowly turnin' 'round.

"Hell yeah. I been ready."

I grin, aimin' the gun at 'im. "Good."

His eyes pop open. "Whhhhaaaaat da fuck?!? Yo listen, I told you, I ain't got no money, ma."

I glare at 'im. "Nigga, please. I ain't pressed for no muthafuckin' money."

"Whha-whaa-what's up then?" he stutters, glancin' round the room.

"You know Juanita, muhfucka?"

He frowns. "Who?"

"Nigga, don't play stupid. The bitch you beat up and left for dead in Brooklyn. Why you do it?"

"Yo, who da fuck are you?" he asks, tryna raise up. *This nigga must think I'm some kinda soft bitch. Therrrssp!* I shoot 'im in his right shoulder. He grabs his shit and screeches. "Aaaaaah, fuck, damn, yo!"

"Muthafucka, you shut ya trap, or I will blow ya face off, right now."

The nigga grunts. Bites down on his bottom lip. "Aaah, fuck. Why da fuck you shoot me?"

"Nigga, don't test my patience. And don't insult my intelligence. Now, I'ma ask you one more time. Why da fuck you do that shit to Juanita when you knew she was pregnant? And before you open ya mouth to hit me wit' some bullshit, you betta take'a deep breath and think 'bout what da fuck you gonna say."

He starts stutterin' again. "I-I-I...yo, listen. I ain't do that shit, ma; on e'erything."

Therrrssp! I shoot 'im in his left knee. "Aaaaaaah, fuck, yo! What kinda crazy bitch are you? Aaaah, fuuuuck! Who da fuck are you?" The nigga is rockin' back and forth in pain, tryna grab his shoulder and his knee.

"You shoulda listened to ya mammy when she told you growin' up not ta eva get in da car wit' strangers." He looks at me like I'm crazy. The nigga's sweatin' bullets. Fear is pasted up on his face, and it makes my pussy drip wit' excitement. "I'm da kinda bitch you don't eva get in da car wit'. And I'm da bitch you don't wanna piss off, that's who da fuck I am. Now, again...why da fuck you beat up Juanita?"

"Yo, I swear to you, I don't know..." I point the gun at 'im again. Warn 'im that I'ma put some heat to his balls if he keeps up wit' the lies. The nigga quickly switches up his story; tries to give me some weak-ass song and dance 'bout he didn't mean to hurt 'er. That he was tryna leave 'er but she wouldn't let 'im. That she kept beggin' 'im to stay, then started fightin' 'im. That he pushed 'er off'a 'im and she fell and hit 'er head on the edge of the table.

"Nigga, shut da fuck up; I don't wanna hear no more 'bout this shit. You still lyin'. Her face was beat da fuck up, nigga. Did you know she was pregnant?" He nods. Tells me that's what they were beefin' 'bout. That he didn't want anotha baby; wanted her to abort it. "So you tried to beat it outta 'er instead."

"No. Things got outta hand."

"And then you fled da state, like that was gonna fix shit. Nigga, because of you, Juanita"—I pull off my wig—"is dead." His eyes widen. "You remember me, muhfucka? Let me refresh ya memory. I'm Katrina, 'er daughter."

"Yo, I swear—"

"Muhfucka, don't swear shit. Because of you, there's a lil' boy layin' up in'a incubator fightin' for his life; because of you, there's a baby I gotta raise now 'cause ya stupid ass had'a kill its mother. And now, muthafucka I gotta kill you."

"No-no...listen. You don't gotta do this, ma..."

"So you think I should just let you go, is that it?"

"Yo, ma...don't do this; don't..."

I stare at the nigga. Take in the blood oozin' outta his shoulder and knee. Glance at his dick. A sly grin forms on my lips. "You wanna live, nigga? Then I tell you what. Lay back and let me see you bust that dick."

He frowns. Looks at me confused. "Whaat?! You want me to play wit' my shit, ma? Are you fuckin' serious? I'm in fuckin' pain."

"Bitch-ass nigga," I hiss through clenched teeth. I walk up on 'im, keepin' my gun aimed at his head. "I don't give'a fuck 'bout ya muthafuckin' pain; I've been pained all my life. Now you eitha start yankin' ya dick or get ya balls blown off. Now which is it gonna be, pain or pleasure?"

The nigga looks shook. And he's definitely in pain. But I wanna see this nigga nut before I shut his lights. The nigga stalls. And it starts to piss me off. "Muthafucka, I ain't gonna tell you again, you eitha bust ya nut, or get da nut bust outta ya."

He takes his bloody hand and starts pullin' at his dick. "Yo, ma, I thought you hated ya moms. Ya'll was always beefin' and shit."

Before I know it, a bitch backhands this muthafucka wit' the back of my gun. "Nigga, what da fuck that got ta do wit' how you beat 'er ass? Or how you ran da bitch crazy? Get that dick hard, or I swear on e'erything I stand for, I will torture ya ass, slowly all muthafuckin' night."

The nigga has tears in his eyes. "Ma, please…can't you see, I'm bleedin' all over the place. Aaaaaah…this shit hurts."

"Then let me add ta ya hurt," I tell 'im, backin' away from 'im. I walk ova to my bag, and pull out maskin' tape. "Tonight, muh-fucka, you gonna wish you neva laid eyes on my mother." I tear off a large piece, then tell 'im to put it ova his mouth. He refuses 'til I cock my gun and prepare to shoot 'im in his otha knee. "The sooner you bust off, the sooner you can get to where you need to be."

He keeps beggin' and whimperin' like a lil' bitch and the shit's gettin' on my muthafuckin' nerves. The pussy nigga has no shame.

Oh, how I wanna fuck! I pull up my skirt, show 'im my pussy. "You wanna smell this pussy, muhfucka? You wanna taste this pussy?" I place one foot up on the bed, stroke my clit, rubbin' my gun along the front'a my pussy. "Look how wet shootin' ya bum-ass got my pussy, nigga." He shifts his eyes away from me. "Muthafucka, look at me 'fore I blow ya muthafuckin eyeballs out."

He looks back at me. I tell 'im to look at my wet pussy. I pull open my lips. The nigga is cryin' and sweatin' and bleedin' all ova the place. "Look at that wet, creamy pussy, bitch…you scared'a this pussy, nigga…"

I press harder on my clit, makin' fast circles over it wit' my two fingas. "Mmmm…you beat up and killed da wrong bitch, nigga… Uhhh…"

I got the muhfucka lookin' at a bitch like she's fuckin' nuts. I help ease his mind. "Nigga, I ain't crazy," I say, dippin' at the knees as my nut builds up inside'a me. "I'm muthafuckin' dangerous, bitch-ass…uhhhh…and you…mmmm…you was a fool…aaaah…to think ya ass was gonna up 'n bounce…oooohhh…and not get got."

"I knew ya ass wasn't no good from da dip, snake-ass muhfucka. You shoulda got that dick hard for me…pussy-ass nigga…mmmm… dick can't even get hard…uhhh…"

Therrrssp! I shoot 'im in the left shoulder. The muhfucka starts howlin' and growlin' like a wounded animal. He's losin' a lotta blood and startin' to look pale in the face. A bitch is startin' to feel pressed 'cause I don't want the nigga passin' out on me before I get my nut off. I speed jack my clit 'til I cum, then run my fingas in and outta my pussy. I pull 'em out and suck off my juice.

I stare at this nigga. "Yeah, nigga…don't worry. You gonna die. I'ma take you outta ya misery." I slip the gun back between my legs, rub it in between my pussy lips, then lick the silencer. "Shootin' ya ass got my pussy so hot, nigga. You don't know how bad I wanna fuck…oh, well. This party's ova."

I spin off, walkin' back ova to my bag. I pull out a travel pack of mango wipes, then wipe between my legs. "You know, Juanita may not have been shit. And the bitch mighta been stupid when it came to bitch-ass niggas like you. But guess what? She was still *my* mother, and you had no muthafuckin' right puttin' ya hands on 'er. I don't give'a fuck how fucked up she was."

The nigga is groanin' and shakin' his head.

I walk back ova to the bed. "Lights out, muhfucka. Thanks for the nut." I press the silencer to his temple and pull the trigger again—*Therrrssp!*—blowin' a hole in his skull. "This is for killin' my mother, bitch."

Next I shoot 'im in his dick and balls. "And this one's for da son you left motherless, you fuckin' bastard!"

I walk into the bathroom, glancin' at my reflection in the mirror. A bitch has tears runnin' down 'er face. I swipe 'em wit' my hand, pullin' out my phone. I call Cash, tell 'im what's what, then fix my face and wig piece. I put back on my glasses, then quietly ease myself on out the room, slidin' outta the hotel. I hop in my rental and pull off, neva lookin' back. I take a deep breath, ready to get back home, anxious to finally be free.

CHAPTER THIRTY-THREE

Still lookin' for change...lookin' for a new groove...tired of all da extras...bitch ready to make a move...ain't tryna be locked down...ain't tryna take no tests...sumthin' gotta give...wanna start things fresh...face da future...butta bitch gotta life to live...step in my way...get a face full'a sutures...

"Yo, sexy ma, what's good? It's Tone."

I smile. "Shit, nigga. Chillin'. Wassup on ya end?"

"Coolin'. You know how it is. Yo, you get them papers yet?"

Oh shit, there's been so much shit goin' on I ain't even had time to go through any'a my mail, I think, walkin' ova to the stack of mail sittin' up on the kitchen aisle countertop. "You know what there's been so much goin' on since I got back here I haven't even given them any thought. Hold on, let me go through my mail." I start siftin' through the pile 'til I come 'cross a letter from the State of California. "Oh shit. I gotta envelope right here from 'em," I tell 'em, rippin' it open.

"Well?"

"Hol' on, hol' on, let me get it open, first." *Ohmigaawd, my hands are shaken.* I pull the letter outta the envelope, and slowly read it. I scream. "Aaaaaaaahhhhh, what nigga, what?! A bitch done passed the exam!"

"Yo, sexy, that's wassup. That's what it is, for real—for real. What you gettin' into tonight, we gotta go out 'n celebrate."

"True-true. And you know this. Wait. Where you at?"

"Oh, damn, my bad. I'm in Jersey, ma. That's why I was callin' you for in the first place. I wanted to link up wit' you before I bounced. But now we definitely gotta get it in tonight, feel me?"

"Yup-yup; I feel you. Well, I'm free tonight. And you can have'a bitch all night," I say wit'out thinkin'. I am startin' to feel overwhelmed. I keep myself from cryin'. Aside from gettin' my high school diploma, this is the first real major shit I've eva accomplished in my life. And it feels real good. No, scratch that. It feels fuckin'good!

"Cool-cool. That's wassup. So what time you wanna link up?" I tell 'im 'round seven. "Oh, yeah…and don't think I didn't catch that last comment."

"Uh, what was that?"

"That I can have you all night."

"Yeah, muhfucka, to celebrate, not run up in my pussy."

He laughs. "Aaah, there you go. Ain't nobody say nuthin' like that. You always thinkin' the worst."

"Yeah, whateva. So you sayin' you ain't on it for no pussy."

"Nah, never that, ma."

I laugh. "You're such a fuckin' liar."

He laughs harder. "Nah, I ain't on it like that."

"Nigga, you know you want some more'a this pussy; stop frontin'."

"Aiight, aiight; only if you tryna get it poppin'. Otherwise, nah…you cool peeps, Kat. I dig how you move. You a real thorough type chick; real talk. Any cat would be a fool not wantin' you on his team."

"Well, since you so full of compliments," I tease, "I might give you a lil' treat and let you eat my pussy. But I ain't suckin' ya dick and I ain't makin' no promises for anything else, muhfucka."

He keeps laughin'. "Yo, Kat, you funny as hell. But I got you. So let me get ya address." I hit 'im wit' the info and directions, then ask 'im where he tryna take me. He tells me he's gotta spot in the city he wants to try. Tells me to serve it up real classy.

I have anotha call comin' in. It's Chanel. I let the nigga know if he ain't here at 'xactly seven, it's a wrap. Let 'im know I don't wait on no nigga, then click ova. "Hello."

"What time you comin' up to da hospital today?"

I decide to go through the rest of my mail while I'm talkin'. There's mostly a buncha bullshit solicitations and a few bills. I glance up at the wall clock. It's ten a.m. "I need to be gettin' my ass in gear soon. I gotta be back here by five." I share my news wit' 'er.

"Ohhmiigod, Kat, that's great. I am so proud of you, boo. So now whatchu gonna do?"

I shrug as if she can see me. "I don't know, yet. I guess at some point, I'ma have'ta go back to Cali for a minute to see what's what."

"Oh cool. Then Zaire can stay wit' me while you tryna get shit poppin' out there."

I frown. *What da fuck?!* "Leavin' Zaire wit' *you*? No, da hell I'm not. When I go, he's goin', too."

"Hol' up, bitch…why you say it like that?"

"Like what?"

"Like, 'bitch, I ain't leavin' my baby wit' ya nasty, stank-ass.'"

I laugh. "Chanel, that's not how I meant it. I'm sayin'…"

"Well, I don't know what you sayin'. But I know how da fuck it sounded." I can tell I done hurt 'er feelin's. "Like a bitch ain't shit. She good enough to be up at da hospital when ya trick-ass is whiskin' all ova, but not good enough to take 'im when he gets outta da hospital. What kinda shit is that?"

Ohmiigaaawd, this lil' nigga got bitches beefin' ova 'im already. And da nigga ain't even slingin' dick, yet. "Girl, I'm sorry. You know that's not how I meant it. It's just that while he's a baby I don't wanna have'ta leave 'im alone wit' anyone unless I really, really have'ta."

She grunts. "Mmmph. You didn't even want his ass; now all'a sudden you wanna be all protective 'n shit. Bitches kill me."

I take a deep breath. "Look, bitch. I said that's not how I meant it. I apologize for it comin' out like that. If you wanna keep draggin' da shit out, then…" I stop in midsentence when I get to a letter from Child Protective Services in New York.

"Hello?"

"I'm still here," I say, rippin' the letter open.

"Well, finish what da fuck you was sayin' so I can continue cussin' ya funky-ass out."

"Ho, fuck you. I ain't thinkin' 'bout ya ugly-ass right now. I got a letter from CPS."

"Well, what it say, bitch?" I read the letter. Tell 'er it says that all allegations against a bitch have been unsubstantiated. That no case will be opened against me. "Now, that's what da fuck I'm talkin' 'bout!" she yells into the phone, forgettin' 'bout the mini-beef she was tryna set off. "We one step closer to bringin' *our* baby home. And, *bitch*…Be clear. I will be takin' 'im, too!"

I laugh, then almost faint when I come 'cross anotha letter. This one's from Brooklyn's Family Court. I scream into the phone. *Ohmiiimuthafuckin'gaawd! Today is my muthafuckin' day*, I think, tearin' the shit open. "Ohhhhhhhhhmiiiigod, ohhhhhhmiiiigod, Chanel!"

"Whaaat da fuck happen? What is it?"

"Bitch, fuck all that one-step-closer shit; we at the muthafuckin' finish line. I gotta court hearin' at Family Court August third at nine a.m."

"Biiiiiiiiiiitch, ohhhhhhhhmiiiimuthafuckin'god, we gotta celebrate!" Chanel screams into the phone. "I knew them bitches couldn't stop ya flow."

"You got that right," I say, grill-cheesin' hard. "A creamy bitch always rises to da top; thought them hoes knew."

"I know that's right. Oh, wait one damn minute. Why da fuck am I all coochie-coo-coo wit' you, bitch, when I'm 'posed to be mad at ya ugly-ass."

I bust out laughin'. "Bitch, we can beef later. You already know I'ma say some otha shit, so save bein' mad 'til then. Right now, we got otha shit to do."

She laughs wit' me. "Bitch, I hate e'erything ya ho-ass stand for."

"Yeah, yeah, yeah…I love you, too, hooker." We go at it a few minutes more, then disconnect.

It's not 'til a bitch is in the shower that it really hits me that all this shit is really happenin' to me, and for me. I stand under the water and fuckin' cry like a baby, excited, nervous, and over-joyed—feelin' like the change I've been hopin' for is finally gonna come.

Once I'm showered, dressed and ready to walk out the door, I open my front door just as the doorbell rings. It's a delivery man. "Delivery for a Miss Rivera."

"That's me," I state, starin' at the white box under his arm. He hands me a clipboard to sign for it, then hands me the box. He tells me the tip has already been taken care of. I thank 'im, then shut the door. I pull apart the red ribbon wrapped 'round the box, then lift up its cover. Two dozen beautiful pink roses are inside along wit' a card. I pick up the card and read it. AYE, YO, ON E'ERYTHING, I'M THINKIN' 'BOUT YOU E'ERYDAY, AND MISSIN' YOU MORE. YA FUTURE MAN!

Nigga, puhleeze, I think, takin' the roses and placin' 'em in a vase, then sittin' 'em on the coffee table. *Outta sight, outta mind.*

The minute I come downstairs, Chanel eyes me, talkin' shit. "Bitch, I hate you," she says, rollin' 'er eyes at me. After meetin' me up at the hospital, she decided she was comin' back to my spot to chill, even after I told the bitch I had shit to do tonight. She claimed she needed a break from bein' in Brooklyn, talkin' 'bout Divine is gettin' on 'er nerves; that the nigga is smotherin' 'er. I was like, "Bitch, puhleeze. Ya ass is full'a lies." But, she's my girl, so here she is.

"Ugh, bitch. What I do now?" I ask, playin' dumb. But I already know what it is. The bitch is gaggin' ova my wears. I'm wearin' a simple, but stylish black Hervé Léger strapless dress I scooped up in Bloomingdales a few weeks ago. I usually don't fuck wit' new designers, but I tried this piece on and loved how it wrapped 'round my curves like a band-aid. So I snatched it up.

"That bitch." She points to my Dolce & Gabbana evenin' bag. *Well, I guess it ain't da wears she's illin' ova.* "Ohhhhmiigod, it's siiick. When you get that? And how much, bitch?" I tell 'er it's a twenty-seven-hundred dollar limited edition. She sucks 'er teeth. "For a bitch who ain't workin' and ain't trickin' a nigga up off'a his paper how is you affordin' all this high-end shit?"

"Layaway, boo," I say, laughin'.

"Bitch, puhleeze. Layaway my ass; it's time you put a bitch on to how you really makin' it pop."

I roll my eyes up in my head. "Ho, we ain't got time for no financial report. My date'll be here soon. Anyway, I told ya dizzy ass to stop givin' out discount pussy and you might be able to bubble-up."

She flicks her hand at me, floppin' back on the sofa. "Whateva." She puts 'er bare feet on top of the coffee table and starts flippin' through the latest issue of *Jet*. "So what's up wit' this nigga you runnin' off wit'?"

I'm in my powder room, applyin' lipgloss ova my painted lips to give 'em a sweet, juicy candy-apple look. I peek my head outta the door. "I ain't runnin' off wit' da nigga. He's a dude I met out in Cali. The nigga's cool and he's 'bout that paper; that's it."

"Mmmph…ya'll fuck?"

I'm glad the doorbell rings. *Right on time*, I think, glancin' down at my timepiece. "Answer da door, nosey, instead of askin' me a buncha damn questions, puhleeeze."

"Yeah, okay. But don't think I'ma forget. I still wanna know if you fucked da nigga. And if da dick was good." I hear 'er open the door. "Come in," she says, lettin' 'im in.

"Wassup, ma?"

"And you are?"

"Tone," I hear 'im say in his smooth, silky voice, "and you?"

"Single, and still lookin'."

I crane my neck outta the bathroom, rollin' my eyes. "Tone, don't pay 'er ass no mind. That's my girl, Chanel. She used to be a clown 'til they revoked 'er happy pills."

He laughs. "It's all good." He looks 'round. "Yo, nice spot."

"Thanks. Have a seat. I'll be ready in a sec." I finish up what I'm doin' then walk into the livin' room.

The muhfucka does a double-take, standin' up. "Daaaaamn, you look good, ma." He walks up on me and gives me a hug. "And you smell even better."

I allow myself to get lost in his strong arms, inhalin' his cologne. "Thank you. Mmmm, you don't smell too bad ya'self. What you have on?" He tells me it's Bulgari. *Yeah, this nigga tryna get some pussy*. I check out his wears. I can't front the nigga is lookin' mad sexy in his custom-fit Armani suit. And his accessories are settin' the shit off. Black Louis belt and black Ferragamo loafers; the nigga's lobes and neck are blingin' on high. I peep Chanel eyein' 'im on the sly, and grin.

"Aiight, hooker, we out."

"Ya'll kiddies have fun," she says, gettin' up off the sofa.

"Nice meetin' you, Chanel."

She smiles. "Oh, da pleasure was all mines." She waits for 'im to walk out the door, then pulls me by the arm. "Bitch, that mutha-fucka is fiiiiine as hell. If you ain't fuckin' 'im, hand 'im ova to me 'cause I damn sure will."

"Bitch, puhleeze. Who won't you fuck?"

"Ya ugly-ass," she says, laughin'.

I laugh wit' 'er. "You'se one lyin'-ass ho. Don't smoke up my shit eitha."

"Bitch, you can't smoke, remember. You 'bout to be a mommy."

"Whateva," I say, walkin' out and shuttin' the door behind me. Tone gets outta the car and walks ova and opens the passenger door for me. He waits for me to get in, then shuts it.

As soon as he gets in the car and pulls outta my driveway, he looks ova at me—lickin' his lips. "Listen, I think I'ma take you up on that offer."

I tilt my head. "What offer was that?"

"Havin' you out all night."

I smirk. "Oh, really. You wanna eat this pussy tonight?"

He grins, takin' my hand and kissin' the inside'a my palm. "What you think?"

I reach ova and grab at his dick. The shit is thick and hard. "Mmmmm...I think you need'a get ya eyes back on da road 'fore we end up tossed upside down in a ditch."

CHAPTER THIRTY-FOUR

Funny how time passes by...nigga been sendin' flowers 'n cards...but he ain't been seen...gotta bitch masturbatin' in a magazine...nigga got da game fucked up...this bitch is done... ain't da type to be waitin' on no one...now he wanna talk... nigga, puhleeze...this bitch comes second to none...

"I miss you, yo," Allstar says, soundin' all down 'n shit. The last three days the nigga's been callin' tryna get back in my good graces. I keep tellin' the nigga it's not that serious. Yeah a bitch was startin' to feel some kinda way, but it's all good. I'm soooo ova the shit now.

"Mmmmph, that's nice," I say, rollin' my eyes up in my head. "You have a funny way of showin' it, though."

"I know, baby..."

"Nigga, stop callin' me that."

"Kat, fuck what you say, ma. I'ma be ya man. And you gonna be my baby, so you might as well get used to it."

"Nigga, you still delusional I see."

"I know I shoulda been callin' you, ma. On some real shit, yo, I've had a lot on my mind da last few weeks. Did you get all the flowers I been sendin' you?"

"Yeah, I got 'em. Thanks. Still a phone call coulda worked, too."

"You right. That's definitely my bad. I really fucked up on that."

"Trust me. It's all good. I wasn't beat to be ya lil' experiment any-damn-way, so you can keep doin' what you doin'.'"

"My experiment? C'mon, Kat why would you say some shit like that? That's what you think you've been?"

"Nigga, you tell me. One minute you sweatin' a bitch all hot 'n heavy, tryna be all up in 'er space and face, poppin' a buncha ooey-gooey shit in 'er ear 'bout how you wanna wife 'er and be 'er man 'n shit. Then the next minute you get ghost. It don't take a rocket scientist to figure out ya ass got some otha shit goin' on. So do me a favor, delete my number from ya phone 'cause I ain't da fuckin' one, okay. I told you da first time I think you tryna play a bitch, I was gonna dead shit."

"YO, what da fuck?! I ain't tryna hear that shit, yo. I told you I'ma tryna sort some shit out. I know it was fucked up for me not to still get at you, but shit's been hectic, Kat. I promise you, once I get this shit handled, it's me and you, ma."

See. I wasn't gonna get into it wit' this nigga, but since he wanna start bassin' in a bitch's ear, then it's lights on up in here. "Nigga, spare me da okey-doke. You told me this shit ova a month ago and you mean to tell me you still goin' through da same shit?"

"True story, Kat; I've been stressin' like a muhfucka, aiight?"

"Let me guess. It has to do wit' some bitch, right?" He gets real quiet. "Ohhhh, a bitch done got ya fuckin' tongue now, huh? Keep shit a hunnid, muhfucka. Is ya stress ova a bitch?"

He sighs into the phone. "Sumthin' like that."

"Just what da fuck I thought."

"But it's not what you think, on e'erything; word up."

"Nigga, *boom!*" I press END, tossin' the phone onto the sofa. The nigga calls back, but I let the shit go into voicemail. *That nigga must think I'm some kinda fool*, I think, goin' down into the basement. I flip on my stereo, then walk ova to the bar and pour myself a shot'a Henny. I toss it back, then pour anotha. *Muhfuckas ain't shit!*

Bitch, you knew what it was wit' da nigga from da rip, so get ova ya'self.

Fantasia's "Angel" comes on through the speakers. I contemplate sparkin' a blunt, but know I can't 'til after this court shit is ova and Zaire is officially mine. I close my eyes and listen to the Fantasia sing. I toss back anotha drink. Then when Indie.Arie's "He Heals Me" comes on, a bitch gets all choked up and wit'out any warnin', I break down and start cryin'.

AT NINE O'CLOCK, I AWAKE LOOKIN' 'ROUND THE ROOM ALL GROGGY 'n shit. "I can't believe I fell asleep down here on da sofa," I think, wipin' the drool from my mouth. I get up and grab the dirty shot glass, step 'round the bar and wash it at the sink, then put it away. Once I get back upstairs I grab my phone from off the sofa in the livin' room, checkin' it for any missed calls. There are eight. I check my messages. I have four. I plop down on the sofa, and wait for 'em to play.

"Hey, sexy. This is Tone. I def enjoyed seein' you the other night. Hopefully when you get back to Cali we'll get a chance to do it again. Stay beautiful, ma."

"Hooker, where da fuck you at? I know you ain't sumwhere down on ya rusty-ass knees, but if you are, rinse 'n swallow, then call me." I laugh at Chanel's ass. *This bitch is a nut.*

"Kat, this is Patrice. When you get a chance, please give me a call." I blink, blink again, wonderin' why the fuck she's callin' me, and leavin' me a damn message bein' all nice. *Uh, no thank you*, I think, hittin' DELETE.

"Yo, I know I fucked up not callin' you, but you gotta believe it ain't what you think. I'm dead-ass, ma. We need to talk. Call me when you get this. I wanna see you." *Oh, now da nigga wanna see a bitch. Puhleeze. Poof, muhfucka. Ya ass is dismissed.*

As I make my way up the stairs, my doorbell rings. I turn back around to see who it is, peekin' through the peephole. *Ohmiigod, what da fuck?! This nigga,* I think shakin' my head. I open the door. Cross my arms, and lean up against up the door frame. "Why are you here?"

"We need to talk," he says, pushin' his way into my house.

"Nigga, have you loss ya muthafuckin' mind? I didn't invite you in, so get da fuck out."

"C'mon, Kat. Look at me. I'm fucked up, yo. I'm stressed da fuck out, aiight?"

I stare at 'im. The nigga looks like he ain't slept in days. I twist my lips up. As mad as I wanna be at this muhfucka for playin' me to the left, a part of me wants to know what the fuck's been goin' on. I take a seat on the sofa. "Well, what's wrong wit' you?"

He sits next to me, takin' me by the hand. "I've missed you, yo; true story."

"Okay, well that's not tellin' me much. What da fuck you all stressed 'bout?"

"You gotta promise me you not gonna start snappin'. That you'll hear me out, first."

I frown. "Nigga I ain't promisin' shit. So speak or get da fuck out; for real, nigga. 'Cause on some real shit, you ain't one'a my favorites right now."

"I fucked up, Kat."

"Yeah, nigga you did. You still wanna be out there fuckin' otha bitches and shit."

"No lie. That's not what I've been doin'?"

"Well, was ya ass locked up?"

He shakes his head. "Nah."

"Okay, what, you fuckin' niggas?"

"Fuck outta here. That ain't my steelo. I don't get down like that, yo."

"Aiight, so then what da fuck is it? Damn."

"That crazy bitch been stressin' me da fuck out, word up."

"What crazy bitch?"

"Ramona."

I blink, blink again. "I thought there was a restrainin' order."

"There is."

"Okay, so then how da fuck is the bitch stressin' you?" He tells me that since that night at the party she had been tryna get at 'im on his Facebook and Blackplanet pages. That she made up fake accounts. Tells me that they were sendin' notes back and forth a few times, then he stopped the shit. The nigga tells me the bitch been talkin' reckless since I rocked her nozzle up in that salon. He tells me the bitch was the one who gutted his tires in my driveway.

My nose flares. "Waaaait one gaawtdamn minute. You tellin' me that bitch knows where da fuck I live. Is that what I hear you sayin'?"

He nods, lookin' all pitiful 'n shit. "Yeah. She's been followin' me."

"Wait a minute, so what you tellin' me is da bitch been stalkin' you."

"Yeah, this ho is a fuckin' nut, yo. She's done threw a brick through my pop's window. And I ain't even stayin' there." I ask 'im if anyone saw her do it. "Nah, but I know she did it. The bitch told me she was gonna keep fuckin' wit' me until I talked to 'er."

I jump up from my seat, slammin' my hand on my hip. "So you

mean to tell me, all this time you been talkin' to that bitch and you gotta restrainin' order against 'er?" He nods. "Why?"

"I was tryna keep peace wit' this broad." I tilt my head, lookin' at his ass like he's a real Fruit Loop. "She's been talkin' real reckless, Kat."

"Then why da fuck didn't you call da police on 'er ass?"

"I did, yo. And them dumb muhfuckas thought da shit was funny, askin' me dumb shit like was I really afraid of 'er, did I really think a lil' chick like 'er could hurt a big nigga like me and shit like that." He pulls out his cell. "But when she started leavin' me all kinda crazy-ass messages, I went down to the station again and played 'em for them muhfuckas." He retrieved his voice messages, then put the phone on speaker.

"Hi, baby. Call me. I miss you. Our baby misses you."

I cringe, pacin' the floor, listenin' to this kook-bitch.

"Alex, call me, big daddy. I need to see you. Why won't you return any of my calls?"

"Alley Cat, you pussy-ass nigga. You scared of this pussy. Stop fucking avoiding my calls, nigga."

"Motherfucker, until you come back where you belong, until you fuck me wit' that big-ass dick, I'm going to keep fuckin' with you."

"Fuck you, nigga. You ain't shit, Alley Cat. I hope you rot in hell, motherfucker! I promise you, you gonna pay for hurting me, nigga. Oh, and that lil' stuck-up bitch you been fucking, the next time I run into her, I'm gonna toss acid in her pretty face. She broke my nose, but I promise you I'm gonna bring a hammer to that bitch's skull. Let's see you run behind that bitch when she's all burnt and banged up."

A bitch is pipin' hot, okay? That stinkin' bitch gonna threaten me. "So this bitch is still out on da muthafuckin' loose, poppin shit."

"I filed a complaint on 'er."

"Well, why da fuck didn't you do that shit in da first place?"

"Them muhfuckas wouldn't let me. They told me there wasn't nuthin' they could do."

I stare the nigga, *down*. "What's that bitch's last name and address? That bitch is barkin' up da wrong muthafuckin' tree and she's 'bout to get chopped da fucked down."

"C'mon, baby. Let da police handle it. I don't want you gettin' caught up in this shit."

"Nigga, is you serious? That bitch has been to my home. She slashed ya muthafuckin' tires in my driveway, did you forget that? And the bitch is talkin' 'bout she gonna do my face. I don't think so. I told you before I wanted that bitch's address, and you fuckin' thought I was playin'. I coulda had that bitch dropped months ago. But noooo, you wanna protect da bitch."

He takes a deep breath, rubbin' his hands ova his face. "It's not like that, yo. You don't understand, this bitch's crazy."

"Nigga, I understand more than you think. And guess what? I don't give'a fuck 'bout that bitch bein' crazy. I want that nutty-ass ho's address. And I want it now!"

"No, baby. I got this."

I glare at 'im. "*No?* You still wanna protect that crazy bitch?"

"Yo, I don't give a fuck 'bout 'er. I ain't protectin' that bitch, yo. I don't want 'er comin' at you; that's all."

"Fuck outta here wit' that dumb shit. You brought da bitch straight to my muthafuckin' doorstep, number one; and number two, ya black ass kept all this bitch's crazy-ass antics from me. Why?"

"I was tryna handle da shit on my own."

"What da fuck?! Muthafucka, you retarded as hell. Why da fuck was you even talkin' to da bitch when you knew 'er ass was a nut from da rip?"

"I know I—"

I'm done fuckin' wit' this nigga, I think, puttin' my hand up to stop him from sayin' shit else. *Strike three!* I stare at 'im, disgusted. "You know what, nigga. Get da fuck outta my house."

He gets up and walks ova toward me. "C'mon, baby. I promise you, da police are lookin' for 'er as we speak. You don't need to get ya'self caught up in this shit."

I huff, grittin' my teeth. "Muthafucka, I'm already caught up in this shit. The minute that bitch stepped to me at that salon it became my shit, too. Now get out!"

"No. I ain't leavin'."

I blink. *"No?* Uh, you ain't leavin'? I tell you what. Hol' that thought. I'll be right back." I run upstairs to my bedroom, swingin' open my closet. *Muhfucka gonna tell me he ain't leavin' up outta my shit. That nigga don't want it. I'ma show his cocky ass.* I open my safe, pullin' out my 9mm. I screw on the silencer, then pop my hips back downstairs. The nigga is sittin' back down on the sofa. *Ohmiigaaawd, this muthafucka is fuckin' crazy.*

I point my gun at 'im. The nigga jumps up, shook. "Nigga, I asked you to get da fuck outta my house. Now I'm tellin' you. Get da fuck up, and get da fuck out, NOW! Or I'ma blow ya muthafuckin' face off."

"Yo, c'mon, baby, why you gotta pull ya shit out on me. All I wanna do is talk."

"Muthafucka, you done said all I need'a hear. Unless you givin' me that slut's last name and address, da only thing I wanna hear is ya ass screechin' outta my driveway."

He stands here lookin' at me all crazy-eyed 'n shit. *This nigga really don't think I'll take his face off.* I cock the gun. "I'ma tell you one more time, then I'ma pop off ya top. Get. Da. FUCK. OUT. NOW!"

He shakes his head, puttin' his hands up. "Aiight, Kat, you got that. You made ya point. I'm out."

"Good. Now get ta steppin'."

I watch 'im walk toward the door and open it. He turns to face me. "Yo, hol' up. Check this out. I didn't do this shit intentionally. A muhfucka thought I could keep that bitch quiet 'til I could figure out how'ta get 'er ass off my back. I didn't want 'er fuckin' wit' you; that's all. And I damn sure wasn't tryna bring drama up in ya space."

"Well, too bad, nigga, you did. Now bounce."

He opens the door and walks out, shuttin' it behind 'im.

I drop down on the step and sit, holdin' my head in my hands. Relieved the nigga left up outta here before I had'a blow his head off. I lay the gun down on the step, starin' out the livin' room window waitin' to see his car lights go on, then disappear outta my driveway.

When it takes the nigga longer than I think it should for 'im to roll out, I get up off the step to see what the fuck he's doin'. As I swing open the door, I see him standin' outside by his car, talkin' to someone but I can't see who it is. And it looks like he has his hands up. I flip on the outside light, then, *Boom! Boom! Boom!* The next thing I know, Alex hits the ground.

"Ohhhmiifuckin'god!" I race back to get my gun, then flee out the door. But whoeva it was that shot 'im, has hopped in they car and sped the fuck off. I race back in the house to get my cell phone, then run back outside, callin' 9-1-1. "Ohhhhmiigod, Alex, can you hear me?" The nigga doesn't respond and he's bleedin' real bad. As soon as the dispatcher picks up, I tell 'im what's what, and tell 'im to hurry the fuck up and get someone here. I drop down beside Alex and try to steady his head. I scoop 'im into my arms and rock 'im, hopin' like hell the nigga doesn't die in my arms. "Hol' on, Allstar…don't you die on me, nigga. Help is on the way."

One of my neighbors—a white man I neva fuck wit'—runs 'cross the yard ova to us, carryin' a buncha towels. "You alright?" he asks, handin' me towels. I tell 'im I am and thank 'im for the towels. "My wife and I saw everything," he says, gettin' on the otha side of Alex. He puts pressure on the wound. "We were on the phone with the police when the woman fired her gun."

"He's losin' a lotta blood," I say, tryna keep my composure. My hands start to shake. *Nigga, why da fuck didn't you give me that bitch's address when I first asked you for it? This shit woulda neva went down like this.*

Just as three cop cars are pullin' up alongside the house, the nigga stops breathin' and it takes e'erything in me not to pass the fuck out.

CHAPTER THIRTY-FIVE

Muhfucka dicked ova a lotta hoes...turned 'em out...then dismissed...gotta nutty-bitch pissed...'bout all da shit she took... horny ho couldn't let go...now da nigga stretched out...wit' bullets in da chest...nigga breathin' done stopped...shoulda gave me da info...crazy ho coulda been dropped...coulda been next on da list...now look...

"Ma'am, can you give me a description of the shooter?" the detective—a medium built brown-skinned man wit' big brown eyes and a thick nose—asked, flippin' open a pad, then pullin' his pen outta the pocket of his white button-up. I notice he has a coffee stain splashed up on the right side. He looks at me, waitin' for me to respond. I think, try to remember what the fuck the bitch looks like.

"Yeah," I say, glancin' down and noticin' there's blood on my muthafuckin' white Louis sneaks. I'm too through. "Give me a minute to refresh my memory." I close my eyes and think back to the day at the salon when the ho stepped to me.

"Take your time," he says, holdin' his pen in his hand, pressin' its tip to the paper.

Once her face comes to me, I say, "She's a crazy-ass, Spanish-lookin' bitch wit' brown hair and brown eyes. She's 'bout five-seven, and a buck-thirty."

"Okay. Did you actually see her shoot him?"

I frown. "I saw someone in all black standin' in my driveway pointin' a gun. No, I didn't actually see da bitch pull da trigga. But, trust me. I heard it. I seen 'im drop. And I know she did it. Alex has a restrainin' order on 'er. And da bitch was stalkin' 'im. That's enough for me to know it was 'er."

"Is there anything else?"

"Yeah, 'er name is Ramona and she—" I stop myself, rememberin' I took the nigga's phone to call his fam. Good thing I had the passcode to his phone; otherwise I wouldn't have been able to contact 'em. I pull the phone outta my bag, then press in the passcode to retrieve his messages. "Here, you listen to these messages and you tell me if you think da bitch did it." I put the phone on speaker and let him listen to 'em. He writes on his notepad, then asks if he can have the phone for evidence. I tell the muhfucka no. Tell 'im that he can get it from Allstar's attorney. I don't know if the nigga has one or not, but that's what I tell 'im.

"Okay, then. Do you have a number where I can reach you in case I have any more questions?" I give 'im my digits, then warn 'im to hurry up and get that bitch off the streets before I do. He looks at me like I'm crazy. "Ma'am, I ask that you not take matters into your own hands. We'll find whoever did this."

I raise my brow. "Be clear. There's a nutty bitch still out there somewhere wit' a gun. And 'er name is Ramona sumthin'. She's already come up on my property twice. And you heard those messages she left on his phone and da one 'bout what she was gonna do to me. So, if you think I'ma sit 'round and wait for da po-po to track 'er ass down, you done banged ya head. So as far as I'm concerned, the bitch should be considered armed and dangerous, so work it out. Get that bitch off da streets. Or I will."

I spin-off on his ass. *Stoopid muhfucka talkin' that dumb shit.* I see Allstar's moms walkin' toward us wit' a tall, buffed, bowlegged older version of Allstar. I know right off the bat it's his pops. *Mygaawd, that old-head is fiiine.*

I speak. "Hi, Missus Maples."

"Hello, baby," she says, walkin' up to me and givin' me a hug. "Good to see you again. Thanks for callin' me." She points to Allstar's twin. "Raynard, this is Alex's friend, Katrina. The young lady I was telling you about. Katrina, this is Alex's father."

I smile at 'im. "Hi, Sir, it's nice to meet you."

He smiles back at me. "Ohhh, so you're the young woman my son keeps talkin' about." He looks me up and down. Oh no this nasty muhfucka ain't tryna get his eye-rovin' on. "He wasn't lying when he said you were a beauty, and sexy, too. It's nice to meet you."

"Thanks," I say, shiftin' my weight from one foot to the otha. While Alex's moms is talkin' to the detective, I tell his father that he had to be rushed into surgery to try 'n stop the bleedin'. Tell 'im he was shot twice in the chest and once in the stomach. Tell 'im one of the bullets barely missed his heart.

"What'd he have to say?" Mr. Maples asks, pointin' ova to the detective when she walks back ova to us.

"He said they're gonna do everything they can to find that *bitch*. That they are puttin' out an all-points bulletin on her crazy ass."

I smirk, hearin' 'er talk my kinda talk.

"Did you tell him about the restraining order?" Mr. Maples asks.

"Of course I did. But he already knew about it." I tell 'er I told him 'bout it. She takes a deep breath, shakes 'er head, then starts spazzin'. "I knew some shit like this was gonna happen," she says, wipin' tears. "I knew one day I would be gettin' this call. He's so fuckin' hard-headed. I told his ass time and time again that him and that fat, black dick of his was gonna get his sex-crazed ass in some deep shit. I told his ass he can't keep fuckin' over these women and not expect one of them to snap."

"Alice, not now," Mr. Maples says, pullin' 'er into his arms. "No need in goin' off about something that has already happened. We need to concentrate on what's going on right now. The most important thing is that he makes it through this."

Ohmiiifuckin'gaawd! I can't believe this shit. I knew I shoulda neva fucked wit' this nigga. Got me sittin' up in this muhfucka wit' blood all ova my fuckin' shirt and sneaks. I take a seat in one'a the chairs. I'm fuckin' drained. I overhear Mister Maples tell his wife that he was goin' to try and find out what was goin' on. Alex's moms watches 'im walk off, then sits next to me. She grabs my hand and tells me how sorry she is that I had to see 'er son get shot. Tells me how he was tryna change his life; how he dismissed all of his hoes. Tells me how much the nigga cares 'bout me.

"I told him to tell you what was going on with that damn girl. But he's just like his father, stubborn and thick-headed. I didn't like that tramp from the moment she tried pinning a baby on him. I knew her ass was trouble." She pauses, takes a deep breath. "He is my only child. And I know he has a lot of shit with him, but I tell you this…" She looks me dead in the eyes. "I will beat… that bitch's…ass if he dies. I promise you that."

I squeeze 'er hand, smilin'. *Ohhhhkay, Momma, let's get it crunked, Boo!* "Mmmph. Well, stand in line, ma'am, 'cause I gotta ass-whoopin' wit' 'er name on it, too."

Alex's pops comes back and tells us that he's still in surgery. I watch as he nervously paces the floor. "Ray, won't you come and have a seat," Ms. Maples says.

"I'm fine," he says, holdin' his head in his hands.

She gets up and grabs his hand, pullin' him ova to a chair next to 'er. "Sit," she says, slippin' 'er fingas through his. I can't help but smile. If Allstar hadn't told me that they were divorced, I woulda neva believed it.

Sittin' here in this waitin' room has me thinkin' 'bout Zaire bein' up in the hospital by himself. It has me thinkin' that this— sittin' here wit' Alex's fam, isn't where I'm 'posed to be. I get up. Tell 'em I'm leavin'.

"Sweetheart, you sure?" his moms asks. I tell 'er I am more sure than eva. She tells me she knows Alex would want to see me when he comes outta surgery. I tell 'er I'm really not interested. Tell 'er that tonight's episode was a bit too extra for me. And I'm exhausted and disgusted by it. She gets up and gives me a hug. "I understand."

I decide to give it to 'er real like a real bitch should. "Missus Maples, no disrespect, but ya son got a buncha shit wit' 'im. And I ain't beat for that. This shit wit' that chick is it for me. I didn't sign up for this kinda craziness. And I ain't tryna stick 'round to wait for anotha nutty-ass ho to come from outta da woodwork. I'm done."

"I understand, trust me." Mr. Maples watches and listens to us talk, but keeps his mouth shut. "Well, I'ma tell you this, and you do what you want wit' it. My son has never expressed any kinda interest in a woman as he has with you. And the fact that he isn't rippin' and runnin' the streets like he used to says a lot." She looks ova at his pops. "Doesn't it, Ray?"

"Yeah," he says, tryna act like he isn't ear-hustlin'. He chuckles. "You got that boy's nose wide open. I never thought I'd see it happen."

"You gotta do what feels right for you," she says, givin' me anotha hug. "But I'd really like to see the two of you together. I think you're the kinda woman he needs in his life. So I hope you'll give 'im another chance."

I smile. "I can't make you any promises." I give 'er my cell number, and tell 'er to call me when he gets outta surgery. Then I reach into my bag and hand 'er his cell phone. I look ova at his pops. Tell 'im it was nice meetin' 'im, then dip.

TWO DAYS LATER, I'M BACK UP AT THE HOSPITAL TO SEE ALLSTAR. His moms had called to tell me that he made it through surgery and was lucky to be alive. She said he was in and outta consciousness. I could tell she was cryin'. I felt 'er pain. The whole time she was talkin', I kept thinkin' that that coulda been me sprawled out on the ground, leakin'. I kept seein' Zaire's cute lil' face and the shit fucked my nerves. If I didn't know before, a bitch knows now. I'm muthafuckin' done! I'm outta this muhfucka. As soon as my court hearin' next week is ova wit' and Zaire is finally able to come home, I'm sellin' my house and gettin' the fuck outta Jersey, and far the hell away from New York. I gotta.

I walk in Allstar's room. He's lyin' up in bed wit' tubes through his nose and there's a heart monitor beepin'. I hate hospitals. His upper body is bandaged. And he has a bandage 'round his head. Apparently when the bitch dropped 'im, he had hit his head and suffered a concussion.

I walk up on 'im. His eyes are closed. I stare at 'im. He looks all fucked up. *Damn, muhfucka, I really dig ya ass. And I dig da dick even better. But good dick attached to a muhfucka wit' a buncha damn drama ain't good for a bitch like me. And it damn sure ain't good for a nigga like you.*

Me poppin' this nigga's top flashes in my head. I blink. The last thing I should be thinkin' 'bout is what if I was the bitch who got nutty for the dick. Unlike that Ramona bitch, when I drop a nigga, it's final.

Speakin' of that dumb-ass ho, they found 'er ass late last night in some project buildin' down in Camden—a part'a south Jersey where e'ry day muhfuckas get it poppin' wit' the gun work like its Fourth of July. Stupid bitch got slapped wit' a buncha charges. Violation of a restrainin' order, attempted murder, possession of a weapon, and two othas I can't remember. All I know is the bitch is lucky they got at 'er before I did.

I reach ova and stroke the side'a his face. He slowly opens his eyes, blinks a few times, then smiles. "Hey," he whispers. "I'm so glad you're okay." He scrunches his face up in pain. "Aaah, this shit hurts." I tell 'im to try not to talk. He bites down on his bottom lip. "She really tried to do me in. Did they find 'er ass, yet?"

I nod. "Yeah, last night."

"Good. Uhh, shit." He shakes his head. "I can't believe this shit. That bitch really shot me." *Believe it, nigga. Ya stupid ass had no muthafuckin' business entertainin' 'er ass.*

I lean in his ear. "Nigga, I feel like punchin' you in ya muthafuckin' chest for bein' so damn stupid."

"I know. I fucked up, baby."

I sigh. "I'm not ya 'baby'."

"Uhh…whatever, yo. Can't you see I'm in pain? I'm not tryna hear that right now."

"Mmmph. Well, hear this then: If you're head wasn't wrapped, I would slap da fuckin' shit outta you."

He tries to laugh. "Aaah, oh fuck…Don't make me laugh."

"I ain't laughin'."

For some reason, this old-school joint starts playin' in my head. I feel like hummin' it. He musta read my mind when he says his moms used always tell 'im it's a thin line between love and hate. I smile. "Why you smilin'?"

"I was standin' here thinkin' the same thing. Actually I was hummin' da song in my head."

He grins. "Damn, you so fuckin' sexy."

I shift my bag from one hand to the other. "Listen, you should rest," I tell 'im, ignorin' the comment.

He reaches for my hand. "I'm so sorry for bringin' that shit to you, baby."

I take a deep breath. "Listen, I'm just glad they got da bitch off da streets. And that you're okay. Hopefully, it'll be a lesson, a warnin', to be very careful who you fuck wit' and how you fuck wit' 'em."

He nods. "You're right. This shit right here is definitely a wake-up call. I'm done. The first chance I get, I'm gettin' da fuck outta Jersey."

Muhfucka, whereva you go, you takin' you wit' you, so if ya mind ain't right, nigga, you ain't gonna be right. And all you gonna get is da same bullshit. I keep my thoughts to myself. Keepin' shit real, I know the shit applies to me as well. I don't tell 'im I'm bouncin', too. Still don't mention anythin' 'bout the baby. Shit, it's really none'a his business.

I glance at my watch, thinkin' 'bout Zaire. *I need to get up to da hospital.* I don't like 'im bein' up there too long wit'out someone up there wit' 'im at all times. Chanel is there for me when I'm not, like now. Still...that's where I'm 'posed to be. Not standin' here fuckin' wit' this nigga. "Look, I gotta go. You take care of ya'self. I'm glad you're okay."

He stares at me. "Damn, you say that like I'm not gonna see you again."

I lean ova and kiss the nigga's soft-ass lips, then look 'im in the eyes. "You're not," I say. He looks sad. When he tries to speak, I kiss 'im, again one last time, slippin' my tongue in his mouth, then walkin' out wit' 'im callin' for me to come back so we can talk. There ain't shit else to say. A bitch gotta know when to keep it cute, and dip on a muhfucka.

WHEN I FINALLY GET TO BROOKLYN, PARK MY WHIP, THEN MAKE my way up to the nursery, it's almost one o'clock. Chanel is holdin' and feedin' 'im. And I can't front. A bitch is feelin' some kinda way 'bout it. *I'm da one who should be feedin' 'im.* Yes, a bitch's jealous! It's a feelin' I ain't used to. But I keep it real cute, and toss my lips up into a smile.

"Hey," she says, smilin' back at me. "He is sooooo cute, Kat. Ohmigod, he's gonna be a real problem."

I nod knowin'ly. "Yup." I go wash my hands, then come back into the room. She hands 'im to me. "Heeeey, snookems," I say, surprised at how much joy this lil' boy brings. "I can't wait for you to get da fu—" I catch myself before I let the *fuck* word slip outta my mouth—"heck outta here."

Chanel is starin' at me, smilin'. "Awww, look at you bein' all fuzzy 'n pink, boo. I neva thought I see da day ya evil ass—"

I cut 'er off, suckin' my teeth. "Ugh, watch ya mouth, ho."

"Girrrl, this not cussin' shi…uh, mess is gonna be a real struggle for me."

"Puhleeze, tell me 'bout it."

"How's Allstar doin?" I tell 'er he's aiight. "Did you tell 'im you wasn't rockin' wit' 'im no more?"

I nod. "Not in so many words. But I think he knows." She shakes 'er head. "What?"

She twists 'er lips. "Nuthin'. When's he gonna get outta da

hospital?" I tell 'er he'll be there for at least anotha week or so from what his moms told me. "Oh, okay." She pauses. Tells me she's gonna come to Jersey tomorrow and stay the night.

I roll my eyes. "What Divine do now?"

She laughs. "He ain't do nuthin'. He's actin' like he got some sense this week."

"Whateva, trick. You da one wit'out any sense."

She keeps laughin'. "Oh, and you should talk. There's a muh—" I shoot 'er a look—"a man layin' up in a hospital room who you know you diggin' and who you know is diggin' you. And you dump 'im. What kinda sense is that?"

"It's common sense, ho. Sumthin' you obviously don't have."

The white nurse on duty catches my eye. She smiles and gives me a slight nod of the head as if she knows exactly what the hell I'm talkin' 'bout. We sit up at the hospital for a few hours wit' Zaire 'til Chanel decides to bounce. I tell 'er I'ma check for 'er in the mornin'. She already know what it is. A bitch ain't goin' no damn where tonight.

CHAPTER THIRTY-SIX

> *Some things ain't meant to be...a smart bitch gotta know when ta dip...lookin' at muhfuckas suspiciously...gotta know when ta cash in da chips...gotta be ready ta change peoples 'n places...see da world thru different eyes...now I gotta baby ta raise...finally I realize...it's time for a bitch ta change 'er ways...*

"Ohhhmiiiigod, Kat, I am so damn happy for you," Chanel says, as we walk outta family court. The judge has given me legal guardianship of Zaire. And today is the day he's bein' released from the hospital—to *me*.

After almost two-and-a-half months of bein' in the hospital, I can finally bring 'im home. He weighs almost seven pounds. On some real shit, goin' up to the hospital e'eryday watchin' that lil' boy fight for his life, made a bitch really start lookin' at shit sideways. A lot'a times I wasn't sayin' shit, but I was constantly thinkin' it. A bitch gotta do better, not just for me, but for him. The first time I held 'im in my arms, he got up in a bitch's heart, and I knew. I knew that that lil' sexy muhfucka was gonna have me wrapped 'round his lil' fingas.

"Girrrrl, I know you are glad this shit is finally ova. How you feel?" I don't have the words to describe what or how I'm feelin'.

Most of what I'm feelin' is new to me. And it's startin' to feel overwhelmin'. I take a deep breath, shakin' my head. I stop walkin', cuppin' my face wit' my hands. I'm all choked up. The minute Chanel hugs me, I start sobbin'. A bitch is scared and excited and nervous. But, most importantly, I am ready—ready for change, ready for the new experience, ready to love. "Hooker," she says, huggin' me tighter, "you ain't gotta say a word. I already know. C'mon, let's get to da hospital to get ya…uh, *our*, baby."

I pull myself together wipin' my face and blowin' my nose, then walk arm in arm with Chanel to the car. As soon as we get in and drive off toward the hospital, I look ova at Chanel and say, "Bitch, I need'a blunt. What you got good?"

She starts laughin', pullin' out 'er stash bag. "Ho, I'm already on it." She sparks it up, takes two pulls, then passes it to me. "Whew, this some good shit, right here," she says, holdin' 'er chest. She slowly blows out the smoke. "This da kinda shit that make a bitch wanna fuck'a horse."

"Chanel, ya ass is so damn stooopid."

"No, fa real. Have you seen how big they dicks are? Whew! Divine and I was watchin' porn da otha night—"

I start coughin' and chokin'. "Bitch, say it ain't so. Tell me ya ho ass ain't tryna get it in wit' animals, too."

"Ewww, no, bitch," she says, laughin'. "I was gettin' ready to tell you, before I was rudely interrupted, that there was this nigga in the movie wit' a dick like a horse's. It was ridiculous. And da bitch he was fuckin' was takin' that shit like a real champion."

I tilt my head. "Bitch, pass me da blunt. What da fuck that got ta do wit' ya freak-ass wantin' ta fuck a horse?"

She busts out laughin'. "I ain't tryna fuck no horse. It was a figure of speech."

I grunt, handin' the blunt back to 'er. "Yeah right. That's not what you said."

"Whateva," she huffs, takin' a pull. I let the shit go 'cause I don't care who she wants to fuck. I decide to tell 'er that after today I'm givin' up blazin'. Well, uh, I'ma try. Shit, today's my first day sparkin' in almost two months. I know I can do it. She looks at me, noddin' like she understands why. "Girl, you gotta do what you gotta do. You know I'm good wit' it. We still pourin' though, right?" I tell 'er not as much. Tell 'er that I need to keep my mind right if I wanna do shit right. She smiles. "Whew, no smokin', no drinkin' *and* no fuckin'? Hooker, you gonna be one cranky bitch."

I laugh. "Ho, who said anything 'bout no fuckin'?"

"Well, now that you ain't fuckin' wit' Allstar anymore, there goes ya steady supply'a dick."

My cell rings. I pull it outta my bag, lookin' at the screen. It's Tone. He's been hittin' me up on a regular, and I been kinda diggin' his convo. *Soon as I get back to Cali, I might have'ta ride down on this nigga's cock.* I grin, pressin' ignore. "Not necessarily, boo; not necessarily."

Chanel hurriedly zooms in and outta traffic so we can get to the hospital to get Zaire, then head to Jersey to hit up Short Hills mall to buy up all the hot shit for lil' boys.

A WHOLE MONTH FLIES BY WIT' ME STILL TRYNA FIND MY RHYTHM wit' havin' a baby in my life. The shit ain't easy. This lil' muh-fucka wanna sleep all day and be up all night, playin'. But, he's so damn cute. So, of course all I do is hold his ass. And he just coos, and drools, and smiles at me. But a bitch is exhausted!

"Oh nooo, Mister Man. Wake ya lil' ass up," I say, unsnappin' the legs of his sleeper, then changin' his Pamper. He fusses, but I don't give'a fuck. I slip the clean pamper underneath 'im, then unfasten the tabs on his Pamper. I make sure to cover his ding-a-ling so he doesn't piss on me. I had'a learn the hard way when he pissed in my damn face. Oooh, I wanted to slap his face. But, then he smiled at me, and I got all mushy. Damn 'im! "We gotta get bathed," I tell 'im as if he can understand what the hell I'm sayin', "then get you ova to the studio so we can flick it up today." We're takin' his first set of pictures today at noon, so he gotta represent. He already has some'a the illest shit out.

The doorbell rings. I glance at the Spiderman clock on Zaire's wall, frownin'. It's 8:24 a.m. "Who da hell is at the door this time'a mornin', huh, lil' man?" I ask, scoopin' 'im up in my arms, then walkin' into my room to throw on a robe before goin' downstairs to see who's at the door. "We got unannounced company, and you know that shit don't fly, ain't that right, lil' man?" He coos as I look through the peephole, shocked. *What da fuck this bitch want?* It's Patrice. This ho has neva dared to come up to my doorstep. I didn't even know the ho knew where I lived. *Keep it cute, bitch. Don't get nasty wit' this chick.* I swing open the door.

"Can I help you?"

She stares at the baby, then looks at me. "I was hopin' we could talk. Can I come in, *please?*" She's carryin' gift bags stuffed wit' items in both hands.

Zaire grabs at my ear, tryna pull on the diamond stud in my ear. I grab his lil' hand. "No, no," I say to 'im, steppin' back to let 'er in. "You have ten minutes."

"Thanks." She walks in, and I shut the door behind 'er. I tell 'er to have a seat. Although I ain't pressed 'bout her tryna get greasy wit' it up in here, I silently hope Zaire doesn't have'ta see me swing 'er through a wall. "Here," she says, handin' me the bags, "these are for da baby."

Bitch, I don't want ya shit. Baby boy wants for nuthin', ho. I take 'em from 'er. "Thanks. And his name is Zaire."

"I like that." She looks 'round my place, takin' a seat. I can tell the bitch's uncomfortable. Shit, I am, too. It's awkward as fuck. "Ya spot is beautiful."

I sit down on the otha side of 'er give. "Sweetie, I know you ain't come here for no social call, so let's not pussy-foot 'round. Get down to da real reason you here."

"I came to see my nephew," she says, starin' at 'im. "And to bring 'im his gifts. They're from his grandmotha, me and Elise."

I blink, blink again. In my head I hear myself sayin', "Bitch, puhleeze. Take ya gifts and ram up in ya slutty-stank pussy." I remind myself that I have a baby in my arms. Remind myself that I said I am tryna change. I swallow back a buncha curse words. "You coulda called, first." She tells me she's been callin' me for the last four weeks, that she's left a buncha messages, and I haven't called 'er back. I shrug. "I didn't wanna talk."

Zaire starts gettin' antsy. I bounce 'im up and down on my knee to calm 'im. She starts talkin' baby talk to 'im and he grins and coos at 'er. "Can I hold 'im?"

Bitch, no da fuck you can't! I hear Chanel's voice in my head. *Ho, it ain't always 'bout ya selfish ass.* I take a deep breath, tell 'er to go wash 'er hands, then reluctantly give 'im to 'er when she returns. She kisses him on his lil' forehead, then holds 'im up against 'er chest. She starts gettin' all emotional 'n shit. "Ohmigod, he's so precious. Kat, we gotta try 'n get ova this shit between us." I tell 'er not to curse in front of Zaire. She apologizes. "I wanna be in my nephew's life. And I'd like to be in yours again."

"That'll neva happen," I say, sittin' back in my seat.

She forces a smile. "We used to be like sistas."

"Yeah, 'til you dropped ya drawers and fu…screwed my man."

"That was a big mistake," she says, wipin' tears. She has Zaire facin' 'er sittin' on 'er knees, doin' more baby talk. He starts fussin' 'n fidgetin'. *Bitch, he don't wanna hear that shit.* She tries to walkin' 'round the room, bouncin' 'im. That doesn't work eitha.

"He's hungry," I say, gettin' up and takin' 'im from 'er. I tell 'er to follow me into the kitchen so I can warm his bottle. "So why'd you do it?" It's a question I neva asked 'er before. It's a question I neva really wanted the answer to. I just cut 'er off and fought 'er e'ery chance I got 'cause I was hurt. She looks at me confused. I grab a burpin' pad, then hand it to 'er along wit' Zaire so she can feed 'im. She's surprised. And so am I. I repeat the question. "Why'd you have'ta sleep wit' B-Love?"

"Keepin' shi...ish real, I was jealous of you. And I was mad that he picked you ova me."

"*Jealous?* For what?"

"Anywhere we went da niggas always ended up pressin' you. You always got all da attention."

"And so did you."

"Yeah, but not da way you did. Niggas saw you as the ultimate catch. Yeah, I was a dime. But they saw you as da fifty-cent piece. I used to really be feelin' some kinda way when we'd be somewhere and muhfuckas would try'n holla at you—first, then me. Or when we'd be walkin' into a spot, all eyes would be on you, then me. Sometimes I felt like I had'a compete wit' you. Even though I know that's not what it was. It was all in my head. Still, I loved you, but secretly hated you for bein' so eff'n fly. So when B-Love kinda dismissed me for you, I was feelin' some kinda way. But then I ran into da nigga a few weeks later and he told me on da sly that he wanted to get at me, too. That he'd run me his dick and lace me wit' wears and paper and shit, but I'd neva be wifey. I wanted da wifey slot, Kat. But he made it clear that only you'd have that title."

I grunt. "Mmmmph. So you let ya jealousy fu...eff up our relationship all 'cause ya schemin'-ass, hot pussy wanted what I had?"

She nods. "Kat, I was all effed up back then." *And ya slutty-ass probably still is*, I think, starin' at 'er. Zaire has fallen asleep. I get up from my seat, and take 'im from 'er, glancin' ova at the micro-wave clock. It reads: 9:27 a.m.

"Listen, I 'preciate you comin' through wit' da gifts, and I 'preciate you keepin' it real. But, it's time for you ta bounce, boo. Zaire and I got things to do today."

She gets up from 'er seat. "Yeah, I need to head back to Brooklyn, anyway. Thanks for lettin' me see Zaire. He's such a beautiful baby. I'm really surprised you are actually doin' this."

"Doin' what?"

"Raisin' 'im. You neva seemed like da type to wanna be tied down wit' a baby. And we all know how much you hated ya moms."

"True. And at first I wasn't beat for 'im. But after seein' 'im and holdin' 'im in my arms, I had'a change'a heart. Besides, I didn't want ya'll asses to get 'im."

She shakes 'er head, laughin'. "Of course you didn't; that's just you. But, it's all good. He's right where he needs to be—wit' his big sista. I'm glad we had'a chance to talk. I hope we can do it again, soon. I know ya grandmotha and Elise would like to see Zaire, as well."

I buck my eyes. "Listen, don't push it. I let you up in here. But don't get it twisted. I ain't beat for no family reunion-type shit. I don't want nuthin' to do wit' ya moms." *Kat, it ain't always 'bout ya selfish-ass.* "Not right now, anyway," I add, shakin' Chanel's voice outta my head, again. "Listen, I don't like you, Patrice. So we ain't eva gonna be what we used to be. And I ain't gonna be fake 'bout it. But, I'm not gonna keep you away from Zaire just because I got issues wit' you." I know she saw the FOR SALE sign out on the lawn when she pulled up, so she gotta know I'm bouncin'.

But since she ain't mention nuthin' 'bout it, I ain't offerin' shit. The bitch'll figure it out soon enough when all'a my numbers are changed, again. And there's no forwardin' address.

She smiles. "That's all I ask." She stares at me for a second, then says, "Kat, people can change. We may not eva get close again. But, hopefully, we can work on bein' civil to each otha."

"Sweetie, whateva happens it's gonna be for da sake of Zaire. That's it."

She leans in to kiss Zaire on the cheek. "Thanks."

"Oh, and—da next time you wanna come through, make sure you call, first. Don't show up at my door 'cause if you do, you won't get in."

"Then you need to answer ya phone."

Bitch, puhleeze. I swing open the door. "Goodbye Pa..." I stop in midsentence, surprised at who's standin' in front of me, preparin' to ring the bell.

CHAPTER THIRTY-SEVEN

Nigga showin' up outta da blue...seein' his face...standin' in my space...gotta bitch all twisted...nigga wanna make me see...his point'a view...tryna apologize...tryna make amends... bearin' his soul...offerin' up his love...tellin' me shit he's been dreamin' of...askin' me to let 'im love me....

He peeps Zaire sleepin' in my arms, then blinks. "Whose baby is that?" I tell 'im mine. "Yours?" he asks, lookin' puzzled. "How old is he?"

"What does it matter? He's mine. And his name is Zaire."

"Why haven't you returned any of my calls or texts?"

"'Cause I've been avoidin' you."

He tilts his head, starin' at Zaire, then me. I can tell he's tryna figure shit out in his head. I let 'im think what he wants. "I thought you weren't fuck—" I check his mouth; tell 'im not to curse in front of Zaire. "My bad. I mean, I thought you weren't gettin' it in wit' anyone else. Is it that cat's out there in Cali?"

I huff. "Geezus, nigga, what's up wit' da twenty damn questions? No, it ain't his. And it ain't yours. Now why you here?"

He reaches for me. "I came here for you."

Fuck all this censorin' shit! I step back. "Well, sorry to bust ya bubble. But, I ain't here for *you* so you can bounce back to whereva you came from. Go find ya'self a bitch whose gonna trick 'er money up on ya ass. And run behind ya ass, beggin' 'n cryin' 'n shit. And shootin' ya ass up when she can't have you."

"That's not da kinda woman I want on my arm, or in my life. I want you."

I shift Zaire from one arm to the otha. His lil' ass is gettin' heavy. "Well, you can't have me. I don't want da headache. So step."

I try to shut the door in his face. "Hol' up…" He puts his hand up and stops the door from shuttin'. "Yo, all I'm askin' for is fifteen minutes. That's all." I glare at 'im. "Kat, look at me, ma. I'm fucked up here. I haven't slept or ate in weeks. I ain't da kinda muhfucka to ever beg a bit…a woman for shit. But, I'm askin', beggin' you, for *fifteen* minutes; that's it. Is that too much for a muhfucka to ask for? Fifteen minutes for you to give me a chance to talk; and you to listen. And when I'm done, if you still ain't beat, then I'll bounce; real talk. I'll walk outta this door and never bother you, again."

I stare at this muhfucka; take the nigga in. His eyes are red and swollen. The nigga looks like he hasn't slept in days. I feel the urge to slap the shit outta 'im for comin' into a bitch's life, pushin' his way into my space. Forcin' a bitch to feel shit she ain't tryna feel.

I step back, pull open the door, and let 'im in. "Ten minutes, then you need to leave." He brushes past me. I shut the door, then tell 'im to give me a minute take the baby upstairs to put 'im in his crib.

When I come back downstairs, he's sittin' on the sofa, holdin' his head in his face. He lifts his head when he hears me. "Kat, listen to me, baby…"

I stand in the middle of the floor, fold my arms. "Nigga, don't *baby* me. Hurry up 'n get to da point, so I can go back to doin' what I was doin'."

"Yo, why da fuck you so fuckin' mean and evil? What did I ever do to you for you to treat me like shit?"

"You came into my life, disruptin' my flow, nigga. That's what you did. You brought drama to my muthafuckin' door, nigga."

"That wasn't my intention," he stands up, walkin' ova to me. "I'm really sorry 'bout that."

"Nigga, sorry don't cut it. A bitch shot ya ass right in front of me. You knew that bitch was a Looney bin graduate and you still was fuckin' wit' da bitch on da sly."

"Kat, I swear to you. I wasn't fuckin' wit' that broad. I put that on e'erything I love. Straight lace, baby, I was only talkin' to 'er ass, tryna keep da peace. Da bitch was talkin' real reckless, so I tried to defuse da shit."

I glare at 'im. "So you tellin' me you was only talkin' to da bitch on da phone?"

He shifts his eyes, shakin' his head. "Nah, I saw 'er a few times. But it wasn't nuthin'."

"Besides 'er, who da fuck else was you seein'?"

"Kat, I wasn't seein' 'er da way you sayin' it. I wasn't seein' anyone else. I told you, on some real shit, that I was really into you."

I sigh. "Why couldn't you step da fuck off when I was brushin' ya ass off? Why'd you have'ta keep pressin' a bitch?"

He touches the side of my face. "'Cause, on some real shit, da first moment I saw you wit' ya girl walkin' through da hotel in Arizona, I knew I had'a get at you. I knew you were da kinda woman I could fall for. And that's on e'eryting. Even when you was playin' a muhfucka to da left, that shit only made me wanna get at you more."

"Then you a damn fool," I tell 'im, sidesteppin' 'im. I take a seat on the sofa.

"Nah…that makes me a man who knows what he wants. Da first time we spoke on da phone, and I heard ya sexy-ass voice, I knew what I already felt—that you were da one for me."

"You don't even know *me*."

"But a muhfucka knows what he feels. I ain't ever felt no shit like this for any female before. And that's some real shit, Kat."

"And what's that?"

"Love."

Love? The word slips from this nigga's lips wit'out any effort. And I'm shocked. It's sumthin' a bitch neva 'pected to hear from 'im. I don't know why, but I need to be sure I heard 'im the first time. "What did you say?" He doesn't blink, doesn't flinch. Looks me in the eyes 'n repeats the shit. "That's what I thought you said. Well, you need ta take that shit up wit' another bitch—"

"Yo, why you keep tryna push me away?"

"I'm not pushin' you away. I'm tryna give ya ass a chance to bow out gracefully."

"I'm not lookin' for an out," he snaps, "I'm lookin' for you to open ya heart and let a muhfucka in so he can love you."

"How you gonna love me? What da fuck you know 'bout lovin' anyone other than ya'self? You've neva even been committed to a bitch. So what makes you think a muhfucka like you can be faithful? How da fuck you know you even capable of love?"

"'Cause I'm not that muhfucka I used to be. I knew the first time we rocked them sheets who I wanted in my life. And I know what I feel"—he taps the space over his heart wit' his fist—"right here."

"And layin' up in that hospital bed gave a muhfucka a buncha time to think. I almost died, Kat. And keepin' it a hunnid, that shit scared me. I don't wanna die not knowin' what it's like to love someone. I mean really love 'em, feel me?

This muhfucka is crazy. Would this muhfucka be sayin' all this shit if he knew I was a bitch who laid a buncha niggas down wit'out battin' an eye? Would da nigga be so pressed to love a bitch knowin' she gets off on shuttin' a muhfucka's lights out?

"I wanna understand you, baby. I wanna stand by you. Be the kinda man in ya dreams. I can be that muhfucka, Kat; real talk. Let a muhfucka love you, Kat."

"Da last muhfucka I thought loved me was busy lettin' a bitch who I thought was my friend suck his dick. And da nigga after 'im was caught fuckin' my aunt, so—"

"So, that's their shit. Not mine. I'm not them. I told you, I don't cheat."

"And you neva been in a relationship eitha."

"Yeah, true. But that doesn't mean I don't know what kinda woman I need in my life to push me to be a better man.

"Yeah, well, you say that shit now. But what happens when ya ass starts gettin' bored wit' havin' only one bitch?"

"That won't happen," he says, starin' at me.

"I don't trust you, nigga."

He slowly shakes his head, runs his hands ova his face. "Keep shit gee. Is it me, or ya'self you don't trust?"

I frown. "Nigga, what's that 'posed to mean?"

"It means bein' honest wit' ya'self 'bout what da fuck you really feelin'. No frontin'. Step outta da bullshit, and see *you* for da first time…"

"*Frontin'?* I don't gotta front 'bout shit. I'ma *real* bitch, nigga."

"Yeah, wit' e'ery bitch, *but* you. For once trust what's in ya heart, not what you *think* in ya head. You say I don't know you, but ya wrong, baby. I know you hurt, like I hurt. I know you dream, like I dream. I know you scared of takin' risks. Of lettin' someone get close to you. Like me, you been runnin' all ya life from ya'self."

I blink, blink again. *This muthafucka don't know shit 'bout a bitch like me.* I slam my hand up on my hip, point a finga at 'im, stab-bin' it in the air. "Nigga, you don't know me; you don't know *shit* 'bout what I been runnin' from, so save that psychoanalytical bullshit."

"Check this out, this ain't no playground and I'm not here to game you. I know what I want. And I know what I don't want. You, I want. Them other broads were strictly bitches I wanted pussy from."

I glance ova at the clock. "Aiight, times up. You gotta go."

"No, not until you listen to me." What da fuck?! This nigga must want anotha round of bullets in 'im. "If you wanna run up 'n get ya gun, do you. I already been shot up, so it ain't nuthin' else you can to do 'xcept kill a muhufa."

"Alex, save all that Alley Cat and Daddy Long Stroke bullshit for them dizzy-ass hoes out there. I ain't interested in nuthin' you sellin'."

He lets out a frustrated sigh. "I'm here, not as Alley Cat, or Daddy Long Stroke, or any other stage name bitches have given me. I'm here as Alexander, baby. A man flawed...and yes, fucked up. But underneath all my scars and faults, I'ma man wit' a big heart, but it's been empty. And I've spent my whole life tryna fill up this big-ass hole wit' a buncha pussy. Yeah, a buncha bitches done tossed me the pussy, done let me bust my nuts down in their throats and all ova their faces, and they let me run all through their wallets. But, after e'ery fuck; after e'ery nut, the only thing it did was make me feel more fucked up, had me feelin' lonelier than before, and still empty. What are you so afraid of?"

"I ain't afraid of shit, nigga."

Bitch, stop lyin'. You say you a real bitch, then keep da shit a hunnid wit' da nigga.

"Yo, if you wanna keep livin' ya life in fear, then do you. But, you gonna miss out on some good shit."

I huff. "Like what, *you?*"

"Nah, like freedom."

I frown. "Nigga, what are you talkin' 'bout? I am free."

He shakes his head. "Baby, as long as you keep livin' in fear, you'll never be free."

"I'm neva gone be da kinda bitch you gonna *try*'n run game on. I'm not da kinda bitch you think you gonna hurt and it be all gravy. No, nigga, I'm da kinda bitch who'll put a bullet in ya shit. And unlike that bitch, Ramona, I pop niggas and drop niggas, in one shot." He bucks his eyes. I can tell I done shocked 'im. I walk ova to the door, swingin' it open. "It's time for you to bounce."

"So you really ain't fuckin' wit' me?" I can tell he's tryna keep it together. I can hear his voice crackin'.

I shake my head, openin' the door. "I can't."

"Oh, aiight. Then I guess it's goodbye."

"I guess so." We're standin' in front of each otha. He's lookin' into my eyes. And I'm lookin' into his. I've neva seen this nigga look so broken. "I don't want you to think I hate you, 'cause I don't. Keepin' shit real, I care 'bout you. And I'm sure you have da potential to be a good man, but I can't chance you draggin' me into no dumb shit. I have a baby to think 'bout now. And I don't want drama in my life."

"So you gotta 'nother nigga in ya life?"

"Alex, da only nigga in my life is that lil' boy upstairs. That's da only man I have da energy for right now." He asks me 'bout the sign outside. Wants to know where I plan on movin'. I tell 'im I don't know. Even if I did know, I wouldn't tell 'im anyway. He wants to know if I'm gonna stay in Jersey, or move back to Brooklyn. I shrug. "I seriously doubt it."

"I feel you. Yo, I thought you said I get three strikes? I should have two left."

"Gettin' ya tires slashed in my driveway was strike one. Actin' funny 'n shit and gettin' ghost on a bitch was strike two. And not keepin' shit real wit' me 'bout that bitch was strike three."

I walk up on 'im, and do sumthin' I know I probably shouldn't. I pull him by his shirt down to me, standin' up on my tippy-toes. I kiss 'im on the lips. Let the nigga slip his tongue in my mouth. My pussy starts to pop as his hands start roamin' all ova my body.

"I've missed you so much. Don't do this to us, baby. Give me anotha chance."

Fuck da nigga one more time, ho.

I can't do this shit wit' him.

Bitch, puhleeze. You know you wanna ride da nigga's dick.

I pull away. "I can't."

He hangs his head, lookin' defeated as he walks out. I watch 'im walk to his car, get in, then back out. He's lookin' at me, and I'm lookin' at 'im. I wave to 'im. And he blows the horn. I don't shut the door 'til I can no longer see his car, then I press my back up against the door, closin' my eyes and bangin' my head up against it. *Bitch, you know you care 'bout his ass. You should gave da nigga anotha chance.*

I can't take that kinda chance. I can't let da nigga get all up in my head, then fuck up my heart.

Ho, get ova ya'self. You know da nigga cares 'bout you. You saw da shit in his eyes.

Call da nigga and tell 'im to come back.

Hell no! I can't fuck wit' 'im.

I take a deep breath, walkin' up the stairs to get showered and dressed. For some reason, a bitch is feelin' kinda down. I know, think, in my head, I'm doin' the right thing, but my heart is tellin' me sumthin' different. *Fuck, fuck, fuck!*

CHAPTER THIRTY-EIGHT

Six months later

"Ooooh, bitch, I don't think I can eva forgive you for packin' up and movin' waaaaay out there, and takin' Zaire from me," Chanel says, lookin' at me through the monitor on my laptop. We're up on Skype talkin', which is our new thing. We talk e'eryday, two, three times a day. It's almost like we're right in the same room togetha. I miss this bitch. She presses 'er face up to the screen. Zaire tries to grab the monitor. "Ain't that right, Boo? That mean old-ugly witch done took you from ya Aunt Chanel." He laughs, touchin' the screen. "Ohhh-miiigod, Kat, and he has two teeth already."

"Girl, them things just popped up outta know where. Now all he wanna do is bite up e'erything. This lil' muh…boy, is a piece of damn work."

"Wit' his fine self," she says, wavin' and blowin' kisses at 'im. He waves back at 'er, then gets down on the floor and starts crawlin' ova to the otha side of the room to get his Spiderman toy. I have toys and shit e'erywhere. This boy is has e'ery kinda toy made for lil' boys, then some. He's spoiled rotten. Chanel rolls er eyes, suckin' 'er teeth.

"Why you doin' all that?"

"Kat, why'd you have to move so damn far from me?"

I laugh. She asks me the same shit e'ery time we talk. And I tell 'er the same shit. "'Cause change is good."

Three weeks after I put my house up on the market, I was able to sell it. I dropped ten gees off'a the price but it's all good. A bitch was ready to roll out, so I didn't give a fuck 'bout nickel and dimin' ova a few thousand dollas. I even paid for the closin' costs. I just wanted to be done. It sold and that's all I cared 'bout. The next month, I shipped what I wanted out here and sold e'erything else, then I changed my numbers. It's definitely a different vibe here, and I'ma always be a East Coast bitch at heart. But bein' here is the best thing I coulda did—for me.

"Change my ass. You coulda kept it real cute and found a cute lil' place in Connecticut, or Philly. You woulda been far enough, but still close enough at da same time. But nooooooo, you gotta be all dramatic and shit, movin' way out there."

"Chanel, boo. Let it go. You'll be here for a whole month in two weeks, so…" I look to see where Zaire is, then lean into the monitor and whisper, "…stop actin' like a needy-ass bitch."

She laughs, whisperin' back, "Fuck you, booga." I toss up da finga, pressin' it up at the screen. She asks me what's up wit' the nigga Tone. I tell 'er nuthin'. Tell 'er we straight mad cool. She wants to know if we fuckin'.

Of course we are, but it ain't nuthin' serious. He's my lil' maintenance man 'til sumthin' worthwhile comes my way. I ain't tellin' 'er all that, though. I laugh. "Bitch, stop tryna monitor my pussy. Geesh." Zaire crawls back ova to me, reachin' up for me to pick 'im up. "Okay, Zee alert," I state, lettin' 'er know that Zaire's back in earshot. I lift 'im up.

"Eat. Eat. Eat," he says.

"Ohmigod, when did he learn to say that? He's talkin' away now."

"Girl, all this boy knows is 'eat, eat, eat' wit' his greedy self." He's eight months old and he's almost twenty-four pounds. He says it again, tryna bite my hand. "Okay, Zaire. Wait. Here drink this." I hand 'im a sippee cup of water. He throws it. "No. Bad boy."

He throws his Spiderman toy. "Don't get it crunked up in here, lil' boy. 'Cause you 'bout to get tossed up, okay? Now chill out."

Chanel laughs. "Boo, you gonna have ya hands full."

"Tell me about it. So, you already know I don't have time for no man."

She smiles. "Well, you neva know what might happen."

"Mmmph. Trick, you know sumthin' I don't?"

"Nope." I grab the laptop, carryin' Zaire on my hip into the kitchen. I sit the laptop up on the table, then put Zaire in his high chair. "Kat, I'm so proud of you. Is parenthood what you thought it would be?"

"Yes and no," I tell 'er, movin' 'round the kitchen tryna warm up Zaire's food. He starts bangin' on the tray, yellin' at the top'a his lungs. E'ery since he started daycare he's picked up shit I ain't diggin'. Like throwin' shit and this screamin'. I'm slowly learnin' how'ta ignore his ass when he starts up his tantrums. Hopefully, he'll outgrow the shit, otherwise we gonna have'a problem. And it ain't gonna be cute. "Sometimes it can be…" The doorbell rings. I ignore the shit. The only person who knows where I live out here is Tone. And I know it ain't 'im 'cause he calls first.

"Ain't you gonna get da door?"

"Nope."

It rings again. "Kat, maybe you should get it. I sent a package to you. That might be it."

"Ooooh, what you send me?"

"Don't worry 'bout it. Go open da door and find out for ya'self."

I suck my teeth. "Uggh. Watch da baby," I say, turnin' the laptop facin' Zaire so she can keep an eye on 'im while I go to the door. I laugh, knowin' there ain't shit she can do if he gets into sumthin', but I like sayin' it, anyway. I tell 'er I'll be right back, then walk out into the livin' room, poppin' shit.

I peek through the peephole. All I see is a white box wit' a red bow blockin' a man's face. *Oh, it must be Chanel's package.* I swing open the door. My mouth drops open. "How'd you know where to find me?" I ask, already knowin' the answer. *That bitch can't eva stick to da damn script!*

He grins, handin' me the box. "Can I come in?" I step back and let 'im in. I can't front, this deep, dark nigga looks...delicious! "Damn, I've missed you, Kat."

I smile. "Nigga, I've..." I stop myself, almost forgettin' I left Zaire in the kitchen by himself. I shut the door and tell 'im to follow me into the kitchen. I turn the laptop 'round. "Umm, ho...is this the package you were talkin' 'bout?" I go back to feedin' Zaire. He has food tossed all ova the floor, and all 'round his face. But, he's quiet and happy and that's all that matters.

She laughs. "Hey, Allstar; took you long enough to get there."

He smiles, takin' off his leather jacket, then sittin' at the table. "Wassup, ma? Yeah, I got lost."

"Well, I'm glad you finally made it. She was startin' ta bore me wit' 'er borin'-ass life. Blah, blah, blah." He laughs. I tell 'er to watch 'er mouth. She keeps runnin' 'er trap. Tells me she wanted to tell me that she had run into 'im at some party a few weeks ago, but figured I wouldn't wanna hear it. And she's right. Well, no...not really. Truth is I neva stopped thinkin' 'bout this nigga. But I knew I didn't have any intentions of eva callin' 'im again.

I sweep up the mess Zaire made on the floor, finish cleanin' 'im up, then take 'im outta his chair. I sit 'im on the floor and he starts crawlin' ova to Alex. Alex picks 'im. "Hey there, lil' man. Wassup, dude?" Zaire starts grinnin' and tryna talk. "Give me five."

I laugh when he slaps 'im. "That's right, Zaire, baby. You know he deserved that."

Chanel is grinnin'. "Awwwww, ya'll look so cute. Like one big family."

"Okaaay, bitch, I've had'a 'nough of you for one day."

"Watch ya mouth, Boo."

"Whateva," I say, givin' 'er the finga. "I'ma deal wit' you later, ho." She laughs. I slam the laptop monitor close on 'er. Alex laughs. And Zaire starts laughin' louder. "Now back to you," I say, takin' Zaire from 'im. "Why are you here?"

"I'm here for you," he says, gettin' up from the table. He walks ova to me and Zaire. He hugs and kisses me as Zaire looks on. "I wanna 'notha shot at bein' ya man."

"I'm not givin' out any more shots," I say, walkin' back into the family room. He follows behind me. I can feel the nigga's eyes all up on my ass. I grin. "Stop starin' at my ass."

He laughs. "I can't help it. There's so much of it."

"Whateva." I sit Zaire in his playpen, then turn to face Alex, foldin' my arms 'cross my chest. "Nigga, you tell me why you think I should give you anotha chance."

He walks up on me, wrappin' me up in his strong arms. "I had three bullets pumped in my chest and stomach by a bitch I aint give two shits 'bout and almost died. I'm willin' to take those same three bullets in da heart, and die, lovin' you. Baby, ain't shit changed. I love you. I honestly thought I'd neva see you again. And my moms kept tellin' me I needed to get ova you. But I couldn't. I didn't want to. Then I ran into ya peeps. And she told me e'erything I needed to know."

I squint at 'im, raisin' a brow. "Oh, yeah, and what's that?"

He kisses me on the lips. "That you loved me." I keep my trap shut, lookin' up at 'im. He kisses me again. "That you missed me."

"You a fool for listenin' to 'er."

"Nah, I don't think so." I try to step outta his embrace, but he holds on tighter. "You feel good in my arms."

"Where you stayin'?" I ask, changin' the subject. He tells me he's at the Marriott ova on Fourth Street in San Francisco. I ask 'im how long he's gonna be out here. He tells me for as long as he needs to be. I stare at 'im. "What's up wit' you and ya girl in LA? Ya'll still fuckin'?"

"She ain't my girl. And, no, we ain't fuckin'. I deaded that shit the night I invited you to my spot. I already knew what it was."

I glance ova at Zaire. He's knocked out. "Be clear. I'm not sharin' no nigga wit' anyone, period."

"And I ain't lookin' to let you." I ask 'im how many chicks he's fuckin'. "I ain't had no pussy since you."

I raise my brows. "Nigga, stop lyin'."

"Nah, true story. I've been straight beatin' this dick, fleshlightin' it, and beatin' up my blow-up doll. Who you been fuckin'?" I tell 'im 'bout Tone. "You need'a shut that shit down, today."

I frown. "Nigga, you ain't my man. And you ain't runnin' shit."

"Whatever, yo. Shut that shit down, Kat. And let's make this shit pop wit' us. I'm tryna play for keeps, baby."

I tilt my head. "What are you sayin'?"

He walks outta the den. Tells me he'll be back. That he wants me to open the box he brought me. He walks back in, carryin' it under his arm, handin' it to me. "Open it." I sit down on the sofa, then untie the ribbon, liftin' the lid. The flowers are beautiful. Two dozen orchards and birds-of-paradise.

"Thank you," I say, liftin' up the card, then pullin' it outta the envelope. I read it: I LOVE YOU, KAT, MORE TODAY, THAN THE DAY BEFORE. I WANNA BUILD A LIFE WIT' YOU, BABY. WANNA BE ALL THE MAN YOU'LL EVER NEED. LOVE, YA MAN FOR LIFE...

"The flowers and card are beautiful. But you still haven't told me why I should give you anotha chance."

"There's another box inside there," he says, liftin' up the flowers, then pullin' it out. I blink. "Kat, I'm not goin' anywhere. You've cursed me out, pulled a gun out on me, and moved three thousand miles away, and I'm still here, still standin', still feelin' what I feel." He opens the box. "I love you, Katrina Rivera, and I wanna be ya husband, ya lover, and ya friend. I wanna grow old wit' you. Raise mini-mes and mini-yous. And explore da world, and each otha, wit' you—and only you. I wanna die knowin' I loved you and you loved me back, baby. Will you marry me?"

I feel myself startin' to hyperventilate. It feels like e'erything 'round me has stopped as I stare at the two-carat rock. My words get stuck in the back'a my throat.

"Ya peoples and my moms helped me pick out da ring. If it's not what you want, we can go pick out sumthin' else."

I shake my head. "No, it's beautiful," I say, feelin' myself becomin' overwhelmed. I'ma fly, buttery bitch wit' a buncha secrets. A cold-blooded killer, a ruthless bitch, wit' dozens of bodies tagged wit' 'er name on 'em. And—although I don't plan on bodyin' anyone else, I can't say what I'ma do if I get the urge to pop anotha muhfucka's top, like his if he tries to do me dirty.

"Well, baby…will you be my wife?" I look at 'im wit' tears runnin' down my face. I stare into his eyes as he kisses my tears. "Yo, you my fuckin' heart, girl. Let's make this shit official."

I nod. "Yes," I finally say in a whisper. I lean ova and kiss 'im in a way I've neva kissed any otha nigga. I kiss 'im wit' a purpose I neva knew existed inside'a me. I kiss 'im wit' more passion than I eva thought imaginable. And 'cause I'm *that* bitch, I slip my tongue deep into his mouth, and welcome 'im into the *Kat Trap*.

ABOUT THE AUTHOR

Cairo resides in Northern New Jersey. He divides a lot of his time between Jersey and southern California, where he is working on his next literary creation, *Man Swappers*. His travels to Egypt are what inspired his pen name. You can email him at: cairo2u@verizon.net. Or visit him on his website/blog at www.booksbycairo.com, or at www.myspace.com/cairo2u, www.facebook.com/CairoBlacktheauthor, or www.blackplanet.com/cairo2u

If you enjoyed "Kitty-Kitty, Bang Bang,"
we're sure you'll love this little taste
of Cairo's next novel

MAN SWAPPERS

Coming Soon from Strebor Books
ENJOY!

≈1≈

PLEASURE

My panties are wet and my body is hot and ready. I am so fucking horny watching my sister, Porsha, down on her knees sucking dick. I watch as she bobs her head back and forth, making swishy-popping noises with her mouth as she slurps, gulps, and swallows the thick, eight-inch dick in front of her.

"That's right, Sis," I urge, grinning and sexily eyeing the six-foot-three, two-hundred-and-twenty pound, caramel-skinned stallion she's kneeling before. He palms the back of her head, eyeing me back. My tongue traces my cherry-red painted lips. "Throat that nigga's dick, Passion. Rock his top, like Mommy taught you." She swallows him down to the base, juggling his balls in her hand. "That's my girl. You're making Mommy so proud of you."

Porsha, aka Passion, enjoys connecting with a man's inner spirit, empowering him to be less inhibited. She encourages him to relax, relate, release and...enjoy the moment.

I thumb my nipples and they pop up like chocolate Hershey kisses, eager to be licked, suckled, and devoured by his hot, hungry mouth. But, tonight, there'll be no touching. He is only allowed to look.

"You like looking at these pretty titties?" I ask him, seductively shaking them at him. I lift up my left breast and flick my long tongue over my nipple. He pulls in his bottom lip. I switch to my right breast, then do the same thing. "You wanna suck these nipples?"

He groans. "Ohhh, yeaaaah, baby...aaaaah, fuuuuck..." I can tell Porsha's head game is getting the best of him. He is straining to hold it together; struggling not to spill his creamy yogurt without permission.

"Motherfucker," my other sister, Persia, barks, snapping her whip, "You better not cum until I tell you to. You understand me?"

"Yesssssss...uhhhh, shiiiit..."

My sister, Persia—aka Pain, is domineering and commanding. Tonight, she is the mistress of ceremony, if you will. She enjoys creating scenarios and role-playing almost as much as she enjoys administering pain. Although she'll tell you, quick, that she is not a Sadomasochist, or a Dominatrix, she's the one who enjoys wearing the latex and leather getups with six-inch pencil boots and red nail polish and lipstick, dragging men around by collars and chains. And you can see the gleam in her eyes every time she causes a man to whimper and beg.

And, then, there is me—Paris, aka Pleasure. I am turned on by watching my two sisters bring a man to his knees just as much as I enjoy having him watching me pleasure myself. I enjoy seeing a man experience intimacy, and allowing him to fulfill his hidden carnal desires while connecting with his fantasies. I am the one who lets them watch me fuck myself with fingers or toys, or a combination of the two, wishing it could be them lost in between the slick folds of my pussy. It is in the knowing that he can not touch, that he can not smell, that he can not taste, the essence of my womanhood—unless, I allow him to—that brings me the most pleasure. I enjoy seeing a man experience sensual and sexual gratification. And, it is within the dark confines of his mind that my sisters and I transform deepest desires into flesh-to-flesh reality.

"Yes what, you sneaky motherfucker?' Persia barks, bringing my attention back to her. "Fucking your best friend's sister, you nasty motherfucker." She walks over to him and snaps a nipple clamp onto his left nipple.

He winces. And bolts of electricity shoot through my clit. "Aaaaah…yes, Mistress Pain."

"You like watching his mother, don't you? You like gazing at her big, wet pussy?"

Bitch, you wish. My pussy ain't big, I think, cuttin' an eye at her. I smack the front of my pussy, then spread my lips so he can see for himself how tight it is.

He licks his lips. "Yes, Mistress Pain."

"Tell your friend's mother how pretty she is."

Porsha sucks him ferociously, taking him all the down in her throat while she smacks, pops and pinches her clit.

"Aaah, oh, shit…" he moans.

"Look at his mother," Persia says, turning his face in my direction, "and tell the bitch what a sexy whore she is."

The word *whore* slices through me. But I will play my position and let it go, for now.

"You real fuckin' sexy, ma," he says, gazing at me. He purposefully doesn't call me a whore, knowing it will bring him delightful consequences.

She grabs him by the throat. Her nails sink into his jugular. He winces, then grunts. Porsha's wearing his dick out, sucking it feverishly. "That's not what I told you to say, you defiant little shit. I said to tell her she's a sexy whore."

"Aaaah, shiiiiit…"

"You better not nut, you dumb fuck. Now say it."

I force a grin. Continue in the fantasy, leaning back on my right forearm, using my left hand to massage my clit over my thin silk panties while staring at Persia. Despite my annoyance that she is forcing him to call me a whore, I am still in awe at how well she flips into script and dominates, manipulates, and controls men. She is wearing a crotch-less latex cat suit with cut-outs at her breasts. Her chocolate nipples poke out like sweet pieces of double-coated chocolate Malt balls.

He repeats her words, and she lets go of his throat, mushing him in the face. I can see the imprint of her nails embedded in his skin. He keeps his eyes locked on me, biting down on in his bottom lip.

"You like fuckin' your friend's sister's throat?" Persia asks, clamping his right nipple. He snaps his eyes shut, pulling in a deep breath. "Open your eyes," she says, stepping up on the footstool near him and sticking her tongue in his ear. She bites down on his earlobe. Repeats the question; tells him to keep his eyes locked on me as I part my shapely legs so he can see my swollen petals around the crotch of my panties.

"Yes, Pain. Her throat feels so fuckin'…aaah, shit…good."

Persia walks over to the table, draped with a black tablecloth, and grabs a wooden ruler. She walks back over to Emerson. But tonight he is being called Sammie—this is what he has asked for. To be a horny teenage boy who sneaks into a window to get his dick sucked by his friend's sister while he watches their mother masturbate. I am the mother who walked in on them, then started watching and playing with myself. A role I happily oblige. Persia glides the ruler over his muscular ass. She traces his ass cheeks with it, runs the edge of it down the crack of his ass, then without warning, she whacks him with it. He flinches. She whacks him again, and again. Then, like a razor, she slowly slides it up his ass crack before lighting his ass on fire.

"You wanna nut, don't you, you nasty little Fucker?"

"No, Pain. Only if it is pleasin' to you."

I moan, listening to the smacking sounds of Porsha's dick sucking. "That's right, suck the shit out that fat dick. Suck him how Mommy showed you." I let out a girlish giggle, then grind on my hand. "You have my pussy soooooo wet," I moan, again, gazing at Emerson. "Sammie, you wanna smell my wet panties while you fuck my daughter's nasty little throat with your dick?"

"Yesssss…" he moans.

"You wanna taste 'em?"

He groans, then grunts, nodding his head as Porsha pulls his cock from out of her mouth and begins to coat it with a glob of spit. She jacks him off, then slowly starts sucking on his balls. "Aaaaah, yeah, baby…just like that…"

I lift my legs up in the air and slowly peel off my panties. I spread open my legs, give him a visual of what he can't have. His eyes widen as he drinks in the loveliness of my freshly-shaven pussy. It greets him with glistened lips, smiling at him. He watches as I dip one finger, then two, in and scoop out my juices. I slip my fingers into my mouth and gently suck on them. When I have cleaned my fingers of my cream, I part my pussy lips and allow him to swallow in its pink center, lush and slippery.

I love my pussy. No, seriously…I adore it. The way it looks; the way it feels; the way it smells; the way its muscles constrict and contract—gripping and tugging at a finger, or tongue, or a neat little battery-operated gadget—when being teased, taunted and toyed with. Oh, how I love the way my cunt drips with its own sweet, sticky, delectable honey as it whines and begs and pleads for a deep fucking by a deliciously thick, pulsating cock. Too bad—for him, tonight, there will be no fucking…by choice.

Emerson, uh Sammie, lets out another moan, keeping his eyes glued to my weeping pussy. He knows my cunt cries for his touch. Knows it begs for his thrusts. And I see the yearning in his eyes to give it what it needs, wants, and craves—his tongue, his fingers, his thick, veiny dick!

Porsha slides a hand between her legs, rapidly smacks her pussy and pops her clit a few times while throating Emerson's cock.

Persia removes his left nipple clamp, then twirls her tongue around it. She flicks her tongue over it, then nibbles on it before moving over to his right nipple and doing the same thing. I know she is about to allow him to bust his nut. And he knows it, too. She walks in back of him, drops down and starts nibbling and biting on his swollen ass cheeks. She kisses and licks where she has bruised. I watch as she parts his ass open, then runs her tongue in his crack.

"Oh, fuck…goddamn…ya'll freaky-ass bitches fuckin' my head up…"

"Did I tell you to speak, you dirty, little maggot? Do you want me to paddle your tight ass until he bleeds?"

"No, Pain."

"Then you speak when spoken to. You understand?"

"Yes, Mistress Pain."

"Muhfucka," Porsha says, stroking his dick, "you can say what you want. You know you ain't ever gonna find another set of fly, freaky bitches like us who'll fuck you stress free. So you better shut the fuck up and ask Pain if you can feed us your nut."

"Pain, baby, may I have permission to bust this nut?"

Persia stops what she's doing. "You think you deserve to cum, you naughty little Fucker?" she asks, smacking him on the ass again.

"Yes, Pain."

She walks around to the front of him, grabbing him by the neck, then pulling him into her and forcefully kissing him. I rapidly finger myself. My pussy explodes, watching him greedily suck the scent of his ass off of Persia's tongue. She pulls back from him. "You like how your ass tastes?"

Porsha wets his dick with more spit, then slips it back into her hungry mouth.

"Aaaaah, shit…"

"Answer me, motherfucker," Persia says, pinching and twisting his nipples.

"Mmmm, aaaahhh…yes, Mistress. I like how my ass tastes on your tongue. I love it when you eat my ass."

"Of course you do, you nasty little sonofabitch." She kisses him again, then walks in back of him, again, and squats down. "Keep fucking her horny mouth real good and I'll let you cum." He grunts as she pulls open his cheeks and blows into his hole. "You want my tongue back in your horny, tight ass?"

Porsha rapidly sucks and gulps his cock.

"Ohhhh, shiiiiiit…yessssss, baby. Fuck my ass with your tongue."

"Don't you nut, yet," Persia warns as she buries her face back into his ass and fucks him with her heated tongue.

He dips at the knees, grabs the sides of Porsha's head and face-fucks her relentlessly, moaning. It is all music to my ears. When he can no longer take the intense dick sucking and ass-licking my sisters are giving him—or watching me play in my wet abyss, his body begins to shake. I watch as his head drops backward and his eyes roll up to the ceiling. He lets out a load, rumbling moan. His body starts to quiver.

It is time.

I smile, wiping my drenched pussy with my panties, then get up and walk over to him. I lick his left nipple, pull him by the neck toward me, then slip my tongue into his mouth. I suck on his tongue, his lips. Wipe his face with my cum-stained panties, then stuff them into his mouth. He greedily sucks and chews on them.

"Clean my panties, you nasty nigga," I say, running my hands along his chiseled chest. I allow my nails to lightly graze across his skin. I whisper in his ear, pulling my panties out of his mouth. I smell them. "Mmmm, my pussy smells so good. What do you think my son would say if he caught you fuckin' his sister's pretty little face and watchin' his mother play with herself?" I reach between his legs and grab his balls while Porsha continues bobbing back and forth on his cock. I roll them in my hand, then lightly squeeze.

"Aaaah, fuuuuck...he'd tell me how fucked up I am."

"He sure would. You ready to show him how fucked up you are?" I ask, dropping down to my knees next to Porsha. He will feed the two of us his milk while Persia eats his ass.

"Oh, yes...aaaaah..." Porsha releases his cock from her throat. He grabs it and rapidly jacks it, moaning. I am anxious to feel his hot cum splash up against my lips and tongue. He has two sets of eyes looking up at him, two wet tongues wagging in anticipated delight, waiting to be drenched by his cream.

Porsha and I both lap at his balls, then pull one into each of our mouths. "Aaaaaah, fuuuck...Yeah, suck them balls...aaah...you pretty bitches got a nigga's head spinnin'...aaaah, shit...I cum-min'...ooohhh...here it comes...open ya mouths...come get this nut..."

He scoots back as Porsha and I open our mouths, and say, "Aaaaaaah", wagging our tongues, and flicking them at the tip of his swollen mushroom head. His body shudders as he pumps out a gushing stream of hot creamy nut. He swings his dick from side to side, sprays us with his sticky cream. Persia removes her tongue from his ass, then comes around and tongues him down again. He continues stroking his dick, squeezing out more nut, then allows me and Porsha to take turns sucking out the last few drops of his salty and sweet nectar.

"Daaaaaaaaaaaaaamn…" he says, trying to catch his breath. "That shit was good as fuck. Ya'll got a muhfucka's head spinnin'."

Porsha and I swallow his nut, standing up and licking our lips. We both take turns kissing him, then push him back on the sofa. "We ain't finished with you, nasty boy," Porsha says, rolling a condom down on his dick, then straddling him. "You fucked my mouth, now it's time to fuck my pussy." She reaches under for his still-hard dick. She strokes it at the base, allowing the head to brush up against the back of her pussy. She will not allow him to enter her until I am in position. I stand up on the sofa and look down into his glazed eyes. The eyes of a man seduced and pleasured by three beautiful women—sisters identical in every way imaginable.

Porsha slips his dick into her smoldering hole, then gallops down on his shaft. Persia is now on her knees sucking on his balls.

He moans.

I straddle his face. Allow my smoldering slit to hover over his seeking mouth. He sticks his thick tongue out, rapidly flaps it back and forth. I lower my pussy, barely allowing the tip of his tongue to touch it. He reaches up for me with his hands. I grab them, pushing them up over his head. Pin them against the wall. Then slowly mount his mouth; give him access to my wetness. Grind on his mouth until I cum in his mouth.

Tonight, we have brought this man before us to heightened bliss. We have taken him on a sexual journey like no other. And have allowed him to explore a hidden desire without guilt or shame. Our motto is simple: What one has, the others share—including men. Yes, Porsha, Persia, and I have given this hunk of man a night he will soon never forget. And, together, we are man swappers—three sisters, three insatiable libidos—who share the same man, with one mission in mind. To fuck him—together, and take him to the edge of ecstasy, taunt him, then toss his ass over.